*Dedicated to all the scientists,
nurses, doctors, and volunteers
who are vaccinating us back to life.
I will not forget your sacrifices.*

M. A. Hunter  nce a young age an one. That dream b gned The Missing Children Case Files.

Born in Darlington in the north-east of England, Hunter grew up in West London, and moved to Southampton to study law at university. It's here that Hunter fell in love and has been married for fifteen years. They are now raising their two children on the border of The New Forest where they enjoy going for walks amongst the wildlife. They regularly holiday across England, but have a particular affinity for the south coast, which formed the setting for the series, spanning from Devon to Brighton, and with a particular focus on Weymouth, one of their favourite towns.

When not writing, Hunter can be found binge-watching favourite shows or buried in the latest story from Angela Marsons, Simon Kernick, or Ann Cleeves.

 twitter.com/Writer_MAHunter

Also by M. A. Hunter

The Missing Children Case Files

Ransomed

Isolated

Trafficked

Discarded

Exposed

REPRESSED

The Missing Children Case Files

M. A. HUNTER

One More Chapter
a division of HarperCollins*Publishers*
1 London Bridge Street
London SE1 9GF
www.harpercollins.co.uk

HarperCollins*Publishers*
1st Floor, Watermarque Building, Ringsend Road
Dublin 4, Ireland

This paperback edition 2021
First published in Great Britain in ebook format
by HarperCollins*Publishers* 2021

A catalogue record of this book is available from the British Library

ISBN: 978-0-00-844338-2

Printed and bound in the UK using 100% Renewable
Electricity at CPI Group (UK) Ltd

Content notices: paedophilia, sexual assault, drug abuse, child abuse, suicidal ideation.

When foxes eat the last gold grape,
And the last white antelope is killed,
I shall stop fighting and escape
Into a little house I'll build.

And you may grope for me in vain
In hollows under the mangrove root,
Or where, in apple-scented rain,
The silver wasp-nests hang like fruit.

— *Escape*, Elinor Wylie

Chapter One

THEN

Ruislip, London

The woman staring back at her from behind the glass looked feeble and exhausted. The skin around her eyes hung almost lifelessly, and the pores of her cheeks were swollen and in need of rejuvenation. But it wasn't just the face that made Zara Edwards despondent; the flaps of skin leading from her neck down to where the bra struggled to restrain her chest at an acceptable height were also old and flaky. Where had this sad, old woman come from? It seemed like only yesterday that she'd still thought of that reflection as a frivolous twenty-something with the world at her feet.

A shadow crossed the dressing table, and a suited figure suddenly appeared behind her in the mirror. He pressed his warm hands on her shoulders and stooped to kiss the top of her head.

'I've booked the Uber for fifteen minutes; is that okay?'

She patted his left hand with her right. 'I'll be ready.'

He stooped lower, one knee pushing into the pile of the carpet, so that his head was now in line with her shoulder. 'You have nothing to worry about,' he said reassuringly, pressing his lips to the top of her arm.

'I'm not worried,' she replied uncertainly.

'Remember, it's just dinner with a few chums from university. They're all very friendly, and I haven't seen most of them for years. We'll have dinner and a few drinks, and then we'll be back here. Remember what the counsellor said about us taking it slowly. It's about one step at a time. We go from here to the Uber, then from the Uber to her house. And I'll be with you the whole time.'

She stared at his reflected eyes, and it was almost enough to flood hers with tears. Her rock, for all these years.

'Promise you won't abandon me tonight?'

He kissed her arm again. 'I promise, with the caveat that you let me use the bathroom alone.' He smiled quickly to show he was only teasing. 'If it all gets too much, you only have to say and I'll make our excuses and we can leave. Okay?'

This was a big night for him, she knew, and that was why she'd spent the entire week psyching herself into the position where she'd at least made it to the dressing table to slap on her war paint. There was a time when her voice would have refused point-blank to even consider dinner at a friend's house, especially when she'd never met the host.

She tilted her head so it pressed into the hand still on her shoulder. 'I'm sorry for being such a drag. I don't know why you put up with me.' She sighed gently.

'I don't *put up with you*,' he reinforced. 'I love you, Zara, and I understand you struggle with new places, especially when you're unfamiliar with the people there. I understand it, and I'm happy to support you as you work towards finding resolution.'

He paused and looked away for the briefest of moments, but she spotted it, quickly returning her eyes to the makeup bag before her so he wouldn't see that she'd seen. If he knew the real reason why she was dreading tonight's dinner, he probably wouldn't press for her to go with him. She'd thought about suggesting he go alone – he was sure to have more fun without her hanging on his arm – but she'd bailed on too many nights out before, and even though he hadn't said as much, she sensed he was starting to grow frustrated by the routine.

'I don't know what I'd do without you,' she said, moving her hand to his cheek where the long scar ran from his eye socket down to his chin.

When they'd first met, he'd been shy of his scar, keeping it partially obscured by high scarves and low hats, but she'd managed to show him that the scar wasn't something to be ashamed of. His standing up to his abusive father was precisely what had saved his mother and younger sister. The pink line where the skin had healed over the bottle slash was evidence of his resilience in the face of adversity. It was her favourite part of his face, even if it was his least.

'I'm the lucky one,' he whispered, just loudly enough for her to hear.

'Are you sure you wouldn't prefer to go alone?' The words were out before she had time to hold them in, and she instantly regretted them as disappointment filled his eyes.

'That would be like Robin taking on Gotham's underworld without Batman, or Penfold without Danger Mouse.'

She'd never picked him up on it, but he always framed her as the powerhouse in their relationship, even though they both knew he wore the trousers. They just wouldn't work if she had any level of real responsibility; she needed him more than he needed her.

'Besides,' he continued, 'some of my friends are beginning to think that you don't exist. If I don't drag you out sooner or later, they're going to think I'm some kind of Norman Bates type character, secretly living out two lives.'

This made her smile, and she craned her neck to kiss him on the lips. 'I'll get dressed; why don't you fix yourself a glass of wine while you wait for the taxi? You deserve it after the week you've had.'

He straightened. 'Can I get you a glass too?'

'Not just yet,' she said, with a shake of the head. 'I'd rather wait until we get there.'

She waited for him to leave before rummaging through the makeup bag, extracting lip gloss, foundation, and mascara, and systematically applying each until the woman staring back at her was virtually unrecognisable. She pulled her cheeks into a smile, and brushed her long, brittle auburn hair, until it resembled something less like a bird's nest. Finally, she stood and moved across to the built-in wardrobe in the wall behind her, and slipped the navy dress from the wire hanger. She pushed her arms in, fiddling with the zip at the side until her tired and less-than-poised body was covered. Taking one final look in the full-length mirror on the wardrobe door, she sighed in remorseful satisfaction. It was the best she could do with what she had.

'And when Professor Sweeten entered his office and saw that the engineers had reassembled that bloody MG inside, well I could have wet myself!'

Most of the rest of the guests sitting around the table laughed at Tom's anecdote from their time at university together, as he reached for his glass and took a long swig of wine. He'd always been able to make Zara laugh, but he wasn't the sort of man constantly looking to keep others entertained. She'd wondered whether he'd been a bit of a class clown at school, but according to his younger sister Mable, he had been very shy until university had helped coax him from his shell. In another life he probably could have pursued a career in comedy, such was his ability to find the humour in almost any situation, but then again, in another life she too could have been someone different.

'You're lucky none of you got arrested!' Harriet cautioned. 'How would that have looked on your applications to the bar? Criminal charges on a future barrister's record would not do.'

Harriet was Will's wife – they were hosting tonight's dinner party – and whilst it had been pitched as a party of six, there were now twelve of them squashed in around the large dining table in the cramped room. For etiquette's sake, the men had agreed to use the selection of emergency chairs that had been drafted in to ensure everyone had a place. As soon as Zara had seen the number of guests she'd desperately wanted to turn around and chase after the Uber, but she hadn't mentioned her fear when Tom had checked if she was okay. He deserved better than to have his evening out ruined. He'd been working such long hours recently that it was important he have a break from chambers, and from their two-bedroom house.

Despite his earlier promise not to leave her side, he hadn't challenged Harriet's suggestion that the friends from university sit together, while their partners gathered at the opposite end of the table.

'They'll just be talking about times that none of us experienced,' Harriet had said. 'Far better to leave them to it.'

That meant Zara was now seated between a secondary school teacher and a literary agent, with whom she doubted she shared many interests. She'd spent most of the evening just watching Tom as he regaled those nearest to him with anecdote after anecdote.

'So what do you do for a living, Zara?' the literary agent asked now, dabbing her lips with a cotton napkin.

She felt the heat rise to her cheeks. 'I work in an independent bookshop.'

'Oh really? I'm in the publishing industry too. You've probably got some of my clients' books in your store.'

'We mainly sell specialist reference books, rather than fiction,' Zara corrected. In truth it had been years since she'd worked in her godfather's shop, but it was an easier lie than admitting she'd been made redundant from her role as a legal secretary before Christmas.

'Ah, okay, fair enough. Do you enjoy working there?'

Zara reached for her glass of chilled wine. 'We never get too busy, and most of the customers who come in usually know what they're looking for; in fact, a lot of the time they come in to collect a book they've pre-ordered. I get on really well with the owner who trusts me to lock up at night, and yeah, I enjoy reading up on subjects I know nothing about.'

'Sounds wonderful! Passion for reading is what attracted me to publishing too. I love finding a submission from a prospective client that just grabs me by the shirttails and drags me on their journey. It's hard work sorting the wheat from the chaff, but so worth it when I see a manuscript I've sweated over reach the top of a chart.'

Zara sipped the wine, but it did nothing to cool her cheeks.

'Do you and Tom have children?'

The inevitable question that always seemed to come up at such engagements, and another reason Zara dreaded attending them. 'No we don't,' she replied evenly. 'Neither Tom nor I want them, to be honest. Don't get me wrong, we love spending time with Tom's niece – his sister's daughter – but I'm just not very maternal. You?'

'I did, but my son died.'

Zara quickly covered her hand with her mouth. 'Oh gosh, I'm so sorry. I had no idea.'

'It's okay. It was a number of years ago. A shock at the time – no parent ever expects to bury their child – but I've come to terms with it now. That's not to say I don't miss him like crazy.'

Zara fixed her with a sincere look. 'I am so sorry. If I'd known I wouldn't have asked.'

The agent smiled back. 'Don't worry about it. Really, I'm fine.'

'Maddie, Maddie,' Harriet was calling from the foot of the table, 'you'll be able to help us settle this debate. Deborah was just saying that she'd read a statistic that claimed over a hundred thousand children are reported missing every year in the UK, but we don't get to hear about even one per cent of them. One of your clients writes about missing children, doesn't she?'

Zara felt her chest constrict as the breath caught in her throat, but she remained perfectly still.

'That's right. Emma Hunter is my number one client at the moment. I've heard that statistic too, but you have to bear in mind that a large proportion of those reported cases relate to children who've run away but who *do* eventually turn up. A prime example is that Jo-Jo Neville who was reported missing from Weymouth last month, but then turned up at her aunt's house.'

'Yes, and there was that other girl, wasn't there…?' Harriet continued. 'Went missing from Brighton… ooh, must be thirty-odd years ago now… Do you remember who I mean?'

The hairs on Zara's arms rose as her body temperature instantly dropped.

'The press gave her that nickname,' Harriet persisted. 'What did they call her? Rock Girl? Yes, that was it: the Brighton Rock Girl, on account of the last photograph her parents had taken of her, sucking on a piece of pink rock on Brighton pier. Do you remember?'

Zara looked to her left for an exit to the bathroom, but the teacher's chair was pulled out, blocking her escape.

'Can't say it rings any bells,' Maddie replied.

Harriet's eyes were now glued to her phone as she searched for the story that Zara knew inside and out.

'Here we go,' Harriet proudly announced, as the conversation at the other end of the table quietened. 'She was nine years old, and the family were staying in Brighton for the weekend. They snapped the picture on the pier, and turned to watch the fireworks, and when they looked back she was gone. I remember my parents really freaked out about it, and my brother and I were essentially put on house arrest for months whilst the press kept running stories about the girl.'

Zara leaned towards the teacher and tried to ask her to tuck her chair in without drawing attention to herself. She could feel Tom's eyes on her, but didn't dare look up.

'She was eventually found almost two years later. Some dirty pervert had kept her locked in a room in his house only a stone's throw from the pier. I remember it was all over the press for weeks and weeks. The whole nation seemed to celebrate her return like she was some celebrity or something.'

'Could I just get out? I need to use the bathroom,' Zara whispered again, but the teacher's attention was focused on the speaker.

Harriet turned her phone around so everyone could see the screen. 'This was the image I was talking about.'

Zara didn't need to look into the excited eyes of the girl with straggly orange hair, innocently sucking the end of the piece of mint-flavoured rock.

Harriet turned the phone back and continued reading. 'The girl wasn't able to tell the police much about what had happened to her, but they arrested and imprisoned the man whose house they found her in. Presumably he's dead now, but just think what a traumatic experience that must have been for the poor girl. Can you imagine being torn from your parents and held prisoner for years? God knows what kind of twisted abuse she experienced. I mean, that kind of thing would totally screw up your psyche, wouldn't it?'

Zara stood and leaned closer to the teacher. 'Would you excuse me, please?'

'According to this,' Harriet continued, 'she received counselling, but was never able to fully open up about what had happened. Psychologists concluded that she must have repressed the memories. Don't blame her, really!'

She paused as she continued to read her screen, evidently enjoying being the centre of the party's attention.

'Oh, here we go, it says the girl – Zara Edwards – and her family ended up moving to Brighton to try and escape the intense media speculation surrounding...' Her words trailed off and her eyes moved slowly up to where Zara continued to hover.

Zara would have given anything for a hole to open up in the floor and swallow her completely, but she remained utterly trapped as eleven pairs of eyes fell on her. With no other choice, she shoved the teacher's chair out of the way and tore through to the bathroom, locking it behind her, before lifting the seat and expelling her starter.

Chapter Two

NOW

Bournemouth, Dorset

I resist the urge to rub my eyes, conscious that I don't want to smudge my eyeliner and leave myself looking like a panda, even though the skin beneath them is swollen and bag-like and probably already doing a good job of it. When the French lawyer said he was going to fetch his client, I didn't think he'd take this long.

It's after eight on a Saturday night, and I've been sitting in this boardroom for almost half an hour already. It's an enormous room, but so cold in atmosphere. The long oval-shaped table is large enough to comfortably seat sixteen, based on the number of chairs I can count, and there is a large projector screen pulled down at the end to my left. Above my head a projection box hangs idly from the cream-coloured ceiling tiles. I am facing a wall of glass, though it is difficult to see any signs of life beyond the darkness of the evening March sky. In fact, given the strength of the lights in the room, all I can really see is a hovering ghostly reflection of myself at the table.

I check my watch again, even though it's barely a minute since I last looked. I guess there's a part of me that hopes Aurélie Lebrun and her solicitor can see how frustrated I am growing with the wait for them. It was they who requested I travel to these offices to meet with them, so the delay is maddening. It feels like I've been doing nothing but sitting and waiting for the last month. That's how long it's been since an anonymous stranger sent me an image of Arthur Turgood and Reverend Peter Saltzing sharing a joke with the Met Police's former commissioner Sir Anthony Tomlinson. I know for a fact that Turgood and Saltzing were part of a trafficking ring exploiting children, but I have nothing to tie Tomlinson to it, save for this photograph.

My long-term associate and friend, PC Jack Serrovitz is actively looking for connections between the men, but he's been so busy with it that he hasn't been able to provide any kind of update. I've left messages for him, but I know we have to be so careful not to let on what we're involved in that I don't blame him for not replying. I know he will tell me as soon as he has something concrete. But then that leaves me twiddling my thumbs. I've tried undertaking my own online research, but there's very little about Tomlinson in the public eye. He doesn't have any social media presence as far as I can see, and there have been no new articles about him since he retired from his post more than a decade ago.

There's also been no new photographs sent by my anonymous source. The image of Tomlinson and the others was one of three sent to my agent's office on consecutive business days, and I'd half expected to receive further information, but nothing has been forthcoming. Jack arranged for the postal envelopes to be forensically examined, but no DNA samples were recovered, and all I've learned is that the first photograph was sent from Dover, the second from Reading, and the third from Chichester by someone called Kylie. There's nothing else anybody can tell me, and there isn't security camera footage at all of the possible post box locations to instigate a search of footage on the off-chance I spot a face from elsewhere in our investigation. I don't recall meeting anybody called Kylie, and for all I know it was a false name given to the woman at the village post office who happened to have noted the name on the sender's lanyard.

Jack has asked me not to release any information about the other two photographs I received, as they are part of the investigation he is undertaking while seconded to the National Crime Agency. For now, the identities of Faye McKenna and Cormack Fitzpatrick are off-limits to future books. I want to find some way of linking their disappearances with that of my sister, Anna, but any such connection eludes me for now. The trail has gone cold. I don't know what the sender was expecting me to do with the images, but I feel like I'm facing a dead end, and I hate that I'm allowing myself to give up so easily, but I have exhausted all avenues.

What's worse is that I haven't heard from Freddie Mitchell since Freddie told me what he witnessed at the Pendark film studios. When I phone, it goes to voicemail, and whenever I head to the homeless shelter where he volunteers, it's always as if I've just missed him. I can understand why he would want to avoid me, I just wish I could tell him how sorry I am for making him relive such a painful time in his life.

Hence my willingness to meet with Aurélie Lebrun so late

on a Saturday evening. She was abducted and held prisoner for eighteen years before she escaped the clutches of her captor last year, and I have reason to believe the people who took and sold her are linked to the ring Turgood and Saltzing were involved with.

Since her escape, Aurélie has been recuperating in her native Paris, where her father continues to work in politics and her mother – a retired actress – has been tending to her daughter's needs. I was commissioned by Aurélie's father, Remy, to tell his daughter's side of the story, and despite her reticence, I managed to garner enough detail to produce a manuscript that has been awaiting her final approval before my publishers will go to print. There is great excitement about the book, given the enormous amount of media attention Aurélie's reappearance stirred up, and there is a film company waiting to exercise their rights to develop it for a streaming TV series. However, Aurélie and her legal team have been sitting on the manuscript for the best part of two months without confirming they're happy to proceed.

A knock at the boardroom door behind me is followed by the arrival of Aurélie, flanked by a very tall balding man with hexagonal glasses, and the much shorter, and tubbier French lawyer who met me here. The suited and booted solicitors remind me of Arnold Schwarzenegger and Danny DeVito on the cover of *Twins*, albeit neither is smiling as they take their seats across the table from me. Their harsh stares suddenly make me feel underprepared for this encounter. Should I also have brought a solicitor with me? I was going to ask Maddie to attend, but she said she already had dinner plans she couldn't get out of.

Aurélie looks healthier than when I saw her in her Poole

Hospital bed last year. She's still thin, but her face is fuller, and her torso less gaunt. Her hair has also grown, and clearly been highlighted and sculpted, and I can now see much more of her mother in the naturally beautiful cheekbones. If this was our first encounter, I'd never have believed she'd spent the best part of eighteen years trapped in a small cell beneath the ground, with only fleeting exposure to the sun. But then she pushes up her sleeves, and I see the telltale scars on her wrists where she tried to end her life a month or so after returning to Paris.

'You're looking well,' I say to cut the growing tension in the room. 'Did you fly over or—'

'Eurostar,' she says, cutting me off, no hint of a smile. She looks as keen to be in this room as I feel.

'Thank you for meeting with us today,' the taller of the two solicitors says, his pinstripe suit clashing with the diagonal purple and yellow stripes of his tie. 'The purpose of the meeting is to challenge some of the claims made in your manuscript.'

My heart sinks, and I know instantly this meeting should have been with the legal team at my publishers rather than with me. When I wrote *Ransomed*, Lord Fitzhume's solicitors tried to have certain lines and conclusions wiped from the manuscript prior to publication, but all of that was dealt with by a team of legal specialists.

I clear my throat, trying to hide the ball of anxiety inflating in the pit of my stomach. 'With all due respect, if you have concerns about the manuscript, it's my publishers you should be speaking with, rather than—'

'My client would prefer to deal with the challenges on a one-on-one basis,' he fires back without missing a beat.

'If that's the case, then why has she hired two legal professionals to host this meeting?' I look directly at her. 'Aurélie, we spoke many times on the telephone and when I came to visit you in Paris; all of *this* is not necessary. I shared multiple extracts of the manuscript with you as I was writing it, and you didn't have too many objections then. I don't understand what's changed.'

She leans into the French solicitor and whispers something, before he confers with his taller colleague.

'Mademoiselle Lebrun was not aware that your book would include references to her giving birth while held in captivity,' he says.

I frown. 'The DNA examination proved that the girl she snatched at the park was in fact the daughter she bore. I'm using it as a device to make your client more empathetic to readers.'

'But it potentially jeopardises the anonymity of the child,' he fires back.

'How exactly?' I say, struggling to keep my tone emotionless.

'By even suggesting she exists, you open her up to intrusion from the press, and others who may try to identify her. My client does not want the child to ever know how she came into this world, and the best way to achieve that is to keep their paths separated.'

I should stand up and leave, telling them to contact my publishers instead. I resent being ambushed in this way, and if this had been their intention all along, I should have been warned to bring legal representation myself.

'The last thing I want is to put Crystal in any kind of danger. I haven't used her real name in the book for that very reason. It would take a dogged approach to check dates of birth and adoption agency papers to uncover her.'

'Nevertheless, the possibility remains, and as such my client wants all references removed.'

I stare straight at Aurélie again. 'Do you realise how complicit you will come across in the manuscript without that human side to your character?'

'Please address your questions to me, Miss Hunter, rather than to my client. I have been instructed to speak on her behalf.'

'It's too late for me to change the manuscript at such short notice. The book is in my publishers' hands now, and as far as I understand it's waiting to run on the presses.'

'Not without my client's authority.'

'She's already agreed to the proposal.' My voice is louder and more aggressive than I'd intended. 'I have her agreement in writing, prior to it being sent to my publisher.'

'My client rebukes that authority, as she hadn't had the opportunity to fully digest and understand the contents of your proposal. Now that she has sought guidance on her legal rights in this matter, she has decided against the book in its current form. If you are prepared to make the required changes, then your publisher should be able to proceed with their desired release dates.'

I wish Maddie were here with me now. She doesn't get intimidated by such corporate-speaking bullies. If I didn't know she was enjoying dinner, I'd phone and ask for some advice.

'You're just going to have to take it up with my publisher then, I'm afraid,' I say, opting for the least confrontation.

The two lawyers confer, before standing and exiting the

room, saying they will return momentarily. Aurélie remains where she is, looking anywhere to avoid my gaze.

'I know you blame yourself for what happened to Jemima Hooper when she stayed at the cabin with you that night, but you were under Jasper Derwent's control, and had no means of escape, physically or emotionally. You can't blame yourself for anything that happened after he took control.'

She doesn't respond, but her eyes begin to shine.

'I also know that a part of you is mourning Jasper's passing, but your feelings of love for him aren't real. I don't doubt they feel real, but he manipulated you from the day you met at that auction room. He groomed you, and you were too young and vulnerable to stop him. You were at his mercy, and he took full advantage. You must see that, surely?'

She looks over to the projection screen, squeezing her lips together to keep them from trembling.

'Please, Aurélie, I know there's more you're holding back from me. Some of your memories will have been repressed and buried because they're too painful to face, but you won't find happiness until you can put them behind you for good.'

I can hear the low rumble of the solicitor's voices just outside the door, and know I don't have long.

'Do you remember I told you about my sister, Anna? You made me believe that you'd met her, but then you told me you hadn't. I'm still looking for her, and your memories could hold the key to me learning more about the group that took her; the group who took you. Wouldn't you like to see those men brought to justice? They stole eighteen years of your life, Aurélie. Help me find them for all the other children whose lives they've also decimated. Help me find them for all the children out there who are still being abused. Help me find them for all the children they're going to snatch and hurt if we don't stop them.'

'No!' she shouts, her head snapping round, and the tears escaping.

The boardroom door is flung open a moment later as the solicitors come in to find the cause of the shout.

'Aurélie, I will change the book as much as you want if you just help me find the men responsible.'

The two lawyers converge around her and shepherd her from the room. 'This meeting is over. If you persist in harassing my client, we will seek restraining measures. Tell your publisher to expect my call.'

Chapter Three

NOW

Weymouth, Dorset

I'm disgruntled and exhausted as I make it onto the ward to which Mum was transferred four days ago following another fall at the hospital. According to the care home manager, Pam Ratchett, Mum was walking to her table at dinner when she keeled over. They feared the worst, and when the paramedics arrived on the scene, they confirmed she'd suffered a minor heart attack, and due to the unsteady arrhythmia, admitted her here for observation and monitoring.

Using the hand sanitiser, I rub my hands until they dry and proceed through the doors, receiving a judgemental pair of raised eyebrows from the male nurse behind the console of desks.

'Visiting is almost over,' he mumbles, looking over to the large clock on the wall, before returning to his book.

Does he think I don't realise that? I know that the unnecessary delay with Aurélie, and the hour-long taxi journey back here from Bournemouth means I'm late for visiting hours, but at least I'm here. What right does he have to judge?

I force myself to take several deep breaths to compose myself and ease the tension in my shoulders, then proceed along the brightly lit corridor. There's not as much chatter and noise as I've heard the last three nights, but then I'm usually here at the start of visiting hours rather than the tail end. The danger now of course is that Mum could already be asleep, but I'm determined to see her regardless.

Entering the room, Mum's is one of eight beds, but half of them are empty. Curtains are pulled around another two, leaving one older man visible, but he has headphones on and is watching something on a tablet, offering the occasional chuckle to show he's still alive.

Mum is sitting up in bed, but her eyes are closed and her head tilted to one side. I don't know when she suddenly looked so old, and more like my grandma than my mum. Her hair has definitely whitened in the last couple of months, with now only the odd darker grey patch near her neck, and behind her ears. And the face that was once so bright is dull and faded, as if even her skin knows the end is near and has surrendered to inevitability.

The white patch of bandage above her left eyebrow bears a bloody stain where her wound has been weeping again. She caught the corner of the table on her way down, and there was blood everywhere according to Pam; I'm just glad I wasn't there to witness it. I know I'd have gone into full-on panic mode.

Sliding over the visitor's chair from beside the bed, I'm surprised to find a book of Elinor Wylie's poems face down

22

but open. I have the same copy at home, and there's a part of me that dreams Anna left it here, even though I know it's impossible. I lift it and turn it over in my hands, but when I open the cover I can see it's on loan from the Weymouth library, so Mum must have brought it with her to the hospital. She so rarely wants to talk about Anna, but it warms me that my lost sister isn't far from her thoughts either. I put my bag down on the floor and finally relax into the cold plastic chair.

Mum doesn't stir, and it's probably best if she sleeps through my visit. The heart monitor she's wired to beeps and whirs in a gentle rhythm, and unless anything has changed today, she's not suffered a repeat attack. When I spoke to the consultant on the phone earlier, he said they were still running tests to determine what may have caused the seizure, and I guess she'll remain here until they have confidence that she won't suffer a repeat.

When Pam phoned, I feared the worst. About a month ago, she had one of her good days where she knew exactly who I was, and was positive and chatty. We spent three hours together reliving happier memories from my childhood, many of which I'd forgotten about. I guess, once Anna disappeared, my view of the world around me dimmed, and most recollections focus on the pain etched across my parents' faces, and the sense of loss. However, when we were catching up, a slew of happier memories emerged, and I think I've been too focused on the negatives to realise how often she put on a brave face for my sake.

Since that day, however, she hasn't had any further *good* days. There have been plenty of bad ones, where she couldn't recognise my face, has been abusive, or been incoherent. That one afternoon a month ago was a real blessing, but my fear is that it was the last time I'll properly see my mum.

Wiping my eyes with a tissue, I start when I see Mum staring back at me. 'Mum, hi,' I say, brightening my tone and mood. 'How are you feeling today?'

She doesn't answer at first, and for a moment I'm not sure if she is actually awake, or whether her eyes have just opened during a cycle of sleep.

'Mum? Are you okay?' I say gently, leaning forwards and stroking her hand where the cannula protrudes.

'Drink,' she croaks back.

Reaching for the plastic jug of water, I fill the small beaker and place the straw between her lips, until she's refreshed and spits the straw out. Returning the beaker to the side table, I retake my seat, still leaning forwards so that any conversation won't disturb the other patients who may be sleeping.

'How are you feeling today, Mum?'

Her eyes haven't left my face, but the lack of recognition is painful.

'Mum, I'm your daughter, Emma. Remember?'

She doesn't budge, but her breathing has quickened and she quickly snatches her hand away from mine.

'It's okay, Mum. You're perfectly safe. You're at the Weymouth Community Hospital. You had a fall and banged your head. Do you remember? The doctors wanted to keep you in until you're feeling more like yourself.'

I know she can hear me, but her expression doesn't change, and it's as if the words have been deflected by some invisible barrier.

'Can I get you anything else? Are you in any pain?'

24

A tear suddenly rolls down her cheek, blotting the dry bag beneath. 'Want to go home.'

'You will go home soon, Mum. I know Pam is missing you, as are your other friends. As soon as you're better, you'll be back in your room with all your favourite things.'

Her voice when she speaks again is a low grumble, like a sulking child. 'Who are you? Why are you keeping me here?'

'I'm your daughter, Emma, Mum. And I'm not keeping you here, but the doctors are worried about your heart, and need to make it better. I know this must be frightening, but you've no reason to be scared.'

'Want my mum.'

This throws me for a moment. 'Mum, Grandma – I mean, *your* mum – died a long time ago. I'm so sorry.' I take a breath and I'm willing her fragile memory to fire for just a few seconds so that I can put her at ease. 'Do you know who you are?'

'Of course I do,' she snaps.

'Good. Do you know who I am?'

She opens her mouth to speak, but then shakes her head.

'I'm your daughter, Mum. Do you remember? You have two daughters, Emma and… Anna. Do you remember having two daughters?'

Again, there is the briefest glimpse of recognition, but it's quickly buried by the furrows of her brow.

'I want to go home.'

'I'm sorry, Mum, but you can't go home until the doctors know you're better.'

She suddenly launches forwards, pulling the sheet from her legs and trying to slide out of bed. 'You can't keep me here.'

If she were more supple and agile, she might have managed

it, but her legs don't move as fast as her brain, and she's suddenly tumbling. I just about manage to catch her and manoeuvre her back into the bed. She is weeping uncontrollably now, as she looks at her withered and wrinkled legs.

I press her head into my chest and just hold her, allowing the emotion to escape, and hoping my love radiates through her and brings her back from this abyss.

Her bony arms wrap around me, but a moment later they are clawing and pulling to get me off her.

'Help!' she cries out. 'Help!' Louder this time.

'Mum, please, you're going to wake everyone up.'

'Help me! Someone help me!'

One of the nurses comes hurrying down the corridor, and looks from Mum to me, and then back again. 'Is everything okay, Winnie?'

'I want her gone,' she demands, pointing a trembling finger towards me. 'She's keeping me against my will. I want her gone.'

The nurse takes Mum's hand and rests her head back against the pillow. 'I'll take care of everything; you just rest, Winnie. Okay? Will you stay here while I talk to your daughter outside?'

Mum allows her to tuck the sheet back in, before the nurse nods for us to step into the corridor.

'I-I'm sorry,' I begin. 'She woke when I arrived, and is a bit disorientated.'

She smiles empathetically. 'That's quite all right. We know about your mum's dementia, and we're treating her accordingly.'

My own eyes fill, but I'm determined not to cry in front of

this kind stranger. 'She couldn't remember who I was, nor my sister… She seems to see me as the enemy.'

The nurse is nodding understandingly. 'Unfortunately it's more common than you'd like to think. She's in unfamiliar surroundings, her body is reacting to the cardiac arrest, and she's at a stage of Alzheimer's where nothing is as it should be. Don't take it to heart.' She rubs my arm, and I'm close to breaking point. 'I'm sure you'd rather stay and check she's okay, but it might be for the best if you left us to it. Visiting hours are all but done anyway. I'll get her settled again, and maybe tomorrow she'll have a better day.'

I smile through the pain and nod, as the words stick in my throat. The nurse returns to the room and I see her talking to Mum, and the tears fall because I know that she's in the best place for her right now. I have to be patient and hope that we'll get one more 'good' day together.

Rick is waiting for me as I exit the hospital, and I crumple into his arms as I see the bouquet of flowers he's holding. 'I got you these,' he whispers. 'I figured it might not have been easy. Are you ready for me to take you home?'

My head nods against his firm chest and he puts his arm around me, leading me to his car. Once inside, he doesn't speak, handing me a packet of tissues and just allowing me to get it out of my system. Tonight was supposed to be our third date, having been out for dinner a couple of times in the last month. We're taking things slowly. Given he's four years my junior, I know he's not in any hurry to settle down; it's been a while since I allowed anyone to get too close, and I'm not yet ready to allow him to fully enter my world.

When my tears have dried, I look across at him. He has

such a firm chin when he's concentrating as he is on the road now. He catches me looking and grins as he glances over.

'Are you checking me out, Emma Hunter?'

I look away as heat rises to my cheeks.

'That's okay,' he says, patting my knee. 'You're free to look. I'm sure it's not every day you get driven home by a Community Support Officer as handsome as me. Feel free to take a long look. I'm not shy.'

I know he's only teasing, but the embarrassment quickly subsides.

'Thank you for coming to pick me up. It's been one hell of a day.'

'You're very welcome. Things didn't go well with your mum, I take it?'

I shake my head, but he doesn't press for details. 'I'm sorry. At least she's in safe hands, right?'

'Yeah, I know.'

'Hey, listen, I know you said it was my choice what film we watched tonight, but I figured you probably wouldn't want to watch an action flick so I brought a couple of comedies with me instead.'

I pretend to be offended. 'Just because I'm a woman, doesn't mean I don't enjoy a fast-paced action film with guns and bloody violence. *Die Hard* is still one of my favourite Christmas movies, after all.'

He chuckles. 'Is that a fact? Damn, I wish I'd brought my Jean-Claude Van Damme collection with me now.'

'What did you bring then?'

'Okay, you can choose between *Four Weddings and a Funeral*, *Ferris Bueller's Day Off*, or *The Hangover*.'

'Do you not own any films made this decade?' I goad.

He laughs. 'Hey, you said I should choose a film that would tell you something about me.'

I consider the statement for a moment. 'So, you're telling me you want to get married, you're a bit of a skiver, and you like getting wasted with your best friends?'

He opens his mouth to challenge, before nodding. 'Actually, that sums me up pretty well. Great deduction there. Maybe it's you who should put in an application to join the police.'

'Have you heard back from the last round of interviews yet?'

He shakes his head. 'Should be any day now though. It's amazing to think I first posted the application nearly nine months ago. I could have given birth in the amount of time it's taken.'

I pull a face. 'Only with a miracle of science.'

He laughs again. 'You know what I mean.'

We arrive outside my flat and he stops the engine before unfastening his seat belt. My mobile rings as I open my door and, checking the display, I'm surprised and alarmed to see Jack's name on the screen.

I have to remind myself that there is nothing more than friendship between Jack and me, and that I'm doing nothing wrong with Rick, yet the guilt remains.

'Everything okay?' Rick asks, coming around to my side and maybe noticing the pallor of my face.

'It's Jack… I should probably take it. Do you mind?'

He says no, but his face tells a different story.

Accepting the call, I unlock my front door and head through to the kitchen, flipping on the lights as I go. 'Hi Jack, how are you?'

'Hey, sorry to call so late. I wanted to give you an update on progress. Is now a good time?'

Rick appears in the doorway, but doesn't enter. I lower the phone to my chest and move back towards him.

'I'm really sorry, but it's Jack with an update on the case, and—'

Rick puts an open palm out to cut me off. 'It's okay. I get it; it's work. We can take a raincheck on tonight.'

I don't want to disappoint him again, especially after he came and collected me. 'No, it's fine, I can phone Jack back in the morning.'

Rick takes my hand and presses it to his lips. 'Don't be silly. I honestly don't mind. I know how long you've been waiting for news. I don't mind, Em, I promise. Besides, if we postpone to another night, I'll be able to go through all my action movies and pick out something we'll both enjoy. Okay? Seriously, talk to Jack, and I'll give you a call tomorrow and we'll sort it out from there.' He releases my hand, and heads back to his car.

Closing the door, I return the phone to my ear. 'So Jack, what's new?'

Chapter Four

THEN

Ruislip, London

'Zara, honey, wake up. Wake up, Zara.'

Tom's frantic pulling and pushing finally extracted her from the nightmare, and she sat bolt upright in bed, her eyes searching the darkness for evidence that the trauma was definitely over. The dressing table to her left beneath the curtains was present and correct, though it was all but impossible to make out the paraphernalia on top. The mirror reflected only the darkness of the rest of the room.

She finally exhaled, and felt her heart gradually return to a trot rather than a gallop. Her fringe was practically glued to her forehead with sweat, and her entire nightdress was damp through.

'Are you okay?' Tom asked beside her, as he flipped on his bedside light, bathing the room in its warm yellow glow.

She was relieved when a monster didn't leap from one of the darker, shadowy corners. 'I'm fine,' she lied, not daring to move in case the monster was under the bed, just lulling her into a false sense of security.

'You were screaming,' Tom said. 'I kept trying to wake you, but it was like whatever had you wouldn't let go. Nightmare?'

She nodded, as there was no point in denying the obvious.

'Can you tell me what it was about?'

She shook her head. 'I don't remember.'

Tom dropped his face rather than arguing. 'Was it anything to do with what happened earlier tonight?'

She remained perfectly still, not wanting to lie to the man who had been her rock and compass for so many years, but not wanting to muddy his view of her either. She'd built their relationship on a bed of half-truths and omissions, and she was terrified the house of cards was about to collapse.

When Tom spoke next his voice was low, failing to disguise the hurt initiating the words. 'I can understand why you wouldn't want to talk about... what happened to you all those years ago – and I don't blame you for not wanting to relive it – but why didn't you tell me? In some ways, it explains a lot of the unanswered questions I've always had.'

She looked over to him, swallowing down the urge to sob, and instead pressed her cold hand against his warm cheek. 'I-I'm sorry,' she whispered.

He raised his face and took her hand from his cheek, holding it tightly. 'I love you, Zara, no matter what. Remember? When we got this place together, we both said we were in it for the long-term. We promised each other we would tackle every obstacle together. Do you remember that?'

A solitary tear escaped as she nodded. She could remember the declaration like it was yesterday – and the guilt she'd felt even then, which had remained as a spectre on her shoulder ever since.

'That's what this is,' Tom continued. 'An obstacle for us to face *together*. I'm disappointed that you didn't feel able to tell me about that part of your life, but I understand how difficult it must be to tackle. Not exactly a starter for ten, right?' He sniggered to ease a fraction of the atmosphere. 'But now that I know, I hope you'll find it easier to open up to me about it.'

He paused, wiping the fringe from her forehead with the back of his hand. 'Not tonight, of course. I think you've been through enough for one day. But maybe we can chat about it in the morning? It's nearly 2am on Sunday, but I have no plans for later. Why don't we go somewhere for a cooked breakfast, and then when we return we have an open conversation? Or better still, we could go to that Italian place you like for brunch?'

She still couldn't find the words to respond, and smiled through the pain with a short nod to acknowledge the idea.

'I assumed that your vomiting during dinner was more influenced by what Harriet read out, rather than too much wine like you suggested?'

She nodded again, recalling everyone's eyes on her as she'd emerged from the bathroom, keeping her head bent low as Tom had draped his jacket around her shaking shoulders. They would have heard her pained retching, though none of them spoke a word as they'd watched, mouths open, from the safety of the cramped dining room.

Tom had made their excuses and suggested he get her home safely, and Harriet had practically fallen over herself in apology for putting her foot well and truly in it.

'I'll box you up some dinner to take with you,' she'd said,

hurrying to the kitchen and filling Tupperware with the paella that had been in the kitchen waiting to be served. She'd refused to take no for an answer, even when Zara's cheeks had greened at the intense aroma of the fish and rice dish. Luckily for her, Tom had hidden it in the Uber's boot for the ride home, and had then quickly thrown it in the fridge when they walked through the door.

She'd sensed he wanted to ask her what had caused the projectile vomiting, but he hadn't pushed, and she'd told him she was tired and in need of sleep.

'I think if Harriet had made the connection, she wouldn't have read out the article as she did,' Tom continued now. 'I think she was as shocked as the rest of us.'

Zara didn't doubt it was a genuine mistake, but it didn't make it any easier to deal with the fallout.

'I'm tired,' she yawned. 'I think we should go back to sleep.'

He agreed and was about to turn off the light when she yelped. 'What is it?' he asked, but he didn't need to as she pulled back the covers; the enormous dark patch on the sheet was evidence of what had happened.

'Don't worry about it,' he said, leaping from the bed and yanking the duvet away to reveal the full extent of the damage. 'You go and sit in the living room, and I'll strip the bed.'

She couldn't move. Approaching her forty-fifth birthday and she'd wet the bed. What the hell was wrong with her?

'Babe? Seriously, leave this to me, and go and put the kettle on. Have one of those herbal teas you like to relax you. This won't take me five minutes, and then we can stay up and talk, or go back to sleep – whatever you want.'

'It's my mess; I should clean it up,' she said resolutely, but still didn't move.

'Don't be silly. How many times have you cleaned up after me when I've returned wasted from a night out with the guys from work?' He moved around the bed and crouched down. 'Let me take care of you for once. Please?'

She allowed him to take her hand and lead her downstairs and through to the living room, where he proceeded to pull the nightdress up and over her head before passing her a fresh one, but she didn't want to put it on. Turning to face him, she caught his eyes following the curve of her breasts before he quickly looked away. He turned to leave, but she grabbed his arm, and pulled him towards her, forcing her lips onto his and then prising his mouth open with her tongue.

But she wasn't strong enough to hold him there, and he broke free of her grip. 'No, babe, not like this. I need to change the sheets.'

The rejection was like a fresh kick to the stomach. 'Don't you want me now you know I'm soiled?'

His face folded into a frown. 'What? No, it isn't that.'

'Am I not good enough for you now you know I was raped when I was barely old enough to even know what sex was?'

'No, Zara, please, you're upset, and you're in a fragile state.'

'If you loved me, you'd fuck me right here and now. Come on, Tom, I'm throwing myself at you. You're not usually so shy.'

The confusion remained gripped to his features. 'I'm going to go and change the bed sheets, and then I'm going to come back in here and we can talk about anything you want. I'm not rejecting you, Zara, just the idea of sex right now. You're in a vulnerable state, and I'm not willing to take advantage of you in that way. I love you more than anything, and you turn me on in so many ways, but in the morning you'll see I'm doing the right thing.'

She turned away from him, dejected. 'Do what you like; you always do.'

He didn't retaliate, instead heading back upstairs, where she heard him opening the door of the airing cupboard to fetch fresh sheets.

Zara looked around the façade of the living room where they'd shared so much laughter and happiness, but now it was tainted somehow. None of it was real; not really. She'd created this world for them to live in where the secrets of the past couldn't get at her, but they'd never really left. She'd hidden them away, and tried to ignore them, but the truth never stayed buried forever.

Leaving the room, she headed into the guest bathroom, locking the door behind her and climbing into the shower. Setting the temperature as hot as she could bear, she held her head beneath the stream, dragging the bar of soap over every inch of her body, and then following it up with the plastic brush usually reserved for getting grime from beneath her fingernails. With her skin red raw, and Tom banging on the door to check she was okay, she killed the stream and stepped out onto her towel. The face in the mirror seemed to be telling her she'd brought all this mess on herself. Had she told Tom from the outset who she was, he may not have fallen for her as hard, but at least she wouldn't have broken his heart all these years later.

'Babe? Are you okay in there?' Tom said from the other side of the door. 'I'm worried about you. Please let me in. I'm sorry

I pulled away from you. You've no idea how much willpower that took! Listen, I've changed the sheets and the bed is ready when you're ready. Do you want me to fix you a drink of anything?'

'I'm fine,' she managed, keeping her glare on the reflection staring back at her.

'Okay, well, if you're sure, do you want me to wait up?'

'No, you go back to bed. I'll be up in a bit.'

She stayed where she was, listening until she heard him move along the floorboards and then the telltale sound of the bed shifting beneath his weight upstairs. And even then she didn't leave the bathroom until she heard the gentle rumble of his snoring.

Unlocking the door, she tiptoed along the hall, returning to the living room where she located the fresh nightdress and slipped it over her head. Satisfied that her movement hadn't disturbed Tom's slumber, she switched on her iPad and googled 'Brighton Rock Girl', trembling when the image of the girl with orange hair appeared on the screen adjacent to an archived news article. She heard Harriet's voice saying the words as she silently read them, and pictured all of those eyes staring at her at the moment Harriet read out the name Zara Edwards.

She'd spent so many years burying the past, but the moment she started reading about how the police were called when she was discovered in the locked bedroom of the house, it all came flooding back. She hadn't given up hope that she'd be discovered one day, but when it actually happened, it was one of the most terrifying experiences of her life.

What followed her rescue remained a blur in her mind. It had all happened so quickly. Wrapped in blankets, they'd rushed her to a hospital. Extracts of voices echoed in her mind now as she tried to replay the broken version of her past. Lots of people asking her name; lots of people telling her she was going to be okay; too many indistinct voices to really know who'd said what or when, or even why.

Zara reached for a tissue from the box on the windowsill and dabbed her eyes. She scrolled the screen until she found an article declaring an arrest had been made in the case. Fifty-seven-year-old Callum Gerrard had been arrested while attempting to flee the country.

She closed her eyes as the top of his head appeared at the bottom of the screen as she continued to scroll. This was why she hadn't wanted Tom to find out about the past. He was a barrister and being inquisitive was what made him so good at his job. He wouldn't be satisfied with just reading about the story; he'd want to know intimate details to satisfy his thirst for the truth. She wasn't ready to fulfil that need, but now it looked like she'd have little choice. Of all the things she'd expected to go wrong at the dinner, Tom learning about her history was the last. Eighteen years of love and support and she'd managed to evade the subject, and now that was all over. She wouldn't be surprised if he broke things off with her in the coming days and weeks. Once he started digging and learned the true scale of what had happened, there was no way he'd be able to live with it or with her.

Forcing her eyes open, she glared into the face of the mugshot on the screen, studying every line and scar, and those dead eyes. This man had died behind bars, and it didn't seem fair. She closed the page and deleted her internet search history so Tom wouldn't know she'd been looking.

Then, reaching for a blanket from the pile in the basket in

the corner of the room, she wrapped herself into a cocoon and lay down on the three-seater sofa. She strained to keep her eyes open for as long as possible, fearing the face of the man in her nightmare. The man who had taken her all those years ago. Not the face of the man they had arrested and imprisoned.

Chapter Five

NOW

Ealing, London

I'm starting to get used to catching the first train from Weymouth to Reading, and it alarms me slightly that I've settled into this routine where I sleep for the first hour or so, until the train pulls into Southampton Central, at which point the coach tends to fill up with other commuters on their way to London. It's usually at this point that I order a cup of tea and a packet of biscuits from the trolley service, before reading or researching, and then buying a bacon roll from the small café at Reading station, and finally boarding the overground train to Ealing Broadway. I must have made this trip a dozen times in the last year at least, and although it usually ends up being a long and tiring day, at least I get to spend the day with my best friend Rachel.

I'm at her door just before 10am, carrying a tray with two steaming mugs and a brown bag of selected Danish pastries that I picked up from the bakery I know she loves between the station and her flat. Generally speaking, Rachel is even less of a morning person than I am, so I'm surprised that she's not only fully clothed when she opens the communal entrance to the block of flats, but has a pencil tucked behind her ear and is on the phone to someone.

She mouths hello as she continues her conversation, and leads me through to the one-bedroom flat where I've been allowed to crash on the sofa-bed whenever I visit. Rachel's dark brunette bob shimmers under the kitchen light as she stoops over her laptop on the breakfast bar. Dropping my travel bag near the sofa-bed, I head through to the bathroom to freshen myself up, and when I return she's ended her call but her eyes are still glued to the laptop screen.

'Hey,' she says, without looking up, 'how was your journey up?'

'Yeah, fine, you know,' I reply. 'Have I come at a bad time?'

This time she meets my gaze. 'No, sorry, my editor wants me to make a last-minute change to a piece going out in tomorrow morning's first edition, so I just had to get it back to him.' She closes the laptop lid and smiles broadly. 'But that's all done now, and I can smell that you've brought me pastries, so we should take these drinks and head over to the sofa and slowly devour the creamiest and crumbliest pastry known to man.'

She picks up the tray of drinks and I carry the bag, and then we collapse on the sofa. It's been a couple of weeks since I was last here, but with Rachel it never seems to matter how long we've been apart; we always fall into the same old routine. It's comfortable, and neither of us would have it any other way.

'Saskia will be over with the books in about twenty minutes,' Rachel says, tucking into a vanilla crown, and bringing the topic of conversation back to the real reason for my visit today.

Of course, Saskia – our new hire from Scandinavia who has seamlessly embedded herself in the Anna Hunter Foundation, and quite frankly neither of us knows what we'd do without her. The fact that she brought homemade cupcakes to her interview didn't sway our decision, but it certainly didn't harm her cause.

I chew the end of my fingernail. 'You don't think I'm being overly cautious, do you?'

Rachel swallows her mouthful. 'Overly cautious, probably not; paranoid that the Charity Commission is going to find anything untoward about the foundation, yes. You need to relax. It's a routine audit, and our annual return is up to date. That's why we hired an accountant to work with Saskia on preparing the return, remember?'

'But why are they looking to audit us now? The foundation is still in its infancy. What's sprouted their interest?'

'These audits are undertaken totally at random, Em. I'm sure that's all this is.'

I break off a piece of my chocolate twist and munch it with discord. 'It just seems... with everything Jack and I are doing to unpick this ring of monsters... it just feels like a bit of a coincidence that we secretly go after a senior public official and suddenly the Charity Commission is on our doorstep sniffing for blood.'

Rachel is the only other person who knows about the picture of Sir Anthony Tomlinson with Turgood and Saltzing. Originally, Jack and I had agreed to only tell his boss DCS Jagtar Rawani, but when I couldn't get hold of Jack earlier in the month, and Rachel noticed I was struggling, she had encouraged me to come clean.

'But you haven't gone public with your investigation into Tomlinson, have you? So, as far as the world knows, you're not investigating him, so there's no reason to think that one is linked to the other. It's probably quite common for the Charity Commission to make sure that new charities are being operated effectively when they first start, to resolve any issues before they escalate into bigger problems. I'm certain that's all this audit is about, and everything is in order. Again, that's why we hired Saskia to run operations on a day-to-day basis. Do you remember it used to take me a day per week to maintain the website? Well, the site has never looked so good nor been run so efficiently as when Saskia took over, and it doesn't take her nearly as long to do. We're receiving more requests for financial support each month, and we're using Derek the detective to run background checks to identify the false claimants. You need to relax.'

It feels good to hear her say that, but I'm still not convinced that someone somewhere hasn't tipped off the Charity Commission in an effort to slow down my investigation; an unscrupulous audit would be the ideal way to have me take my eye off the ball.

'Saskia is bringing everything over in a bit,' Rachel continues, 'and then you'll be able to go through it all with a fine-tooth comb. You'll see there's nothing to fear.'

I wish I shared her optimism.

'Where's Daniella today?' I ask, keen to move on.

'Um, what day is it?'

'Sunday.'

'Okay... then she's probably in Morocco... I think. It's

tough keeping track of whichever glamorous location she's due in next.'

'And what's happening in Morocco?'

She narrows her eyes. 'I'm not officially allowed to know,' she whispers conspiratorially, 'but what I can tell you is that it's for a very well-known retailer who makes a habit of producing cutesy adverts in time for Christmas.'

My eyes widen in acknowledgement. 'I see. And things between the two of you are still…?'

'Better than ever,' she grins. 'It's funny, but since we got engaged, it's like when we first got together again. It's tough when she goes away for days at a time on one shoot or another, but when she gets back we can't keep our hands off one another. Sorry, over-share?'

I pretend to choke on my chocolate twist. 'Yeah, but some things never change.'

'Okay, well why don't you tell me how things are working out with you and Rick?'

'Not much to tell, to be honest. We're taking things slowly, and I'm enjoying getting to know him better.'

'How very civilised,' she mocks. 'What I want to know is whether you've slept with him yet.'

The heat rises to my cheeks. 'No, not yet.'

'It is allowed though, you know? You don't have to be betrothed for a bit of hanky panky these days.'

I slap her arm playfully. 'I'm well aware that times have changed, Rach, but it's my decision to take things slowly. I barely know him, and I want things to be on my terms.'

She's grinning wildly again, with more than a hint of mischief in the slant of her eyes. 'Or is it just that you're trying to delay things in the hope that Jack realises what he's missing and comes beating down your door?'

'This has nothing to do with Jack,' I reply quickly, but I'm not comfortable with the high pitch of my voice.

'Yeah, yeah, you say potato, I say pot-ah-to. I wish you'd just tell Jack how you feel about him; you never know, he might say he's really into you too, and then the pair of you can live happily ever after.'

'For the last time, there's nothing going on between Jack and me. We're just friends, and I value that friendship.'

She takes another bite of her pastry. 'I'm not sure which of us you're trying to convince, Em, but you've failed with me.'

I open my mouth to argue again, but she cuts me off with her hand.

'Listen, Em, there *is* something else I've been meaning to discuss with you... Oh, I don't know how to say this without upsetting you...'

I instantly straighten at the hint of bad news. 'What is it? You can tell me anything; you know that.'

'It's just... oh, I don't know,' she sighs. 'The thing is, since the proposal, Daniella and I have been talking. She tends to stay in hotels or crash here when she's in England, and has her own house in Sicily, where she's from... The thing is, Em, we're getting married soon, and this place is barely big enough for me, let alone two of us, so...'

It's sweet that she thinks the prospect of her moving in with her fiancée would upset me, and I quickly pull her into a hug. 'I'm thrilled that you two want to get your own place together, Rach.'

She squeezes me back. 'You are? Oh God, I didn't know how you'd react. I know you like crashing here when you come to meet with Maddie, or you're working with Jack. And I'm not saying that wherever we move to won't have a spare room for you to stay in when you visit, but you'd just have to get used to staying with a couple rather than just me.'

I separate us and fix her with a sincere stare. 'In truth, I probably should stop freeloading on you when I visit London anyway. There's no reason for me not to check into a hotel when I'm here on book business anyway.'

'I like when you come and stay with me though. You're still my best friend, and that will never change, Em.'

We embrace again. 'You know this means you'll have to curtail your wild girls' nights out,' I whisper. 'Once that ball and chain is tied to your ankle, it'll be quiet nights in in front of the television, watching soap operas and eating ready meals from trays on your laps.'

She erupts in laughter and we both sit back.

'Well if you don't hurry up and make a move on Rick or Jack, or whomever, I'll be buying you your first cat for your birthday, and some knitting yarn for Christmas.'

She chuckles to herself as I reach for my ringing phone, surprised to see DCS Jagtar Rawani's name. Although we agreed to exchange mobile numbers so that any calls wouldn't be logged on the police register, this is the first time he's actually called me.

'Good morning...' my voice trails off, as I'm not sure how to address him. *DCS Rawani* seems too formal, but we're not exactly on first name terms.

'Hi, Emma, it's DCS Rawani. Are you okay to speak?'

Even though Rachel knows about Tomlinson, I still feel the urge to move into the kitchen where at least she won't overhear his side of the conversation. 'Sure, what's going on?'

'I wanted to check if you've heard from Jack at all recently.'

'As a matter of fact he phoned me last night.'

'He did? And what did he say?'

'He said he was phoning to give me an update, but didn't actually have all that much he could share. He said that Faye McKenna's and Cormack Fitzpatrick's names had been added to the inquiry following the discovery of their faces on the videos recovered from Turgood's hard drive. He said the team haven't found anything else to link Faye and Cormack in terms of their backgrounds and the nature of their disappearances. He told me he'd been working around the clock on the Tomlinson angle, but was having to tread very carefully to avoid setting off alarm bells with his boss at the NCA. That's pretty much it. We spoke for about fifteen minutes in all.'

'Did he say anything else about what he'd be looking at next?'

I think back to last night's call, but I'd been so tired after the day I'd had that I was actually relieved the call had ended so quickly so that I could get to bed ahead of my early morning alarm.

'He said he still had one more lead he wanted to follow up on last night and that he'd call me back this morning if it amounted to anything.'

'And has he phoned you?'

I'm suddenly all too aware of the urgency in his tone. 'Um, no, he hasn't phoned today. Why? What's going on?'

The hairs are standing up on the back of my neck as I wait for the thundercloud that I can sense approaching like I've just glimpsed lightning.

'He... Jack was involved in a road traffic accident last night.'

My heart skips a beat and my hand shoots out for the countertop to steady myself. 'Is he…?'

'He was rushed to the Emergency Department at Hillingdon Hospital in the early hours of this morning…'

Oh God, oh no, please don't say it!

'Is he…?' I try again, but can't bring myself to finish the sentence.

'He's alive, but unconscious.'

My knees wobble and I exhale.

'I'm trying to establish whether the accident was simply bad luck or—'

'Whether there's something more sinister at play,' I finish for him.

'Exactly. Did he happen to mention to you where he was going or what this lead was?'

'No, I'm sorry, he didn't say, and I didn't push. Can I see him?'

'Sure, I can arrange it. How long until you can get to London?'

'I'm already here. I'm in Ealing.'

'Great. I'll meet you at the hospital in half an hour.'

Chapter Six

NOW

Hillingdon Hospital, London

I'm relieved that Rachel offered to drive me to the hospital as I can't focus on anything but seeing Jack. It feels so unreal that I was only speaking to him thirteen hours ago, and now he's in a hospital bed fighting for his life. Rachel messaged Saskia and asked her to drop the books around later, which I feel guilty about, especially as it was me who insisted on looking at them ahead of next week's audit. She was very understanding, but I know how annoyed I'd feel being messed about like that.

'Did DCS Rawani tell you where Jack is being treated?' Rachel asks as she spots a sign for the hospital.

I can't concentrate on remembering his words. It was as if my mind blocked out everything after he said Jack had been in an accident.

'He was taken to A&E this morning, but Rawani wasn't

specific about where he is now,' I reply, aware of how lame a response that is.

'Okay, well I'll park near the main building, and then perhaps we can phone Rawani and find out where he is. Sound good?'

I smile in acknowledgement, but my mind is far from at ease. As we pull in beneath the security barrier for the car park, however, I spot Rawani standing by the entrance, looking at his watch. At first I hardly recognise him in navy jeans and a salmon-coloured polo shirt. I've never seen him out of uniform before, but due to his height and the tight wrapping of his turban, he does tend to stand out in a crowd. Him checking his watch would suggest that we're a few minutes late, so I exit the car and allow Rachel to park while I hurry over to him.

'I'm sorry I'm late,' I say, panting. 'Traffic along the Uxbridge Road was foul.'

He glances at his watch again. 'That's okay. Shall we go in?'

I nod, quickly typing a message to Rachel and asking her to wait in the car.

Rawani leads me in through the automatic doors, and I'm relieved that he seems to know exactly where he's going. We sail along the corridors until we arrive at the Intensive Care Unit. He shows the nurse at the station his identification, and explains we're here to see Jack. The nurse leads us through the next set of doors until we arrive at a private room where a single patrolman is sitting guard.

'A precaution,' Rawani mutters under his breath, before addressing the officer. 'Any trouble?'

The patrolman shakes his head.

'Good. Go and get yourself a coffee and be back at your post in fifteen minutes.'

The patrolman leaves without a word, and I guess that's a sign of the power that this Detective Chief Superintendent wields over his people, whether it's derived from fear, respect, or a combination of both.

I struggle to control my breathing as he opens the door and steps aside to allow me to enter first. Jack is sprawled out on the bed, his eyes taped closed, with obvious swelling on one side. His right wrist is covered in a protective cast, and I recognise the wires leading to the heart monitor as it's the same one that sits behind Mum's bed in Weymouth. When I left her at the hospital last night, I didn't imagine I'd be back in a hospital so soon after.

'His car was recovered after a collision with a telegraph pole,' Rawani explains, 'but judging by the damage to the wing of the car, it's possible another vehicle was also involved in what happened. Bruising on his knuckles and around his ribs suggest he fractured his wrist prior to the accident. From what I understand, his injuries indicate he may have been involved in some kind of altercation before he started driving.'

My mouth drops open. 'But Jack isn't violent. He wouldn't hurt a fly.'

Rawani raises his eyebrows. 'His injuries would suggest otherwise on this occasion. I know you've already explained what the two of you discussed, but will you go over it once more for me?'

He scrapes a chair across the room for me to sit on, while pulling another over for him. 'You should know Jack is in safe hands here. I have had an officer stationed outside his room since he was moved up here. It's purely a precaution in case his altercation results in some kind of retaliation.'

I look over to Jack again as his chest rises and falls in time with the whirring of the machine beside him. There is a tube poking out of his mouth attached to the respirator. I know they don't intubate as a precaution, and Jack is in a worse state than Rawani initially suggested. It was me who led Jack into this investigation, and if he dies as a result of that, I will never forgive myself. If I hadn't agreed to him looking into Anna's disappearance, he wouldn't have found her face on Turgood's hard drive, and he wouldn't be here now.

'This is all my fault,' I whisper, as tears pool behind my eyes.

'I don't see how,' Rawani replies matter-of-factly. 'Now, tell me *exactly* what Jack said to you when he phoned last night.'

I close my eyes, clearing my mind of the panic that I may never get to hear Jack's voice again, or see that goofy way he grins when he's trying to be funny.

'He spoke about Faye and Cormack, and—'

'No, after that,' he interrupts. 'Tell me what he said about this lead he was following up on.'

I concentrate on Jack's voice and try to put myself back in my flat. The microwave had just pinged to announce my warm milk was ready, and I trapped the phone between my ear and shoulder while I stirred in the drinking chocolate powder. He asked me what I was doing, and I was too embarrassed to say I was making a hot chocolate, and instead I said I was tucking into a glass of chardonnay. I don't know why I lied; maybe it's because I was trying to sound more sophisticated, but I'm not sure. I responded by asking him whether his daughter Mila was with him, and he said he was having her over to stay on Wednesday night instead this week. I think I made a joke about him leaving his social calendar open, and…

'He said he was on his way to meet someone who might

have information relevant to the inquiry,' I tell Rawani. 'I asked him who, but he gave me the usual spiel about not wanting to confirm until he was certain. I laughed because even though what we're doing is a kind of private investigation off the books, he's still such a stickler for the rules. It was only at that point that I realised he was talking to me via the Bluetooth system in his car.'

'So he was physically driving somewhere while on the phone to you?'

I nod.

'Good, then if his phone was in use while he was driving, we should be able to triangulate his position at the time of the call, and hopefully track his movements thereafter. It won't tell us who he was meeting, but might indicate where they met.'

I hadn't thought of that, but then again my head seems to have been out of order since he called.

'Can you do that without giving away what we're doing?' I ask, conscious of what it could mean for the investigation if Tomlinson got wind that he's a potential target.

'One of my officers was involved in a road traffic accident with a telegraph pole. Even if he wasn't on duty at the time, I have a responsibility to discover what caused that accident. I will handle the matter personally until I know what happened. Plus, you have to remember that this simply could have been exactly that: an accident. For all we know, Jack had an argument with his ex-partner's new husband, and in his haste to get away crashed his car. There is nothing concrete to confirm it has anything to do with our inquiry. Whatever lead Jack was following, it may well have turned out to be nothing, or possibly he didn't even make it there. I don't want to speculate on what might have happened until I've had the chance to look into it.'

I know he's trying to calm me down, but my instinct is telling me that this is definitely connected, just like the surprise audit of the foundation by the Charity Commission. The problem is we don't know just how high the conspiracy could go. If Tomlinson *is* implicated, it doesn't mean it stops with him.

I suddenly have a flashback to something Lord Fitzhume told me when I was looking for his missing granddaughter: *there are always spies amongst us.*

'I'm not going to let them intimidate us into submission,' I say defiantly. 'I've been fighting all my life for the truth, and this won't stop me.'

Rawani doesn't answer at first, but I can feel him watching me.

'What?' I ask eventually when I can't take the silence any longer.

'It might be an idea for us not to meet again for now. Just in case. What are your writing commitments like at the moment?'

'We're battling with some lawyers to get my last book into print. I've not agreed on a new project yet. I've sketched a piece about Faye and Cormack, but I promised Jack I wouldn't submit it until after the investigation. What's with the sudden interest?'

'Not interest as such. I thought it might be an idea if you kept your head down just until we know what's going on. Maybe take a holiday somewhere.'

Something stirs in the back of my mind, and I don't want to listen to what the voice is telling me, but I can't ignore it. It was Jack's idea to involve Rawani in our discovery of Tomlinson's photograph, and I allowed Jack to convince me that his DCS was trustworthy, but I don't know all that much about him. Our exchanges have been limited, and he has gone out of his way to support our investigation, but is that because he genuinely wants to help or because he's serving an ulterior motive? The fact that he personally wants to oversee Jack's accident could be out of some kind of obligatory sense of honour, but could equally be an opportunity to cover up the truth.

'We should go,' he says, standing. 'We don't want anyone seeing the three of us together, just in case. Do you need a lift anywhere?'

I can't bring myself to look at him in case he reads the mistrust in my face. 'No. Thank you, but my friend is waiting in the car park.'

'Okay. I'll leave first, and you can follow in a few minutes. Remember, radio silence until I contact you again.'

I wait until he's gone before I let out my tears of dread.

Chapter Seven

THEN

Ruislip, London

The restaurant wasn't as busy as Zara had anticipated, and Tom's phone call had guaranteed them their favourite table, out of the glare of the front window, where passers-by would stop to gawk at whatever the diners were eating, but also out of the thoroughfare between front door and kitchen. This table allowed them a view of the front window, but in a nook where conversation wouldn't be overheard by the myriad other tables.

He hadn't said much since he'd found her asleep on the sofa. He'd entered, wrapped in his dressing gown, carrying her a fresh mug of tea and telling her he was going to run a bath. She'd wanted him to confront her about last night's outburst, but he'd made no reference to it. And when he'd emerged from the steamy bathroom with a freshly-shaven face and his jet-black hair sculpted back with gel – resembling a Sicilian hitman, rather than an Oxbridge graduate – he'd simply reported that brunch was booked for eleven.

It annoyed her that he wasn't angry about her throwing herself at him; it annoyed her that he wasn't the least bit upset about her wetting the bed; it annoyed her that they'd argued, and it hadn't grated with him as it had with her. She'd tossed and turned on the sofa, trying to predict how the next confrontation would play out when they were both in the cold light of day. From the way he'd emerged from the bedroom with a freshly pressed shirt, sports jacket, and winning smile, it was as if none of last night had happened.

Was that his plan? Just to ignore the revelation about her past? Was he simply going to bury it, and paper over the cracks in their relationship? If only it was that easy for her too. She'd spent years plugging holes in their sinking ship, but now that the fault lines were visible, she didn't want to keep filling them. Her truth was out, and he needed to at least acknowledge that nothing could ever go back to how it was before Will and Harriet's disastrous dinner party.

She'd dressed in a simple lime-coloured one-piece silk summer dress, accompanied by a thin cream-coloured cotton cardigan and matching heels. With makeup applied, at least she *looked* the part, even if she didn't feel it. Conversation in the car ride to the high street was stilted, and when Giuseppe – the restaurant owner and a former client of Tom's – escorted them to their table, Tom seemed back to his usual self, sharing an anecdote with the young Italian.

Everything on the menu always sounded so delicious, but as she read the familiar list, nothing tempted her. She eventually settled for eggs benedict and a blood-orange soda to go with the double espresso. Tom ordered an all-day breakfast calzone and a cappuccino, and silence once more returned to the table.

'They reckon temperatures could reach as high as twenty-two later today,' Tom said, studying his phone's screen. 'Perhaps after brunch, we could drive out of London and find somewhere for a nice walk, and maybe an early evening dinner in a country pub? What do you think?'

Was this what they'd now become? A couple who went on drives and slowly worked their way through fancy menus in one establishment or another? She knew he needed more than that, and in truth so did she. But this wasn't the place to confront the elephant lurking in the room.

'Sounds nice,' she replied instead.

'More rain due by Wednesday though, and then a significant drop in temperatures. They're predicting snow by the end of the month.'

'We'd best make the most of today then.'

She inwardly cringed at the lack of anything else to say.

He locked his phone and placed it screen down on the white table cloth, appearing to reach for her hand, before stopping himself. 'How are you feeling now?'

She didn't know how to answer. Did he want her to tell the truth and admit that she doubted she'd ever feel herself again? Or was he hoping she'd simply say she was fine, and attempt to move past last night? In the end, she simply shrugged.

His fingers edged closer to hers. 'You know, there is something I've been meaning to talk to you about for a while, but I've been putting it off, trying to find the right time... As you know, work is going well, and I'm being kept plenty busy with new cases and consultations, and there's every chance Sir Robert will be retiring from chambers in the next six months, and I'm in with a shout at progression... So, what I was going to—'

He didn't manage to finish as an ear-splitting ringing erupted directly over their heads, and both pairs of hands shot up to protect their hearing.

Zara could barely keep her eyes open as her mind sucked her back to a place she had hoped she would never see again.

The mirage of the restaurant faded before her eyes and she was back in the confines of the box room at the top of the house. The cacophony of noise remained, however, and as she squashed her back into the door, she felt it vibrate as *he* banged and bashed at it. But she'd managed to drag the bedframe across the thick wood, and with her pressed against it, the door wouldn't budge.

'Screw you then!' he shouted through the door, swiftly followed by the thundering echo of his steps as he retreated down the stairs.

Her ears were in agony as the alarm noise reverberated off the small walls, and she could feel the wet of tears on her face as she willed the noise and the pain to dissipate. But then something tickled at the back of her throat, and she erupted into a coughing fit that only seemed to grow worse as the room filled with a thin layer of grey smoke. It tasted like she was eating coal, and she could almost feel the black tar coating her gums.

Standing, she hurried to the tiny window, but the lock had been painted shut, and no matter how she tried to dig her tiny fingers beneath the latch, it wouldn't budge. Thumping her fists against the pane of glass, the sound was muffled by the smoke alarm that was now the beating heart of the house. And if she couldn't hear the thumps on the window, what chance was there that a neighbour or passing stranger would be able to hear it?

Rushing back to the bed, she yanked it away from the door, and reached for the handle, but as she depressed it, she realised he must have slid the lock across on the other side, sealing her inside. She pulled and tugged as she had so many times before, but it wouldn't budge.

And that was when she saw the cloud of grey wafting up from the gap beneath the door.

Spluttering, she dragged the duvet from the bedframe, and squashed it down towards the gap, temporarily cutting off the smoke supply. But it was only a fleeting reprieve.

The room was warming rapidly, and she couldn't begin to predict how long it would be before the growing orange flames would engulf the room. She was safe from him in here, but what was the point if death came knocking first?

She returned to the window and tried to look out, hoping someone – anyone – would just glance up and realise she was trapped in here and call the fire brigade. But what she could still see of the street was empty of life. The smoke was now billowing from the kitchen below her room, and it was becoming more and more difficult to see anything through the glass. Although she'd managed to slow the stream of smoke, the room was still filling, and as panic set in, she was struggling to breathe between coughing fits.

What had they taught her in school about fires? Wasn't it to stay low, and wait for help? But what if help didn't come? Then what was she supposed to do?

Giving up on the window, she returned to the door. She reached for the door handle again, before quickly withdrawing her hand and yelping as the metal burned her palm. The flames crackled and spat just beyond the wooden door, and she didn't need to be told that the fire had taken control of the upstairs landing. Even if she manged to open the door, her path out would probably be blocked anyway.

So this was it? How many nights had she lain awake on the thin and bumpy mattress, willing her life to end so that she'd no longer have to suffer at *his* hands? She'd prayed for reprieve, but now that it was here, she desperately didn't want to die.

Dropping to her knees, she closed her eyes, and between coughs recited the 'Hail Mary', begging for someone to take her from this place, or for death to be quick.

The room was now spinning as her entire body seemed to be leaking water, such was the heat in the room now. Lying down on the carpet, she closed her eyes and accepted her sentence, but seconds later, there was a rumble and scraping sound and a gust of wind followed the cracking open of the window frame. An angel dressed in bright yellow trousers and helmet with a plastic face covering appeared through the cloud. He lifted her up and over his shoulder, and as she continued to retch and heave, she felt her body being slowly lowered, and something being pushed over her own face.

'Zara? Babe? Zara? Can you hear me?'

She forced her clammy eyes open, and all she could see was Tom's pained concern staring back at her.

'Babe? Can you hear me? Zara?'

'Y-yes,' she stuttered, her head pounding. She was suddenly aware that she could no longer hear the smoke alarm. 'W-what happened? Where am I?'

She searched her surroundings, relief slowly washing over her as the familiar shop fronts of Ruislip High Street filled her periphery. A few yards up from them she saw Giuseppe apologising profusely to the small crowd of diners surrounding him who were asking what had happened.

'Chip pan fire,' Tom explained quietly. 'Apparently, one of the sous-chefs stepped outside to take a phone call, leaving the pan unwatched, and the stove caught ablaze, setting off the smoke alarms. They evacuated the dining room as a precaution. Where did you go though? As soon as the alarm sounded, I stood up and said we should follow everyone else out, but you were rooted to the spot. Your eyes were open, but it was like you were frozen in time or something. In the end, Giuseppe had to help me carry you out here.' He paused and pressed his hand to her forehead. 'You're freezing cold. Are you okay?'

She could still taste the charcoal stench of smoke from the bedroom. 'I must have had a panic attack,' she bluffed, looking at her palm where the door handle had scarred her all those years ago.

'Well, Giuseppe has said he's going to give everyone free drinks by way of an apology. Our food is probably nearly ready. Shall we?'

He pressed his fist into his hip to make a loop of his arm, but Zara didn't move.

'I can't,' she said, her eyes filling. 'Please, I just want to go home.'

Tom searched her eyes for answers, and finding none, slowly nodded. 'Okay. I'll let Giuseppe know something's come up and settle the bill.'

He began to move away and she reached for him. 'I'm sorry, Tom. For everything. I'm sorry.'

He patted her hand on his arm. 'I'm really worried about

you, babe. I feel like there's so much you haven't told me, and I want to help you get through this, but you have to let me in. I think we should speak to someone to help put you at ease. I have an idea. Let me sort things with Giuseppe, and then I'm going to make a call. We can get you through this.'

Chapter Eight

NOW

Ealing, London

I've never felt so out of place, in both life and location. The air reeks of stale beer and tar carried on the breath of those whose expressions of despair and loss aptly reflect how I'm feeling. The guy behind the bar stares at me with mistrust as he takes my order and almost smirks when I ask if there's a wine list. He points at a sheet of glass dripping with condensation at knee height, and I tell him to pick. He opens the refrigerator door, extracts a bottle, and swills the contents before pouring a measure into the glass he's placed on the sticky bar.

I nod for him to make it a large and drop a crisp ten pound note on the damp-looking bar towel to my left. The first swig stings my cheeks and reminds me why I only drink as a last resort, but the second gulp warms my throat and briefly lifts the cloud inside my head.

I flip over my phone as it jars on the bar and I see it's another message from Rachel asking where I am. I don't want her to see how much I'm struggling, especially when her future has never looked so rosy, but looking at the two skinheads propped up against the fruit machine who keep glancing in my direction, I don't feel totally safe. This was a bad idea, but I didn't think twice before crossing the road and bowling in. I don't want to think about what Jack would say if he could see me now.

I reply to Rachel's message and confirm the name of the bar. Two blue ticks appear beside my message confirming she's seen it, but she doesn't reply. I take another drink from the glass, allowing my arms to press against the edge of the sticky bar, before the weight of my thoughts crushes me.

I still can't come to terms with Jack lying so helpless in that hospital bed. My focus all this time has been on why he ended up that way, but I've been avoiding the question of who caused his injuries, and potentially ran him off the road. And to what end? A warning? An attempt to stop us? What if I'm being watched now? Should we have been checking for a tail? What if whoever hurt Jack was at the hospital waiting to see who else was involved in the investigation? How many more of my friends' lives am I going to endanger in this quest?

It's only when I feel Rachel reaching for my arms and placing her hands around my shoulders that I cave and admit what drove me in here.

'I'm the reason he's there,' I tell her, and although my eyes are dry of tears, the guilt weighs heavy on my heart.

Rachel shakes her head. 'Don't do this to yourself. Jack is a grown man with a mind of his own. You have this – frankly *irritating* – habit of taking responsibility for everyone else's poor decisions. Ever since I met you, you're so quick to admit culpability, but you're one of the smartest and most caring people I know. I know you blame yourself for Anna wandering off that day, but it was *her* choice to go without telling your parents. I'm sorry if that sounds harsh, but it's the truth, and you're only going to run yourself into the ground if you keep taking on others' blame.'

She takes a breath, and then frowns with empathy. 'I'm sorry, but you need to snap out of this, Em. I can see you're worried about Jack so I won't ask how he is, but you're seeing conspiracy where it doesn't exist. The Emma Hunter I know and love wouldn't be seen dead in a place like this.' She glances up and shrugs apologetically at the barman, who's watching us closely. 'The warrior I know would tackle the obstacle head on and find out what lead Jack was chasing, and pick up the baton where he left off.'

She's right that I'm not going to be any use frantically worrying, but my head is all over the place, and I don't know what to do for the best. Generally when I feel a blockage like this, I'd go and visit Mum at the home, as the walk helps clear my head. Maybe it's all the low-hanging smog of London that's causing the blockage. I'm certain if I could smell the salt in the air, and hear the waves crashing on the sand opposite my flat, I wouldn't be so blindsided.

She takes a sip of the wine and grimaces. 'And if your plan is to bury your troubles at the bottom of a bottle, I won't allow you to do it with this piss. Let me take you back to mine, and we can make a plan.'

I don't move, but she's right about the wine.

'Thank you,' I tell her, straining to smile in appreciation. 'I know you're right, but I feel so lost right now. In truth, I've been lost for the last month. It doesn't seem to matter how hard I try, I can't tie the loose ends together. I thought we were making progress on tracking down the people who snatched Anna, but now this wall we've come up against feels unscalable. Do you know what I mean?'

'What you need is a distraction,' she says, pushing the wine glass away and dragging me from the pub. I open my mouth to argue, but I know deep down she's trying to save me from myself, and I don't put up a fight as she crosses us over the road and returns us to her car. Once inside, she reaches over and opens the glovebox, removing three glossy magazines and resting them on my lap.

'I need your help and good taste in selecting a wedding dress and honeymoon destination.'

At first I think she's joking, but the look of concentration on her face as she flips open *Brides* magazine shows me she's serious. I want to push the magazines to the footwell and remind her that Jack is fighting for his life in hospital, that Freddie is refusing to speak to me, and that any chance of finding my sister shrinks by the second. But I now see that her eyes are just as troubled as mine, even if for a different reason.

'Obviously, I've got no chance of looking as beautiful as Daniella will, but I want her to know that I've made an effort. She's so glamorous and on fleek, and I don't want to embarrass her. Ordinarily, if I wanted fashion advice I'd ask her, but I want to surprise her on the day, so I can't discuss it with her.'

I look down at my jeans and suit jacket. 'I'm hardly a style icon, Rach. You must have other friends more in the know than me.'

'I'm not trying to compete with Daniella. I want something understated—'

I raise my eyebrows.

'But with a touch of sophistication,' she quickly adds. 'I've narrowed it down to half a dozen dresses that I like the style of, but I want your opinion about them before going to find something similar. If we can narrow it down to a couple of styles, then I'll know better what I'm looking for.'

I'm flattered that she'd ask for my opinion, but she should know I'm out of my depth when it comes to this sort of thing. I dress for comfort rather than to any kind of trend, but there is an eagerness in her eyes that I don't want to disappoint.

'Can't you just go on one of those programmes where they do it all for you? Isn't there one called *Dress to Impress*?' I mean it as a joke, but her eyes widen with excitement.

'Would you go on that show with me? If I applied they'd reject my application, but if international bestselling author Emma Hunter agreed to appear too, I'm sure—'

'Rach, I was joking,' I sigh, flipping open the magazine on top. 'Why don't you show me your picks and then I can tell you which I think would best suit you. I can't promise you'll agree with me, but as your maid of honour, I guess this does fall within my remit.'

Her eyes brighten instantly and I can't help but admire her enthusiasm.

'I've never seen you as happy as you are right now, and I'm so pleased that you've met someone who puts such a warm smile on your beautiful face. I never thought I'd see the day when you were looking at wedding brochures and trying to pick the perfect honeymoon. You've come a long way, Rachel Leeming.'

Her eyes mist over, and she pulls me into her arms. 'I couldn't have done it without you, Em. I want you to know if there's anything I can ever do for you, you're only to say. Do you hear me?'

I'm about to respond when I feel my mobile buzzing in my pocket, and see that Maddie is calling.

'Hi Emma, is now a good time? I have a favour to ask.'

I'm feeling woozy, the wine having gone to my head. I exit the car, welcoming the cool breeze and splashes of rain as they flush my cheeks.

'Emma? Are you there? Can you hear me?

'Sorry, yes, I'm here. What's the favour?'

'It's a bit delicate. Are you still in London?'

'For now. I'm with Rachel. Why? What's going on?'

'Are you? Oh that's fab! I need you to come over to my place if you can? There's someone here I'd like you to meet.'

I groan at the thought of Maddie trying to match-make, but she quickly corrects me. 'I met someone at a party last night that I think will interest you. Do you remember the "Brighton Rock Girl"?'

Chapter Nine

NOW

Edgware, London

Rachel parks us outside the address Maddie texted to me. I don't know what I was expecting her home to look like, but this wasn't it. Given how organised and pragmatic she is in her working life, I suppose I've always pictured her in some high-end penthouse apartment overlooking the Thames, chewing the fat with friends from across the globe until the early hours, before grabbing a couple of hours' sleep and racing to Blackfriars to put the publishing industry to rights. I realise now that my impression of Maddie's home life has been duly influenced by the film *Wall Street*.

Maddie's three-storey townhouse is on a reasonably new estate, judging by the orange glow of the brickwork, and the narrow semi-detached properties across the road. There's even a large fenced playground with swings, slides, and a skate ramp in the centre of the estate. It's the kind of place that looks welcoming to younger families using government funding to help them buy their first home. The fact that none of the thirty or so properties in the estate are up for sale speaks volumes.

Even Rachel looks surprised as we exit the Uber, and she stares up at the townhouse. 'You sure this is the place?' she asks sceptically.

I show her my phone's screen. 'This is where she said.'

We approach the door, passing Maddie's old rust-covered VW Beetle she affectionately calls Gertie. Maddie loves this car more than any other possession and I've often thought that when it does eventually give up the ghost, she'll have it immortalised in some kind of garage or museum. She says it's cheap to run, has low mileage, and one very careful owner. I've never felt safe being driven in it to meetings, but there's something endearing about the way Maddie stands by Gertie through thick and thin.

'This is definitely the place,' I say, nodding at Gertie, and hovering my hand over the bonnet at the rear and feeling no heat rising.

A laminated sign has been screwed to the doorframe warning cold callers not to stop at the door, as she won't buy goods or make charitable donations on the doorstep. Maddie being as pragmatic as ever. Searching around the rest of the door frame, there's no sign of a doorbell, and so Rachel raps heavily on the PVC door, until we see movement behind the frosted glass, and Maddie opens it moments later.

'Oh, it's you,' she says, making no effort to hide her disappointment when her eyes fall on Rachel.

The fact that my best friend and my mentor can't see eye to

eye is one of my greatest frustrations. They both have my best interests at heart, and perhaps that's the reason the conflict exists.

Maddie's eyes quickly brighten when she sees me lurking behind, and she ushers us inside, closing the door before advising us to head upstairs to the sitting room. I'm a little surprised Maddie isn't offering a tour of her abode, given I've never been here before, but the urgency with which she's shooing us up the stairs suggests there's more going on here than she let on in her phone call.

I managed to perform a quick internet search about the 'Brighton Rock Girl' on the ride over from Ealing to jog my memory of the case, but I didn't learn much more than that Zara Edwards was abducted thirty-five years ago, and was later recovered when police were called to a house fire not far from the pier where she went missing. According to what I read, the perpetrator was arrested and imprisoned and later died behind bars. I don't quite understand why Maddie seemed so keen to discuss the case other than that she thinks the subject could make for a good follow-up book to Aurélie's story. Given the age of the case, and the fact that it was resolved before I was born, I don't really see what fresh angle I could bring to the table.

I start upon entering the sitting room, finding two people already inside, the man sipping from a mug of coffee and the woman standing at the window with her back to me. With the net curtains flapping around her in the breeze from the open window, there's something ghost-like about her.

'Emma Hunter, may I introduce Tom and Zara?' Maddie says proudly.

The apparition at the window turns at the mention of her name, and I now see she's older than I'd expected from the deep-red highlights in her hair. The welts beneath her eyes and downcast lips indicate she's already cried today. Maybe she can sense the same thing from me.

I extend my hand to the man first as he is closest to me, and he stands and shakes it.

'Tom,' he says in a baritone voice that seems to perfectly suit his combed-back hairstyle, sports jacket, and dress-shirt look. If I had to guess I'd say he's probably a surgeon or barrister; definitely a white-collar profession of some sort.

I then move across to the woman, who reluctantly takes my hand but limply enough that when I shake mine, her grip breaks. 'I'm Emma,' I confirm as if it was necessary, 'and this is my friend and some-time collaborator Rachel.'

Rachel remains behind Maddie and nods politely at the two of them.

'Great!' Maddie declares, clapping her hands together. 'Now that everyone's acquainted, can I fix anyone a fresh drink? Tom? Zara, would you like something now?'

She shakes her head and returns to looking out of the window. Tom shakes his head and then Maddie looks to me. To be honest, my head is still spinning slightly from the bitter wine at the pub so I shake my head too.

'Well, I should leave you to it,' Maddie continues, moving past Rachel to the door. 'If you need anything, I'll be downstairs in the kitchen.'

Rachel and I sit on the corner sofa, the opposite end to Tom who continues to drink his coffee in silence. Although Maddie didn't say, the fact that the woman by the window is called Zara, and that that's also the name of the 'Brighton

Rock Girl', leads me to think I'm not making too many assumptions to guess that this is the girl from the famous photograph.

I remember now researching the case when I was first looking for Anna while at university. I read up on so many missing child stories in a desperate effort to find links to Anna's case, but I don't recall anything particularly standing out about Zara's story in terms of similarity.

'Have you travelled far?' I say when the silence in the room becomes overwhelming.

'Ruislip,' Tom replies cheerily, 'so, no, not too far. You're from Weymouth aren't you?'

Will I ever get used to perfect strangers knowing more about me than I do about them? I doubt it.

'That's right,' I say, hoping the warmth in my cheeks isn't visible to the others in the room. 'But I was at Rachel's flat in Ealing when Maddie called,' I add, pointing at Rachel.

I don't know if I've said before, but I don't do idle chit-chat very well. There are some who are blessed with the ability to make small talk with new people they meet, but I'm not. I'd sooner they just tell me why they wanted to meet me.

'Babe, do you want to come and sit down?' Tom asks Zara, but if she hears him, she makes no acknowledgement.

My fingers tap my lap, as my mind blanks of any further conversation starters. I'm adamant I won't mention the weather, but moments after this thought, I bowl out with, 'It's surprisingly warm for the time of year, isn't it?'

I instantly cringe, especially when Tom tells me they're predicting snow later this month.

I look to Rachel for help, but she shrugs.

Sitting forward, I grimace as I speak. 'Sorry to be blunt, but

I'm not exactly sure why I'm here today… Is there something specific you want to talk about?'

Tom looks over to his statuesque wife before resting his mug on the carpet. 'It's difficult… Um, we met your agent – Maddie – at a dinner party last night. She's um… a friend of a friend, you know. Anyway, she was telling us about the work that you've been doing with your writing – you'll have to forgive me, I haven't read any of your books – and how you've become something of an expert in locating missing children.'

'I'm no expert,' I quickly caution.

He frowns. 'Oh, right… Yeah. Anyway, long story short, Zara was… abducted when she was a child, and it was quite the human interest story in the press for a long time, and when she was found, and returned to her parents… the nation celebrated.'

'I read about it on the way over,' I say, nodding.

'Okay, good… So what do you think?'

'About what?'

'About helping Zara? There was a… thing last night, and then another *thing* this morning… Sorry, it's all rather awkward.'

I look over to the window where Zara remains frozen. 'From what I understand, the man who snatched and held you – Callum Gerrard – was caught shortly after you were recovered?'

There's the slightest jolt, but she doesn't answer.

'Can you tell us what *thing* happened that you're so concerned about?' Rachel asks, cutting through the silence.

Tom shuffles awkwardly in his seat. 'Well, she… she had quite a bad nightmare last night, which I think was probably triggered by me learning the truth about her history.'

Rachel and I exchange glances.

'So you weren't aware of Zara's abduction?' Rachel clarifies for the both of us.

Tom looks down at his feet. 'Not before last night, no. It was as much of a shock for me as those at the dinner party.' His head snaps up. 'But that isn't important. I understand why Zara wouldn't want to share that part of her life, but now that I do know, I'm keen to help her through it in any way I can.'

I look back to Zara and say her name to get her attention. 'Zara? Was the nightmare related to what happened all those years ago?'

She turns to face me and nods.

'Can you tell me about it?'

She looks over to Tom and then back at me. 'I don't think I can… I remember feeling terrified, but apart from that, no, I don't remember what the nightmare was about.'

'Have you had nightmares about that time of your life before?'

'Not for a long time. I think I did have nightmares – a lot of them – once I got home, and I don't really remember when they stopped, other than that they did. That period of my life feels like another lifetime; do you understand what I mean?'

I stand. 'I do, yes. Listen, I have an idea if you're up for it? Why don't you and I go for a walk outside – just the two of us – and we can talk one to one? I could certainly do with a breath of fresh air.'

She looks back to Tom, as if seeking his permission, but he nods his encouragement. It's funny, but I'm sensing it wasn't Zara's idea to come here today. My hope is that she'll be more willing to open up if we're alone, but hopefully Rachel might also get some useful information out of Tom without Zara around.

Heading down to the front door, I stop to advise Maddie we're just popping out for some air, but she's on the phone with someone, and I'm not sure she quite understands.

The air outside is warm and muggy, and if I were to guess, I'd say that a storm is brewing somewhere nearby.

Chapter Ten

THEN

Brighton, East Sussex

35 years ago

Squashed into the side of the picnic bench, Zara placed the headphones over her ears and adjusted the thin metal frame over her hair until the sponge pads rested comfortably. Her mum had agreed to Zara bringing her Walkman for tonight's festivities, in case the bangers were too loud. Zara had wanted to say that the louder the better as far as she was concerned, but had felt a rush of responsibility that she'd been allowed to bring her most expensive present out for the evening. On her ninth birthday back in June, her mum had told her they would both start treating her differently now that she was older, and that meant Zara herself would have to start taking greater accountability for her own actions.

They had seemed like big words at the time, and until this holiday they hadn't really treated her much differently.

However, when they'd come away to Brighton three days earlier, her mum had given her a purse with five pounds in – a little holiday money from Grandma – and Zara had been allowed to carry it in her mini handbag, with the freedom to choose how she spent it.

'That's all the money you'll have,' her mum had cautioned. 'Once it's gone, it's gone, so think wisely before spending willy-nilly.'

And Zara had bided by that warning. She'd seen plenty of things as they'd twisted and turned through the Lanes today. Nobody had warned her just how disorientating the streets of Brighton could be; a maze of alleys interconnecting, and each offering treasures aplenty. At one point, she'd lost sight of her mum and panic had started to set in, until she'd spotted the tail of the mustard-coloured scarf disappearing behind a sheet doorway and had hurried after. Then, behind another cloak-like door, Zara had followed her nose and found a tiny shop where the chocolate-laced air smelt heavenly. The little man – was she allowed to call him a dwarf? – behind the counter had eyed her suspiciously, enquiring as to where her parents were, right before her mum had come through the curtain. His suspicion quickly turned to delight, as he held out a plate of sugared mice, and encouraged her to taste a sample.

She'd succumbed and bought ten, feeling proud when he'd handed her the little brown paper bag, and she'd squashed it into her handbag, next to her purse. That still left her four shiny gold coins of her own to spend, and she wasn't going to waste them. The trip from shop to shop had continued until lunchtime, when they'd met up with her dad. Her mum hadn't been happy that he was late getting to the bus stop, but he'd promised to make it up to them with a fish and chip supper for lunch. What Zara hadn't expected was that their supper wouldn't be out of a newspaper like she was used to, but in a restaurant. Not only that, but her dining choice hadn't been limited to a small cod and chips.

'Have whatever you want,' her dad had said, smiling broadly at them both from across the table.

'How are we going to afford this place?' her mum had asked wearily, keeping her fluorescent tracksuit top hidden by her pale blue anorak.

'Cos I had a good day,' he had replied with glee, before producing a wad of notes that he used to fan himself.

'Jesus!' Mum had exclaimed. 'You rob a bank or something?'

He'd quickly hidden the cash, conscious that such extravagance could draw unwanted attention. 'Mate of mine at the track put me onto a sure thing, and voilà!'

Mum had scowled at the admission. 'The gee-gees. Where'd the money for the stake come from, Keith?'

Zara had kept her head down as the inevitable argument over money had ensued, and had been grateful when the gum-chewing waitress had arrived at the table to take their order. The waitress was wearing a collared shirt, but had tied the tails into a knot, revealing her belly button, despite the cold November temperature outside. Her hair was in a scruffy bob, and her face heavily made-up. Zara had envied her confidence, and had wondered whether her mum would let her buy some gum and makeup with what remained of Grandma's money.

'And my daughter will have scampi and chips,' Dad had concluded, winking at Zara as he placed the order.

She'd never had scampi before but had asked to try it

several times. She was pleased he'd remembered, and taken the decision out of her hands.

'How about we save some of your winnings to help pay for next month's housekeeping,' her mum had chided when the waitress was gone.

'If my princess wants scampi, then that's what she'll have,' he'd fired back, winking at Zara again.

She'd smiled back. She loved it when he referred to her as his princess. She wasn't the prettiest of girls – her long ginger plaits often referred to as *rat tails* by some of the older girls at school – but when her dad called her his princess, she felt like a beautiful swan.

Dinner had arrived, and she'd wolfed down the scampi and chips with a large dollop of ketchup from the bottle. Her dad's good mood meant that he'd bought them both an ice cream along the promenade, and they'd finished the afternoon at the amusement arcades. Zara had been reluctant to go in at first, seeing the games as a potential waste of her holiday money, but her dad had then handed her a fresh five pound note and sent her off to the teller to collect a bucket of change. Even her mum had had a go on one of the clutch machines, but despite her best efforts she hadn't managed to win Zara the teddy she so desperately wanted. At age nine, she didn't usually crave soft toys anymore, but this particular one was in the shape of a crab, with a smiley face, and it perfectly summed up the holiday to that point.

When she wasn't looking, her dad went and spoke to the teller, before producing the crab teddy for Zara. He didn't tell her how much it had cost to buy outright, but she hadn't cared. It had been the best day, and as they huddled on the bench, and the dark sky drew in, she had been excited about what tomorrow would bring.

Now, as the Communards began the first bars of 'Don't Leave Me This Way' – the cassette single had been a back-to-school present from her mum – the cold air was starting to feel uncomfortable. Pressing her face and shoulder into her mum's arm, she was soon being snuggled.

'Are either of you hungry?' her dad asked.

It had been hours since the scampi and chips, and Zara had all but forgotten about the sugared mice in her handbag. 'I am,' she said.

'Me too,' he chuckled. 'How about I go and see if I can find us something sweet to eat; the fireworks are set to start at eight, and we should go and find a good spot on the pier to watch them from.'

He left without another word.

'Are you cold sweetheart?' her mum asked, pulling Zara closer into her anorak.

'A bit, but I'll be okay,' Zara replied, bobbing her head to the music.

The bench was across the road from the pier, and even though the sky was darkening by the second, she could see more and more people starting to gather at the pier's entrance and beyond where the pavilion's lights looked like a beacon. It was impossible to separate the sand from the sea now, but she could hear the waves crashing nearby.

'We should live here,' she said, imagining how much fun it would be to have the beach on their doorstep.

'You'd soon get bored of the beach,' her mum said, as if reading her mind. 'It's a treat when you come somewhere like this for a break, but I bet most of the locals rarely frequent the beach. Besides, it wouldn't be very practical for mine and your dad's jobs, would it?'

'You could get different jobs though, couldn't you?'

'Well, how about this, when *you're* older, and get to choose where you live, you could rent a place near a beach. How about that? Then me and your dad can come and visit you here.'

Zara's eyes widened at the idea. 'Then we could spend Christmas Day swimming in the sea.'

Her mum chuckled as the bitter wind stung their faces. Her dad was coming back across the road and ushering for them to come and meet him.

'We'd better go,' her mum said, standing and taking Zara by the hand. 'Oh, Zara, your fingers are freezing. Where are the gloves I told you to bring?'

Zara knew precisely where the gloves were: on the end of her bed at the caravan where her mum had placed them, before reminding her to bring them with her. Zara shrugged.

'Well, put your hands in your pockets to get them warm,' her mum suggested, as they caught up with her dad.

'Who fancies a bit of mint rock then?' he said, producing the large pink stick.

'What have you bought that for?' her mum sighed. 'It's enormous. It'll rot her teeth and give her an upset tummy.'

He smiled as he uncoiled the twisted plastic wrapper and passed it to her. 'You need to suck on it until it softens.'

The freshness of the mint flavour caught in her throat and she coughed initially, but it quickly passed and the sugary sweetness was soon shutting out the cold.

'Here, I got us one of them disposable cameras too,' her dad said, showing off the second of his purchases. 'Thought we could get some photos by the rollercoaster they've constructed where the theatre used to be.'

They continued across the road, beneath the canopy at the entrance where temporary stalls had been erected, selling sugared almonds and toffee apples. Zara would have happily exchanged the hard lump of rock for a toffee apple, but her dad had looked so thrilled when he'd handed it to her that she continued to suck at the hardened treat.

'There used to be a big theatre here, known as the Palace Theatre,' he said, leaning in and having a lick of the rock. 'They used it in a *Carry On* film in the early 70s, do you remember the one I mean? Where the toilet factory workers come to the beach for the day.'

She nodded, vaguely remembering watching it with him one Sunday afternoon when it had been on television.

'It got damaged, mind you,' he continued. 'There was a huge storm ten or so years ago, and the end of the pier was crashed into by a boat and they demolished the theatre, building this rollercoaster and these arcades instead. You want a go on the rollercoaster before the fireworks start?'

Zara looked up at the looping track, and whilst she'd thought it a good idea when they'd been on the bench across the road, up close it was much higher than she'd realised, and the squealing riders on it at the moment didn't instil any sense of confidence.

Zara shook her head. 'Maybe tomorrow?' she added when she saw his face was crestfallen.

'Well, let's at least get some pictures to treasure this moment, eh? You go and stand by the rollercoaster's entrance, and I'll take your picture.'

She did as instructed, before her mum quickly hurried over and tidied the trailing plaits.

'Hold up your rock,' her dad called, squinting into the camera, clicking the snapper with a bright flash before winding it on and taking extra shots in case the first didn't come out.

A whizzing noise was followed by a trail of green light shooting into the sky before exploding into a million yellow lights overhead.

'They're starting,' her dad said, draping an arm around his wife's shoulders and ushering Zara to join them.

Zara reached for her mum's hand, before being reminded to keep her hand in her pocket for warmth, and swapping the rock over when her right hand was too cold. Zara didn't hear the second part as a red and blue trail shot into the sky with a whoosh. Everyone else on the pier had now stopped what they were doing and had gathered around to watch the spectacle. Zara kept her headphones in place to muffle the bangs and gnawed at the pink rock.

More and more people moved closer, all with necks craned to watch the light show in the sky. Zara tried to maintain her ground, but found herself being bustled until she could no longer see the fireworks whizzing and exploding. Tugging on her mum's arm, she tried to explain, but even though her mum stooped to listen, it was impossible to hear anything over the whooping of the crowd and the exhilarating explosions.

Taking a few steps backwards, Zara reversed through the crowd, keeping her head bent upwards, until she could once again see the light show. Checking she could still see her mum's yellow scarf, she watched with wonder as blues, reds, whites, and greens intertwined against the black canvas, starting at each bang but thrilled by the experience all the same. Lowering her face just long enough to wrap the end of the rock in its crinkling plastic wrapper, she wasn't expecting to feel something soft pressed roughly over her face. The chemical smell made her want to gag and kick out, but her vision quickly blurred, and the last thing she saw was the yellow scarf snapping around as her mum began to look for her in the crowd of bodies.

Chapter Eleven

NOW

Edgware, London

Removing my suit jacket, I tie the sleeves around my waist. At first I can't quite match Zara's pace. It's not a slow stroll, nor a steady pace, but somewhere between the two, which I'm not used to. She is only a few inches taller than I am, but her legs are disproportionately longer, which means one slow stride for her is two medium steps for me. I almost feel like a ballroom dancer following a quick-quick-slow step.

'What is it you do for a living, Zara?' I ask to break the ice.

'Nothing at the moment... I worked as a legal secretary in a local firm until they got taken over by another firm and then I was made redundant just before Christmas.'

'Oh, I'm sorry to hear that.'

Her head is slightly bent, her eyes concentrating on the dry ground immediately ahead of her. 'It's fine. I wasn't enjoying the role, to be honest. It was a means to an end, and they gave me a fairly generous package to go quickly. Tom knew my heart wasn't in it, and he said I should take some time out to think about what I really want to do. At forty-four, it's probably a bit late to start a new career, but if I can find something that brings in steady pay without too much stress, I think I'd find contentment.'

'How long have you and Tom been together?'

'Nearly twenty years,' she replies, her response guarded.

'You can tell,' I offer quietly. 'His love for you is deep-rooted, I think. The way he looks at you, it's more than that new love and longing… Love transcends all normal feeling after a while; it evolves into something greater than any other. It's why it stings so much when we lose someone close, and why in the moments of pure fear, our first thought is for those we love.'

She muses on this for several steps, before cocking her head slightly in my direction. 'Do you think that kind of love can survive something like this?'

I'm not entirely sure what *this* she's referring to at first, so I play for time. 'True love can survive anything…' but then I think of how my own parents' marriage ended in such a mess, and I don't finish what I was going to say.

'I feel like there's something you want to say to me,' I continue, trying a fresh approach, 'but something's holding you back. Would that be a fair assessment?'

Her foot hovers temporarily in the air, before she places it down and continues forwards. The momentary pause catches me out, and I have to adjust my own footing to stay in time.

'Why are you here?' Zara asks.

'I came because Maddie said you wanted to talk to someone about your experience.'

She snorts. 'Is that what he told you?'

'Who? Tom? I didn't speak to him, only Maddie.'

'*He* wants me to talk to someone about… all of *this*. I'd sooner it all remained where I left it.'

This isn't a turn I'd anticipated, but I'm experienced enough now to overcome most bumps in the road when speaking to victims who can't be sure who to trust.

'It must have been difficult for you… after you returned, I mean. Your abduction was front-page news across the country, and your return widely celebrated.'

She grunts at this as a memory stirs behind those dark and resolute eyes. 'You can't begin to understand what it's like having everybody know who you are and what you've been through.'

'Actually, you'd be surprised,' I reply with a wry smile. 'I went from being an occasional journalist to a bestselling writer overnight, and I wasn't ready for it; I'm still not. It freaks me out whenever I go somewhere new and some stranger in the street recognises me from the picture on the inside cover of one of my books, or from a television interview where they've seen me. I know I can't complain because it's what pays my bills, and it means that I've managed to give my subjects a much-needed voice, but it isn't always easy. I suppose for you, returning to school must have been the hardest part?'

She keeps her eyes averted to the ground, but even I can see they're starting to moisten. 'I didn't want to go back, but I wasn't given a choice. They said it would help to get back into a normal routine, and be surrounded by my friends, but they didn't understand… They couldn't understand what I'd been through, and I couldn't talk about it with anyone.'

A cat scampers across the pavement and pauses to consider

us, assessing our threat level, before continuing across the road.

'It was like I was a different person. *Everyone* treated me differently. Some walked on eggshells, which was unbearable, while others tried to treat me as I was before, but that was impossible to get used to. Nobody could see me for who I was, and I think that's why I struggled so much. I'd missed nearly two years' worth of work, and although the teachers offered additional support, I just couldn't see the point. Not after... after what had happened.'

'I'm sorry,' I offer sincerely. 'I can empathise to a degree.' I take a deep breath. 'When I returned to school after my sister went missing, I could almost hear everyone's thoughts. You know? *Oh, there goes that girl whose sister disappeared. I wonder if she knows where she is. Did the parents kill her and cover it up?* In fairness, the interest in me was restricted to school and the occasional passer-by at the supermarket, and they did lose interest in me as the investigation dried up, but I'll never forget hating that feeling of being the centre of attention.'

Zara's head cocks again, but this time she looks straight at me. 'You'd never know. I've watched you being interviewed about your first book, and the trial that put those monsters behind bars. You spoke so passionately about how you couldn't stop digging until you'd discovered the truth and could prove their complicity. I never would have guessed you didn't enjoy the spotlight.'

It's my turn to look away as my cheeks redden. Is that really how people see me? Someone who craves attention and limelight? I suppose it's easy to jump to conclusions about people we've never met and have to accept at face value when they're made-up, and their wardrobe has been carefully selected for the cameras.

'So is that why you came here today?' Zara asks, finally looking back out at the path ahead of us, her shoulders relaxing a little.

'I don't follow, sorry.'

'You see me as your next project to tackle,' she clarifies.

'No,' I answer honestly. 'Maddie said you needed someone to talk to, so that's why I came. I'm actually knee-deep in an investigation right now, and not looking for new projects. Sorry.'

'Don't apologise. I'm glad. I'm not looking to sell my story to the highest bidder.'

Something clicks in the back of my head. Her refusal to speak when we were inside; choosing a spot out of the window to focus her attention on; her reticence to talk about her experience.

'It wasn't your idea to call Maddie, was it?'

She shakes her head, and I catch a glimpse of a smile. 'Tom wants to know what happened, but he loves me too much to ask me directly. I think he hoped I would open up to you and then he'd hear through the grapevine.'

'But that's not what you want?'

The stern expression returns. 'No.'

'Can I ask you a personal question?'

She stops still, fearing the worst. 'That depends what it is.'

'If Tom hadn't found out the truth last night, would you ever have told him about your history?'

'Would you? If you had buried such a dark and despicable secret – something you're ashamed to remember, even for just a split second – would you be willing to share that with the person you love more than anything in the world?'

It's a fair question, and I'm not going to patronise her by claiming I have any idea how much she has suffered since that night thirty-five years ago.

'Honestly, I don't know, but then I've never been so in love with someone that I'd be willing to share everything about myself. I can see how much he loves you, and how he only wants whatever is best. I genuinely believe that. I appreciate it's your story to tell, but doesn't he deserve the chance to understand your journey too?'

She spins on her heel and strides back the way we've come, head down and steps so fast I'm practically jogging to keep up.

'Zara, I'm sorry,' I pant. 'Please, I didn't mean to upset you.'

She stops, nearly sending me plunging forwards. 'I've worked for years to bury my past, and now, despite my best efforts, one throwaway comment from a woman I barely know has dug up everything I hate about myself. I would give anything to go back in time and yank that phone from her hand before she said my name, but I can't do that. All I can do now is manage the fallout as best I can. And if that...' She stops to try and compose herself, but the tears are flowing despite her best efforts. 'And if that means calling time on me and Tom, then so be it. I've reinvented myself before and I'm prepared to do it again to keep that shadow from ruining my future.'

'Zara, listen, I know you don't want to speak about your past, and I don't blame you. I'd like to help you if I can, but only when you're ready.'

She tries to move on, but I reach for her arm. 'I know what

the monsters who snatched you are capable of. I lost my sister more than twenty years ago, and I am hunting those responsible. I have met so many victims of that kind of horrific abuse, and although each of your stories are different, there's one thing you *all* have in common: you're resilient. You're all survivors, and that's something nobody can take away from you.'

'What do you want from me?'

I release her arm and offer my palms in a calming gesture. 'I don't want anything, other than for you to know that I'm here if you ever do want to confront your past. I'm not talking about writing about your life, I simply mean two people with shared experiences talking openly.'

She wipes her eyes with the back of her hand, but I reach into my bag and offer her a tissue from the packet I keep there for such occasions. She accepts it, and nods her thanks, dabbing at the tears.

'Can I say one more thing before we head back inside?' I ask, knowing that the words might drive a bigger wedge between us, but feeling compelled to stay honest. 'You've done incredibly well to keep this thing buried for the best part of thirty-five years, but things like this eat away at you from the inside, and it's very rare they remain buried forever. I'm a firm believer in fate shaping my future, and the fact that you and I have met at this time when my investigation has reached a wall, and you're temporarily unemployed, is telling me that we could help each other.'

I pass her my business card. 'If and when you feel like you're ready to stop running, please call me. All I want to do is help you in any way I can. Please think about it.'

She stuffs the card into her clutch bag, along with the tissue, before taking a deep breath and walking up the path to Maddie's front door. It wouldn't surprise me if I never hear from her again.

Chapter Twelve

NOW

Edgware, London

With Tom and Zara gone, Rachel and I take stock in Maddie's living room while she pours us all a large glass of something white and chilled. So far, Maddie and Rachel have been perfectly civil to one another, and I dare to hope this could become their new normal, and a crack appearing in the ice wall they've both maintained for so long; or maybe it's just wishful thinking.

'He's really worried about her,' Rachel explains when we're all seated. 'Apparently, he had no idea about her history. He said she doesn't talk much about her childhood, but he'd just assumed it hadn't been too pleasant. Apparently her dad died some years ago, and she and her mum had a big falling out just after Christmas and don't really talk these days, save for the obligatory birthday and Christmas card exchange. He said it was such a shock when the truth was revealed at that dinner party last night.'

'It was a shock for all of us!' Maddie chimes in. 'I was sitting right next to her, and I've never seen blood drain from someone's face as quickly. She made no attempt to deny it, nor claim it was just a shared name. I think that's what I would have done. I'd have brazenly claimed it wasn't me, and all would have been forgotten. It must have really caught her off-guard.'

'We can only begin to imagine what she went through while being held by that brute,' I offer, to add some context for why she kept the truth hidden for so long from her partner. 'She told me she's ashamed of that part of her life and just wants to keep it buried in the past. I don't blame her, if I'm totally honest. She's built a new life with Tom in which that chapter of her life didn't happen, and isn't that what we all deserve? A chance to put the sins of the past behind us? It wasn't her fault that she was taken and subjected to horrific abuse, so if she would prefer to forget about it, then we should abide by those wishes. I got the impression it wasn't her idea to reach out to you, Maddie.'

'Tom admitted as much when the two of you went out,' Rachel says, taking a sip of her wine. 'He said she woke him up screaming with a nightmare during the night, but she couldn't remember exactly what had scared her so much.' She pauses for another sip. 'He also said the nightmare resulted in her wetting the bed, which is why he's so worried about her. He's not looking for her to share everything with him, but he's worried that the more she runs from her past, the more it will eat her up inside.'

I recall her reaction when I mooted the same idea: stone cold, and stuffing my business card into her purse.

'Pressuring her like this isn't the answer though,' I warn

them. 'I remember when I was first speaking to Freddie about the abuse he suffered at the hands of Arthur Turgood and the others. Deep down he *wanted* to tell me what had happened – he's admitted as much subsequently – but he didn't know *how* to tell me, or whether he could trust me. That's probably why Zara is so reluctant to speak to Tom about all of this: she's terrified he'll see her for who she truly is and run a mile.'

'I don't think he will,' Rachel says. 'If anything, the longer she refuses to confront her past, the more likely it is she'll push him away.'

There's probably a lot of truth in that statement, but it isn't my place to force Zara to do something she doesn't want to do. I've given her my contact details, so if and when she feels ready to reach out, she can. I worked hard to earn Freddie's trust, and it took time and gentle probing, but he ultimately *wanted* me to dig; I don't get the same impression from Zara, and that's why I don't feel I should put any more pressure on her.

'Tom also said there was an incident when they went out for brunch this morning,' Rachel continues. 'Did she mention anything about that to you?'

I take a sip of the wine and grimace at the bitter aftertaste. 'No, what happened?'

'Apparently something caught alight in the restaurant's kitchen and it set off the smoke alarm. The owner tried to clear the place but Zara froze and was in a trance-like state until Tom carried her outside. He said it was like someone had frozen her like a statue. He's worried that if there was a real fire at their home and he wasn't around to get her out, she'd be trapped. I looked it up and apparently she was trapped in a burning house when she was found by the fire brigade and that's when they realised who she was and reunited her with her parents. It sounds like she's still suffering with PTSD from that experience.'

'Presumably she must have received some kind of counselling after what she went through?' I say.

Rachel shrugs. 'It was the mid-80s; things like PTSD and psychological counselling weren't as common as now, and usually reserved for the rich and famous. I'm not sure it would have been mandatory for the police to put her in touch with a psychiatrist or have a psychologist review her situation. It's possible she's never explored what happened, and that could be what has manifested since the dinner party.'

I reach for my glass again, before stopping myself. 'Maddie, what is this wine?'

'Oh, something the wine club sent me. Why, do you like it?'

I shake my head. 'A tad bitter for my palate, I'm afraid.'

'Oh, that's a shame. I can open up something else if you prefer? I've got several bottles out there that they've sent me over the last few weeks, but I just haven't had the time to sample them. The subscription was a Christmas present from one of the girls in the office. Sweet really, but I've no idea how she thought I'd get through a case of wine a month on my own.'

'I could get through a case of wine a week,' Rachel declares, before they both laugh. I do believe that's the first time they've ever shared a joke.

'You're welcome to take a bottle or two home with you, if you want,' Maddie offers. 'Better than them going to waste on my wine rack.'

Rachel glances at me in surprise, before nodding. 'Thank you, I appreciate the offer.'

'Oh, Emma, I was meaning to ask, how did you get on with Aurélie Lebrun yesterday?' Maddie asks, sitting up with interest.

I'd totally forgotten about the meeting at the solicitor's office, but now I turn up my nose. 'Not great, to be honest. It was an ambush. She'd brought two solicitors with her and basically said they're planning to fight the publication of *Trafficked* as it paints Aurélie in a negative light.'

Maddie frowns. 'Does it? The book I read shows a woman manipulated into believing she was in love with her captor and being subjected to ill-treatment. Sure, her lying to the police in order to try and escape with him was unfortunate, but just a reflection of how deeply the psychological abuse had impacted on her. It's a compelling story, and I really don't think there's anything for her to be worried about.'

'Try telling her solicitors that,' I say glumly. 'I told them they'd need to take it up with the publisher.'

Maddie muses for a moment. 'I bet it's just a stalling tactic to try and get us to up her share of the profits for the sale of the serialisation rights. I've had Reflex Media waiting for us to confirm the sale for months. I bet if the publisher refuses to budge on the requested changes to the manuscript they'll counter with an offer agreeing to leave it, based on a higher share of the profits. We'll fight back of course, but if one extra per cent will be enough to smooth the transaction, then it might be worth considering.'

This is exactly why I employ Maddie to look after the business side of my writing career. I was floundering in that office last night, whereas Maddie knows how to play tough and talk the talk. I'd be lost without her.

'It will be good to finally see *Trafficked* published,' Maddie concludes, 'but more importantly, are you working on anything new for me to read?'

Although Rachel is aware of the private project Jack and I have been working on, Maddie knows very little, and I'm not ready to include her in talks indicating Tomlinson's possible involvement in the ring without Jack's agreement.

'Nothing concrete at present; I'm still trying to uncover the identity of the person who sent you the pictures of Cormack Fitzpatrick and Faye McKenna for my attention, but I've drawn a blank. I take it you've not received any other envelopes for my attention?'

'Not after the third one a month ago, no. Can't that policeman friend of yours shed any light on it? What's his name again? Jack?'

Jack's prone body in the hospital bed with the heart monitor beeping behind him fills my mind, and I suddenly feel my eyes welling up.

'What is it, Emma? Are you all right?' Maddie asks.

Rachel must have read my mind, because she quickly explains that Jack was in a car accident overnight, and all I can do is nod when Maddie tells me she's sorry and I've nothing to worry about. In truth, I'm not worried about me; I'm worried about the position I've put Jack in, and the impact that could have on his daughter, Mila. Does she even know that her dad is fighting for his life? I presume Rawani will have notified Jack's next of kin, but would that include his ex-wife and daughter?

I use a tissue from the packet in my bag to dry my eyes and take several breaths to compose myself again. I think back to what I told Zara about fate aligning things like pieces on a chessboard. It's safe to say mine and Jack's investigation has stalled, and I'm not going to be able to progress anything until he wakes from the coma. I don't have the energy to fight Aurélie over her interpretation of my last manuscript, but Maddie will take that on. What does that leave me to do, apart from try to help Zara? I know she won't be forthcoming, but that doesn't mean I can't do some digging of my own. Maybe if I can find out more about the man who took her, I can ease her mind about that period and help her realise the benefits of counselling.

'Can you do me a favour?' I ask Maddie, sliding my glass of wine over to Rachel to finish. 'Can you contact Tom and tell him I'd like to meet again? Something tells me that our paths have crossed at this point for a reason, and I can't ignore that.'

Chapter Thirteen

THEN

Harrow, London

Tom's car rattled and bounced along the road, but the silence on the inside was painful and was making the journey home drag. There were comfortable silences – between two people who knew each other intrinsically – but this wasn't that. Tom's occasional glances towards her hadn't gone unnoticed by Zara who kept her head faced towards the window, though not really seeing the trees and pavement blurring through the glass.

'Listen,' Tom finally said, the sigh pained, 'I'm sorry for suggesting you speak to Emma Hunter. I only want to help, but I see now that was wrong and I'm sorry.'

They were stopped at a traffic light and she could see his eyes reflected in the glass. It broke her heart to see that anguish and regret, but she wasn't prepared to forgive and forget so quickly. Too many people had been there making decisions for her – all in her best interests, or so they'd claimed – but at forty-four years of age, wasn't it time she was allowed to make her own decisions and mistakes?

Her parents had been the same after she returned to their home. She hadn't realised it at first, but looking back on it now, they'd been pulling the strings for most of her teenage life. If she'd wanted to go out and see her friends, it wasn't that they'd refuse her request, rather make insinuations that it wasn't a good idea, convincing her to reject the offer. Or when Jimmy Marcus – one of the most popular lads in Fourth Form – had asked her to the school disco, and she'd finally felt like she could put the past behind her. They'd insisted on meeting Jimmy beforehand, and her mum had given him the tenth degree until he had decided she was more trouble than she was worth, and subsequently took Karen Campbell instead.

Control seemed so important to those around her, and yet she'd never felt so out of control. The redundancy before Christmas had been a shock for a time, until she'd realised it was a blessing in disguise. But three months on, she was still no closer to figuring out what it was she wanted to do with her life. It was all right for people like Emma Hunter who'd discovered their natural talent and were exploiting it. But what was Zara's talent? She'd never been sporty, wasn't particularly creative, and although she could cook, she lacked the flair to pursue it with any gusto. She'd been good at her job as a legal secretary, but that was more down to her organisational skills than a desire to be the best she could. And even that choice of profession had been semi-influenced by her parents.

'You want a good job with decent pay and benefits, where you can make a difference,' her mum had said the day she was looking at UCAS options.

She turned and met Tom's gaze for the second before it

returned to the road as the lights turned green. Despite her reservations about the degree she'd pursued, had she not, she never would have graduated and gone on to meet Tom and they wouldn't have spent the last near-twenty years together. That was longer than the average marriage these days. She didn't want to lose him, and it was hardly his fault that he'd learned her secret. He hadn't been chasing the truth, and he hadn't pressured her to reveal more about her upbringing, but his decision to drag her to meet Emma Hunter today spoke volumes.

Why couldn't he just let it go and pretend like last night hadn't happened?

'Can we just go somewhere, instead of going home?' he asked, glancing back at her. 'I'm enjoying the drive, but the silence is killing me.'

'Where did you have in mind?'

'Somewhere nobody knows us, and we can move silently through crowds, just the two of us. Windsor's not too far. It's been ages since we've been there. We could walk along the river, maybe stop for an ice cream?'

It sounded good, and reminded her of a time before all of this.

'And I promise we won't mention anything about... you know,' he added.

She nodded and looked away before he saw the shine in her eyes, focusing once more on the window.

Parking just along from Windsor train station, they hurried along the road, back towards the town centre. The earlier warmth of the air had vanished, the sun hidden behind a blanket of white and light grey clouds, and unlikely to penetrate anytime soon. Neither had packed anoraks, and they would just have to take their chances should a shower strike.

The main bulk of the town was as busy as ever with tourists of all colours, races, and creeds mingling around the enormous castle and local shops offering souvenirs of their visit. Tom and Zara avoided the main strip, circumventing the road towards the river and stopping at a quiet ice cream stall.

'What did you go for?' Zara asked when Tom joined her beside the water's edge.

'I got you a salted caramel, of course,' he said, handing one of the wafer cones over. 'And I went for rhubarb and custard. You want a lick?'

She nodded and leaned in, running her tongue over the yellow and pink scoop. 'Mmm, reminds me of school crumble,' she commented, savouring the sweetness.

'I know, right? It reminds me of going to my grandma's house on a Sunday afternoon as a kid. She was always making crumble with some fruit she'd grown or found on one of her walks in the country. I think the weirdest combination we ever had was boysenberry and nettle. It was this hot-pink colour,' he laughed. 'Not to my liking so I left the fruit and just ate the crumble topping.'

They moved on from the wall, watching as a crowd gathered to feed the ducks and swans that were amassing just short of the footbridge.

'How's yours?' Tom asked.

'Delicious,' she replied, savouring the salty flavour that contrasted with the sweetness of the caramel. She looped her arm through his and pressed her head against his upper arm, and that's how they moved forward – united.

'Do you remember when we came here after you got your first legal-secretary job?' Tom asked, resting his ear on the top of her head.

'Vaguely,' she said, allowing herself to relax for the first time that day.

'We walked along this very river after lunch because we'd both eaten far too much, and I think that was the day we said we'd be together forever. Do you remember?'

She could recall several walks along this river both as a couple and with friends, but no memory immediately jumped to the front of her mind.

'Vaguely,' she encouraged.

'Come on, you must remember it. We'd been to the all-you-can-eat buffet at the Chinese restaurant just down from the castle. We had tickets for a tour of the castle that afternoon, but we agreed not to use them as we were feeling too full. Remember? I thought I was actually going to throw up, so you led me to this enormous expanse of grass inside a quiet park, and you told me to lie down on my back and just rest my head on your thigh. You told me that the best thing to do when feeling like I might throw up was to lie flat and still and just focus on my breathing. Then you told me to rub circles over my belly to settle it.'

The memory was starting to shine through the cloud. 'That's right. I would have said anything to stop you talking about being sick, because it was making me feel sick too,' she chuckled.

She felt his head nodding in agreement. 'That's right! That was it. You told me a few days later that you were terrified I would actually be sick because that would cause you to vomit immediately after. You kept saying that it wouldn't look good on your first day at your new job if we'd both been arrested for throwing up in a park.'

It was an interesting memory for him to dig up now, but not exactly the romantic trip down memory lane she'd anticipated. That was probably why she'd struggled to recall it at first, buried as it was along with the other worst moments of her life.

'What of it?' she asked.

'I don't know,' he mused, 'it just popped into my head, that's all. I think that was the first time I knew that you'd always be there for me. You took good care of me, and made me feel a hundred times better. I knew I loved you that day, and my feelings for you have only grown stronger every day since.'

She squeezed his arm in acknowledgement. He'd never told her that was how he'd interpreted that particular event, and she wondered now whether things would have worked out differently had she just allowed him to be sick that day. But it wasn't in her nature to watch others suffer if she was able to make a difference.

'That was also the day I told you I would love you forever and that I would spend every remaining day of my life putting you first and making your life as good as it could be. I'm sorry I didn't achieve that today.'

She almost chocked on the well of emotion that exploded within her in that moment, the familiar sting of tears close by. She squeezed his arm again. He'd promised he wouldn't bring up recent events, but a second apology was more than a nod to it.

'I love you, Zara Edwards. Do you know that? I love you because you're my first thought when I wake, and the last thing I see at night. I love you because you know how to make me laugh, and you don't complain when I leave stray hairs in the bathtub after I've showered. I love you because you make me a better person whenever you're near to me. I love you because I can't imagine how bad my life would have been had I not met you.'

The sting in her eyes was close to breaking point. 'I love you too, Tom.'

He stopped and took her left hand in his. 'Please, let me finish.'

She looked around uneasily. They were standing in the middle of the walkway, meaning other people would have to skirt around them. 'Tom, if there's something you want to say, can you just spit it out? We're in everyone's way here.'

'I don't care,' he smiled with sincerity. 'I only care about the woman who's standing before me right now with salted caramel lips.'

She licked her lips, her cheeks reddening a fraction.

'That day in the park when we were both trying to think of anything other than being ill from all the noodles and tea we'd consumed, we also made another promise to one another. Do you remember what it was?'

She allowed her eyes to wander as she tried to work out what he was going on about, amongst the tuts and sighs of those passing around them.

'Tom, we should move up onto the grass verge; people can't get past.'

'To hell with *them*! Listen to what I'm trying to say, would you? There's something I've been meaning to ask you for weeks now, and it's never quite felt like the right time.'

A flourish of bright yellow coming closer caught Zara's eye.

'I wanted to find the perfect setting,' Tom continued, 'but something always seems to crop up and interfere with my plans.'

The bright yellow coat was waving at them now, and as Zara studied the figure closely her heart sank.

'What I'm trying to say, Zara,' Tom continued, 'is—' he took a deep breath.

'Zara and Tom, fancy bumping into you two!' Harriet declared, wrapping the arms of her neon jacket around the two of them. 'It's such a small world at times, isn't it?'

Tom opened his mouth to speak, but words failed him.

'I'm glad I've run into you actually,' Harriet continued. 'I wanted to apologise again for what happened last night. If I'd had any idea of who you *really* were, I'd have kept my big trap shut. Will said I should phone and apologise, but it just felt so impersonal. I'm so sorry, Zara. Is there anything I can do to make it up to you?'

Tom was still floundering, and Zara couldn't bring herself to meet either of their stares, as the beautiful moment, when she'd dared to believe that she and Tom might be able to put everything behind them, died.

Chapter Fourteen

NOW

Edgware, London

For some reason I'm not altogether surprised when Tom returns to Maddie's townhouse without Zara in tow. He makes excuses for her – blaming fatigue and a headache for her absence – but I'd have to be blind not to see how eager he is to be here. I feel like I've been trapped inside Maddie's for hours, and so I suggest we go for a walk, though it's much cooler now than when Zara was beating the path earlier. I want to get Tom alone as I haven't had the chance to find out why he arranged the meeting even though Zara seemed so against it.

I don't immediately launch into the list of questions peppering my mind, but after two minutes of virtual silence, I can bite my tongue no longer. 'It can't be easy, for Zara I mean, living with everything she's been through.'

His pace slows momentarily as if my comment has struck a nerve, but he doesn't speak, just nods considerately.

'They say often in these cases, the victim can suffer from survivor's guilt,' I continue, 'and it can be easier to repress and bury the memory than it is to acknowledge it.'

He still doesn't respond, and whilst I have no clue where this footpath is going to take us, he doesn't look concerned about getting lost.

'How do you feel about all of this?' I try, in an effort to be more direct.

'My feelings don't really come into it, do they? Zara's the one who's been living with this burden for all these years.'

It's an honourable response, but not one I totally believe. I feel like he wants to believe the words, but he's holding back.

'It must have been a shock for you too though, no? Learning that the woman you've built a life with has suffered such pain and trauma and tried to protect you from it. Can't have been easy for you to learn she's kept such a huge secret from you for so many years.'

He stops abruptly, but continues to stare ahead, as if awaiting an onrushing locomotive. 'I don't blame her, if that's what you're getting at.'

'It wasn't,' I say quietly, conscious of burning this bridge at its foundation stage. 'But I don't think you should suffer guilt about feeling hurt by this sudden admission. It's one hell of a shock to deal with, and you strike me as someone who would put Zara's feelings above your own.'

I can't tell if I've overstepped, but he remains frozen to the spot.

'In fact, I'd imagine it's probably eating you up inside, isn't it? You don't want to question her motives for keeping such a secret from you for so many years, and you want to offer her the support of a loving partner, but it isn't easy to do both.'

'I just want what's best for her,' he says after a beat, and his shoulders sag in defeat.

I take a step closer to him and gently rub his arm. 'In my experience, those who've suffered any kind of traumatic experience like that can be reluctant to open up about it.' I picture Aurélie Lebrun as I say this. 'It's very likely that she's terrified about what it will mean to relive the memories, particularly if there was violence and abuse involved. You might also find that part of her reticence is in an effort to protect you.'

He looks up again, but continues to listen intently.

'Think about it from her point of view: she knows you love her, and you have a picture of how she looks and who she is. She's probably terrified that if she confides in you about what happened, your impression of her will change, as I guess it naturally would. That's not to say you wouldn't still love her – it might even bring you closer together – but it's a huge risk as far as she's concerned. Would you say the two of you were happy before the revelation last night?'

He nods. 'Absolutely. I'm not saying life was perfect, but yeah, on the whole I'd say we were happy with our lot.'

'Okay, so now imagine your worst secret, something from *your* past you're either too embarrassed or ashamed to admit to. I don't want to know what it is, but we all have *something* we wish we could erase from history, right? Imagine if Zara then found out that truth; wouldn't it worry you that she would no longer see you in the same way?'

'I suppose you're right,' Tom admits, the tension in his frown softening. 'I hadn't thought about it like that.'

'Imagine now if once she'd found out your deep, dark

secret, she forced you to talk about it with perfect strangers, and wouldn't allow it to drop.'

His lips curl up slightly. 'I imagine that would be pretty frustrating.'

I nod in agreement. 'So did the two of you have an argument after you left Maddie's townhouse in Edgware?'

'Actually, no. She was very quiet in the car, and I suppose I was feeling guilty about putting her in that position, so I suggested we go for a drive. We ended up in Windsor, which is one of our favourite places to go for a walk and relive old memories. I was all set to—' He stops himself from speaking, but then considers whether to continue. 'Can I show you something?'

'Of course.'

He reaches deep into the pocket of his trousers, and fiddles with something for a moment, before extracting a small ring box and opening it for me to see. The engagement ring sparkles despite the thick grey clouds above our heads robbing the sky of brightness. It's as if he has plucked a star from the sky and trapped it in the box.

'I've been carrying it around in my pocket for weeks, waiting for the right moment to give it to Zara and propose to her, but whenever I think it's the right time, something happens to prevent me. I'm beginning to think it's fate's way of telling me not to bother.'

'Do you think she knows what you're planning?'

He shakes his head vehemently, pocketing the ring box at the same time. 'We always said we didn't need a piece of paper to prove how we felt about each other, but...' he sighs. 'Maybe it's because I'm getting older, but it's more than that now. I want the world to know how I feel about her, and that to me she's the most perfect woman in the world.

'I spent ages trying to find the perfect ring. Zara's not into flashy jewellery, but I remember her telling me how her grandmother used to wear a ring her grandfather had scrimped and saved to buy, so that's what I did. It cost me three months' salary, but she's worth every penny in my eyes.'

'She's lucky to have you, Tom,' I say, and mean every word. Life dealt Zara a cruel hand, but she's risen above that and found what most of us only dream of.

'I took her to Windsor this afternoon and was going to drop down on one knee in front of everyone and just bowl out with the question. I thought it would prove to her that I don't need to know about her history, because I want her for who she is now.'

'But things didn't go to plan?' I question.

He shakes his head.

'Can I let you in on a little secret about us ladies?' I say, leaning closer like I'm going to reveal some unknown truth. 'It doesn't have to be the perfect moment for a marriage proposal. Sure, we appreciate a bit of effort on our partner's behalf, but the main thing is the way the question is asked. Don't give up.'

'I'm worried that when I do ask, she'll mistake it for some grand gesture on the back of what I found out, and she'll say no.'

'I think it's obvious that she loves you, Tom, but in fairness, now might not be the best time to make the proposal. It might also be worth mooting the idea before getting down on one knee, as there might be other reasons she doesn't want to get married. I'm not trying to put you off – God knows, you never know what tomorrow might bring – but I think you just need to be there for her at the moment. If and when she's ready to open up about her past, I'm sure she will.'

He nods, but I can't tell if he's listening or just acknowledging.

'Zara mentioned that you had a sister who went missing as a kid too, right?'

My eyes moisten as I see Anna striding off in the direction of Grandma's house. 'She's still out there somewhere,' I say, but the words sound hollow on my lips.

'Did the police ever... did they ever figure out what happened? Was she taken like Zara, or did she run away?'

I'm not sure I'll ever know for certain, I don't say. I shrug instead.

'The thing is,' he adds, 'Zara told me that the man they arrested – the one who was allegedly holding her at that house – he wasn't the one who snatched her from the pier that night.'

My ears prick up at this statement as I try and recall reading anything to corroborate it.

'I don't know all the ins and outs, and I'm not sure Zara will be willing to say any more, but I just wondered...' He catches himself, as if he's already said too much.

'You're suggesting the man who grabbed Zara could be the same person who took my sister?'

I had asked myself the same question when I was at university and reading up on every known child abduction case I could lay my hands on, but there certainly wasn't enough about Zara's abduction that resonated. But then, at the time I thought they'd caught the man responsible. It feels too coincidental that the two events could be related, and yet there's a part of me that wants to believe this is fate's way of pointing me towards destiny.

He shrugs. 'Sorry, all I was thinking was, if the man responsible for taking Zara was never brought to justice, then maybe he could have been involved somehow in what happened to your sister. I'm sure you've probably already considered that.'

He checks his watch, his pink cheeks telling me I'm not the only one suddenly feeling awkward.

'The thing is,' he continues, fixing me with a sincere stare, 'if you were able to find out who took Zara all those years ago, and could bring him to justice, maybe it could be what Zara needs to put all of this behind her once and for all.'

I want to tell him that what he's asking is an impossible task, but he doesn't give me the chance.

'Zara and her mum Angie had a falling out just before Christmas. I don't know what it was about, and she doesn't like to talk about it, but I reckon Angie might be willing to talk to you about that time, if you were interested. The two of them haven't spoken in months, but Angie has always been a hoarder, and I'd bet good money on her having clippings of every newspaper story from that time in the loft. It might save you a bit of effort, and it's unlikely to get back to Zara.'

There's a desperation in his eyes that I've seen when looking in the mirror, and it's a look that's almost impossible to say no to.

'I'm not saying that you would have any interest, but in case you do, I'll text you Angie's phone number and address when I get home. She still lives in Brighton where it all happened, though God knows why. I'm not sure I'll ever be able to go back there, not now I know what... what transpired.'

We walk back to Maddie's townhouse in silence, and he offers little more than a smile and a wave as he climbs back into his car and pulls away. The wind whips around me as I feel the pull of my sister's memory dragging me out of the gloom. It's almost as if I can hear her voice whispering my name on the wind.

Chapter Fifteen

NOW

Ealing, London

Our stomachs are rumbling on the drive back to Rachel's flat, and so Rachel detours to pick up some takeaway. It's been a long day for us both, and neither of us is in the mood to cook. I'm salivating with the smell of the peri-peri as we head back through the town. I can't stop thinking about the possibility that the man who led Zara to hell could have done the same to my sister. How many others have suffered a similar fate as a consequence? It's ringing alarm bells of what Aurélie has told me of her own abduction from Worthing. Whilst it was a young woman who tricked her, there was a hand-off involved. Did whoever took Anna, sell her on as well?

'If Daniella knew what we're about to tuck into, she would be so jealous,' Rachel grins as we near her flat.

I try to rein in my imagination and focus on not spoiling

Rachel's night. 'Well I won't tell her if you don't,' I say back, my stomach growling in dissatisfaction that I haven't yet fed it.

I take control of the paper bags as Rachel unlocks the door at the communal entrance, but then freezes when she sees two uniformed police officers at her door talking to one of her neighbours.

'Oh, here she is,' says Mrs Duvitski from upstairs. 'Rachel, dear, there was a break-in.'

Neither of us is ready for that news, and I almost drop the food, only just managing to recover it in time.

'A break-in?' Rachel questions. 'At my flat?'

One of the officers turns to face her and nods grimly. 'Miss Leeming?' she asks. 'It's a bit of a mess in there, and it would really help us if you could have a look around and see if there's anything obvious that's been taken.'

From the look of disbelief on Rachel's face, I'd say it hasn't yet sunk in. 'I don't understand,' she says, frowning. 'Why would somebody break into my flat? I don't own anything of particular value... Are you sure they broke into *my* flat?'

'There was smoke,' Mrs Duvitski explains. 'I was on my way back from feeding the ducks at Walpole Park, and I saw all this grey smoke billowing from your front window. I hurried inside, and that's when I saw that your front door wasn't closed. I poked my head around the door, calling out your name, and that's when I saw all the mess. The smoke was coming from a small fire in a metal bucket in the middle of the room, and so I poured a couple of glasses of water on it before it was able to spread. Then I phoned the landlord to see if he could give me your phone number so I could let you know, but he refused of course – something about data protection – and suggested I phone the police. Heaven forbid he actually comes over to sort out the problem and earn his rent. Anyway, I waited by your door to make sure nobody else could go in until these officers arrived.'

My face is cold with the shock, but Rachel's is glowing with ire. 'A fire? You're saying somebody broke into my flat and started a fire? Who the hell would do that?'

The female officer shrugs. 'Could just be kids. It looks like they used something like a crowbar to gain entry to your flat, and I don't know if you left your front window open, or they opened it to clear the smoke.'

'My window was closed,' Rachel is adamant. 'I live on the ground floor, so I'm not in the habit of encouraging burglars. If the window was open, they must have done it, whoever *they* are. Have you dusted for prints yet?'

The female officer looks despondent. 'It's not standard practice to do so in situations like this.'

'Situations like *this*?' Rachel challenges.

'There have been a spate of burglaries in the area in the last three months, and entry is generally with a crowbar when the occupant is out. These are opportunistic thieves. Maybe they witnessed you going out earlier, or happened to glance in through your window, saw the place was empty, and took a chance.'

'But why start a fire?'

She shrugs again. 'I'm sorry, Miss Leeming, but it was probably just bored kids. It's the weekend, so no school or college, and it's been a surprisingly warm day... If you wouldn't mind having a look to see if there's anything missing, my colleague and I can file a report and give you a case reference number for you to pass on to your insurance company.'

Rachel flashes a look at me, and I offer her a hug for solidarity. 'Do you want me to come in with you?' I ask.

'And who are you?' the officer asks, her eyes assessing my appearance.

'I'm Rachel's friend, Emma. I'm staying with her at the moment,' I reply.

'Well, Emma, it might be best if Miss Leeming enters alone for now, so as not to disturb the scene.'

I wait patiently with the two officers and Mrs Duvitski, who could return to her own flat but who seems more interested in watching the unfolding drama.

'Oh my God!' I hear Rachel exclaim painfully from inside. 'They've ruined everything!'

The female officer sends her colleague inside to take notes of missing items.

'Have you two been somewhere nice?' the police woman's tone is plain and inoffensive.

'Work,' I respond, not wanting to go into the detail of meeting Zara and Tom.

'And what is it you do?'

'Rachel is a journalist with a broadsheet, and I'm an author.'

There's no trace of recognition in her eyes. 'I've always wanted to write a book. What sort of books do you write?'

Mrs Duvitski's interest has also been piqued, but now doesn't feel like the time to talk about my books. 'Crime,' I answer simply.

'Anything I might have heard of?'

'Probably not,' I reply, my appetite waning as I hear Rachel moving about inside and swearing as she begins to tidy some of the mess.

'I'd love to be a romance writer,' the officer continues, 'in the style of a Jojo Moyes or Jenny Colgan. Is it easy to get started?'

I appreciate she's probably just trying to make conversation to restrict any kind of awkward silence, but her choice of topic feels contrived and I'd prefer the silence. I'm grateful when her colleague emerges with his notebook, and nods for me to enter. Even though I've heard Rachel's profanity as she's been moving about inside, I'm not prepared for what I see when I get there.

The main room looks as though a bomb has gone off. Mrs Duvitski may have extinguished the fire, but a cloud of grey smoke still hangs just below the ceiling, and it's going to be a while until the smell diminishes. The cause of the fire appears to be one of Rachel's plant pots – the plant it was holding I now see has been tossed onto the bedspread in Rachel's room. The sofa-bed where I have spent many a night over the last couple of weeks has been cut with a knife of some sort, and most of the stuffing ejected. The floor is covered in books from the upturned shelving unit, and the kitchen linoleum is hidden beneath broken crockery.

'They've taken my laptop, iPad, and the money I was saving in my building society book in my bedside table,' she says glumly.

'Oh Rach, I'm sorry.' I squeeze her tightly. 'Was everything on your laptop backed up to the cloud?'

She nods. 'In this day and age it does it automatically, thankfully, but it's still bloody annoying that some bastards have wrecked my home. It gives me the creeps just knowing they've been in here.'

I have nothing but sympathy for her, but am relieved I had

my laptop with me when we went out. I too back up everything to the invisible cloud in the sky, but the laptop to me is more than just information. I bought it shortly after graduation, and although it's slow and scratched, it's been with me during my journey to becoming a professional writer and I couldn't bear to be apart from it.

'I know this is going to sound lame,' Rachel says, 'but do you think we could find a hotel to check into for tonight? I don't think I have the strength to tidy this mess right now.'

'Of course, of course,' I tell her. 'I'll look for somewhere on my phone in a minute, and then you and I can give this place a proper tidy up in the morning.'

The female officer enters the room and offers her condolences. 'I'd ask your landlord to send someone round to secure your front door if you're not planning on staying tonight,' she advises. 'If, when you start to go through the mess, you realise something else is missing, then give us a call and let us know, and we'll add it to the casefile. Given the list of items that were taken, it suggests it probably was kids looking for stuff they can easily sell on, which is why they will have left your television. People are less likely to notice kids carrying laptops and iPads, but carrying a forty-inch television down the street sets alarm bells ringing to most passers-by.'

Stepping into the kitchen I locate two plastic plates from the rubble on the floor, and dish out our food. No wine glasses appear to have survived the break-in, and so when Rachel unscrews the lid of the wine and swigs from the bottle, we accept this as the best option.

Rachel's phone vibrates on the counter, and she swears when she sees Saskia's name in the display.

'Oh God,' she gasps, 'I'd totally forgotten she was supposed to be coming back here.'

I'd forgotten too. We postponed her visit when Rawani told me about Jack, and I didn't even think about her when Maddie called asking us to meet with Tom and Zara.

I cringe. 'Can you tell her I'm sorry, and I'll rearrange to view the books after we've tidied this place up tomorrow?'

Rachel nods, and accepts the call. 'Hi, Saskia, sorry we weren't here when you came back, it's been a monster of a day, but if you... Wait, what? Who is this?'

The anxiety in Rachel's voice distracts me from my food.

'You're not being serious! Oh my God! Well is she... is she okay?' Rachel lowers the phone and covers the mouthpiece with her hand. 'It's a nurse in the Emergency Department at Ealing Hospital. Apparently Saskia was knocked over in a hit-and-run accident at lunchtime today, and is in a critical condition.'

My mouth drops as the news sinks in.

Rachel listens in again, before lowering the phone for a second time. 'She says that a witness said they saw a dark BMW leaving the scene, but nobody got the licence plate details. She said it happened just up the road from here.'

Poor Saskia. I can't help but assume that the accident could have occurred when she was on her way to see us, while we were on our way to see Jack at the hospital. It's my fault that she was bringing the books over to be reviewed.

'Is she all right? How badly injured is she?' I ask.

Rachel listens in to the call again. 'She's conscious but has a dislocated shoulder.'

'What about the books?' I ask, now concerned that the

foundation's financial information could be flapping about in the wind.

'Was she brought in with anything?' Rachel relays. 'We believe she might have been carrying our company's account information.' Rachel shakes her head at me as she continues to listen. 'Can we see her?'

I feel sick to my stomach. I know there will be copies of the accounts online, but the thought of the financial statements and account details falling into the wrong hands fills me with dread. And then another thought enters my head which sucks the blood from my upper body.

'Thank you,' Rachel declares before hanging up.

'She said we can go and see her if we want, but she's still being examined at the moment, so it might be best to wait until tomorrow.'

I don't respond, my mind racing with paranoid thoughts and conclusions that I don't want to be true.

I swallow hard and force the words from my mouth. 'What if it's all related? The burglary and the hit-and-run, I mean.'

Rachel frowns. 'Why would you say that?'

'Think about it: the sudden audit from the Charity Commission; Jack's car accident and the hospital; the burglary here; and now Saskia knocked down by a car. What if it's all related? What if this is someone's efforts to stop our investigation?'

Rachel's look of disbelief speaks volumes, but now I can't think of anything else.

Chapter Sixteen

THEN

Brighton, East Sussex

35 years ago

Peeling one eye open, Zara's first thought was that she'd woken from a horrific nightmare. Behind her eyes she could still see the frantic look on her mother's face as she'd started searching through the crowd for her, and the bleach-like pong still clung to her nose hairs. But as her second eyelid finally opened, confusion instantly hit, squeezing the ache that already clung to her head.

Although it was dark in the room, the bare grey wall looked nothing like home, or any hotel she could remember. Was she still dreaming now? Reaching out, she gently ran her fingers along the surface of the wall, shuddering at the cool touch as the rough concrete scratched at her fingertips. She pulled her hand back, as if the wall could somehow swallow her up like a sleeping monster.

Suddenly aware of how cold she felt, she ran her hands up and down her arms as quickly as she could, surprised when she saw vapours of steam escaping her mouth as she breathed in and out. Looking down she saw she was still wearing the black *Ghostbusters* T-shirt she'd chosen for yesterday, but there was no sign of her coat. Her denim skirt and tights were doing little to provide warmth and comfort, and there was no sign of her trainers in the near vicinity. The hard floor was as cold and rough as the wall, and she scurried back across it as far as she could go until she met the firm grey wall behind her. Wherever she was, the space between the walls was less than her room at home, and she estimated only one and a half versions of her could lie down without touching either wall.

Allowing her head to roll from one side to the other, her red hair fell over her face as she did; there was no sign of the hair tie that her mother had used to secure the strands in place yesterday morning before they'd headed out to the shops, and then on to the fireworks. She thought then about the sound of the explosions and the gasps from the crowd as one colourful explosion followed another, but here there was no sound whatsoever, as if this tiny room was held in a vacuum.

She couldn't quite see the wall to the left, but there was a tiny sliver of light at the top of the right wall that immediately drew her attention. Standing unsteadily, and wanting to shriek as her tights-covered feet touched cold concrete, she pressed her body against the right wall in an effort to get as close to the light as she could, but even stretching her arms as high as they would go, and standing on tiptoe, she couldn't get anywhere close to the window. Moving backwards across the room until her shoulder blades struck the furthest wall, she craned her neck. It was definitely a window of some sort, but it was still too high to see anything through it. The thin sliver of light seemed to be caused by daylight rather than an artificial source.

Grinding of metal against metal was followed by a loud popping noise and an elongated creek as a door to her left slowly opened. She scurried to the far corner opposite the new source of light, dropping to her haunches, as if she would have any chance of avoiding contact with the dark and round figure now entering the cell.

'Good, you're awake,' the figure grunted.

She opened her mouth to speak, but terror and dehydration kept the scream in her throat.

'You're not going to give me trouble, are you?' the figure grunted again.

'W-where am I?' she whispered, though could barely hear her own voice.

He froze, his head tilting as he considered her for a moment. 'How old are you?'

'N-nine,' she gasped, a cloud of air escaping her trembling lips.

'Jesus! They get younger every time,' he muttered, before stopping himself from sharing any more of his own opinion of what they did here. 'Listen, keep your head down and do as you're told; that's the best advice I can give you.'

He moved closer again and she buried her face between her knees, but it made no difference as he lifted her into the air with ease, tucking her slight frame under his arm and turning back to face the door. This was the moment the fight returned to her body, and she pelted him with elbow blows and knee knocks, but after twenty seconds of writhing, it was only she who was out of breath and bearing the brunt of the blows. He continued forwards as if she were nothing more than a pesky insect searching for an escape. She couldn't see where they were going on account of how he had lifted her, and as much as she tried to twist herself into a position that would allow her to see, his grip remained firm, and his tread, although heavy, was taken in very precise, purposeful steps.

She noticed large metal doors to her left and right along the corridor, each with a different number crudely painted onto the surface. They'd passed seven, eight, and nine, so she could only assume her door was number five or six, though she had no idea of the significance of the numbering system. The corridor certainly didn't share any of the characteristics of the hotel her family had been staying in for the weekend. No soft carpet, flock wallpaper, or dainty spotlights here. The occasional single bulb hanging from the concrete ceiling was barely enough to light the dim corridor.

They finally stopped when they reached the end of the corridor and the figure thumped his hand against a metal door there. The door opened, and she had to squint as her eyes adjusted to the harsh bright light escaping into the gloom.

'This her?' a voice called out from behind Zara, the German accent as harsh as the light.

'Yep. Number five,' the large figure replied.

'Leave us.'

The large figure gently lowered Zara to the ground, but blocked her path as she tried to run back out of the door.

'Remember what I told you,' he muttered, before leaving and closing the door behind him. The sound of metal grinding unwillingly against metal followed as he locked her in.

'Turn around and let me see you then,' the voice behind Zara instructed, and with little other choice she obeyed, quickly shielding her eyes from the glare of light targeted at her.

She couldn't see his face, just a silhouette bobbing behind the spotlight on the large desk. The room wasn't much larger than the one from which she'd been carried, but it certainly appeared more furnished. Two large filing cabinets were positioned against the wall below the small, high window. The desk itself resembled the one in her daddy's office, but where his was covered in framed pictures of her and her mum, this one had a tall stack of folders on one corner and a large open pad, about the size of the school register, beneath his small and hairy hands. She recognised the smell from the cigarette he was smoking, and as he exhaled a large grey cloud drifted up and above the spotlight.

'From now on, your name is Number Five,' he instructed. 'You are only to speak when you are spoken to. Do you understand?'

This had to still be part of the original nightmare, and she felt ready to scream and cry, but sheer terror was keeping both at bay. If she could just scream out for her mum or dad, she knew they would come running and wake her, and cuddle her, and smother her in their affectionate kisses. But their names remained buried.

'If I say your name, Number Five, then you will answer me. Do you understand, Number Five?'

'Y-yes.'

'Good. Now remove your clothes.'

She froze, still unable to properly see his face.

'I said *remove your clothes*, Number Five.'

Still she remained frozen to the spot, her body no longer responding to the messages her brain was sending. She'd taken her clothes off plenty of times, so it wouldn't be any kind of challenge, but the voice of warning in the back of her head wouldn't allow her to yield to the command. It was just wrong. She didn't know where she was, how she'd got here, who this man was, nor why he wanted her to take off her clothes. Too many things didn't add up, and so she remained locked in the beam of light.

The man slammed his hairy hands against his large notebook and the clap echoed off the walls around her. He stood and moved out from behind the desk, and as his shadow blocked out the harsh beam, she felt something warm and wet trickle between her legs. The man didn't notice, but the palm of his hand suddenly crashed hard against her cheek, lifting her off the floor and sending her crashing to the hard concrete floor.

'On your feet, Number Five, and *remove* your clothes. Don't make me tell you again,' he grizzled, planting his feet, the glow of the light hugging him.

Zara remained where she was on the floor. The tears that were now flowing from her eyes were doing little to cool the burning heat in her cheek where his slap had connected.

'I'm going to count to five, and if you haven't started to remove your clothes, I will do it myself. One…'

She heard the numbers as they rolled from his tongue, but it was as if someone had frozen her limbs in place. When he reached five, she screamed in panic as he grabbed her ankles and dragged her towards him.

She couldn't remember the last time she'd tasted food. Locked in the cell with nothing but the hard and rough concrete floor for companionship, she'd drifted in and out of sleep more times than she could remember and had soiled the one-piece robe he had given her to wear when he'd torn the *Ghostbusters* T-shirt from her near lifeless body. He'd then dragged her back along the corridor, all the way to room five, leaving grazes the length of both her legs, grazes which had remained untreated and now itched more than they stung. No amount of crying and calling for her parents had brought her out of the nightmare, and when she wasn't dozing she sobbed.

She almost didn't hear the now familiar sound of the grinding metal before the door popped open, and she made no effort to try and hide, nor to look into the face of whoever had entered. She didn't even struggle as she was lifted into the air, and carried in the arms of the larger figure who'd checked on her a couple of times since her return to the cell.

'You hungry?' he muttered now, but she didn't have the strength or will to respond.

She felt weightless, and for a moment it was as if the angels had descended and were carrying her to paradise. The walls of her prison had disappeared from her periphery and the air even tasted sweeter somehow. She snapped awake when she was lowered to a softer floor. She could feel the divots and uneven surface of the wood, and as her fingers scrabbled around she sat up, knowing that wherever she was now, she hadn't been here before. She didn't expect to see the room full of other robe-wearing girls, all kneeling with their heads bowed forwards. This room was much larger than any of the cells, and three of the walls had the high windows, meaning the room was much brighter than she'd been expecting. She had been left in the middle of the circle of girls, and as she sat up she hoped to make eye contact with just one of them. She counted at least twelve, though it was difficult to remember where she'd started counting, as they all looked so similar. One-piece robes hung from each of their bodies, hiding their gaunt frames beneath, and each of them had long, dark hair, ranging from auburn to chestnut. It was almost as if she'd been left in a hall of mirrors. She now noticed that each girl had an empty metal bowl before them, but there didn't seem to be any space for her to join the circle.

'Number Five, welcome to The Sisterhood,' the German voice called out. 'All of the girls you see before you have sat where you are now. Each has learned how to behave, as you will too. You now have a decision to make. If you want to join The Sisterhood, you must choose someone's place to take. If you refuse you will be returned to your cell without food or drink. Do you understand?'

She could barely hear the words, and the panic that had held her in its grasp when she'd first heard the little man's harsh accent held her firm once more. Confusion flooded her mind as she tried to replay the man's words. He wanted her to choose one of these girls to swap places with? Was that what he meant?

'Number Five, you have until the count of five to select your place. One...'

She forced herself to stand as hunger pangs took control, and looked around the room once again, willing one of the bowed heads to make eye contact, or to volunteer to swap places. None of them moved.

'Two...' the voice echoed from somewhere outside of the circle.

What would happen to the girl she selected? Would she simply be taken to Zara's cell and starved for two days? Could she really inflict that on a perfect stranger?

'Three…'

Or maybe she would be freeing that girl from this hell hole; that was an easier thought to stomach. The girl would be freed and allowed to return to her family and life and live happily ever after like in all the fairy tales she'd heard in her short life. Each of those stories contained a malevolent character like the hairy-handed man.

'Four…'

There was another possible outcome for the chosen girl that she refused to allow herself to consider.

'Five.'

The thought of returning to her cell without satisfying her thirst was more nightmarish than the choice.

Zara hurried across to the girl directly in front of her and thrust out her hand, pointing at the crown of the girl's head.

Not another word was spoken as the hulk of the man stepped out of the shadows and lifted the chosen girl into the air, then indicated for Zara to take her place. 'You did well,' he muttered, turning before Zara could see his face.

Zara promptly dropped into the now vacant space and watched as the gorilla in the suit carried the girl from the room. An ear-splitting shriek was the only sound as the chosen one realised her fate.

Chapter Seventeen

NOW

Ealing, London

Neither of us have slept well as we emerge from our hotel room and head down the stairs towards the tiny room set up for breakfast. Rachel and I take one look at the single table offering small boxes of breakfast cereal, a bowl containing overripe bananas and apples, and a second basket filled with seeded bread rolls, and decide to pass on the hotel's offer of a continental breakfast buffet. Instead, we return to our room, collect our bags and swiftly check out. The hotel, which was apparently the closest available to Rachel's flat in Ealing, is in fact in Alperton, a short bus ride away. Neither of us is up for a walk in the early morning drizzle, nor standing at a bus stop, and so we catch a taxi back and are on the familiar streets of Ealing Broadway fifteen minutes later. Buying a bag of pastries and two large black coffees on the way, we almost feel human again as Rachel's flat comes into view.

'I don't feel safe going in,' she tells me on the way, and the look accompanying the statement isn't one I've seen before. It is regret mixed with fear and disgust. Suddenly the flat that has been her home – a part of her DNA – for the best part of six years seems foreign and tainted.

Despite the vandals' use of a crowbar, the lock has just about managed to keep the door secured to the frame. I must admit that my pulse is racing as we open the door and head inside, half-expecting the same vandals to leap out from some dark corner and attack us. This doesn't happen of course; the curse of an overactive imagination taunts me. I had hoped the cold light of day would make the damage and destruction more palatable, but if anything it feels more personal. The stench of smoke still hangs in the air above our heads, and I'm not sure how long the windows would need to be opened to shift it.

Depositing our drinks on the debris-free countertop, I pull off one of the black sacks we bought on the way back, and flap it open. Despite the eruption of noise, Rachel remains frozen to the spot, and I can only assume she's struggling to recall what the place looked like before the devastation.

'Do you want to leave me to do it?' I offer. 'I don't mind. You could go out for a long walk, and I'm sure I could have it looking in a more reasonable state within an hour or two.'

She smiles, but I can see how much of a strain it is for her to do so. She sighs and holds out her hand for the bag, crouching down and lifting a small wooden frame that's just about holding itself together by a solitary tack. The glass plate is no longer inside the frame, but is at least intact, so I'm surprised when I see her place both inside the bin liner, only preserving the crumpled photograph of herself dressed in graduation garb.

'Do you remember graduation day?' she asks, as she places the photograph beside the cardboard cups on the counter top. 'Do you remember how terrifying it was knowing we'd have to find jobs and places to live? I was just about to secure my internship at *The Telegraph*, but you were still writing freelance for the *Dorset Echo*. I told you that you should move to London with me, that I'd take care of you, and that it wasn't nearly as threatening as they made out in the movies. You were adamant that you wanted to return to Weymouth, and I could never understand your fear of the big city. I guess you were right all along.'

Her shoulders sag, defeated.

'No I wasn't,' I reassure her. 'If anything, my work in the last few years has revealed that nowhere in this country is as safe as I once assumed.'

'Not too many burglaries in your neck of the woods though, are there?'

'I'm sure there are plenty. Poverty and desperation aren't unique conditions reserved for London, you know.' I take a breath. 'I know you're in shock about what's happened, and I don't blame you for feeling low about it all, but you will find somewhere new that will give you that feeling of security again. Think about it: you and Daniella are due to get married later this year, and you were already talking about getting a place of your own, remember? This could just be fate's way of pushing you to move quicker. It's a horrible situation to be faced with, but there could be a silver lining.'

She looks close to tears, and so I delicately place my arms around her shoulders and just hold her.

'I don't know how you manage to stay so positive,' she whispers into my shoulder. 'When I think of all you've been through with your sister disappearing, your dad's sudden death, and now your mum's dementia… My life by comparison is a fairy tale.'

'Come on,' I say, pulling away, 'let's crack on with this, and then maybe we go and visit Saskia, and check she's feeling better?'

She strains a smile again, but nods her affirmation.

'Why don't you start in the bedroom, Rach, as I'd prefer not to be rifling through your underwear?'

She actually chuckles this time and heads through to the small bedroom, leaving me to pick at the mess. Starting in the kitchen, I carefully deposit the smashed plates and bowls into a fresh bin liner, managing to recover two plates, a single bowl, but alas no wine glasses. Sweeping sections with a dustpan and brush as I go, I'm secretly pleased with my efforts within fifteen minutes, and save for the virtually empty cupboards, and the bulging bin liner that I almost can't lift, you'd never know the place had been vandalised.

Ripping off a third bin liner, I shake it open and move into the open living room area. This is probably the worst hit of the rooms, particularly as the soil from one of the two pot plants has been crudely shaken over the mess in the centre of the room, making it almost impossible to pick up anything not covered in mud. Not a single photo frame remains on the wall, and despite my best efforts, none of the glass is salvageable. I gather the photographs in a pile beside our cups, reminding myself that new frames can be purchased once Rachel has found her next home. It wouldn't surprise me if she decides to stay in a hotel for a second night, though I doubt she'll choose the same place on account of the lumpy mattress and flat pillows.

I continue to work around the room until I've sorted the debris into those items that might still be of use – there isn't much, mainly books – and three bags containing the rest. Locating the hoover in the small cupboard by the front door, I go to work on the soil, but it takes two empties before it's all gone, and the place looks liveable, save for the slashed sofa-bed which definitely hasn't survived. Most of the stuffing is now in one of the black sacks.

Rachel emerges from her bedroom and gives an impressed nod at my efforts.

'I've made a note of the items I've put in the bin bags,' I tell her, 'so you can let your insurance company know.'

'Thank you,' she replies, 'but there probably wasn't enough to cover the excess on my policy. I'll tell them about my stolen laptop and iPad, but I'm not sure they'll cover the stolen money.' She pauses, and sighs again. 'I really hope the little bastards who did this suffer a karma bitch slap imminently.'

I share the sentiment that whoever has caused such heartache deserves to suffer a similar fate, but it brings my mind back to last night's discussion. The police officers were pretty confident it was merely the work of bored vandals, but I can't ignore the possibility that the flat was targeted because of the work Jack and I have been doing. I know it could just be coincidental, but my overactive imagination won't let it drop. I told you it could be a curse as much as a blessing.

'Was there anything else missing?' I ask, relieved when she shakes her head.

'No. They pretty much emptied all my drawers onto the bed and floor, and save for the soil on the bedspread, there's no particular damage. Looks like their focus was the living room. I'm amazed at how quickly you got it tidied. Thank you for helping today, Em. Don't think I could have faced this on my own.'

I rub her upper arm. 'Anytime. Are you up for going to see Saskia now? I could phone ahead and check if she's allowed visitors, but by the time I get through to someone, we might just as well go there.'

Rachel agrees, and we leave the tied sacks in the middle of the room. Mrs Duvitski catches us on the stairs as we close the door. It's impossible to tell whether she's headed out or just returning as it looks as though she's putting on her coat, and yet her shopping basket has a baguette poking out of the top.

'Have the police managed to catch those responsible?' she asks, to sate her curiosity for gossip.

'I doubt it,' Rachel replies, nodding for me to keep moving.

'I remembered something else,' she calls, causing both of us to stop and turn back.

'There was a man here earlier yesterday,' she explains.

'What man?' Rachel asks.

'He said he was from the gas board, come to read your meter, but he was very apologetic when I told him we're all on smart meters here so there was no need.'

'Describe him to me.'

Mrs Duvitski pushes the large spectacles up off her nose. 'Tall, dark hair, very handsome. Reminded me of a movie star, like Cary Grant.'

'Why didn't you mention this to the police yesterday? What time was he here?'

She considers the question. 'It must have been mid-morning, maybe just before lunch?'

That was the time we'd gone to Maddie's to meet with Zara and Tom.

'Can you remember anything else about him? Did he say which gas company he worked for?'

'No dear, but that was the odd thing that stuck in my memory: he was dressed in a dark suit and white shirt. Looked more like a bouncer at a nightclub than someone here to read a meter. Anyway, as I said, he was very apologetic and left soon after, claiming he must have been given the wrong address.'

Rachel looks at me and I nod that it sounds suspicious, but it doesn't give us a lot to go on.

'Thank you, Mrs Duvitski,' Rachel says. 'If you see him again, would you phone me?' She hands over a business card. 'It's really important.'

'Of course, dear, but I doubt he'll be back now that he knows you have a smart meter.' She heads back upstairs, dragging the shopping trolley behind her, oblivious to the fact that the handsome stranger was almost definitely not from the gas board.

Ealing Hospital is as grey and drab as you might expect for a facility built in the late 70s. This is now the third hospital I've visited in as many days, and it's really starting to feel like a personal attack on my own sanity. I've never been a fan of hospitals. Although I appreciate they are there to heal and treat the sick, and that the doctors and nurses who toil every day should be awarded medals for their service, I don't recall any visit that didn't leave me filled with dread.

Saskia is awake when we enter the ward we've been directed to, and although her arm is in a sling and she looks in some discomfort, she smiles when she sees us. 'You didn't

147

have to come in and see me,' she says, brushing the fringe from her eyes and revealing bruising and grazes around her eye. 'They're due to let me out later, hopefully.'

I place the box of chocolates on the bedsheet over her legs. 'Couldn't find any grapes,' I say apologetically, 'but these should give you plenty of energy.'

Her eyes light up when she recognises the brand – her favourite – and she encourages us to sit.

'How are you feeling?' I ask lamely.

'Not too bad, all things considered. I don't really remember the collision, which is probably for the best. I woke here late last night and was in a panic until the nurse explained what had happened. I remember walking down the pavement and had my head buried in my phone,' she rolls her eyes with shame, 'and the next thing, I was in here. They said the driver didn't stop, which is naughty, but it could have been a lot worse.'

'I bet your shoulder is painful,' Rachel questions. 'I dislocated mine when I was a child and I remember it ached for weeks afterwards.'

'The painkillers are certainly helping,' she smiles again, 'but I might need a few days to get back into action. Is that all right? We've never discussed sick pay and the like.'

'Take all the time you need,' I assure her. 'I'm sure Rachel and I can manage the foundation's work until you're back on your feet.'

'Thank you. I'm just glad I managed to drop the books off with you before the accident. I hate to think what would have happened had I been carrying them when I was hit.'

My heart skips a beat. 'Wait, what? When did you drop off the books?'

Her brow furrows with confusion. 'I left them at Rachel's flat and was on my way home when the accident happened.'

I look at Rachel. 'You didn't find the books when clearing up this morning, did you?'

She shakes her head. 'Not a trace.'

My mind is performing a thousand calculations and it's hard to focus on any one strand. 'Wait, how did you get into Rachel's flat to leave the books?'

'Oh, I didn't. I left them with your friend Jack.'

'Jack?'

'Yes, that is his name, isn't it? PC Jack Serrovitz?'

'You left them with Jack Serrovitz?'

Saskia nods eagerly. 'Yes. He was just coming out of the flat when I arrived. I have to say he's far more handsome than you make out in your books, Emma.'

I feel physically sick, but take several breaths to restrain the urge. 'How do you know it was Jack?'

'He showed me his identification. I read his name on the card, though come to think of it... his thumb was over the picture. He said Rachel was out and you were just headed into the shower, Emma, and he said he'd put them inside the flat for me.' Her confusion is descending into panic. 'Did I do the wrong thing? I know you two work together so I thought it would be okay.'

I look back to Rachel and as the blood drains from her face, I can only assume she's reached the same conclusion as I have. 'Jack's still in the hospital,' I say to her.

'Mrs Duvitski described a tall, dark, Cary Grant-like figure—'

'Yes, that's who he reminded me of,' Saskia interrupts.

'And you saw him leaving Rachel's flat?' I ask her.

'Yes, that's the only reason I believed his story. He hadn't quite closed the door, and when I explained who I was and why I wanted to go inside that's when he said you were getting in the shower so he'd put them in. I saw him go back inside, so I didn't think any more of it. I was messaging you to let you know when the car struck.'

So many thoughts are pulsing through my mind right now, and the ones concerning me the most are: who is this man; why did he have Jack's warrant card; and what has he done with the foundation's books? I have no doubt now that Jack's accident and the burglary at the flat are connected, and it suddenly feels like we're being watched even now, and I just want to run until my body has no more left to give.

Chapter Eighteen

NOW

Uxbridge, London

Jack fighting for his life, the vandalism at Rachel's flat, and now Saskia's hit-and-run are all connected. I can't prove it, or understand what connects them, but I feel it in my bones. Jack was pursuing a lead into Tomlinson's links to the trafficking ring, and now someone posing as Jack was seen at Rachel's flat at the time of the break-in, and also collected the financial books from Saskia. All I know for certain is that I've never been as terrified as I am right now.

My fight-or-flight instinct is telling me to run before any more of the people I care for become embroiled in this mess, yet I can't abandon my friends if they are in danger. The only person who can tell me what really happened to Jack on the night of his accident is Jack himself, and that's why I beg Rachel to drive us there, but this time she insists on coming into the hospital with me. She's trying to hide it, but I can see that Saskia's revelation has rattled her too. I hate that my actions have put her in jeopardy, but I've never been more grateful to have her at my side. If I had to choose one person to face danger with, there's nobody else I'd rather have.

Rachel insisted I phone DCS Rawani and inform him that someone is using Jack's warrant card, but I still don't know whether I can place reliance on him. Jack once told me there's nobody else he trusts more than Rawani, which is why we went to him about the Tomlinson connection in the first place, but sometimes I just get an odd vibe from him, and I can't place what it is that puts my nerves on alert. I relent and leave a message for him to meet us at Jack's bedside. I know he said we shouldn't risk being seen together, but a part of me wants there to be witnesses, just in case.

I recognise the officer standing outside the room, and he tells me my name is on a small list that Rawani confirmed could have access to Jack. He stares quizzically at Rachel until I offer assurances that she can be trusted, but he is adamant only I am allowed to be admitted. Rachel pats my arm, and tells me she will wait outside, but in my eyes it isn't her integrity that should be questioned.

I start as I enter the room and see Mila in school uniform hunched over the bed, her fingers entwined in Jack's and her head resting gently on his chest. She looks so angelic and at peace, and I'm tempted to leave the room and give them the space they deserve.

'Emma!' Mila calls out as I eye the door, and suddenly she's rushing over to me and wrapping her arms around my waist. 'Mum, this is Dad's friend Emma that I told you about. The writer.'

It's only now that I spot a young woman standing with her back to the window. She is a fraction shorter than me, with hair as dark as night. She's dressed in an open denim jacket, pink jogging bottoms, and her hair hangs loosely at her sides. For someone who gave birth in the last six weeks, she looks incredible. Yet there is a true sadness to her eyes that makes me instantly want to hug her despite my own reservations about physical contact.

'Lovely to meet you,' she says, crossing the room, and extending her hand to shake. 'I'm Jack's— I'm Chrissie.'

'And you,' I quickly retort, 'though I wish our first meeting was under better circumstances.'

Her gaze turns to Jack in the bed, and she dabs a tissue against the corner of her eye. 'Typical of him to get us in the same room and then duck out of the introductions,' she says, returning her stare to me and smiling through the obvious pain.

'I'm sorry to turn up unannounced. If I'd known the two of you were here, I'd have waited outside until you were finished.'

'Don't be silly,' she smiles again, warmer this time. 'Jack needs his family around him, and from what Mila tells me, you've practically become family to him now anyway.'

I almost choke on spittle in my throat. Is that really how they see me? Has Jack said something to Mila, or is it just the overactive imagination of an eight-year-old girl who adores her father?

I look down at her and put on my bravest smile to try and reassure her that everything will be okay, even though I don't feel it.

'And how are you doing, Mila? It feels like an age since we met at Hyde Park for the Christmas fayre, and I'd swear you've grown taller since then.'

'I'm the third tallest girl in my class now,' she declares proudly, 'and the sixth tallest in the year.'

How I long for the days when height was the only measure of importance.

'Come on, Mila,' Chrissie says, running a hand through her daughter's hair, 'we should get back. I promised your teacher I'd have you in before the lunch bell.'

Mila instantly releases her grip of my hips, and rushes back to the bedside, straining to lift herself onto the bed and kissing the top of Jack's head, before hurrying back to her mum. As they move towards the door, she stops and looks back at me.

'You will look after my dad while I'm not here, won't you?'

My heart warms in an instant as I see Jack's goofy grin shining through her cheeks. I've never realised how much she resembles him, although it's hard to tell with the mask covering his mouth and his face still so swollen and bruised.

'I promise I'll do whatever I can to keep him safe,' I vow, and her smile widens with this news. She waves as they disappear through the door.

I wipe my own eyes with the back of my hand and slowly approach the bed, looking for any sign that Jack's drug-addled mind is alert enough to sense my presence. If only he would open his eyes, or stir in some way so I know he will actually pull through this and fully recover. But there is no movement, even when I start as the door opens behind us. Spinning around, I see Rawani enter in full dress uniform and come over.

'I warned you that we shouldn't be seen together,' he begins, but I cut him off and quickly relay the news about the break-in and Saskia's hit-and-run. He only seems interested when I mention the Jack impersonator at Rachel's door.

'Did she get a good look at the man? Could she help us put together a composite so we can check if we have a record for him?'

I honestly don't know, but I'll ask Saskia if she's up to it. There may also be some merit in having Rachel's neighbour Mrs Duvitski check Saskia's description in case it's the same man she described as Cary Grant.

'Was Jack's warrant card on him when he was brought in?' I ask, but I can tell from the way he lowers his eyes that it wasn't.

'I'd assumed he'd left it at home, but I'll follow up on it.'

'Have you made any further progress on what happened yet? You said you were going to be checking traffic cameras.'

'It's still a work in progress, Miss Hunter. We will get to the bottom of it one way or another.'

There's that weird vibe again. He must know how close Jack and I have been working and that he doesn't need to worry about my discretion.

'Do you agree that all of this is connected?' I ask next, deciding to call him out on it.

'All I know is that Jack's altercation is out of character, and that we may not know the real reason he was where he was until he wakes.'

That doesn't answer my question, but that doesn't come as a surprise.

'Do you think your life may be in danger?' he asks, keeping his eyes on Jack.

'I didn't until you just mentioned it. Do you think my life is in danger?'

This does make him look over, but he neither nods, nor shakes his head. 'I can't offer you any physical protection, Miss

Hunter, but if you have somewhere you can go and lie low for a few days, I'd suggest it would be good to go.'

Is the concern at the edge of his eyes genuinely for my safety, or does he just want me out of the picture so he can help cover up the mess that was created when I received that photograph of Tomlinson with Saltzing and Turgood?

I don't want to leave Jack in this state, but I'm invisible in this gargantuan city and I've never felt truly safe in London.

'Promise me that nothing else will happen to Jack. If I go, I need to know that he will have trusted people watching over him. Swear to me.'

'Can I be honest with you, Miss Hunter?'

I nod, though it does beg the question as to whether everything that has gone before was less than honest.

'If you're right, and Jack's accident is someone's attempt to influence your investigation, then these actions are probably nothing more than warnings and intimidation. If someone wanted Jack dead, I imagine he would be already.'

I don't like his dismissive tone, and now wish he hadn't been so brutally honest, but I don't know if he is capable of empathy or compassion.

He says nothing more before departing, leaving me alone with Jack and only the sound of the breathing apparatus cutting through the deathly silence.

All of this started because I asked Jack to review my sister's casefile, and I never would have predicted this is where it would lead. For the past month I've been desperate for some kind of break in the case, but this avenue is closed until Jack regains consciousness and points the finger. So what does that leave me with?

And that's when Tom's words trigger somewhere in the

back of my head: *if the man responsible for taking Zara was never brought to justice, then maybe he could have been involved somehow in what happened to your sister.*

In an instant I know what I need to do, and where Rachel and I can lay low for a few days.

Chapter Nineteen

THEN

Ruislip, London

Switching off the vacuum cleaner, Zara welcomed the silence as it returned to the cluttered living room. Tom had been gone before she'd woken at eight, after what was a restless night's sleep. She'd spent two hours of it sitting up in bed on the iPad, once more staring into the dead eyes of the man charged for her abduction.

Callum Gerrard had been fifty-seven when he was caught attempting to flee the country at the docks at Portsmouth. He'd refused to go quietly, and had even jumped from the ferry while it was still moored, and had to be fished out by the Coast Guard. He denied the charges, but was found guilty at court and sentenced to fifteen years in prison. He was deemed sick and perverted by the press after his sentencing at Brighton Crown Court, but such behaviour wasn't as prevalent in the public eye at the time and so he was never likely to escape a custodial sentence.

Why he'd chosen to accept culpability for her abduction remained a mystery to Zara, but what frightened her more was the knowledge that the real guilty party remained at large. In the thirty-five years that had passed since she was taken, she had imagined that he was probably dead too, but she didn't know that for certain, and that was what continued to bother her now, as she straightened the furniture in the living room.

What if he wasn't dead, and had been up to his twisted antics in all the time he should have been in prison alongside Gerrard? How many more children had suffered at his hands because she hadn't been brave enough to admit that Gerrard was just one in a string of men who had beaten and abused her?

What if he's still out there?

Switching on the Dyson again, she ran it over a stubborn patch of fluff in the corner beside the coffee table that she must have missed first time around, yet still the voice in her head remained, rising above her attempt to drown it out.

You could have stopped him.

Releasing the handle, she dropped to her knees and covered her ears with both hands, but still the voice taunted her.

You're to blame.

'I was only a child!' she screamed at the empty room as the tears burned.

There was more truth to that statement than anyone could understand. She had been nine years old when she was taken, and eleven when she was rescued by the fireman on the ladder. The police had interviewed her several times, delicately asking what had happened, but they had never asked her whether Gerrard was the man who'd snatched her years before. She had been in no position to tell them they had the wrong man, and they probably wouldn't have listened anyway. It was a big win as far as they were concerned, and all they'd wanted was to tie a big bow around his capture.

When Tom finds out the truth, he'll leave you too.

'Stop it! Stop it! Stop it!' she yelled at the room.

Then you'll be all alone again, like you deserve.

Dragging herself from the carpet, she switched off the vacuum and stormed to the bathroom, opening the medicine cabinet and pulling out two packets of ibuprofen before turning and heading into the kitchen. Tears fell as she reached into the cupboard and removed a small glass, filling it from the tap and placing it unsteadily on the counter. The hazy sunshine glinted off the large blade on the drainer, as if it was calling to her, and she quickly scooped it up.

'Is this what you want?' she demanded, raising her eyes to the ceiling.

Dropping the knife, she opened both packets of ibuprofen, and started popping pills onto the counter beside the glass. It wouldn't necessarily be enough to kill her, but that many pills would stop her phoning for an ambulance after she'd punctured the veins in her wrist.

Brushing the pills into the palm of her hand, she looked up to the heavens again. 'Is this what I deserve? If you want me to end it, then give the word and I'll do it.'

The voice in her head didn't respond, but she remained where she was, willing it to taunt her further, but it was gone. For now.

Slamming the contents of her palm onto the counter, she took a step backwards, but continued to grip the edge of the counter for support, focusing on deep breaths, until her legs felt strong enough to support her once more. She grunted with derision at the powdery mess before her, ashamed to have allowed such a weak routine to surface.

Pills and a knife? That wasn't the way she was going to go out of this world. Zara knew deep down that she'd never have the courage to go through with such a stunt. At the very least she wouldn't want Tom to return and find her. *He* deserved better.

Taking one further deep breath, she scooped up the pills and packets and threw both into the dustbin, before collecting the kitchen knife and returning it to the vacant slit in the wooden block. With her cheeks still burning with the shame, she moved unsteadily back through to the living room, ignoring the fallen Dyson, and dropped onto the sofa. She remained still for several minutes composing herself before collecting the iPad from its charging stand, and switching it on.

Maybe it was just this house that was getting her down. Seeing the same walls and furniture day in and day out was bound to have an impact on her mental health, but the thought of going out to browse through shops that held no interest repulsed her. Opening a search engine, she typed in last-minute holidays and scanned the results that appeared on the screen. A break away with Tom sounded far more appealing.

Images of tropical beaches, city landscapes dominated by high-rise office buildings and skyscrapers, and crisp white mounds of snow filled the screen. Any and every possible kind of holiday available to peruse at her fingertips. She hadn't expected such a broad choice of options. But which one to choose?

Tom loved to explore and immerse himself in other cultures, but that didn't necessarily rule out a beach holiday, so long as they didn't spend every day on the sand and in the sea. They'd never been skiing, but ice-cold temperatures didn't necessarily appeal right now, though the thought of après-ski around warm crackling fires sounded heavenly. She didn't care where they went, so long as it was sufficiently different to the current norm. At least the monotony of work had kept the barrier to her past firm and rigid; had helped her build this false life, and almost allowed her to believe the house of cards was her reality.

Almost.

Tom would appreciate a surprise holiday, wouldn't he? Would it be enough to distract him from Harriet's revelation?

Zara wasn't sure the answer to either question would be what she was hoping to hear. And it terrified her that his actual answer might be that he *didn't* want to go on holiday with her at all. When they'd been in Windsor yesterday, she'd sensed he'd wanted to tell her something by the river before Harriet had interrupted, and once Harriet had moved on, Zara hadn't allowed him to continue, just in case he'd delivered the termination she was dreading. They would have to talk about Saturday night's revelation at some point, but she was determined to delay it for as long as possible, hoping time would give him the perspective and capacity to forgive her the years of deceit. It probably wouldn't, but she had to cling to the possibility.

She clicked on a site and searched for popular destinations, hovering over the Seychelles when a beautiful apartment with a sea view presented itself. The price was on the high side, but she could almost taste the on-beach cocktails in one of the photographs. She'd never been to the Seychelles, but it ranked as one of the destinations she'd dreamed of visiting. She should really check whether Tom could get the time off work before booking anything, yet still she continued to click through the photographs, excitement building with the butterflies in her stomach.

They could fly from Heathrow, which was only a short taxi ride away, and despite the thirteen-hour flight, they could be there by next weekend. The cursor hovered over the reserve button, but she hesitated.

What if Tom came home and said he didn't want to go away with her, and was angry that she'd booked a holiday without checking with him?

Simple: she would book it with her own money and tell him it was her treat; he couldn't be angry then.

Opening a new internet window, she logged onto her online bank account, gasping when she saw just how low her balance was. She knew she'd been dipping into the redundancy money here and there, but hadn't realised just how little was left. Tom hadn't asked for any support with the monthly utility bills and rent, but she'd felt guilty about letting him shoulder the burden. She immediately closed the holiday pages, and focused on the small figure in her account.

Could it really be accurate? Had her funds been so depleted in the months since the payout had been made?

She hadn't realised it was so bad, and now guilt suffocated the earlier excitement. There was only one solution to this new dilemma: she would have to find a new job. They said change was as good as a break, and maybe finding something that would demand she leave the flat every day would help beat the post-revelation blues. Given it was possible that Tom was contemplating ending their relationship, she would need to find a means of supporting herself financially, but that opened a whole new flux of questions, the main one being what did she want to do as a job?

She'd been efficient as a legal secretary, but she didn't desperately want to return to such a pressurised environment. Could her experience and organisational skills be put to use as some kind of receptionist? It certainly didn't give her the buzz of excitement she was hoping for. Opening a job search window, she began to look at recruitment companies, but quickly grew bored. She wasn't in the right mental space to start updating her CV and cover letter template; besides, Tom was better at things like that, and she'd need his help. Determining she'd ask for his help when he returned later, she was about to switch off the iPad when another thought struck. Searching for Emma Hunter's name, she found that Emma had published three books to date. She downloaded the first, *Monsters Under the Bed*, promising herself she would only read the first chapter, but soon she had lost herself in the pages.

Chapter Twenty

NOW

Brighton, East Sussex

'Is this the place?' Rachel asks, craning her neck to stare up at the tall grey office block, where half the windows have been boarded up by thick yellowing wood.

I check the address on my phone, comparing it to the fading street sign on the corner of the road, and the broken name sign above the double door entrance. 'Looks like it must be,' I respond, unable to keep the self-doubt from my tone.

'Maybe the charity went out of business?' Rachel offers.

'Not according to their Facebook page,' I quickly counter. 'Says the helpline is open eight till ten every day, and this is where it's allegedly operated from.'

The office block we're standing before looks like it was once a thriving hub of activity, but has long been forgotten about. Across the road, the street is littered with abandoned sandwich shops, independent cafés, and a newsagent, with only the latter not shut up with graffiti-stained metal shutters. But it's the lack of people which most makes it feel like we've stumbled into a ghost town. We've been standing on the pavement for at least ten minutes and nobody has emerged from or entered the building; nor have there been any vehicles driven past. If this really is the hub of the runaways helpline charity, then they're doing a cracking job of covering their tracks.

I nod at the newsagent's. 'No harm in asking,' I suggest, quickly crossing the road with Rachel in tow.

A small bell rings as I push open the door. A woman in a painfully-bright sari bolts up behind the counter as if connected to a mechanism that stirred her into action at the push of the door.

'Good morning,' I say, hurrying to the counter, and ignoring the tall rack of glossy magazines to my right and the rack of chocolate bars to my left.

She nods in response, though her eyes don't leave the open magazine on the counter before her.

'I wondered if you could tell me anything about the office block across the road,' I ask, as I arrive at the counter.

The woman in the yellow and pink sari finally makes eye contact, but her lips remain tight for several seconds before she eventually speaks. 'What specifically do you want to know?'

There is no trace of an accent, and it wouldn't surprise me if this tiny shop had been in operation for decades. The woman across from me has a stern face, and I sense she doesn't suffer fools gladly. Despite the lack of obvious passing trade, she's not bending over backwards to encourage us to make a purchase.

'We're looking for the "Gone But Not Forgotten" helpline, which I believe rents some desks in the building.'

She nods. 'They're in there. Maybe five or six at a time. It used to be more, but times are tough. Not always easy to get people to give up their time to sit and wait for calls.'

It's a relief to hear our trip down to Brighton today hasn't been in vain, but I still don't know for certain whether Zara's mum, Angie, is scheduled to be on duty. I could simply call the helpline and ask, but I'd hate to take the slot of a runaway who's made the decision to reach out and seek help.

'Ah, that's great to hear,' I say, offering a smile of gratitude. 'Do many of the volunteers come in here?'

She shrugs. 'Hard to say; I don't interrogate every consumer.'

It's impossible to miss the agitated tone in her voice, and I guess as far as she's concerned, we've already outstayed our welcome.

'Can I buy two bottles of mineral water?' I ask, nodding at the tall refrigerator cabinet beside her, before reaching for two bags of cheese and onion crisps from the basket on the counter.

'Still or sparkling?'

'Still, please.'

She opens the fridge and selects two bottles before quickly closing the fridge door.

'Thank you for your help,' I say, once I've paid, and she returns to her stool, eyes immediately back to whatever she was reading. 'It's definitely the place,' I say to Rachel once I'm back outside again, and have handed her a bottle of water and a bag of crisps.

'So, what do you think?' she asks, opening the bottle and taking a long drink. 'Do we hang around and wait to see if she turns up, or go and see if we can get inside?'

It's too cold to hang around outside the newsagent's, and

there's little by way of protection from the bitter wind despite the six storeys of office block before us. And call me paranoid, but I can't help feeling like we're being watched, even though there isn't another soul in sight.

'I think we knock on the door and ask to go in,' I suggest. 'Worst they can say is no.'

Crossing the road, we locate a panel of switches beside one of the double doors, but none of them are labelled, so I systematically press each one until finally a gruff voice crackles through the intercom.

'Yeah?'

'Hello, I'm trying to get hold of anyone from the "Gone But Not Forgotten" helpline,' I reply as airily as my dry throat will allow.

'Delivery?' she croaks back.

'No, not exactly.' I look uncertainly at Rachel. 'I'm a reporter, and we were looking to do an article about the rise in missing people along the south coast. Is there a manager or trustee we can speak with?'

There is a pause before the door buzzes. 'Second floor, but you'll have to use the stairs; lift's out of order,' the voice crackles again.

Heading inside, there is no sign of a security guard behind the dust-covered desk in the entrance way. Passing through disabled security barriers, we locate a bank of three lifts, which all have crudely scrawled 'Out of Order' signs stuck to them. The fire escape is clearly signposted, and it is this we use to climb the two flights of stairs. When we emerge on the second floor, another handwritten sign has been stuck to the door segregating the office space from the lift space. Again, there is little by way of security keeping us from opening the doors and proceeding through. I imagine the whole building was once a thriving contact centre for some bank or other financial institution, long since abandoned.

The floor stretches beyond what I can see, but the only activity seems to be from a dozen desks to our left where four women and one man are chatting. One of the women stands when she sees us and removes the headset from her neck. Leaving the group to chat, she comes over to us, and the stench of tar and tobacco is so overwhelming that I take an involuntary step backwards.

'Hi, I'm—'

'Emma Hunter,' she cuts me off, reaching for and shaking my hand vigorously, her broad smile lifting the bags beneath her eyes. 'Gosh, I know who you are. We all do. Everyone, look who it is!'

The conversation hushes as the group turns and stares, though none seem brave enough to come over and introduce themselves.

'We're huge fans,' the woman continues, mobile phone suddenly in hand. 'Could I get a selfie with you?'

Diana – according to her name badge – is old enough to be my mother, and her greying hair is tightly permed, but her mobile phone is far more advanced than my own, so when she thrusts it into the air, I don't have the heart to tell her that this is the part of my job I loathe. Straining my lips into a smile, I try not to blink as she snaps more than a dozen images in quick succession.

'Come in, come in and take a seat,' Diana ushers Rachel and me in, returning to the small group and fetching a couple of spare chairs. 'Have you really come to write an article about this motley crew?'

There is a murmur of tittering amongst the other four at this description. Looking at them, *crew* is too urban a noun to describe the group. All are white, sixty-plus in age, and middle-class, but there is a common bond between them: they've all lost someone close to them. I guess that means I have more in common with them than I would have assumed.

'I'm actually looking for Angie Edwards,' I say, looking for any other name badges, but not seeing any.

'Oh,' Diana replies, crestfallen. 'Angie isn't scheduled to be in today, I'm sorry.'

'Do you think you could give me her address so I can call round and see her? I really do need to speak to her today. It's about her daughter, Zara.'

Diana is already nodding before I've said Zara's name. I guess each of the volunteers on the helpline knows each other's war stories inside and out. 'I don't think I can give you her address for data privacy reasons, but I don't mind giving her a call and seeing whether she can pop down to see you though? I think she said she had an orthodontist appointment this morning, but I'm sure she'd be super keen to meet you too. Can you hang on, and let me call her?'

'Sure,' I nod, 'thank you.'

Diana pulls the headset back on and moves away to a different desk, leaving the rest of the group somewhat gawping. I really don't know what to say to them. I don't respond well when the spotlight is suddenly thrust upon me, as I become very self-conscious of saying the wrong thing.

'Are you staying in Brighton, or are you just here for the day?' the woman beside Rachel asks. She is probably the youngest of the group – either that or she's the only one who chooses to colour her rich red locks.

'Hoping to stay at least one night,' I reply, glancing at Rachel for confirmation. She's been surprisingly quiet, but I now see the small smirk at the corners of her mouth; she must realise just how much I'm struggling.

'And is your next case going to be about Zara then? God knows, Angie deserves some good news after all this time.'

The comment catches me off-guard. I recall Tom mentioning something about an argument between mother and daughter, but I would have thought that surrounding herself with so many other stories about lost loved ones, she'd be grateful to have her daughter back.

I'm about to ask what she means when Diana bustles back over to the group. 'Angie said she can be here by two, if you're all right to hang on?'

I look to Rachel again who nods her agreement.

'Great!' Diana declares. 'Can I fix either of you a cup of tea or coffee?'

I hold up the water bottle and shake my head. 'We're fine, thank you.'

A ringing reverberates around the room, and the only male in the group sighs and turns back to face the computer behind him, and answers the call. 'You're through to Clive at Gone But Not Forgotten, how can I help you today?'

Chapter Twenty-One

NOW

Brighton, East Sussex

Having fielded questions from Diana and her so-called 'motley crew' for the best part of an hour, I'm relieved when the door to the tiny contact centre opens, and a woman in a long brown leather coat steps in, waving at Diana, who hustles over and must be quietly explaining what I've already shared. A moment later, Diana is beckoning Rachel and me over, and introduces us.

'Angie, this is the lovely Emma Hunter, and the equally lovely Rachel Leeming. Can you believe it? The two of them here in the flesh. How many times have we said how great it would be to meet the two of them? I keep pinching myself, thinking it's a dream.'

Angie Edwards smiles brightly, but is more restrained than her colleague. 'Delighted to meet you both,' she says, proffering her hand.

'They're here to talk about Zara,' Diana continues, raising

her eyebrows expectantly. 'Can you imagine seeing her story in a book?'

This is certainly not something I have promised, and I don't appreciate Diana putting words into my mouth. I'm about to correct her, when Rachel steps forward. 'Diana, would you mind if we took Angie for a cup of tea? I'm sure you all have plenty of calls to answer, and we'd just be a distraction.'

Diana doesn't initially grasp the hint, and frowns.

'I think that's a good idea,' Angie pipes up, 'as I haven't eaten yet, and we wouldn't want to get in the way. I'll pop back up when we're done,' she promises.

Diana looks disappointed, like a child whose parents have come to collect her from a friend's house. 'Of course, of course, you don't need me and the others eavesdropping, do you? Make sure to mention the charity,' she adds with a wink and a nod at Angie.

Heading back down the stairs and out of the building, Angie is quick to apologise for her enthusiastic friend. 'Diana is one of your biggest fans,' she explains when we're seated in a small independent coffee shop around the corner, and on a much busier street. 'She set up the helpline, ooh, must be almost thirty years ago now.

'Her son Gavin ran away from home when he was fifteen, and she really struggled with her mental health. He'd fallen in with a crowd pushing drugs. Remember, this would have been back in the early 90s when heroin was the drug of choice for most disillusioned young people. The day he left home, he stole several hundred pounds from Diana's purse and disappeared. The police did eventually find him four years later... fished out of the River Ouse. They reckoned he'd been in there, somehow trapped beneath the surface, for at least two years. She understandably went to pieces – blamed herself, when it wasn't her fault. That's what we parents do, isn't it? When our children put themselves in harm's way, we always question whether we could or should have done things differently.'

'You wouldn't think she'd been through such heartache to meet her,' I empathise.

'That bright and upbeat demeanour? It's all an act. She tries to put a brave face on it for the others – desperately trying to instil some semblance of positivity in what is a tough role – but I've seen her after hours when she goes home to her dingy flat and just sobs. The helpline gives her a purpose and a reason to get out of bed every morning. Even though it's totally voluntary, she's in the office *every* day, even Christmas and Boxing Day. She's a saint.'

'I presume the charity doesn't make much money from the helpline?'

Angie shakes her head glumly. 'Relies on donations from the public, which just aren't enough most months. The landlord of the office block is a personal friend and agreed to charge a reduced rent to us, just so that the land isn't totally going to waste, but I know that Diana personally fronts some of the expense herself. I try to help when I can, but my pension only stretches so far.'

I feel for her, and part of me just wants to write about Zara's story with all profits going to Gone But Not Forgotten, but there would be so many hurdles to traverse before that could happen, including obtaining Zara's agreement to me investigating and writing it.

'I wanted to talk to you about Zara,' I begin, but she's

already nodding as she takes a bite of the tuna sandwich she ordered.

'I figured someone would come calling at some point. The thirty-fifth anniversary of her disappearance is just around the corner, but I didn't expect *The Telegraph* to cover the story.' She looks directly at Rachel as she says this.

'Oh no, um, I'm not here in that capacity,' Rachel quickly clarifies. 'It's Emma who has the interest in the story.'

Angie turns back to me. 'So Diana was right, and you're looking to write about Zara then?'

This isn't the position I wanted to find myself in. I only came at Tom's suggestion, and I don't want to lie to Angie about my true motive.

'Not exactly,' I stammer. 'What I mean to say is, I have an interest in what happened to Zara, but I don't yet know what that will develop into. My agent introduced me to Zara and Tom yesterday, and I... I just want to help her find some closure.'

Angie considers this for a moment before changing the subject. 'You could write a piece about the helpline. I know Diana can be a bit much, but her heart is in the right place.' She chuckles. 'You know, it's funny, we refer to ourselves as Mum's Army sometimes – you know, in honour of the wartime sitcom? There's about ten of us in total who volunteer over the course of a year, and we're all at an age when we could be enjoying retirement, but still we come in, standing guard as the last line of defence. Clive and Stuart are the only men who are involved. Stuart is Clive's son, and I think he only comes along once a month to stay in his dad's good books. And we all have that common purpose: we want to help reunite lost people with their families, because we know what it's like to lose touch and not hear back. Well, as you do too, Emma. How long's it been since you last saw your sister?'

I cringe inwardly at the prospect that Angie knows far more about me than I do about her. 'Twenty-one years.'

'So you understand what it's like. We are so reliant on public donations, but it feels like we're shrinking in the city. Diana set it up so that those who've lost loved ones could call and cry when they needed to, but also to allow those who find themselves lost to reach out for support. Without advertising and an increase in donations, I fear it will only be a matter of time until the line gets switched off permanently.' She turns back to Rachel. 'Is there any chance you can do something with your paper? A bit of national coverage could go a long way.'

I feel for Rachel as she shuffles awkwardly in her chair. 'It's not really my area of journalism, but I'll speak to my editor and see what he suggests.'

I think we all know that's a no, but Angie smiles gratefully regardless.

'Can you tell me about the day Zara disappeared? I've read a variety of stories in the press about how you were on holiday and at the pier to watch a fireworks display, but I'd like to know what wasn't included in the press reports.'

She looks annoyed at the change of direction, but it's only momentary. 'No parent should have to go through that. Do you have children of your own?'

We both shake our heads.

'Well, it's a different feeling to that of losing a friend or sibling. When you become a parent, you sign this invisible contract that you will go to all lengths to keep your child safe from harm. It isn't always easy, but that's why despite any arguments, children are always the last thing on their parents' minds last thing at night. I felt like a failure; I still do. If only I'd held her hand, or kept her nearby, or warned her not to wander, but I didn't, and I will live with that regret for the rest of my life.' Her hand shoots up to her face, but the tears remain at bay.

'I'm sorry, Angie, the last thing I want to do is upset you, but Tom has asked me to help Zara find some peace, and she's not going to open up to me until I can understand what's keeping her trapped in the past.'

She smiles at the mention of Tom's name. 'He's a nice boy, is Tom. Well, I say *boy*, obviously he's a man now, but he's good for her, I think. Cares a lot.' She pauses. 'Part of me died that day. I remember waking every day for a week and believing it was just a terrifying nightmare, until the realisation hit. It was like losing her all over again each and every day. But I never gave up hope that one day I'd find her.'

'You must be something of an icon to the others at the helpline,' I suggest.

Angie frowns and picks at something in her teeth. 'In what way?'

'I mean, because *your* daughter came home. Yours is the ultimate success story, right? You found her.'

She narrows her eyes, but doesn't respond.

'I read up about Zara's story as research into my sister's disappearance,' I continue as the awkward silence gets to me. 'It's so incredible that she was found twenty-one months later when many would probably have given up hope, and so close to the abduction site.'

She fixes me with a hard stare. 'I did what any mother would do to try and keep the investigation alive. I even quit my job and roamed different parts of the city endlessly, showing pictures, asking questions, begging for help. I petitioned the local MP to talk about Zara in Parliament and to pressure the local force not to allow the investigation to grow cold, but it's hard when you're only one voice.'

I don't disagree; I've fought every day since I was twenty to revive interest in my sister's case, but not even Maddie is willing to consider it. I know my mum worked feverishly to maintain local interest in Anna's disappearance, but eventually had to give up the fight when it became too much.

'Had she changed much in the nearly two years she was away?'

She scoffs at the question. 'She wasn't my little girl anymore, if that's what you mean. Those precious years were stolen from us, and even a life sentence in prison doesn't feel sufficient punishment for such a cruel act. Bring back capital punishment is what I say. Men like that – *monsters* – who prey on the vulnerable should be pulled out and disposed of like weeds. It shouldn't be acceptable just to lock them away and try to forget the past. An example should be made.' She hushes, suddenly aware of her raised voice. 'But I can't change any of that, so I do what I can, and that's how I became involved with Diana and the helpline. It's my hope that if just being on the end of a phone can give one person some hope when they need it most, then that's one person I've helped. It really would mean the world if you could do anything to help raise awareness of the work we're doing. I appreciate it's far from Weymouth, but—'

'I'll do what I can. Rach and I run a charitable foundation that offers support to families who need it, and there must be some way we can link up with Gone But Not Forgotten. As soon as our administrator Saskia is back on her feet, I'll have her reach out to Diana.'

Angie smiles for the first time since we sat down.

'Have you spoken to your daughter recently?' I begin, trying to steer the conversation again.

Angie's reaction is odd though, as if my question is a slap in the face. Again I recall the argument Tom mentioned and wonder if there's still a raw nerve.

She finally sighs and wipes the corners of her mouth with a paper napkin, and drops it on what remains of her tuna sandwich. 'No, Emma, I haven't spoken to *my* daughter in years. Almost thirty-five of them actually.'

Rachel and I exchange glances. 'I don't follow.'

'Okay, well let me explain it to you in plain English, shall I? My daughter was abducted in 1986 from this city, and hasn't been seen since. The eleven-year-old girl who was returned to us is *not* my daughter.'

Chapter Twenty-Two

THEN

Brighton, East Sussex

34 years ago

Months had passed since Zara had been taken from the pier, as best as she could determine, but it had reached the point where she wasn't even sure she'd ever been on that pier at all. She continued to cling to the memory of her parents and that trip to Brighton for the fireworks, but as far as she knew now, it could all have been a dream. The thought of that minty rock and the colourful explosions overhead was now blurry around the edges, like a recording on a video tape that had been overused and was about to split under the strain. In fact, everything before the moment she'd woken cold and alone in that cell felt like it was just days away from being ejected in a spaghetti-like spool of dark tape that would be impossible to reassemble.

As her mind slowly wakened, she tried to picture her

mum's face, wrapped in that yellow scarf against the chill of the November breeze.

Don't leave me, Mum, she pleaded silently. *I need you. You need to find me.*

Had she been wearing that woollen coat her dad had bought her from Marks & Spencer's? The grey tweed one that was so rough to the touch that Zara had compared it to sandpaper, but that her mum had vehemently defended.

'It's so warm inside that I reckon I could scale Everest, just like that Sir Edmund Hillary,' she would argue.

But *was* that the coat her mum had been wearing? She didn't like it when it got wet, so would she have even brought it on the weekend break in early November when rain was likely? But if she hadn't been wearing *that* coat, what had she been wearing? Why couldn't she remember something so simple?

Gentle rumbling somewhere in the darkness beyond her closed eyes indicated she wasn't alone, but her brain wasn't prepared to let go of the rapidly blurring picture of her mum and dad. If she couldn't sharpen the image now, she was terrified she'd never be able to focus on their faces again, and that was a worse torture than she'd already experienced.

Temporarily moving away from the image of her mum, she tried to recall her dad's voice. He was a good ten years older than her mum, and a lifetime of smoking cheap tobacco had left him with a gravelly rattle, especially when he laughed so hard it made him cough. Not that there had been a lot to laugh about recently. She knew there were things her mum and dad weren't telling her. Conversations suddenly hushed when she entered the room; letters with hospital insignia quickly shuffled into drawers and out of sight with an ominous, 'We'll discuss it later.' Her dad chose to shave his head now, and was always in a flat cap when they went outside, but he rarely complained about the cold. He'd definitely had that flat cap on when she'd last seen him, because he'd hidden his winnings beneath it – a habit he'd had since childhood, or so he'd claimed.

Yes, the image of her dad was much sharper than that of her mother. He'd been happy at the pier, hadn't he? Happier than she'd seen him for a while. And he'd bought her that pink rock, telling her it reminded him of his own childhood trips to the seaside. She could just about remember how sweet that first lick had tasted. He'd told her she couldn't just bite the sweet, but that it was worth the wait. He'd tried to hold her hand when they'd first walked onto the pier, but she'd told him her hands were cold. Why hadn't he insisted?

The rumbling in the darkness was louder now, but it wasn't a rumble; it was voices. Two voices, in fact, though the fuzz in her ears was still too heavy to allow her to decipher what the voices were discussing, or just how close they were. Impossible to know if they were in the room with her, or just beyond it.

She tried to picture her mother's face again, but the rumbling voices were becoming too much of a distraction. Her mum's face was blurring further, now no longer able to decipher what colour her eyes were. Brown? Hazel? Green? She had no idea.

A sharp pain erupted behind her eyes, as if a pointy blade was being pressed against the skin there, and instinct forced her hands to her temple. Her mind blanked, only able to concentrate on the agony of what was rapidly taking total control of her body. She could no longer feel anything but the internal burning, was unable to process anything other than the wish for the pain to stop.

She'd experienced a headache before, and her mum would usually give her a dose of Calpol and a cold flannel, and it would eventually disappear. But this was like nothing she'd ever experienced, and in the darkness she prayed for anything that would take the pain away.

The voices grew louder.

'I don't know what you expect *me* to do about it. None of this was my idea.'

She didn't immediately recognise the voice but as she fought against the continued burning in her head, she wasn't even certain she hadn't just imagined the voice speaking. The heat in her head was spreading and she could taste it now in her throat, like that feeling immediately after being sick when it feels like no amount of water or toothpaste will remove the burn. But still the heat descended, finally bringing a fraction of relief to her head – or it could have just been her brain's need to firefight the pain receptors elsewhere in the body.

She tried to prise her eyes apart, but the lids felt so heavy that the task was mammoth. She finally managed to get one open, using her trembling fingers to aid the process, but she didn't immediately recognise her surroundings. She wasn't in her usual cell. The familiar grey walls had been replaced by some kind of dark wood panelling.

She tried to blink, and this time managed to get her second eye slightly open. Yes, there was definitely some kind of wood panelling on the wall, and as she tried to straighten her head, she now took in the fireplace and hearth.

Was it all in her imagination? Were her eyes even open? She couldn't move properly, and didn't have the presence of mind to pinch herself awake, and yet she was certain she wasn't actually dreaming.

'Well, what are we going to do about it?' the second voice challenged the first.

'He said we have to take care of it, so what do you *think* he wants us to do?'

'No. No way. Not a kid.'

'We don't have no kind of choice in the matter. He says she's too hot to handle right now, and the police are turning over every stone looking for her.'

Zara flinched at the words, sensing the *she* and *her* they were referring to was in fact her. She closed her eyes again, allowing her head to once again rest against the seat cushion, and focused all her efforts on the two male voices. She now recognised the second as Clyde, the gorilla who'd first carried her from her cell.

'I don't think I can... Not to a kid,' Clyde said now, sounding vulnerable as he spoke.

'What difference does it make? It's not like what we do here isn't going to see us burn in Hell for eternity, is it? Don't tell me you've suddenly grown a conscience! You wasn't worried when you was collecting your pay, was you?'

Zara couldn't work out why Clyde was so reluctant to undertake whatever assignment had now been bestowed on him, but she'd seen enough to know that Clyde would eventually cave and do whatever had been asked of him, regardless of his own view about events.

In the weeks since she'd first arrived, she'd grown accustomed to the daily routine, and despite early setbacks involving shouting, beatings, and withdrawal of basic rations, she'd learned it was easier to go along with the programme.

Clyde, it seemed, was just as institutionalised.

The heat in her chest continued to expand, and she could feel it creeping along her arms and legs, sucking the strength from her aching limbs as it wound around every muscle and sinew, until she silently begged for anyone to take it away.

'She's waking,' the first voice acknowledged. 'Do you reckon she's craving it yet?'

Clyde didn't respond at first, but his heavy breathing revealed his true feelings. 'You know the craving starts after the first couple of hits. By now, it'll be eating her up inside.'

She heard footsteps moving towards her, followed by the sliding of a drawer somewhere off to her right.

'Shall I do the honours?' the first voice said, now so close that Zara felt as though she could reach out and touch him if only she could control her arms.

'Can't you just leave her be?' Clyde asked, still some way back.

'Do you really want her to suffer more? She'll be grateful for the hit. It'll take away all the pain, won't it, Number Five?'

Her shoulders tensed at mention of her name, but she found herself involuntarily murmuring in response.

'You want me to take the pain away, Number Five?' the first voice taunted.

'Yes,' she mouthed, as though she was nothing more than a ventriloquist's dummy.

'See, Clyde, she wants the hit.'

'Doesn't mean you have to give it to her,' Clyde grunted back. 'We could *not* give her the hit, let her ride out the down, and then let her go.'

'Are you out of your *fucking* mind? Do you realise what

they would do to us if we did that? I don't know what's wrong with you these days!'

Zara didn't struggle as she felt cold, bony fingers coiling around her left forearm, nor did she wince when the shoelace was tied around her upper arm and tightened.

'Tell me, Number Five, should I do as your dumbass friend Clyde wants and leave you to suffer?'

Zara forced her eyelids open once again until she was looking into the face of her captor, and gently shook her head.

He lifted the syringe into the air, and although her vision couldn't quite focus on the sharp point of the needle, she knew the promise that it held.

'It isn't right,' Clyde was mumbling out of sight. 'She's just a kid.'

'Oh, I don't know about that... She's old enough to know her own mind, aren't you, Number Five? Why don't you tell Clyde how much you want the pain to stop?'

'Please,' she mouthed, the words catching in her throat.

'In fact, I bet you'd do anything I wanted for this, wouldn't you?'

This was the part she always dreaded, but even as her broken brain tried to fight against the inevitable, she knew deep down she'd eventually cave and do whatever was asked of her. Ashamed that her spirit could be broken so easily, she pushed all thoughts of her mum and dad from her mind and focused on the only thing that would take away the pain.

The scratch as the needle entered her vein brought a gasp of anticipation, and as the warm liquid entered her bloodstream, it was as if someone had opened a window and allowed her to escape the dim and dreary prison.

'See how much she loves it here? Would you really want to deny her such pleasure?'

Clyde didn't respond.

'The way I see it, we've got two choices: we kill her and dump the body, or we sell her on to someone else and make her their problem rather than ours.'

Chapter Twenty-Three

NOW

Brighton, East Sussex

The mood in the café is decidedly frostier than when we arrived, and it has nothing to do with the bitter wind blowing through every time the door opens. Angie's last statement has left my mouth gaping, but she is continuing to eat her tuna sandwich as if she's merely rolled out a fact everyone is already familiar with.

It takes Rachel's common sense to break the ice. 'You mean metaphorically, right?'

Angie pauses mid-bite, as if she's genuinely considering the question. 'What I mean is that the eleven-year-old Zara who returned was barely a shell of the nine-year-old we lost. Whatever they did to her in there... So much had changed. I lost my daughter that day, and I don't feel like she ever really came back. The little redhead with pigtails and a heart of gold, with just a little mischievous twinkle in her eyes, never returned.'

The articles I read didn't go into too much detail about the experiences Zara suffered at the hands of the man who took her, but given what Aurélie described to me about her time in captivity, I can only imagine the sorts of horrors Zara faced. It would certainly explain why she's so keen not to relive her past, and why she's been running from the truth for so long.

Freddie's face suddenly pops into my head, and I'm temporarily transported back to the days before *Monsters Under the Bed* became the bestseller it is; back when I was just a simple freelance writer trying to help a down-on-his-luck guy who'd asked for help. It was many interviews in when he first described some of the abuse doled out by Arthur Turgood and his cronies at the boys' home. Graphic detail that I didn't share in the book; *couldn't* share in the book. Like any abusive relationship, it centres on power and control, but it isn't just about the abuser taking control; the victim needs to surrender their power at the same time. If you think about it as two people perfectly balanced on a set of scales, the victim has to willingly hand over the weight keeping the scale balanced until the abuser has it all.

Freddie's sorry eyes fizz through my mind for the briefest moment and it's like I've been kicked again.

Angie finishes her sandwich and wipes her lips with the paper napkin again. 'Before Zara was taken she wanted to be a nurse when she grew up. I asked her why a nurse and not a doctor, and she said it was because she wanted to help others, not just fix them, which I guess is a fair designation. Whenever she would play dress-up from a toddler onwards she would always dress as a nurse, take guests' temperatures, and treat them with absolute kindness.' She breaks off and smiles at the memory. 'She had such an incredible bedside manner. I remember being holed up in bed one winter with a nasty cold; she came and visited me every day, bringing freshly picked flowers, and ordered her dad to ferry food and drink backwards and forwards to me. I knew she would make a fantastic nurse, and was a little jealous that she was so switched on about her career at such a young age.'

The cool air of the room is making the hairs on my arms stand up, so I roll down the sleeves of my jacket and reach for my mug of tea.

'Fast forward to her return in 1988, and so much had changed. Facially she still just about looked like my little girl, but the sparkle in her eyes was gone, replaced by despair. And the mood swings… it was like she'd become a teenager overnight, stomping about and slamming doors whenever she couldn't get her own way. As far as the world knew, we were back together and lived happily ever after, but let me tell you that was far from the truth.

'She'd lost interest in becoming a nurse, as if all her empathy had been sucked out, leaving just an impossibly large black hole inside her. It sounds silly, I know, but it was like she underwent an entire personality transplant while she was gone. Not that I'm blaming her, but I'd spent all that time yearning for my little girl to be returned, but when she was it felt like I'd been cheated… that they'd brought back the wrong child.

'I know that sounds selfish, and I should be grateful to have been reunited – especially considering the situation with you and your sister – but it's difficult to accept that things were so different.'

There is a sheen to her eyes, and I don't want to upset her

further but I still feel as if we've barely scratched the surface so far.

'She was offered specialist counselling though, right?' I check.

Angie nods. 'It was offered, and we made her attend for the first few weeks, but it didn't really help, I don't think. The counsellor she met with was lovely, but was bound by a code of ethics and unwilling to share what the two of them talked about in their sessions. I did insist on attending one of the early sessions, but Zara refused to speak and we spent virtually the entire sixty minutes in stony silence. After that, the counsellor suggested I not attend as I was prohibiting Zara's recovery. At the time I was offended – after all, this was *my* daughter; she should have been able to speak freely in front of me – but looking back on it now, I think she was probably right. I've read your books, Emma, and I can only begin to imagine what she went through.'

A waitress approaches our table and collects Angie's plate, before returning to the kitchen.

'Tom said you and Zara haven't spoken since an argument,' Rachel says, cutting through the delicate rapport I've been trying to build. 'Can you tell us what the argument was about?'

I'm expecting such a direct question to get Angie's back up, but she smiles as if it was nothing more than a polite enquiry about her health. 'Have you spoken to Zara about the argument?'

I shake my head. 'It was Tom who told us. He didn't seem to know what it was about, but said that you haven't really spoken since.'

She nods, thinking about how to respond. 'It was before

Christmas, right after she'd been told she was being made redundant from that solicitor's firm. She came to Brighton to visit me – not that she was happy to be back here. She came to stay at the house for a few days. I think Tom was away on a friend's stag do, and she hadn't told him about the redundancy notice because she didn't want to ruin his weekend. I was pleased to see her, and I felt like we were finally properly talking about things. What you need to understand is that conversations between the two of us – probably as much my fault as Zara's – have been stilted since she came back. When she was still young, it didn't take much for her to be moved to tears, and I think I reached a point where I was constantly walking on eggshells when she was around. Her dad would tell me not to upset her, and I tried my damnedest not to, but that meant I wasn't able to really get too involved in her life. When she was choosing colleges to attend I dared to mention her previous desire to become a nurse, but whenever I talked about the past she would snap, and it almost felt like she was going out of her way to turn her back on the girl she once was. I swear to this day that her decision to study Law at university was to spite me.'

I think back to my own university choices, and how my mum was so terrified I'd leave home, become dazzled by the bright lights of a big city, and never return. Part of the reason I chose Bournemouth as my university was so that I was close enough that she'd panic less. I doubt Zara's choice to study Law was purely to get back at Angie, but I don't contradict her statement. Parents do things with their children's best interests at heart, but don't necessarily understand why children make the choices they do. It's a mystery as old as time.

Angie sits back in her seat and allows her eyes to wander

around the small café, nodding when she recognises a woman sitting at another table. 'Anyway, when she returned before Christmas, it felt like she was really opening up to me. She told me how frightened she was that she wouldn't find another job straight away, especially as not many employers recruit before Christmas, and she told me she wasn't sure she wanted to continue being a legal secretary. I was surprised by her admission, but listened, and when – and *only when* – she asked my opinion, I offered it. I mentioned how much she'd enjoyed pretending to be a nurse as a child, and she flew off the handle. I've never seen someone go from calm and relaxed to seething and vicious so quickly. She threw her dinner plate at the wall, smashing it, and told me I had to stop living in the past. She said that that Zara was gone and would never return, and the sooner I accepted it the better for all concerned.

'I tried to apologise – I hadn't meant to upset her – but she stormed out and drove straight back to London, even though she'd had two glasses of wine, and was legally over the limit. She didn't phone or message to let me know she'd arrived safely, and after a week of her not returning my calls or text messages, I reached out to Tom, and he suggested I just let the dust settle. He messages me now once a week to update me on how she is, but she hasn't contacted me directly since.'

Her eyes are misting again, and this time I reach into my satchel and hand her a tissue. 'I think your daughter needs help, Angie,' I tell her as she dabs at her eyes. 'Tom is worried that they won't be able to move on until she finds some kind of closure, but she's resisting. I need to find a way through.'

'Are you sure that's what you want, Emma? Why are you doing this? What's driving you?'

Rachel asked the same question before, and whilst I want to

say it's just my desire to help, the truth is something quite different, and she deserves to know. They both do.

'My sister,' I say, unable to meet their gaze. 'One day, if I do manage to find her... I need to be armed with ways of getting through to her. I believe she's still out there somewhere and needs help to come home. My gut is telling me Zara also needs a guide to bring her home, and I want to be her guide if she'll let me.'

Angie stretches an arm across the table and clasps my hand. 'Thank you. I want my daughter home as well. I'm certain she's never forgiven me for allowing her to be taken in the first place. Do you know the number of times I've played the What If game with myself? What if we hadn't come to Brighton that weekend? What if we had stayed in the hotel that night rather than going to the pier? What if we'd stayed sitting on the bench across from the pier? What if...' she breaks off as her voice cracks under the strain. 'What if I had held my daughter's hand, rather than worrying about keeping my hands warm in my pockets?'

Rachel and I don't speak as her tears fall. Nothing more needs to be said. The What If game is one we've all played when trying to handle remorse. It's a game nobody ever wins.

Chapter Twenty-Four

NOW

Brighton, East Sussex

I feel exhausted when we emerge from the café, and all I want is a shower and a lie-down, but we've yet to book a hotel and it's already after four. If the town is fully booked, we'll have to think about driving back to London. Rachel hasn't mentioned it, but I can see she's as shattered as I am, and stifles another yawn.

'We should think about dinner at some point,' she suggests. 'I'm thinking fish and chips out of the paper. That's what people do when they go to the seaside, right?'

I try to stop myself smiling at such a generalisation, though it is true that the fish and chip shops in Weymouth do a roaring trade in the summer.

'Sounds perfect,' I say instead. 'We should probably look for some digs too. I don't really fancy the drive back to London today. I also feel like there's more that Angie wanted to say, but for some reason she was holding back.'

199

Rachel nods in agreement. 'Oh good, I thought it was just me questioning what she told us.'

I frown. 'You think she was lying?'

'Not lying as much as maybe not feeling she could totally trust us. Wait, let me correct that. I'm not sure she trusted me; she seems to be a fan of yours though. It might be worth you trying to meet with her again, maybe under the guise of supporting the helpline in some way, and then see if she opens up more when you're alone.'

We move away from the café. The street is as empty as when we first arrived here a couple of hours ago, the only difference now that the newsagent's has shutters pulled down over the door and window.

Despite the emptiness of the street, my inner voice is telling me that we're not safe here, and we head back towards the main road, back towards the city centre and coastline. Checking my phone, I see I've missed two calls from Rick, and my pulse quickens when I hear his recorded voice asking me to call him back.

'Bad news?' Rachel asks, picking up on the paling of my face.

'We're about to find out,' I reply, pressing the phone to my ear. I'm grateful when Rick answers quickly.

'Hey,' he says, 'how are you?'

I'm not expecting him to sound so relaxed. 'W-what's going on? You said to call urgently.'

'Did I? Oh yeah, sorry, I forgot… Um, I called by your place and couldn't see any signs of damage at all. I tried the door and it was secure. All the double-glazing at the front was also fine. I couldn't get into the back to check properly, but if I couldn't get at it, I'm not sure any kind of burglar could either.'

I exhale for the first time since hearing his message. 'You're sure?'

'One hundred per cent. What's going on, Emma? You sound terrified.'

'Long story,' I reply, flashing Rachel a thumbs up.

'Is your friend okay after the break-in at her place?'

I look at Rachel who is walking beside me, staring at her own phone's screen. 'Yes, I think she's coping. Bit of a shock for us to come back to, that's all.'

'I understand totally. I've seen what an emotional toll a break-in can have on victims. Are the police up there taking care of things?'

I recall the officer's words: *it was probably just bored kids.*

'They're not confident of catching those responsible,' I tell Rick.

'You mentioned earlier that you thought it wasn't a random attack. Are you worried someone's coming after you?'

I picture Jack in the hospital bed with the machine helping him breathe, and I don't want to put Rick in an equally precarious situation.

'You don't witness what I have without developing a certain level of paranoia, I suppose. Probably just my overactive imagination and the shock of the break-in. It's been a funny couple of months, you know?'

'I know… Don't beat yourself up about it. Are you going to be away from Weymouth for a considerable time?'

I sigh. 'Honestly, I don't know yet. I don't really want to leave Rachel to handle this by herself.'

She silently shakes her head and mouths the word *no* at me in protest.

'So it'll probably be a few days until I'm back.'

'Of course – your friend needs you. How about I keep an eye on your place while you're away? I don't mind stopping by at the start and end of my shift, just to double check.'

'I can't ask you to do that for me, Rick.'

'Nonsense, it's all part of the service of your local Community Support Officer, and if it will help put your mind at ease, then I'm only too happy to help.'

I stop, snapping my head round to check the street behind us, but there aren't any strangers following us, or lurking in bushes. In fact, the only person I can see is a woman pushing a pram in the opposite direction.

'Thank you, Rick,' I say, hurrying to catch up with Rachel. 'It means a lot.'

'My pleasure. Let me know when you're back in town, and then maybe we can catch up over dinner or something?'

Jack's face flashes back into my head momentarily, but I shake it away and close my eyes. 'That'd be nice. I'd better go; Rachel and I need to find somewhere to crash for the night.'

'Okay. Take care. Oh, and Emma, if there's anything else you need, just shout. Okay?'

I thank him again and hang up.

'Everything okay back home?' Rachel asks.

'Apparently so. Maybe it was just kids after all.'

'Good, well while you were sorting that, I managed to find us a room for the night. It's eighty pounds for a double, but figured we could share a room if you're happy to go halves?'

I check behind us once more, grateful that I won't have to spend the night on my own.

Chapter Twenty-Five

THEN

Ruislip, London

She heard them before she saw them: footsteps shuffling across the dusty, concrete floor, and before she could react, they had a bag pulled down over her face, and her wrists tied with something hard that dug into her skin.

'No, no, no,' she screamed, her imagination instinctively fearing the worst.

They didn't speak, but she recognised the familiar cigarette smoke on their breath as she was lifted into the air and flung over someone's shoulder, knocking the wind from her. She opened her mouth to scream, to alert the others as to what was happening, but the sound wouldn't come.

The car boot lid squeaked like a mouse as it was opened, and a moment later she felt weightless as she was dragged from the shoulder and dropped inside.

'Make a fucking noise and we'll bury you where you'll

never be found,' one of them growled, prodding her face with something hard and metallic.

And then the lid was slammed shut, and she was trapped as the vehicle moved and bounced, and she was rolling about inside and feeling as though she was a stray sock inside a tumble dryer.

She pulled the rough hessian bag from her face but there was no light inside the box, and she clamped her eyes shut as she felt the world spin and almost retched.

And suddenly the boot lid was being lifted, and a bright light burned her eyes as the beam was shone at them. Her tiny hands offered little resistance, but she couldn't look as the men around her argued and discussed, finally agreeing a price, and the bag was quickly back over her face as one took her arms and the other her legs, and lifted her from the boot.

She was about to scream in an effort to attract attention, but a fist to the gut knocked the wind from her lungs and the fight left her.

For a moment she wondered whether they were planning to bury her this way, or throw her into a nearby river tied to rocks, but they didn't. Instead, they carried her into a cold building, one at either end like she was nothing more than a roll of carpet.

'Up the stairs, turn right, and then last door on the right. The front room. Where it's boarded up.'

She instantly pictured the grey and white stubble, acne-covered forehead, and shaved head of Callum Gerrard and her skin froze.

Almost instantly she was on the bed, trapped inside the room, hearing him shouting through the door that he was going out, and then she was down at the front door, holding the flickering candle. As if no longer in control of her body, she moved the orange flame to the bottom edge of the curtains and watched as it licked the seams, before engulfing the whole bottom section, quickly spreading up the curtain like a swan spreading its wings in defiance.

Suddenly filled with fear at how Gerrard would react when he saw the damage, she patted the material with one of her pillows, but then that caught alight too, and she had to throw it away, only managing to land it on the rug beneath the window, and that was soon flickering and urging her towards its promise of redemption.

And then she was back in the room, covering her face with her duvet as smoke filled the room from beneath the door, and she willed death to come for her.

'Zara? Zara?'

It couldn't be. That was Tom's voice. But he couldn't be here now. She wouldn't meet him until years later.

'Zara? Zara? Wake up.'

Zara shot upright in bed, her nightdress clinging to her body like a second skin. Tom's sweet face was beside her in the bed, the look of concern gripping his features, born out of love. Her eyes darted to the bedroom door, but the hole she'd just bashed into it was gone. The only glow in the room was the warm light from the spotlight on Tom's bedside table.

'You were screaming out my name,' Tom said now, picking up her hand and holding it tenderly. 'You were having another nightmare, weren't you?'

Her eyes filled with tears and she nodded grimly, her lips

trembling as she dared her voice to speak.

Tom remained still for a moment, the light catching the scar on his face and casting a weird shadow with his nose, but although his face was strained and tired, he'd never looked so handsome. He pulled his arm around her shoulders and held her close, and she pressed her fingers into the skin by his shoulder, willing him to never let her go.

He rested his cheek on the top of her head. 'It's okay,' he cooed. 'I'm here, and I'll take care of you. I love you, Zara Edwards.'

She couldn't echo his words verbally, as her lips continued to tremble, but her heart screamed them loud enough that she was sure he must have been able to hear them.

'You don't have to tell me about your past,' he conceded, holding her tight against his bare chest. 'I don't need to know where you came from, because I love you for the woman you are now. I know I will never understand what you went through, but I'm prepared to accept that if you'll allow me to build a future for us. Together.'

He loosened his arm, and then his warm hands were on her shoulders, turning her to look at him, his face strained. 'Will you just give me a minute?'

She nodded slightly, desperate to prevent the tears from escaping, and watched as he climbed out of the bed, opened the bedroom door, and disappeared into the hallway. For the briefest moment, she thought maybe she was still dreaming, and that somehow it would be Callum Gerrard who returned in Tom's place, so relief filled her heart when Tom padded back into the room a minute or so later, his hands held behind his back, as if he was carrying something he didn't want her to see.

Coming around to her side of the bed, he knelt down unsteadily, and squirrelled away whatever he'd been holding, allowing him to reach for her hands once again. 'I love you, Zara Edwards, and I have been in love with you since the first time we met. I know I can be an insufferable bore when I talk about fishing or the test match, and I know you hate it when I drink too much wine and spend the night snoring like a bear with a sore head.'

This made her smile slightly, and although her instinct was to press her hand against his cheek, he held them firm.

'I realise these are just a handful of my many flaws, and if I were to ask you outright you could probably list at least a dozen more—'

'Probably closer to two dozen more,' she giggled.

What remained of his concern disappeared in an instant, and his broad grin broke out, somehow brightening the room around him. 'Okay, yeah, two dozen probably is a closer figure, but despite those chinks in my armour, I want you to know that I am your knight on a white steed, and I will do everything within my power to protect you from now until the day I die.'

She felt the first tears free themselves, but unlike what she'd been restraining, these were tears of pure love.

'And I know we discussed it a long time ago, and both of us agreed that we didn't need some silly piece of paper to define what we have...' He released one of her hands and reached down beside the bed.

Zara's hand shot up to her mouth, and her heart skipped a beat as it suddenly dawned on her why he was being so kind, and was down on his knees. Her instinct was to stop him before he asked, but some invisible force held her firm.

'But after all this time together, I *want* the world to know that I'm your man and that they will have to walk over my dead body before they can get to you again. I love you, Zara, and I've been carrying this ring around in my jacket pocket for weeks, waiting for the right time to ask you, but I realise now that *this* is the perfect moment, because it's just you and me, and that's all I want.' He breathed in deeply. 'Will you marry me?'

His hand came up, holding out the open jewellery box, the sparkling diamond ring enclosed in the dim light from the bedside table.

They'd agreed so many years before that they were comfortable being civil partners rather than husband and wife, and she'd never pictured herself ever accepting a proposal from any man, least of all Tom. But as she stared into his eyes and saw the love, she found herself nodding.

'Y-yes,' she stuttered, 'I will marry you, Tom Faust.'

His eyes lit up and he whipped out the ring, sliding it delicately onto her finger. 'You're serious? You will? Oh my God, I was certain you'd say no.'

He pulled her into him and kissed her on the lips. And she kissed him back hard, all images of the previous nightmare evaporating into tiny dust-like fragments. Yanking the wet nightdress over her head, she pulled him onto the bed, desperate to feel the love inside her and responding to his warm touch as he pressed his body against hers.

And as they made love, she knew that the time was right to stop running from the past. The secret she'd buried thirty-four years ago would have to be revealed, but with Tom at her side, she no longer feared what it would mean for her future. For *their* future.

Chapter Twenty-Six

NOW

Brighton, East Sussex

Noises in the corridor have me on high alert. At first there was a hen party singing shortly after 2am, with one of the party loudly whispering to the others to be quiet. Then, about an hour later, a screaming baby in the room next to us was swiftly followed by a bitter argument between stressed mother and father, as they (loudly) debated which of them should be doing the early feed. Rachel somehow managed to sleep through both disturbances. But I'm not letting her sleep now.

'What is it?' she begins to ask, before I quickly cover her mouth and press a finger against my own.

She is half-asleep and confused as hell, but then she hears it and her eyes widen. I nod to confirm that we can both now hear someone trying to get into our room.

My heart is racing, and I'm not sure I've ever felt this

scared, but I need to keep it together. And I definitely need to ignore the voice of paranoia raging through my overactive imagination. Rachel, who's usually the more gung-ho of the two of us, has now pulled her knees to her chest, and is physically trembling beside me.

'You go,' she whispers.

My mouth drops in shock, but before I can say anything the fumbling at the door handle stops.

I think about Jack lying helpless in the hospital. I think about the break-in and fire at Rachel's home. I think about Saskia being knocked down and left for dead, and about the foundation's stolen books.

Enough is enough.

Peeling the duvet back off my legs, I slide them out in silence and yank my hand free of Rachel who is slowly shaking her head, and mouthing the word *no*. Searching around the room, I can't see anything obvious to defend myself with. I eventually settle for the toilet brush I see standing just inside the bathroom door. It won't inflict any serious damage but maybe he'll be repelled by the germs.

Tiptoeing towards the door, the toilet brush gripped over my shoulder in as menacing a manner as I can strike, I take a deep breath before flicking on the light and pulling on the door handle. My eyes are clamped shut as the bright lights of the corridor bathe me in their glow. There is no sound, so I crack one eye open, and stare out into the empty corridor. Opening my other eye, I lean forward, searching for the telltale sound of some creep beating a hasty retreat, but there is nobody in sight.

Disappointed, I allow the heavy door to close and return my weapon to its sheath.

'Well?' Rachel asks, her voice barely more than a whisper.

I shake my head. 'Nobody there.'

She frowns. 'Did we imagine it?'

I shake my head again. 'No, we both definitely heard someone at the door. They must have chickened out or changed their mind, I guess.'

'It was probably just someone at the wrong room,' she rationalises, ever my voice of reason. 'You know, like they thought they were at room 215, instead of 212 or something.'

She looks less convinced than I do, but that doesn't stop her clinging to the theory. 'All these rooms and corridors do look the same, don't they? Like in *The Shining*. It's easy to become disoriented.'

Could she have picked worse iconography to back up her argument? Now I can't stop picturing the river of blood exploding from the lift doors, and the two little girls chasing the boy in his go-kart.

'We can phone down to reception and report it,' Rachel tries again, clearly keen to put the whole situation behind her.

'No,' I say, climbing back into bed and pulling the duvet over my legs once more. 'We should get some sleep,' I say firmly, and it does the trick, as I feel her head press down on the pillow beside me.

I don't go back to sleep, however, instead keeping my eyes and ears glued to the door.

Breakfast passes without incident, but there isn't enough coffee in the world to make me feel less tired. Rachel doesn't mention what happened this morning, but I can see she's still thinking about it as she picks at the wholemeal toast she ordered, tearing at the crust. Lying awake all night, I've now had time to rationalise it, and am feeling less spooked than I was.

Ultimately, all the doors in the hotel are controlled by electronic key passes. There are probably a couple that would act as skeleton keys with access to all the rooms, but these would be used by the cleaners or held at reception. And there's no way the person at the door could have had one, as he or she didn't manage to make it into our room. Rachel's explanation about another guest mistaking our room for theirs makes sense, but given the time of night, and everything that's been going on, I can't fully commit to believing it. What I need is something to take my mind off all the paranoia, and Rachel doesn't fail to deliver.

'I've made us an appointment to speak to Henry Weisz,' she tells me matter-of-factly.

'Okay,' I respond sceptically, drawing out the vowel. 'Who is Henry Weisz?'

Her face brightens. 'He was the unofficial biographer of the Brighton Rock Girl.'

I scrunch my nose in confusion.

'He published a book about the disappearance and recovery a year or so after the events. He claimed to have the inside track, but I don't believe his book was ever formally endorsed by the Edwards family or local law enforcement.' She unlocks her phone and shows me an open Amazon page of the book in question. 'He was a reporter at *The Argus*, Brighton's local newspaper, and he was the chief reporter on all things to do with Zara's case. I found him online while you were in the shower last night, and I messaged him and asked if we could pick his brain about events at the time, and he agreed. He still lives in the city and has invited us to his house at ten, so we'd better get a move on.'

I pass the phone back to her. 'How come I've never come across him before? His name and the book certainly don't ring any bells.'

Rachel is nodding her understanding. 'Well, from what I've managed to find, there was some controversy about his book. I think initially he saw an opportunity to make some money out of the story, but as soon as Zara returned, the Edwards family wanted nothing to do with him. I imagine they just wanted life to return to as normal a state as possible, and the book would have just prolonged the trauma. He seemed to take it to heart, and focused his side of the story on Callum Gerrard.'

'The man who was arrested for the abduction,' I clarify, recognising the name.

'Exactly. But interestingly, his book suggested that the police didn't catch the right man.'

My brow furrows. 'But they found her in *his* house, and she picked him out of a line-up.'

Rachel swallows down another piece of toast. 'Oh yes, there was no question that he was the one who kept her locked up, but he privately maintained that he wasn't the man who abducted Zara to begin with. At least, that's what Henry Weisz claims in his book.'

This is news to me, and I don't recall ever reading anything challenging Callum Gerrard as the perpetrator. I briefly studied his background when I was looking for answers about who might have abducted Anna. Given the similar nature of their disappearances – one second they're there, and the next gone – I did explore the possibility that he might have snatched Anna too. That theory was quickly disproved when I realised he'd already died in prison when she was taken.

'But he was found guilty and sentenced,' I say.

'The CPS never brought a charge of abduction against him as there was insufficient evidence. Given they had a strong case for false imprisonment and sexual assault on a minor, I presume the other part was ignored. He was fifty-seven when he was arrested, nearly fifty-nine when the trial finally ended, so he was unlikely to ever make it out of prison alive with what they had him on. I think it's worth having a chat with Weisz before we head back to London. Can't do any harm, can it?'

Given that most, if not all, of the officers who would have worked on the original investigation are probably retired, Weisz could give us a good insight into matters. We settle the hotel bill and check out, lugging our small holdalls back to the car.

It takes fifteen minutes to drive to the address Weisz sent to Rachel, and the bungalow isn't quite what I was expecting. In a small cul-de-sac, with prominent neighbourhood watch signs and a motorhome parked in the driveway, it's only when Weisz opens the front door that I even remember he must now also be retired. He is dressed in a camel-coloured cardigan, and although his hairline is massively receded, the long silver ponytail draped over his shoulder suggests there is life in the old dog yet.

He smiles warmly and steps aside to allow us in. The smell of baking bread drifts through from the kitchen at the back of the property and it sets my taste buds off.

'Something smells good,' I say, as he shows us into the spacious front room.

'Thank you, the loaf should be done soon, so if you hear an alarm sound, don't panic. Can I fetch either of you a hot drink? An herbal tea perhaps?'

Even though it's not that long since breakfast, I nod enthusiastically. In my experience, accepting a hot drink helps prolong the amount of time we'll be welcome in the house.

Weisz leaves us and disappears out to the back of the bungalow. There is one two-seater sofa at the back of the room, facing the large and bright bay window. A leather reclining armchair is directly in front of the window, and looks well used. It's currently facing a small television screen, but it's what's behind the set that catches my eye. The main wall is covered by three large shelving units, crammed with books. One whole shelf contains copies of Weisz's own book, but the rest are a vast collection of non-fiction tomes. Books about abductions, serial killers, and famous crimes. I could spend a year in this room reading! There's even a copy of *Ransomed* on the shelf.

He returns minutes later, carrying a tray with three mugs and a small plate of digestive biscuits.

'Ah, you're admiring my collection,' he says, spotting me ogling the books. 'I've always been fascinated by the criminal mind. Not so much the motivation for committing the crime, but what drives career criminals to keep breaking the law. Is it the thrill of the chase? Or an imbalance? Fascinating stuff.'

He balances the tray on a small table behind the main door before passing over the mugs. He sits back into the recliner, and we perch on the sofa.

'You're here to talk about Callum Gerrard then,' he begins. 'One of the laziest miscarriages of justice ever seen.'

'In what way?' I ask, blowing on the rim of my mug.

'Before I answer that question, may I ask one of my own?'

I glance at Rachel, uncertain how much she will have shared with Weisz in their message exchange. 'Of course.'

'After I received the invitation to meet with you, I put my thinking cap on. Presumably your interest in Callum has to be related to the Brighton Rock Girl case, right?'

I'm not sure how best to phrase my response, so I take a moment to consider the options. 'My interest is personal, rather than professional,' I say ambiguously.

He smiles at this. 'Playing your cards close to your chest, I get it. Very smart. It's interesting to finally meet you, Emma. I've watched your career blossoming over the last few years, and I was cheering you on when the case against Arthur Turgood made it to court. Bravo on that. And then your publicised involvement in the discovery of Cassie Hilliard, again, bravo! You're a woman after my own heart; someone who can smell wrongdoing and won't rest until it's corrected. Am I right?'

My instinct is to correct his assumption, but I don't want to alienate him when he seems so willing to talk, so I simply nod and smile instead.

'I wish you'd been around when I was writing my novel; we'd have made a fine pair. I bet with you on board, we could have got poor Callum's story into the mainstream media. I did discuss serialising the novel in one of the London red tops, but they bottled it. Too controversial, I suppose.'

'But Callum Gerrard was banged to rights; I thought he admitted to holding Zara prisoner?'

Weisz's smile drops. 'He admitted to looking after her at his house, but it was as a favour to someone else. I'm convinced that the wrong man was locked up. And what's more, I believe I can prove it.'

Chapter Twenty-Seven

NOW

Brighton, East Sussex

Henry Weisz's left hand is stroking the end of his white ponytail, as if it's a pet hanging from his shoulder. The stroking is subconscious, as far as I can tell, as he continues to rifle through the box between his feet with his right hand.

'I'm sure it was in here,' he mutters under his breath, trying to convince himself rather than Rachel and me.

He releases the ponytail and pushes the box away with his right foot, systematically lifting the next brown cardboard cube down from the table beside him. He opens the flaps and begins to flick though the pages in this one, this time using both hands to expedite the process.

'Perhaps if you told us what you're looking for, Rachel and I could help search for it?' I suggest with bated breath.

His head flies up and his eyes burrow into me initially, but the pained expression quickly disperses. Clearly the thought of anyone else touching a single volume of his research appals him in some way.

'Thanks, but I was sure I'd filed it in one of these,' he says, plastering on a fake smile to paper over his annoyance at the disruption. 'This is the evidence collated by the police *after* Callum was arrested, you see? So these boxes should include all witness testimony from neighbours and other busybodies in the street around the time that Callum was living there. In my opinion it's all worthless as it's nothing more than hearsay and anecdotal opinions.'

He snatches up a sample of stapled pages and skim reads the top sheet. 'Here, for example, Mrs Sheila Rifkin who lived six houses away from Callum. She claimed – and I quote – "I never did much take to him; he had one of those faces where you just knew he was up to something rotten, but it was impossible to know what. As soon as we found out why he'd been arrested, my Alan and me said he was guilty." How can they count that as evidence?' Weisz rolls his eyes. 'This box is full of such nonsense.'

I keep trying to catch Rachel's eye to try and get a sense of whether she's finding this encounter just as awkward, but her head's been buried in her phone for the last ten or so minutes, and she seems oblivious to my advances.

'Aha!' Weisz declares proudly, hoisting a laminated sheet from the box. 'I knew it would be in here somewhere.'

He stands, brushing digestive crumbs from his lap, and leans across the table so I can take the sheet from him. I accept it, and read quickly. When I've finished, I look back to Weisz who has sat back down and is grinning at me, his eyebrows raised in expectation.

'What exactly is this?' I ask, confused.

'That is *proof* that Callum didn't abduct Zara.'

I look back at the laminated page. It is a typed and signed statement bearing the Sussex Police header. 'Who is Gabriel Laing?'

Weisz's eyes twinkle at mention of the name. 'After Callum's very public arrest and denouement, Laing came forward to Sussex Police and made the statement you're holding. In it he states that on the night of the abduction, Callum was in fact with Laing on the other side of the country. Well, on the Cornish moors. This sworn testimony *proves* that Callum could not have abducted Zara.'

In my head I'm already thinking of dozens of questions that would challenge Weisz's conviction, but I bite my tongue. 'Okay, let's say for a moment you're right, and Callum Gerrard wasn't on the pier the night Zara was abducted. What difference does it make? She was held prisoner in *his* house, and was subjected to physical and mental abuse under *his* watch. If you ask me, the right man went to prison.'

A scowl replaces Weisz's grin. 'Not so. I don't deny that Callum was involved in the horrific suffering of that poor girl, but only *after* the fact. In his words, she was only at his property for a matter of days before she started the fire and escaped. Incidentally, no charges of criminal damage were ever sought against the girl, but I suppose that's neither here nor there.'

I look to Rachel again, but whatever she's reading has her complete attention.

'I'm sorry Henry, but I'm not seeing the point you're trying to make,' I try again.

'Callum didn't abduct her,' he repeats. 'Don't you see? I thought you were supposed to be intuitive.'

I bite my tongue for a second time. 'Forgive me, Henry, I didn't sleep well last night. You're saying that Callum Gerrard didn't abduct Zara based on Gabriel Laing's statement.'

'Exactly! Laing made the statement to the police two days after the arrest, but they didn't follow up on it. Don't you see? It's evidence that they bungled the investigation. No charges have been formally sought against anyone for the abduction of the girl.'

I look down at the laminated sheet again. 'What can you tell me about Gabriel Laing? Is he a friend of Gerrard's?'

'Sort of… They're ex-cell mates.'

Suddenly I'm starting to see why the Sussex Police might not have put too much faith in the statement I'm holding. 'What was Laing inside for?'

'Possession of indecent material, but,' he breaks off excitedly, 'that doesn't mean he wasn't telling the truth. When I met with Callum after the trial he told me all about their trip to Cornwall, and when I interviewed Gabriel, he was able to show me receipts confirming he was in Cornwall at the time of the abduction.'

'And did Callum Gerrard have corroborative evidence of the trip?'

Weisz shakes his head in disappointment. 'Alas, he wasn't one for keeping hold of receipts and mementos, but we know that Gabriel was in Cornwall, and he swears Callum was as well. Whether or not you believe Gabriel, the police didn't pursue the possibility that Callum didn't abduct Zara. When I interviewed him behind bars, he told me that the girl was delivered to him about a week before she escaped. His house wasn't set up adequately to look after a guest, and so he wasn't surprised that she managed to escape. He was adamant that the physical abuse she suffered happened before she arrived at his house.'

He's yet to tell me anything that convinces me that Gerrard shouldn't have been locked up, but I know from Freddie's story that mistakes can happen. 'So how did Gerrard come into contact with Zara? If he didn't take her, who did, and how did she end up at his house?'

Weisz shuffles uncomfortably on his chair. 'He wasn't willing to give me a name; all he'd say was that the people responsible would kill him if he talked. I was making progress – he was beginning to trust me – when he died inside. They think their secret died with him, but I know they're out there. You know who I'm talking about, don't you, Emma? I've read *Ransomed* and *Isolated*; we both know there are people out there operating in such circles. That's why I was so excited when Rachel messaged last night. You and me: it's meant to be.'

I don't like the excited snarl plastered across his face.

'Think about it,' he continues, before I can correct him. 'My inside knowledge of the case, and your contacts in the industry; we'd be an unstoppable force.'

Could he be right? Could the same ring who were involved with making the videos found on Turgood's hard drive have been involved in Zara's abduction? The same ring who I'm certain are trying to stop mine and Jack's investigation? There's nothing concrete to link the situations, and I don't want my meddling to put Henry Weisz's life in danger.

'I'm sorry, Henry, but I'm here in a personal capacity, not to open an investigation into what went on nearly thirty-five years ago. Even if Gerrard wasn't the abductor all those years ago, he was the one holding Zara when she was found. Whether he was the main culprit or an accessory after the fact,

I have no doubt he probably got the justice he deserved. Why are you so keen to dig up the past? Gerrard is dead now, and there isn't any interest in the story.'

He looks put out as he puffs out his chest and stares down his nose at me. 'Have you spoken to Mrs Edwards yet?'

I decide to keep our meeting with Angie to myself. 'Why do you ask?'

'I spoke to her after Callum was sentenced and as soon as I suggested there could have been wrongdoing in the investigation, I saw in her face that she felt the same way. In fact, she was only too happy to speak to me before Zara escaped the house fire. She was encouraging me to write articles and even agreed to endorse my book. At that time there were serious questions being asked about why Zara hadn't been found so long after her disappearance. But as soon as she was found, it was as if a switch went off in her head and she washed her hands of me. She knows more than she's let on all this time. Mark my words.'

'We need to go,' Rachel says, standing, eyes still glued to the screen.

'Why? What's going on?' I ask, picking up on the anxiety in her voice.

Rachel is close to tears as she meets my curious gaze. 'My editor wants me in the office this afternoon. Rumour is, redundancies are looming.'

Chapter Twenty-Eight

THEN

Brighton, East Sussex

34 years ago

She was still coughing as the fireman carried her slowly down the ladder. He'd warned her to keep her eyes closed as they made their descent, as the view from over his shoulder would be disorientating. He smelled of sweet cologne, not dissimilar to the stuff her dad had once worn, and it provided just a modicum of comfort.

The scene on the street was like something out of a movie. Two fire engines were blocking off the street she'd watched from the window for the past week, an ambulance was parked just beyond them, and two men in bright green uniforms were stationed ready to gather her up onto a trolley as soon as the fireman released her. They manhandled her onto the firm mattress and pillow, pulling at her clothes, a mask of cool air pressed over her mouth and nose, and a stethoscope pressed against her chest.

She couldn't concentrate for the strange faces coming and going from above her, each taking it in turns to look down at her and provide a reassuring smile. Some asked questions, but it was almost as if they were speaking a foreign language, and she couldn't answer. The more she coughed, the more of the air in the mask she inhaled, and the dizzier she became.

So many times she'd looked out of the window, staring down and praying just one person would walk past, but being at the end of the cul-de-sac, nobody came down this far unless their intention was to call at the property; and the only person who'd done that was *him*, and he'd had no interest in looking up at the terrified girl trapped behind the glass.

A crowd of neighbours had now formed just beyond the fire engines and ambulance, all keen to see what the fuss was about and whether the fire would spread. It was probably the most excitement they'd seen in years. She wondered whether *he* was in the crowd, observing the scene unfold. He was out before the fire had taken hold upstairs, but that didn't mean he'd gone far. And it didn't mean he wouldn't be back for her. She'd be safe surrounded by doctors and police – surely he wouldn't come for her with them around?

She thought about the day she'd arrived at the house, the way *he'd* removed his belt and held it so menacingly above his head, the way he'd leered at her before whipping the buckle down across her lower back. She'd yelped and crashed to the hard mat, and he'd simply laughed. Well, he wouldn't be laughing now.

The paramedics bumped and bustled the trolley into the back of the waiting ambulance, and as one of them slammed the doors shut, she welcomed the silence that temporarily ensued.

'Try and take normal breaths,' said the paramedic who'd remained in the back of the ambulance with her. 'I expect you've inhaled a fair amount of smoke that you'll be coughing up for a few days, but we need to take you to the hospital to examine you. Can you tell me your name?'

She tried to answer the question, but as she opened her mouth, another fit of coughing followed.

'It's okay, try not to speak for now,' he said, pressing a stethoscope against her chest again. 'Can you tell me if it hurts anywhere?'

Apart from the ache in her chest from the cough, she couldn't feel any new pain beyond the healing scars on her back, and shook her head.

'That's good,' the paramedic cajoled. 'You're lucky we got to you when we did.'

She didn't feel lucky, but was relieved to hear the engine roar to life and the roll of the vehicle as it started to move.

She must have passed out, as the next thing she knew was that she was in a bed somewhere new. She knew enough to realise it was a private room in a hospital. She was familiar with the unoriginal format of the square ceiling tiles and blocks of fluorescent bulbs overhead. She'd spent enough time in similar rooms to know she was under observation.

Straining to lift her head, she spotted a woman in a green uniform buzzing about at the side of the bed, reading dials on the machines just out of sight.

'Ah, good, you're awake,' the nurse said with a warm and welcoming smile. 'Do you know where you are?'

Zara tried to nod, but something was restricting her neck.

'Oh, try not to move, sweetheart,' the nurse counselled. 'We've put your neck in a brace for now, just as a precaution. When you came in we found some nasty bruising to your back and neck, and the doctor wants a few X-rays taken to be sure there's no lasting damage. Do you know what an X-ray is?'

She did her best to nod, but it was all but impossible with the cushioned material pressing into her chin.

'How are you feeling now?' the nurse asked.

Zara couldn't respond as her eyes quickly filled with tears. Was it really over? The months of torment and abuse gone, or was this just some dream she'd wake from?

The nurse pressed a cold hand to Zara's forehead. 'There, there, it's okay, you're safe here now. We're going to take great care of you, I promise.'

The tears rolled down her cheeks and she quickly reached up and wiped them away with her fingers as she'd been trained to do.

'I bet what you'd like to see is a friendly face,' the nurse continued. 'Now that you're awake, do you think you'd be up for a visitor?'

'Yes,' Zara croaked.

The pretty nurse's smile grew wider, and she dabbed at the tears with a fresh tissue. 'You just stay right there, and I'll be back.'

The nurse disappeared from sight, and a door was opened nearby. A moment later the nurse returned with a woman whose face was a veil of tears.

'Look who it is,' the nurse exclaimed. 'Your mum has been so desperate with worry. I'll give you two a moment to get reacquainted.'

The crying woman buried her head in the pillow beside the

girl's head. 'I can't believe you're back,' she said. 'It feels like a dream. I never thought I'd see you again, my darling.'

'Wh-who are you?' the girl in the bed asked.

The woman lifted her face and wiped at her own tears. 'It's Mummy, Zara. Oh, would you look at you! You already look so much older than I remember. And they've cut your hair, but don't worry about that, it will soon grow back.'

The girl felt for her short hair and tangled the curls around her fingers; it had always been short, hadn't it?

'Oh my darling, please don't cry; I promise everything will be okay from now on. I won't let you out of my sight ever again. Do you hear me? I am so, so sorry we let him take you. The police will find whoever is responsible and lock him away for life. Nobody will hurt you again, I promise.'

The words were ones she'd longed to hear for so long, but there was still an element of doubt in the young girl's mind, and it still felt out of sync with the life she'd become accustomed to in such a short time.

'As soon as your X-rays are done, they'll bring you some supper. What would you like to eat? They don't have your favourite on the menu, but they've got sausages and mash, if you fancy? I know it isn't toad in the hole, but we could just pretend for tonight. And then, as soon as I have you back home, I will bake you the *largest* toad in the hole ever seen. How does that sound?' The woman broke off as fresh tears filled her eyes. 'It's so good to have you back, Zara. Wait till your dad gets here too. He's been so distraught with worry too.'

Zara opened her mouth to speak, but thought better of it. The room seemed to be swirling in bright colours and she must have passed out, because when she awoke she was alone in the room again, and the protective foam around her neck had been removed.

It was dark outside the window now, and the overhead light had been switched off. A small, low light somewhere behind her remained on, casting a dim glow over the foot of the bed. She sat up in bed, surprised to find the face mask now gone. The effort to straighten caused a small cough, but nowhere near as bad as she had been suffering earlier. There was a small plastic device attached to one of her fingers, which she pulled off and allowed to crash to the floor. A machine bleeped in dissatisfaction.

It was a strain to look behind her and the machinery she saw made little sense, but she spotted the source of the light and adjusted it. Something moved in her periphery at the back of the room, and she quickly pulled her legs up, tucking them beneath her chin as some kind of defence. She gasped at the shadowy figure there, and for the briefest of moments she thought *he'd* found her, and that the nightmare would return.

But the figure didn't appear to be moving, and as she fiddled with the light again she realised it wasn't a figure at all, just a coat stand, with a large overcoat and brimmed hat hanging from it. She released the breath she'd been holding, and laughed at the ridiculousness of her mind's trick.

The door to the room opened a moment later and a young woman in a white uniform appeared and made her way across to the bed. 'Is everything okay, Zara?' she asked, her accent from somewhere further north in the country.

'I-I'm thirsty,' she croaked.

'Of course you are,' the nurse replied, handing her a beaker of lukewarm water, waiting for the girl to have a drink, before returning the beaker to a small table. 'And are you feeling hungry? You've missed supper, I'm afraid, but I could probably do you a slice of dry toast to tide you over until morning.'

'W-where's—'

'Your mum? She's been sent home for the night, but she promised she'd be back first thing in the morning with your dad. The doctor should be around by eleven and if all is well, you might be released just after lunch. I bet you can't wait to be home again, you poor child. I didn't realise who you were at first, and I can't believe they've found you after all this time. You're famous now, you know? I should probably ask for your autograph or something.' She chuckled at this, as she reattached the small plastic device to the girl's finger.

'I'm n-not who you think,' the girl tried to say, as the nurse plumped the pillows.

'What's that, dear?'

'I-I'm not… I don't know who that woman is, but she's not my mum… There must be some mistake.'

The nurse frowned and tilted her head. 'I know all of this must be so confusing, you poor, poor thing. I think what you're probably suffering from is called post-traumatic stress disorder. Do you know what that is?'

She shook her head.

'It means that because you've suffered a great ordeal, your mind is a bit all over the place, and things are going to feel a bit weird for you for a few days, maybe even a few weeks. It's perfectly natural to feel confused and out of place. Don't worry about it for now. We've arranged for you to speak to a specialist counsellor who will be able to help clear up any confusion. She's lovely and will be around after breakfast.

She'll help you get things straight in your head. Now, how about that toast?'

Zara gave a gentle nod, and watched as the nurse left the room and headed down the corridor. Lying back on the pillow, she fought against the tears slowly blurring her view of the ceiling tiles. Maybe the nurse was right, and it was the stress of the last two years causing the confusion. But one thing she was certain of beyond all else was: whoever the mum and dad coming to see her in the morning were, they weren't *her* parents.

Chapter Twenty-Nine

NOW

Hillingdon Hospital, London

The drive back to London saw Rachel ride the rollercoaster of emotions. Disbelief that the newspaper was planning *more* job cuts; anger that she might be one of the casualties; bitter that there would probably be less-deserving (and higher paid) journalists who would keep their jobs because they were part of the old boys' club; and finally acceptance that there was nothing she could do to change the future.

I offered reassuring words, but they sounded as worthless as they were. With a delicate economy flirting with recession, there are no employment guarantees anymore. Rachel is a brilliant writer, and I have no doubt that one door closing will inevitably lead to another opening, but where and when that will be is beyond us both. It couldn't have come at a worse time for her, what with the wedding to pay for in a few months, and just when she and Daniella were talking about

233

moving to a new forever home together. I don't doubt that Daniella could probably afford to support the pair of them for the immediate future, but Rachel is too proud to accept such generosity, even from the woman she loves.

I don't fancy returning to her flat on my own and pacing the floor in nervous anticipation for her to update me, and so I ask if she'll drop me at the hospital to see Jack. Ironically, seeing a friend banged up in hospital might be the lesser of two evils.

'Let me know what they say,' I tell her, as I climb out at the side of the road where she's pulled over. 'And good luck!'

Rachel's face is ashen as she attempts to pull her face into a resolute smile before pulling back into traffic.

What a terrible year it's been so far! If I'd known Aurélie Lebrun's legal team would give me so much hassle about my book, *Trafficked*, I never would have written it. Not that my publishers gave me a lot of choice after Aurélie's father – a politician once again running for office in Paris – requested I tell his daughter's story in my words. I'm pretty sure my editor would have encouraged me to politely decline had they realised the energy that would be wasted trying to edit the manuscript into a version accepted by all parties.

Next was the discovery of Faye McKenna's bones in a suitcase on the site of the former Pendark Film Studios. That seemed to have been the catalyst that sent Jack and me into the black hole we now find ourselves in. And whoever tipped us off about the identity of Faye McKenna is the same person who has indicated that former Met Police Commissioner Sir Anthony Tomlinson is embroiled in the conspiracy to cover up the activities of the ring who may or may not have abducted my sister Anna. I've never felt so far away from finding out the truth.

And to top it off, the person who got me asking uncomfortable questions to begin with isn't speaking to me. I miss Freddie's flamboyance and ability to make me laugh even when he's not in the best of places. No amount of apologising is going to show him how sorry I am that I kept pushing him until he admitted more about his involvement with the ring. But that doesn't mean I don't desperately want to make it up to him – if only I could find him.

The silly thing is I don't hold any animosity towards him for any actions during that time in his life. He was a vulnerable young man who had been physically and mentally abused, and it has scarred him for life. When I met him and tried to put him back together again, I had no idea I was using such badly damaged cogs. My only hope is that if I can finally expose the conspirators and help the police seek appropriate justice, Freddie might find it in his heart to forgive me.

I'm close to tears as I make it up to Jack's ward, and having identified myself to the uniformed officer sitting outside Jack's room, I head in. It's dim as the blinds are still closed, and as I approach the bed, I start when I see the purple and yellow bruising covering Jack's face. My chest tightens. He looks so helpless, wrapped tightly beneath the hospital sheet – so lifeless. And it appears his condition hasn't improved much since the last time I was here.

'There's been no change,' a deep voice echoes from behind me, and I start again.

Turning, I see DCS Jagtar Rawani is sitting in the far corner of the room, behind where the door would have opened, which is why I didn't notice him when entering. He stands now and moves out of the shadows, his usually pristine beard carrying extra growth, his tie pulled into a small knot and swollen skin beneath his eyes. I recognise the signs: this is a man who has barely slept in days. I wonder now just how many hours he's spent in that corner waiting for signs of life.

'They scanned him again today,' Rawani continues, clearing his throat, 'and there is still swelling to the brain, which is why they're keeping him under for now.'

'You look like you could do with some rest,' I say. 'I don't mind staying for a bit while you get off home.'

His eyes remain fixed on Jack's prone body, and he doesn't acknowledge the suggestion. 'My team found Jack's car on traffic cameras and traced it to a pub in Richmond called The Lucky Horseshoe. Security footage acquired at the pub shows Jack entering, apparently looking for someone before confronting a barrel-chested IC-1 male. They appear to argue, before the landlord asks both to leave. Once outside, the argument continues, based on the pub's outside camera, and there is some pushing and shoving, and then Jack appears to throw a punch. He misses because the recipient ducks out of the way, and throws a retaliatory punch that catches Jack square in the jaw. Probably accounts for some of the bruising on Jack's face, with the rest a result of the car crash.'

He's speaking so matter-of-factly – he's so detached – when my mind is racing with question after question.

'Jack stumbles,' Rawani continues before I can interject, 'and then lunges at the other man, but he is easily blocked, and ends up flat on the floor. The second man points and shouts something before heading back inside the pub where he remains until closing, according to the security feed and the landlord. Jack skulks off with a limp arm and climbs into his car, before driving off.'

Despite the myriad questions, one leaps out. 'What happens then?'

'He returns home by an alternative route, and the team is still looking for the exact route so they can find any kind of evidence to enlighten us. Right now, we simply don't know how he ended up crashing into the telegraph pole.'

'The man he confronted, I presume you've identified him?'

Rawani stares blankly at me. 'Dean O'Farrell. Amateur boxer by all accounts. He was picked up and interviewed yesterday. Claims he doesn't know Jack, but that their children go to school together. According to O'Farrell, Jack was angry about an incident between O'Farrell's daughter and his own.'

'What sort of incident?'

Rawani's gaze doesn't shift. 'Name calling and hair pulling, according to O'Farrell. Something of nothing, from what he says. For whatever reason, Jack took exception to it and confronted O'Farrell while off duty.'

It doesn't sit right with me, and I shake my head. 'Does that sound like Jack to you? Has he ever struck you as violent?'

Rawani cocks an eyebrow. 'The one thing I know about PC Serrovitz is how protective he is of Mila. I never would have had him down as a violent man, but I've seen the security camera footage from the pub, and it does support O'Farrell's version of events. Either way, it explains why Jack was over that way when the accident with the RTC occurred.'

He's right about Jack's sensitivity when it comes to Mila, but I still can't imagine him going all that way to pick a fight with another parent, especially an amateur boxer. Is that really where he was headed when he phoned me on Saturday night?

Something doesn't add up, and yet Rawani seems so willing to accept the explanation.

'O'Farrell has lodged an official complaint against PC Serrovitz, so now I have a Professional Standards investigation hanging over us. It's not the best timing.'

I don't like Rawani's tone, and can't bite my tongue. 'Have you even spoken to Mila's mum, Chrissie, to check whether there really was an incident between the girls? For all we know, O'Farrell is making up the story to protect his own back.'

It's a lame argument and I regret it the moment it leaves my lips.

Rawani narrows his eyes. 'We haven't spoken to her directly, but the school administrator has confirmed the children had a spat and had to be separated in the playground last week.' He moves away from the bed, before turning back, his cheeks darkening with ire. 'I know you may think that some of us don't know how to do our jobs properly, but I can assure you that I'm not treating any of this with any less due care and attention. Jack is part of my team, and even if it does feel out of character for him to behave in this way, it isn't beyond the realms of possibility. Until he wakes and sets the record straight, I will treat this matter as I would any other, and I'll appreciate you not to second guess my judgement.'

I'm blushing by the end of the tirade, and I can see from the regret in his face that I'm not really the target of his frustrations.

'I'm sorry,' I offer. 'Jack trusts you, and that's good enough for me. For the record, I have nothing but the utmost respect for what you and your colleagues do.'

An uncomfortable divide has sprouted up, and I'm relieved

when Rawani says he has to return to the station, leaving me alone in the room with Jack. Dragging the chair from the shadowy corner, I sit beside Jack, and take his non-bandaged hand in mine. It is cool to the touch, probably a result of him lying down for so long.

It pains me to see him like this. The Jack I know is so full of life and always cracking lame jokes. The person before me now is nothing but an empty shell of the man I care for. I don't want to picture my life without his clumsy and obtuse observations.

My tear splashes against the pristine sheet, and I use the back of Jack's hand to catch the remainder.

'Please wake up, Jack,' I whisper quietly. 'I need you.'

Edgware, London

As I'm leaving the hospital, my head bent low and unable to stop thinking about how Jack's appearance in Richmond could be connected to our investigation, the last thing I'm expecting is a phone call from Maddie, asking me to hightail it over to her place. I try to explain that I'm really not in the mood for being sociable, but when she tells me it's specifically to do with Zara Edwards, I yield and order an Uber.

Forty minutes later, and with fatigue starting to set in, I arrive at Maddie's address once more, though it feels isolating not having Rachel or Jack alongside me. Rachel has yet to phone and update me on her work situation. I don't want to chase her up, but I'm worried about her, so I send a message to advise her where I am, and tell her to call me whenever she's ready. I just hope for her sake it isn't the news she's dreading. It feels like the last thing we need is more bad news.

There is an unfamiliar Jaguar parked across Maddie's driveway as I approach the three-storey townhouse, and as I look up at the living room window on the first floor, I'm sure the man leaning up against the glass is Zara's partner, Tom, but his back is to me so I can't be certain.

I suppose he might have come to Maddie's to say he's changed his mind about Rachel and me digging into Zara's past. I can't think of any other reason he'd be here, but then my brain doesn't feel at its sharpest right now.

I ring the bell and Maddie opens the dark brown UPVC door a moment later, air kissing my cheeks before leading me inside. I can smell apple and cinnamon hanging in the air, and it warms my heart, reminding me of trips to my grandma's house when she would have baked crumble on a Sunday. But as we head into the kitchen, there is no sign that Maddie's been cooking. The countertops are clear of flour, sugar, and apple cores, and a thin sheen of dust on the glass plate of the oven door suggests it hasn't been in use for days, let alone this morning.

'Tea?' Maddie asks absently, filling the kettle at the tap.

'Thank you.'

'Tom and Zara are just upstairs, but I thought I should give you a heads-up before we join them.' Maddie returns the kettle to its stand and leans closer so she won't have to shout over the sound of the boiling water. 'Tom phoned first thing and said Zara had something she wished to share with you, and could I arrange a meeting. I explained you're very busy but I'd see what I could do.'

'Have they said what they want to speak about?' I ask, pushing thoughts of Jack and Rachel from my mind.

Maddie shakes her head glumly. 'Couldn't get it out of them. Zara said she didn't want to repeat the news, and wanted to wait until you arrived. They've only been here fifteen minutes themselves.'

Curiosity can be the curse of a journalist because I instantly want to race up the stairs and interrogate Zara, but I know I need to be patient. If she's suddenly remembered some important detail about her abduction, she will need space to reveal it. Thankfully, patience is a virtue I've developed, and so I wait beside Maddie while she fixes the drinks, and then follow her up to the living room. The smell of apple and cinnamon is stronger up here, and I now spot an air freshener plugged into a socket at the top of the stairs.

Zara is perched on the edge of the armchair beside the window, holding firmly onto Tom's hand as he stands directly behind her. I smile warmly at them both as I enter the room, taking a seat on the sofa with Maddie at my side. It's an odd sensation, but the room feels cooler than downstairs, as if a cloud is hanging over the room. I sip my tea to overcome the feeling.

Zara is dressed in navy-coloured skinny jeans, and is wearing a cream jacket not dissimilar in shade to my own. In fact, looking at her choice of outfit, we almost resemble two participants at a lookalike competition, with only her flame-like red locks distinguishing us. Strangely, I'd argue she looks more serene than the last time we were here, as if she's made her peace with the Damocles sword above her head. Tom too looks more relaxed than when I last saw him at Maddie's.

Zara moves her left hand up and squeezes Tom's as a sign for him to release her other hand, and he duly obliges. The sunlight catches on the sparkler on her ring finger, which I'm certain wasn't there the other day, but that surely can't be the news she's come to share, can it? When we first met, she never let her guard down once, and surely there must be other friends higher on the list of priority people to share the news with.

I'm pleased for Tom though. When we met at Maddie's house he showed me the ring she's now wearing and spoke of how he'd been waiting for the perfect time to propose. Clearly the moment must have presented itself in the days since.

Zara takes an audible deep breath. 'I suppose I should begin,' she says, her hands immediately coming together between her knees and awkwardly intertwining. She doesn't speak again for a moment, struggling to find the right words, her gaze distracted by the ring.

'If it's easier,' I encourage, 'I find just bowling out with it is the most painless method, like ripping off a plaster.'

She looks up and catches my eye, hers filling instantly. 'Even a plaster that I've been wearing for nearly thirty-five years?' She snorts at her own inside joke and takes another deep breath. 'I didn't realise how hard this would be. I spoke to Tom first thing, and that was tough enough, but to now admit it to you two...'

Tom's hand comes down and rests on her shoulder, and I see the gentle squeeze of support he offers, before he leans down and whispers something in her ear, concluding with a kiss on her cheek. She nods at whatever he's said, and then he straightens.

'I...' she starts, before pausing again. 'I am... not who you think I am, Miss Hunter.'

'Please call me Emma.'

She strains a smile, but I can see from the lines beside her mouth just how difficult she's finding this. 'When we spoke outside the other day, you told me you would listen to whatever I had to say whenever I was ready to talk about it. After Tom proposed last night, I guess I realised I can't keep running from the skeletons in my closet. If I'm to move forward,' she catches herself, and looks back up to Tom. 'If *we're* to move forward, then our story has to be built on the truth. No more lies, and no more hiding.'

I don't reply, giving her as much time as she needs, but I can feel Maddie edging further forwards beside me. Resting my hand on her knee, I give a subtle shake of my head. Alas, patience is not a virtue bestowed on my agent.

Another audible breath. 'Oh gosh, here goes: I... I don't believe that I am Zara Edwards.' She exhales heavily. 'I did believe it for a long time... Rather, I think I convinced myself that I was who they said I was, but I've been having these intense dreams – nightmares, really – and the walls that I put up are starting to crack. Maybe it's because of my age, or the approaching anniversary, I don't know.'

I can feel the frown settling on my face, but even as it does some jigsaw piece behind my eyes slots into place. 'You're telling us that you're *not* the Zara Edwards who was abducted from the pier in Brighton?'

She shakes her head, and as she does, the first tear escapes and rolls the length of her cheek, unobstructed. 'I don't think I am. When I was rescued from that burning building, I was very confused. I can't recall a lot of what was done to me while I was away, but... I remember the psychologist telling me afterwards that it's quite common for victims of significant trauma to bury and repress their experiences. And once I was out, I didn't want to dig any of that up. I was terrified of reliving it, and so I buried it along with my internal doubts about Angie and Keith Edwards. The moment I first saw them at the hospital – I dreamt about that exact moment a couple of weeks ago – I knew they weren't my parents. But the strangest thing was that they were convinced that I *was* their daughter, and I got carried away on the love they were so willing to offer me.

'Again, I buried my confusion and doubt, and ploughed forwards. I was convinced someone would eventually realise the truth, but even when I returned to school, and none of my so-called friends' faces looked familiar, nobody questioned that I wasn't who I claimed to be. I think I genuinely reached a point where I thought it was *my* memory that was wrong. The counsellor spoke a lot about scar tissue in my memory altering perception, and I accepted that as it was easier than confronting the truth which now feels inescapable.'

She stops talking, and takes several shallow breaths as she wipes her eyes with a handkerchief Tom hands to her.

This was certainly not the admission I was anticipating when I received Maddie's call, and it's caught me totally off-guard, yet I'm not sure why it has. Angie told us that Zara didn't seem the same when she returned; how her passion for nursing had diminished, and how even her handwriting looked different. Back then, I suppose, DNA testing wasn't anywhere near what it is now, and if both parents confirmed that their daughter was home, maybe there wasn't much way of disproving it. Add in Henry Weisz's assertion that Callum Gerrard wasn't the person who abducted the real Zara from the pier, and the story makes more sense.

'Why come clean now?' I ask, taking another sip of my tea,

and trying to pretend that what she's just told me isn't a huge shock.

'Mum – I mean Angie – showed me nothing but love and support growing up, and although we didn't always see eye to eye, her love was unconditional.' Her voice breaks as she continues. 'I've robbed her of the truth for nearly three decades, and she deserves to know what really happened to her daughter. I know it will break her heart, but better that than living in ignorance.'

Her tears are now flowing freely, and I feel the sting in my own eyes.

'Tom tells me that you saw her recently,' she continues.

'Yesterday,' I smile, thinking about the conviction Angie has shown to try and reconnect families with their lost loved ones at the helpline. 'She's fit and well,' I add, remembering the two of them haven't spoken since before Christmas. 'Is this what caused the argument between you?'

Zara looks away before returning my stare and offering a short nod. 'I was already having doubts at that point, and I didn't want to admit it to myself. When she started on about pursuing some career in nursing, something snapped in my head, and I knew I needed to get out of there before I admitted the truth. Looking back on it objectively, I think I triggered the argument as an escape route. And the reason I've failed to contact her since is because I don't want to lie to her anymore. I suppose that sounds pretty selfish.'

I'm the last person who can judge people for selfish motives, and if what she's saying is true, it's not a situation many of us would find ourselves in. It's virtually impossible to truly appreciate how difficult it will have been to live with such pain.

'What do you want to do from here?' I ask, willing my own tears to stay away.

Zara glances up at Tom, who once again gives a reassuring nod, before she fixes me with a hard stare. 'I want to find out what really happened to Zara Edwards, to provide Angie with the truth she's entitled to. Will you help me, Emma?'

Chapter Thirty-One

THEN

Edgware, London

With Emma having excused herself to make a phone call, Zara took the opportunity to step outside for fresh air, grateful that Tom joined her without the need for her to ask.

'You won't let me out of your sight now we're engaged, will you?' she teased in an effort to lighten the tension she sensed coming from the tightness of his jaw.

He didn't share in the humour, taking both her hands in his, but holding them delicately, as if they might be porcelain capable of shattering into a thousand pieces. Leaning forward, he pressed his forehead against hers, and her heart surged with love at having him with her, even if she did sense he was about to burst the bubble.

'Are you sure this is what you want to do?' he asked quietly, his voice barely more than a whisper.

'I don't really have a choice, do I?' she replied softly. 'I've spent the last thirty-four years living a lie, and I don't want to anymore.' She held her breath. 'Do you think I'm making a mistake?'

His head rubbed against her fringe as he slowly shook his head. 'No, not a mistake, but are you sure you understand the repercussions of your choice? You told me you hated all the furore that hounded you in the weeks and months that followed your recovery from the house fire… I'm just worried about how this detail coming out is going to affect *you*.'

She took a solitary step backwards so he could read her eyes as she spoke. 'I'm not planning on broadcasting this to the world. I want Emma to help me learn the truth about who I am and what happened to me and the Zara who was taken, but that's all. As far as I'm concerned, the fewer people who know the truth, the better.'

His jaw remained fixed, and his face adopted a grey hue. 'That's all well and good, but surely you must see that something like this is bound to get out into the public forum; it's inevitable. Even if you choose not to announce it, Maddie and Emma in there already know about it, and I daresay whoever Emma's now talking to on the phone knows too. Of course you'll have to tell your mum – sorry, I mean Angie – and how do you think she's going to react? Even if she doesn't believe you, it won't stop her talking about it with her friends at the helpline. This is a huge deal, my love, and no matter how hard you try to control the fallout, it will spread.'

She broke free of his grasp and turned away, hurrying down the footpath to the main street so he wouldn't see the fresh sheen washing over her vision.

'Zara, wait,' he called after her, but it only made her quicken her pace, eventually breaking into a sprint as she swallowed up paving slabs despite the slapping of her shoes against the stone.

Deep down she knew he was right, and she was disappointed with her own naivety at not realising the obvious truth. In her mind, she was old news now – a story children tell their friends to frighten them: *Watch your back or you might get snatched like the Brighton Rock Girl!*

But it wasn't that simple, was it? How many people had read and empathised with Angie and Keith when Zara had been snatched? There had been nationwide sorrow. And then the outpouring of relief when the little girl with ginger hair had been found. It may have been thirty-four years ago, but there was nothing like a scandal to stir up the British media. All it would take was one slip of the tongue, or someone out to make a quick buck at her expense, and then it would be flashing camera bulbs all over again.

What was the alternative though? Say nothing and live the rest of her life knowing that she was the cause of a mother's loss?

Tom was only looking out for her, and to his credit he hadn't chased after her, giving her the space she needed to get her head straight. She'd told him at breakfast this morning, even though she'd been terrified he would storm off. Instead, he'd listened and considered, and then told her it was okay. He hadn't shouted, hadn't criticised, hadn't blamed her even. All he'd said was it didn't change his feelings for her, and that he would remain at her side to support her.

She didn't deserve such kindness, she knew, but she'd accepted it at face value.

Poor Tom, he didn't deserve any of this. He'd been nothing but supportive after the redundancy, and even after the nightmares had started, he had been her knight in shining armour. This was his perfect excuse to cut his losses, but rather than doing so, he'd asked her to marry him. Her heart filled once again as she caught sight of the beautiful stone in the ring, and she reduced her pace to a slow jog, sucking in lungfuls of breath to aid her recovery.

How would *he* cope with their lives suddenly being thrust into the limelight? After all, it wasn't just her life they'd be scrutinising. She'd witnessed tabloid intrusion first hand, and it wasn't something she'd welcome back lightly. And how long would his faith in her continue? Would he start to question other things in their time together? She'd lied to him for the best part of eighteen years, so how could he trust anything else she'd told him?

Would things have been different had she spoken up that first day? She'd tried, of that she was certain, but nobody had been prepared to listen. If the same thing happened today, DNA testing would quickly have revealed her lie. If only it had been so simple to convince the world of her lie back then.

No, she knew what she had to do, and even if that brought a mountain of trouble down on her, there really wasn't a lot she could do about it. Walking slowly back to the estate, she found Tom waiting for her on the doorstep.

'I'm sorry,' he offered, before she had a chance to echo the sentiment. 'The last thing I want is to put more pressure on you, and I—'

She stretched up and kissed him to break the apology. 'I'm sorry too. For running off, and for keeping something so big from you for so many years. I think I convinced myself that if I kept running it would never catch up with me. But it's time to stop running. I'm not saying it will be easy, and I don't doubt there will be times when we regret starting out on the journey, but it's the right thing to do.'

He kissed her back and then nodded. 'Shall we go back inside then?'

She followed him in, and as they reached the upstairs landing, they found Emma had finished on her phone call and had set up her laptop on the large dining table in the second room.

Maddie joined them a minute later, carrying a tray of plates and glasses. 'I ordered some pizza,' she said as she laid out the crockery. 'I hope that's okay?'

Emma's eyes widened at mention of the food, but her gaze remained locked on the laptop screen.

'Perfect,' Zara offered, pulling out a chair beside Emma, with Tom sitting on the next chair over.

Emma adjusted the screen so that all three of them could see it, before opening a webpage. 'This is the missingpeople.org site that would be the first place I'd come when researching people who have gone missing in the UK. I'm assuming – given nobody reported you speaking with a foreign accent in the early days – that you were from the UK to begin with, so it's as good a place as any to start from.'

Zara nodded at the explanation, her heart fluttering at the anticipation of starting. She recognised the cold sweat and increased heartrate from standing on the start line of a race during sports day as a child.

'There are filters on the site to narrow down the criteria. So we'll filter for female children who've been missing for more than three years initially to reduce the options. What does that leave us…?'

The three of them stared at the screen, while Maddie waited downstairs for the pizza to be delivered.

Zara watched as the list of faces refreshed slowly on the site as the filters were applied. 'I can't believe there are so many,' she said, more to herself than anyone.

'Tragically, there are more children that go missing each year than anyone else,' Emma echoed glumly. 'Thankfully, more are found than not, but the success rate is far from one hundred per cent. I imagine it would be a lot worse without resources like this. And locating missing people quickly has been improved by the advance of social media. Ironically, the dark side of social media has probably contributed to the increase in people going missing to begin with, so...' She left the statement hanging. 'Can you remember anything about the time when your disappearance started, to help narrow the list further? Do you know where you're from, for example?'

Zara closed her eyes, but shook her head. 'It's difficult to remember anything of life before the fireman rescued me... I get flashes – glimpses really – of memories, but not enough to provide much insight. There's something fleeting about an animal enclosure; possibly a memory of being at a zoo, maybe, but I can't be certain. And it isn't obvious whether it's a memory from before or after I was found. I can't think of any place other than Brighton, but that's probably because that's where Angie and Keith raised me after my return. I'm sorry.'

'It's okay,' Emma soothed. 'This is going to take us time. Look, there are some of these we can automatically rule out, based on appearance. Can I ask a personal question? About your hair. One of the corroborating factors as to why the authorities were so quick to hand you back to Angie and Keith was your fiery hair. This is your natural hair colour, I take it?'

Zara felt the locks that had helped her quash the voice of doubt in those early years. 'Yes, it is. Darker now than it was, but I never changed it intentionally.'

'Okay, well presumably we can assume that if you were reported missing, then the image they would have used of you would have been one that reflected the colour.'

Zara frowned. 'Wait, what do you mean by *if* I was reported missing?'

Emma scrunched up her nose. 'This website relies on the families of the absent person reporting the disappearance, specifically reporting the disappearance to the police. I would imagine, ninety-nine times out of a hundred, it would be a given that your real parents or guardians would have formally recorded your absence, but… depending on the circumstances, there is a prospect that we won't be able to find you.' Emma quickly raised her hands in a calming gesture. 'That's not to say we won't be successful; I just want to prepare you for the possibility, and the only reason I do say that is that thirty-five years ago there was no doubt in the investigating team's mind that you were the missing Zara. I would have assumed that, given the amount of media exposure your story garnered, if there was a second family out there craving news about their missing redhead, they would have come forward to challenge.'

This was a question that hadn't occurred to Zara previously, but now she couldn't ignore it: why hadn't her real family come looking for her?

Scrolling through the passport-sized images on the screen between them, panic slowly rose in her throat. What if she couldn't find out who she really was? What if she was lost forever?

Chapter Thirty-Two

NOW

Edgware, London

Scrolling through the faces on the screen, I know I need to be concentrating, but my mind is elsewhere. I've tried phoning Rachel four times, but the call has rung through to her messaging service each time. I've recorded three voicemails asking Rachel to phone me back, but as yet those messages have gone unanswered. I'm probably just being paranoid, and it could simply be that she's just caught up with a story, or the meeting with her editor has run over, but... it's been nearly three hours since I last saw Rachel, and I know she will have made it to her office in that time. What if the meeting was bad news, and now she's gone to drown her sorrows? Or worse still, what if she's been involved in an accident, and doesn't even realise I'm trying to get hold of her?

Curse of the writer's overactive imagination again.

I look up at Zara, forcing myself to remember how important this search is for her. It has taken tremendous courage for Zara to impart her secret to me, and she deserves my full attention and cooperation. If Rachel would just phone me back and let me know what her editor has said, I know I'd be less distracted.

My gaze returns to the screen, but there's part of me that feels like we're wasting our time here. Even though I've applied a filter to show the faces of girls who have been missing for over three years, there are still so many, and the majority have foreign-sounding names and the wrong skin tone, which means we can quickly rule them out as a match for the woman before me now. On top of that, I can't escape the fact that if there really is a family out there looking for her true self, then surely questions would have been asked when the authorities believed they'd discovered Zara.

The breath catches in my throat as a very recognisable face suddenly appears on the screen. It shouldn't have come as a surprise given the filters that have been applied, but catching sight of my sister sends my pulse spiking; it's almost like coming face to face with her for the first time all over again. I don't think Zara notices me quickly scrolling on.

Hovering the mouse over each image presents us with a name and a date from when they went missing, which is only as helpful as being able to rule out any images of girls who went missing after Zara was found in 1988. The page is slow to refresh and add new images, and while we wait I offer both Zara and Tom a reassuring smile, but neither looks comfortable with what we're doing. After ten minutes of looking at vulnerable faces, we're no closer to finding out who this Zara is.

'Is that it?' she asks when no new faces load to the screen.

I reluctantly nod. 'I'm sorry, it appears so.'

She looks over to Tom, her lip trembling.

'There must be more missing children than this,' Tom says, refusing to be beaten. 'I assume there are other websites?'

'There are,' I admit, 'but this is one of the more popular ones. It's difficult without knowing a little bit more about your life before 1988. Are you sure there are no other details you can recall from your time before you were discovered in Callum Gerrard's house? Anything at all could be useful. A location, or a face, or a name. Anything?'

Zara's lip continues to tremble, like that of an orphaned child being asked to trust her life into the hands of new guardians. 'I...' she stops herself, and a frown slowly takes control of her forehead. She closes her eyes, lowers her head, and her hand comes up and massages her temple. 'There's a voice... in the dreams I've been having. A woman's voice, quiet, but confident... It's... it's angry with me, I think. It calls out when the dream is darkening from behind my eyes... right before I wake up... It's calling out... calling out to me, I think. If I could just...' Her eyes snap open, and she looks straight at me. 'Ruth, or Ruthie. That's what the voice is calling out. I think... maybe... my name might have been Ruth.' She looks back at the screen. 'Is there any way to look for missing girls called Ruth?'

I turn my attention back to the screen also and scroll back to the top of the page, hoping the list of faces has refreshed to reveal new images. 'Alas, on the site we're using, all we can do is look at the faces and names; there's no way to filter by name. I could do a standard search for missing girls called Ruth, but is there anything else you can remember? You don't know where you lived before Brighton?'

She shakes her head ruefully. 'I'm sorry, no.'

Tom takes her hand and leans forwards, as if what he's about to say will bring redemption for us all. 'What if we tried something like hypnosis? The fact that Zara is having dreams – sorry, nightmares – about her earlier experiences suggests that the memories are there, just hidden away. I read about this hypnotherapist who specialises in unlocking repressed memories and experiences; maybe she could help unlock some of that history.'

Zara looks at me expectantly.

I so want to offer them hope, but I won't lead them down the garden path. My face folds in on itself as I prepare for the backlash. 'I wouldn't place too much hope in that sort of thing. From what I've heard and seen of so-called hypnotic regression, it's pretty hit and miss, and requires the subject to be open to the power of suggestion. There's no way to prove for certain whether what the subject is revealing is *actual* memory, and not just what the imagination has created to make life easier. It's why the police can't place any reliance on witness statements based on hypnotic sessions, and why they're not considered evidentiary in court.'

'But I'm not talking about regressing her through previous lives,' Tom sits forward, as if raising his voice will be sufficient to change the facts. 'A hypnotist could plant a seed that encourages Zara's subconscious to unlock those memories whether in a dream-like state where it's safe for her to do so, or once she's out of the session. It's worth trying, surely?'

Passive aggression is clearly a tactic he's used to succeeding with in court, but I'm not intimidated.

Zara is still looking to me for agreement to the idea, and I desperately want to satisfy her need for reassurance. 'It's up to you,' I hear my voice say, despite my better judgement. 'If you think it will help, then I guess there's no harm, but I would just warn you that there are no guarantees. I'd hate you to spend a fortune, believing it's the answer to all your problems, only to be let down.'

'What do you think I should do?' she asks verbally, even though her body language has been screaming the question for minutes.

'If it was me... I don't think I'd bother. There are still other avenues we could pursue in terms of trying to find out who you are. The names and faces on the missingpersons.org site are not an exhaustive list. What we've seen today are priority cases based on the administrators' interactions with the police and those still actively searching for the victims. There are thousands of missing children cases that remain unresolved with the British police – and that's assuming you went missing on British soil. Even if you were born in the UK, had you been resident in a foreign country at the time of your disappearance, it's possible your family wouldn't have notified the UK authorities.'

Zara frowns at this statement, but Tom appears to have taken it as a dent to his pride.

'You've heard her speak, and there's no trace of a foreign accent,' he argues, his voice elevated.

I offer my hands in a calming gesture to them both. 'I agree that thirty-five years later there's no obvious accent to Zara's voice but, hypothetically, if Zara was born and raised in the UK until her seventh or eighth birthday, and then her parents moved to the US or Canada, for example, and it was there that she was taken and brought back to the UK, there's no reason that anyone would be able to hear it in her voice.'

'I do remember a plane,' Zara says quietly, her eyes once

again closed as she searches the recesses of her memory. 'At least, I think I do... I can picture a woman in a blue uniform – a stewardess, I think. She's handing me a cushion and telling me I should get some sleep. I can't see my parents, or anyone I recognise, but I have a feeling of pure dread.'

My eye catches the picture of Anna on the screen again, and I can't help being drawn to it. What if she too had been returned to the wrong family after she went missing? Would she have grown up knowing something wasn't right, as Zara had done? Could she still be out there now, ignoring the voice in the back of her head?

I shake the thought from my mind. When Zara returned in 1988, DNA testing as a means of identifying individuals was still in its relative infancy. Breakthroughs were being made in both the UK and USA, but it wasn't until the early 90s that DNA testing began to resemble what is now so commonplace and effective. Anna went missing in 2000, by which point a national DNA database had been established in the UK, and I know a sample of Anna's DNA is held there for the possibility that it's ever required for identification purposes. If she had been discovered and returned to the wrong family, the police definitely would have performed a DNA test, and I wouldn't still be looking for her.

'Do you think that's what happened then?' Zara asks quietly, but the hope is dripping from every syllable. 'You think I was taken while in another country?'

'What? No, that's not what I meant,' I clarify. 'I'm just saying it's a *possibility*. I doubt that's what happened, and there could be a hundred other reasons why we can't find your picture on this website.'

Tom releases Zara's hand and moves away from the table,

starting to pace by the window. I can see he's frustrated – as we all are – but he's doing a terrible job of hiding it.

'You're the expert here, Emma,' Zara says, shuffling closer to me, 'what do you think we should do next?'

'I'm hardly an expert,' I quickly counter.

'Not so. You found Cassie Hilliard and Sally Curtis when everyone else had given up. Please don't give up on me.'

She must know I'm a sucker for a heartfelt plea. Closing the laptop, I let out a heavy sigh. 'I won't give up on you, Zara, I promise, but I think you need to prepare yourself for the prospect that you may never find out the truth about where you're from and who you are. Thirty-five years is a helluva lot of water to have passed under the bridge. I'm not sure what else I can do to help.'

She is crestfallen, but nods in acknowledgement.

What if this was Anna appealing for help? I'd want someone to move heaven and earth to reconnect us. Zara isn't all that different to Anna; both have experienced a level of abuse that I refuse to allow my brain to think about. They both deserve a happier ending.

A thought fires in the back of my mind. Her story *is* a lot like Anna's, and if that is the case then it's just possible she might have been exposed to what was happening at Pendark when Arthur Turgood and his cronies were there.

Snatching up my phone, I make my excuses and head down to the kitchen, closing the door so I won't be overheard. When Jack and I were trying to ascertain whether Faye McKenna and Cormack Fitzpatrick had appeared in the videos recovered from Turgood's hard drive, Jack took me to the NCA office in Vauxhall and introduced me to his colleagues Jasminda Kaur and Geoff Macaulay. They were able to perform a facial recognition attempt of images in a matter of seconds. Dialling the office, I'm relieved to recognise Jasminda's voice.

'Hi, Jasminda, it's Emma Hunter. We were introduced last month by Jack Serrovitz.'

'Sure, you're the writer. How is Jack? We heard about the car accident.'

'He's...' I don't know quite how to answer, and how much they've been told about his condition. 'He's still in hospital,' I settle for.

'Will you pass on our best when you see him next,' she says empathetically.

'Yes, of course. Listen, Jasminda, I don't have long, but I was wondering if you could do me a favour. I'm going to email you a picture of a girl Jack and I are trying to trace. Do you think you could run the image against the stills taken from the Turgood videos, and let me know of any potential matches?'

'Sure, no worries.'

I clench my fist in satisfaction. 'There's one other thing too... Could you run a search on the missing persons database for a girl called Ruth who would have gone missing pre-1988?'

Chapter Thirty-Three

Edgware, London

Tom hasn't stopped pacing since I came off the phone to Jasminda, and even Maddie coming in with the delivered pizza has done little to distract us from the elephant in the room. Jasminda promised she'd phone back as soon as she has an update, but it's already been twenty minutes and I'm tempted to phone her back.

For Zara, it's a matter of potentially understanding more about who she was, but for me there's far more at stake. If Jasminda does find a match to Zara's younger self on the Turgood videos, it potentially opens a fresh angle for mine and Jack's investigation. But it's not necessarily a welcome angle. If Zara does feature then it means the ring of traffickers and paedophiles was active long before Freddie and my sister became implicated. I dread to think about how long they've gone undetected, and what lengths they've gone to in order to keep off the radar.

Zara has been chewing at her nails since her revelation about the name Ruth, but she looks up and forces a smile whenever she catches me glancing over. I know she's trying to put a brave face on things, but it can't be easy knowing that your whole life has been a lie. I haven't asked her whether she recalls being videoed during her time away, because I don't have the heart to shake her foundations further.

The smell of pizza hangs in the air, but food is the last thing on any of our minds. Despite Maddie's less-than-subtle attempts to encourage us all to tuck in, thus far she's the only one who's taken a slice, and even that remains virtually untouched on her plate.

My phone rings, and I answer it before the first ring stops. 'Hi, Jasminda, hi... Yes, well?'

'I've run a check on the two pictures you emailed over. It doesn't look like the face in question appears in the videos; at least, there's nothing higher than a twenty per cent match to the stills we pulled. As I'm sure Jack told you, some of the footage is so grainy that it's impossible to identify enough features for the software to attempt a match. I'm sorry it's not better news.'

I look over to Zara who's staring back at me, trying to read my reaction to the news. If anything, it's the best news we've heard today. I don't know how I'd find the strength to tell Zara about the videos on Turgood's drive.

'That's okay,' I tell Jasminda. 'Thank you for checking for me. Did you have any luck on the name Ruth?'

There is a notable pause on the line that has me double-checking the strength of my mobile phone signal.

'Jasminda? Are you there? Can you hear me?'

'Yes I can... Listen, I need to check your interest in the name Ruth. Do you have a surname you can tell me?'

'No, that's all I've got, I'm afraid. There's a woman who I believe was abducted in the mid to late 80s, but her name is all I've got; the name and that she had fire-red hair.'

Another pause. 'And this is part of the work you're undertaking with Jack?'

I don't want to lie to her, but given Jack's comatose state, it doesn't feel right to mislead her.

'Sort of,' I try, but not even I'm convinced by the lie.

'The thing is,' Jasminda begins, 'I'm sorry, Emma, I've been told I'm not at liberty to confirm details of any missing children with you.'

My brow thickens. 'I don't understand. You can't tell me if there are any open investigations involving the name Ruth?'

'I'm sorry, but I've been told I can't share the details of *any* missing children cases with you.'

'Wait, told by whom?'

'My DCI. Listen, I'm sorry, I shouldn't even be phoning you back, but I know how much Jack rates you, and so I wanted to be courteous. I should go.'

'No, Jasminda, please, just hold on a second. Just so I'm clear, your DCI has given you a direct order *not* to speak to me?'

'Yes. If he knew I was on the phone to you now, he'd be furious.'

'What's his name? Your DCI, I mean?'

'Harry Dainton.'

I recognise the name. He's Jack's lead at the National Crime Agency. I met him briefly at the ruins of Pendark when Faye McKenna's skeleton was recovered in a suitcase. Jack described him as a good guy, but then also told me he plays golf with former commissioner Sir Anthony Tomlinson. Is it possible Tomlinson has told Dainton not to cooperate with me? With no evidence it'll be impossible to prove.

'Can you tell me exactly what Dainton said?'

'There was a team memo saying your work with Jack was coming to an end and Jack would be returning to his post in the Met immediately.'

The late afternoon sun is making the room feel like it's spinning.

'Why haven't I been told any of this? Does Jack know?'

'The memo came round the day before his accident... I would have thought he'd have told you. Listen, Emma, I'm sorry, but I really need to go.'

'Wait, Jasminda, please, just tell me one thing: did you find any open cases involving a child called Ruth in the mid to late 80s?'

She pauses again, and for a moment I think she's hung up on me, but then I hear the mouthpiece being moved closer to her lips. When she speaks she is whispering. 'You're still friends with Jack's DCS, right?'

I picture Rawani's tired eyes this morning. 'Yes.'

'Good. Ask him to look into Ruth Swaile. I'm sorry, that's all I can tell you; I have to go.'

This time the line does die, and as I return the phone to my satchel, I can feel Zara's eyes burning into me.

'Any luck?' she asks with a desperate gasp.

I don't know what to make of Jasminda's message, nor why Jack wouldn't have told me the investigation was being closed; maybe he just didn't know how to tell me. Either way, I won't know more until he wakes from the coma.

'Nothing she could share over the phone,' I say.

Zara looks despondent, her eyes dropping to the pizza on the table but her body making no effort to reach for a slice. 'Oh, well maybe I made a mistake. Do you think Ruth could have been a sister's name or something?'

'I don't know,' I say with a shrug. 'It could be something or it could be nothing. It's not the end of the road, though. There is something you can do to set the wheels in motion, but it won't be easy.'

She frowns at me. 'What do you mean?'

'Well, there is one way we can prove you're *not* Zara Edwards. We could have a sample of your DNA compared to that of Angie. You'd have to speak to her though, and come clean about why you want the test performed.'

Her face drains of blood as, I imagine, she pictures that conversation with Angie. I certainly don't envy her. Zara stands and puffs out her cheeks, falling into step with Tom's pacing.

'What do you think?' she asks him.

He stops and rubs his forehead with his palm. The strain is clear to see and as he puts on an affectionate smile, his love for Zara radiates.

'Honestly, I wish you'd never realised any of this. For your sake, not for mine. I can only imagine how this is eating you up inside. But I meant what I said before: I am in this for the long run. If you think it's for the best, then I think we should go to Brighton and speak to your mum... Sorry, I mean Angie. It won't be easy, but she needs to know the truth as well.'

Zara's face hasn't regained its colour.

'I'll be right there with you,' he adds quickly.

But Zara is shaking her head. 'No, it's something I need to

do alone. If you'll drive me to Brighton and take me to her house, then I'll start the conversation.'

She looks over to me and it pains me to see the melancholy in her eyes. 'How was she when you saw her?'

I think back to our conversation in the café near the office building. 'Honestly, I think she probably half expects a bombshell like this. The way she spoke about you after your return... She pretty much said it was like you were a different person. I'm not saying the conversation will be easy, but I don't think she'll doubt what you're telling her.'

'Can I phone you after I've spoken to her?' Zara asks, gathering her bag from the carpet. 'Assuming she agrees to giving a DNA sample, I'm not sure how or where to go about getting it tested.'

'Sure,' I nod, 'I know a couple of labs that could do the work. Just let me know when you're ready. Hey, and listen, if after you've spoken to Angie you decide you don't actually want the test, that's fine. Nobody is going to judge you, least of all me.'

Zara thanks me and puts on a brave face as she and Tom leave. I'm not sure if they're planning to drive straight to Brighton now, but if it was me trying to have that conversation with my mother, I'd need days if not weeks to prepare.

'Well I certainly wasn't expecting that,' Maddie comments when she's shown them out and returned to the first floor. 'It could make an interesting follow-up to *Trafficked* if Zara will agree to be your protagonist.'

A part of me is disappointed at Maddie's comment, until I remind myself that she is there to protect my commercial interests. I know she doesn't mean to be so ruthless.

'Well, that all depends whether Aurélie and her legal team

will finally approve the manuscript, I suppose. Have you heard any more from them since Friday's meeting?'

'Can't say I have, but I'll follow up with your publishers in the morning. I know they were keen to get things resolved sooner rather than later. The world is crying out for the next Emma Hunter book.'

I wish I shared her enthusiasm.

'Are you going to eat any of this pizza?' Maddie asks. 'It's too big for me to manage alone.'

My appetite hasn't returned, but I agree to take a slice with me when I leave. Right now I have two calls to place: the first is to Rachel to find out why she's not been in contact, and the second is to DCS Rawani to find out why Jack's secondment at the NCA has been ended prematurely. These last couple of months have had my paranoia on high alert, but now I'm almost certain there's more to it than whimsy.

Chapter Thirty-Four

THEN

Ruislip, London

The drive from Edgware back to Ruislip was made in stony silence, with Tom occasionally glancing over to Zara to check how she was coping with the shock of what had been discussed. The radio played low and was a welcome distraction to the lack of talking. Zara would never admit as much to him, but she too was full of regret. Would it really have been so difficult to keep her feelings bottled up? The big secret had hung over her for so many years, always lurking in the shadows, and she'd never been able to forget the prospect that it would leap out when she was least expecting and sweep the rug from beneath her feet. That was why she'd come clean about her own doubts about her true identity, but it was yet another weight for Tom to bear too.

This past week had been hard enough on him – not that he'd ever openly admit it to her. Learning that his fiancée was associated with the Brighton Rock Girl case must have been tough enough, and bless him, he'd handled himself with grace. However, he hadn't anticipated the latest bombshell, and what hurt her most was the fact that he now knew that she'd lied to him. Twice. Would he ever be able to truly trust her again? She didn't feel as though she deserved his trust and support.

'Do you want to go to Brighton tonight?' he croaked, before clearing his throat and repeating the question.

She didn't really, but she also sensed that if she didn't strike while the iron was hot she'd find further excuses to put it off. And if they didn't go there today, she'd doubtless spend the night tossing and turning, dreading the trip and conversation tomorrow. A part of her wanted to tell him she'd changed her mind, and didn't want to ever have that conversation with Angie. Couldn't Emma just do some digging without Angie ever finding out the truth? It would be cruel, and yet wouldn't it be less cruel if Angie never had to know? Zara felt confident she could fake being Angie's daughter for a few more years, and would even go out of her way to be a better daughter, and smooth things over. *That* was what Angie really deserved, wasn't it?

'Babe? I said, do you want to go to Brighton tonight? I can get a couple more days off work. Jacob knows we've got family stuff we're dealing with.'

She turned to meet his stare, her brow furrowing. 'You told Jacob about me?'

'No, not exactly,' Tom quickly backtracked. 'What I mean is, I told him we've got a few family things to sort out. That's all I've said. He doesn't know about any of *this*.'

It pacified her for now, but she also knew it wouldn't be healthy for Tom to bottle up his own feelings. He'd offered her words of encouragement and support over the last few days, but he hadn't told her how *he* was feeling about all of *this*, as he'd put it.

Had she heard a tone when he'd answered? Did that indicate he wasn't happy, and was hiding it from her?

'I keep playing over what I'll say to her,' Zara said absently, her gaze returning to the passing houses beyond her window. 'I don't want to just blurt it out, but I don't think it's something I can sugar-coat.'

They drove past their local corner shop and Tom indicated, waiting at the junction until he could pull into their road.

'Maybe you should phone ahead, so she knows we're coming,' he suggested. 'I don't mind phoning if that would be easier? Better that than just turning up on her doorstep unannounced.'

Zara was considering the idea as they reached the large hedgerow and the driveway cut through the middle. Tom stopped suddenly, a yellow Mini blocking their entrance. He parked at the side of the road instead.

'Looks like the mountain has come to Mohammed,' he muttered under his breath, unfastening his belt and climbing out.

By the time they'd pulled alongside the Mini, Angie was already clambering out herself and offered a large bouquet to Zara. 'I was beginning to worry the two of you had gone away. I hope you don't mind me coming unannounced. With the way things have been between us since before Christmas... I thought it best just to come and apologise. I'm sorry, Zara.'

Zara couldn't get the words past her throat. She snatched at the flowers and hurried inside, before the tears escaped and the lies came tumbling from her mouth.

Angie and Tom followed behind, Tom explaining that it

had been a difficult day, and that they should give Zara a few moments to compose herself. Zara hurried to the bedroom, locking the door behind her, but all the while listening to the gentle hum of Tom's voice as he made Angie welcome and put on the kettle.

Angie's sudden appearance had to be a sign, of that Zara had no doubt, but she couldn't be certain what it was a sign of. On the one hand it could be fate's way of forcing her to have the conversation tonight, especially as she was already yearning for opportunities to get out of it. That said, maybe Angie turning up out of the blue could have been fate's way of telling Zara *not* to have that conversation, and to just make her peace. After all, Angie had appeared with flowers and an apology.

A knock at the bedroom door was followed by Tom asking, 'Do you want a cup of tea?'

She'd need something stronger than tea if she was going to detonate the bomb tonight. 'Please,' she replied. 'I'll be out in a minute.'

Zara waited until she heard that Tom and Angie had moved into the living room, before checking that her makeup didn't give her away and then joining them. Tom was in the single armchair, forcing Zara to sit on the sofa with Angie, and as the two of them looked the other up and down, it soon became clear that Zara wasn't the only one with something to say.

'How have you been?' Angie started, sipping her tea.

'We're fine,' Zara replied, although the question hadn't directly included Tom. 'And you? Are you still working with Diana at the helpline?'

'Oh yes, more and more in fact. That's kind of why I

wanted to come and see you today.' Angie lowered her cup and saucer to a coaster on the table beside her, before reaching out and taking Zara's hands in hers. 'I had a visitor at the office yesterday. That writer, Emma Hunter, was asking questions about you and about that time in our lives. She didn't say directly that she'd spoken with you, but I sensed you in the background somewhere.'

Zara looked over to Tom, who was quietly observing the two of them. He offered a gentle nod in her direction.

'She was asking me questions about what life was like after you returned, and it stirred up a lot of old memories for me... and I came to realise that whilst I thought I was making your feelings the centre of my world, actually a lot of what happened in the months and years after you came back to us wasn't about your best interests. I knew you'd been affected by what had happened, and my goal became about fixing everything, when really that wasn't what you needed. We sent you for counselling to help you find closure for what had happened, and keeping you in the same school around your old friends... I genuinely believed that would help bring out the old you – the one from before you were taken – but I now see that probably wasn't the best thing for you. I see now that living in the same house and following the old routines only served as a constant reminder of what had happened.'

Zara opened her mouth to speak, but her trembling lip made enunciation almost impossible.

Angie squeezed Zara's hands. 'Looking back on that time, I wish we'd started afresh elsewhere with new identities and purpose. And I'm sorry that we didn't. I'm sorry for so many things – too many things to recall – and I'm hoping that we can wipe the slate clean. Speaking with Emma Hunter reminded me that there are mothers out there who don't have the opportunity to be a part of their daughter's life, and I don't want to dishonour their battles. So, please forgive me for being a bad mother, and help me to make it up to you.'

There was so much Zara wanted to say, so much she wanted to apologise for, but as she watched Angie's desperate plea for forgiveness, there was nothing she wanted more than to accept it.

Thrusting her arms out, Zara hugged Angie tightly. 'I'm sorry too, Mum.'

Chapter Thirty-Five

NOW

Uxbridge, London

Rachel still isn't answering her phone, and my overactive and paranoid imagination is driving me to irrational conclusions. What if she never made it to the office, and has been involved in an accident? What if she *did* make it to the office, but it was bad news and now she's harmed herself in some way? What if the same person who burgled her flat was also stalking Rachel, and has…?

I don't finish the thought, because even I can see how unfounded these feelings are. But what other explanation could there be for Rachel switching off her phone when she *promised* she'd let me know what was going on? With no better idea, I phone Daniella's mobile, hoping that if Rachel was inconsolable then she would inevitably reach out to her fiancée first, but Daniella's phone is also switched off, and I have a vague recollection of Rachel saying Daniella was in Morocco, which could be why it's switched off.

At times, I can be incredibly patient, but when I've got the bit between my teeth, I just want it chewed without delay. I'm not usually given to reckless abandon, but short of just returning to Rachel's flat and *hoping* for good news, I know there's nothing more I can do until Rachel reaches out to me. That said, if I haven't heard back from her by tonight, I will contact the police and share my concerns. If only Jack was on duty, I know he wouldn't hesitate to phone around the local hospitals and see if anyone matching Rachel's description had been brought in. I've already tried that but those emergency departments that did answer were forthright in telling me they couldn't divulge that sort of information to the general public.

I've always felt so in control of my life and like I'm driving myself towards destiny, but right now my future has never felt so unrestrained. It feels like I've been pushed out of a plane without a parachute, and I'm flailing through the air, waiting to be saved – or for the rapidly approaching ground to catch me first. What I need to do is slow my descent for as long as possible. And that's why I am now standing outside Uxbridge Police Station, a building I have visited many times in the last eighteen months. It's the place where I first met Jack when he was assigned to help me sift through the Cassie Hilliard casefile. How far we've come since that initial awkward encounter.

How I wish he was waiting for me inside.

Staring up to the window I know belongs to DCS Rawani's office, I'm pleased to see there's light peeking out around the edges of the closed blind. He's definitely up there; whether he'll be willing to see me so late in the day is another matter, but I won't know unless I go inside.

Every passing minute is another chance to turn it all around, my dad would tell Anna and me whenever we were upset about something not going to plan. Peeling off my jacket, and straightening my fringe in the reflection of the front door, I take a deep breath, clear my mind of negativity, and approach the front desk.

I vaguely recognise the young woman behind the glass screen, but her name escapes me at first. Her head is dipped, but that bright, short bob is unmistakeable. She raises her eyes from the report on the desk in front of her when I clear my throat, and she smiles warmly as her eyes recognise me. The lanyard she's wearing identifies her as Constable Denier.

'Hello, Emma,' she gushes. 'It's good to see you again. How's the writing going?'

There are two questions writers regularly get asked by friends, family, and acquaintances: how is the writing/sales going, and do you have a spare copy of your book I can read?

Both are equally frustrating. The first question is not always easy to answer, particularly as it's difficult to determine how well writing is going until the manuscript is complete, and Maddie as my agent oversees sales. She updates me on volumes occasionally, but only anecdotally. I receive a statement of sales volumes twice a year from my publisher, but I don't tend to pay too much attention to those as that's very much Maddie's area of expertise.

The second question suggests I have a treasure trove of author copies of my books that I'm happy to donate free of charge to any Tom, Dick, or Harry who fancies one. The truth is I receive maybe a dozen copies of the books on publication day, but most of those are sent to charitable organisations as raffle prizes. Also, expecting me to give away my book –

which, let's face it, is months or years of work – free of charge belittles the effort that has gone into it.

I don't share any of this with young Officer Denier, who I now realise looks different because she's had the metal braces removed from her teeth. I smile instead, and give my standard answer.

'The writing's great, thanks. Would you be able to let DCS Rawani know that I'm here, and that I need to speak to him urgently?'

She smiles again, and I have to credit her orthodontist on a job well done. She tells me to wait by the two chairs near the main door, while she picks up the phone on the desk and places the call.

'Is he expecting you?' she asks, as she dials his extension.

'Not exactly,' I admit, 'but he'll want to hear what I have to tell him.'

She relays the message into the receiver while I move across to the chairs – not that I sit.

'He says he's finishing something up, and asked if you'd mind waiting for him down here.'

What else did I expect? Jagtar Rawani has never been impressed by my writing track record, and in fact for a long time I was convinced he didn't care for my writing in general; that was until I saw a copy of *Ransomed* on the shelf in his office. Not that he's shared his thoughts on the book or his role within it.

I use the delay to try Rachel again. I've lost count of the voice messages I've left on her mobile, and if she had a landline I'd have left twice as many. I'm tempted to search for the number of the newspaper office and demand to speak to her editor to find out what he said to her, but I don't want to unnecessarily embarrass Rachel like some naïve parent chasing after their errant child who's simply forgotten to phone.

I turn back to face the front desk when I hear the door being buzzed open and find Rawani standing there, suit covered by an enormous overcoat, a leather briefcase in his left hand. The bags beneath his eyes are as painful as they were when I found him at the hospital this morning. He doesn't speak as he passes me on his way out of the building, and Denier offers an awkward shrug when our eyes meet, so I hurry after him.

'Jagtar?' I try, almost breathless trying to maintain his brisk walking pace.

'Not here,' he replies through gritted teeth. 'Just walk.'

The sun is setting over the town as we head in the opposite direction, snaking through the quiet streets of Uxbridge, away from anything resembling normality, finally stopping when we reach the entrance of a graveyard shrouded in darkness. Rawani doesn't stop to ask how I might feel about heading into such an isolated arena with someone I barely know, and I do think twice about following him in, before curiosity gets the better of me. He heads past the preliminary gravestones, his sight and motion focused on the low-hanging branches ahead. He eventually stops at the final grave, but makes no effort to offer reverence, still staring at the overhanging wood and leaves.

'What do you want, Miss Hunter?'

Despite telling him time and again to call me Emma, he prefers the formality of titles.

I take a deep breath to compose myself. 'When were you going to tell me that Jack's investigation had ended?'

His shoulders tense. 'I was called into Commander

Fielding's office on Friday morning. It was a routine check-in to discuss operational targets and plans for the coming quarter, but as soon as I got there I knew something was off. The Deputy Assistant Commissioner was in the room too. Commander Fielding explained that she wanted to come by and congratulate me on reaching twenty-nine years of service, and to thank me for everything I had achieved in my distinguished career in the Metropolitan Police. She stayed and spoke for five minutes, finishing by saying Commander Fielding would struggle to fill my boots when I've retired. That's when I realised I'd been ambushed. She left the room, and he proceeded to tell me that it was time to start planning my retirement.'

I wouldn't have said Rawani was old enough to be considering retirement, but then I don't actually know how old he is. Whilst I would have placed him in his fifties, he could easily be older.

'It wasn't a request or suggestion. Commander Fielding has determined that I'm to be put out to pasture, and has already shortlisted half a dozen applicants to replace me. My rodeo is over.'

It's clear from his tone that this isn't a decision he is comfortable with, but there is resignation there too; he doesn't have the strength to fight against fate.

'I'm sorry to hear that,' I say genuinely, knowing Jack will be disappointed to lose his mentor. 'When's the big day?'

He sighs. 'Less than three weeks away now.'

'Oh, wow! I hadn't realised it would be so soon.'

'I had some holiday still to book, so Commander Fielding has suggested I tidy up any loose ends and then take what remains in the run-up to my departure.'

'I'm sure it will be a challenge to replace you. I bet your wife is happy with the news though?'

Rawani has a framed picture of his wife and two daughters on the desk in his office, but he's never spoken of them to me.

'Once I returned from Commander Fielding's office, I received a phone call from DCI Harry Dainton at the NCA. It was a courtesy call to advise me that Jack's investigation had borne little fruit, and the decision had been taken to wrap it up and redeploy resources to more crucial cases. He told me Jack hadn't reacted well to the news, and I was to ensure all Jack's notes on the investigation be handed over to Dainton's team.

That means Jack definitely knew the investigation had been closed when he phoned me on Saturday night, but he chose not to mention it.

Rawani spins and the reflection of the setting sun catches in the glaze of his eyes. 'I've been in this profession for too long to accept coincidence as a reasonable explanation for anything, Miss Hunter. My retirement and Jack being reassigned stinks, and the only logical deduction I can make is that somebody knows what we're trying to prove.'

He isn't saying it, but the glare he's giving me suggests he suspects me of letting something slip. 'I've told nobody about Tomlinson,' I say firmly, 'and I'm sure Jack wouldn't have said anything either. We made a pact in your office not to mention his name to anyone unless we had tangible evidence linking him to Arthur Turgood, Reverend Peter Saltzing, and the others in the ring.'

'That's what I thought you'd say, which is why I didn't want to speak to you at the station. If none of us spoke about the investigation, then they must have had some other way of hearing.'

A shiver runs the length of my spine, despite the relative warmth of the spring evening.

'You think your office has been bugged?'

He doesn't respond, his gaze wandering over the gravestones beyond me. 'Do you know why I like to come here?' he asks.

I turn to try and see what he's specifically looking at, before shrugging.

'It serves as a reminder that we're all on the same conveyor belt heading towards the same conclusion. No matter what walk of life we're from, our lives are fleeting, and no matter how we spend our days, and how much wealth and knowledge we accumulate, ultimately one day we will end up in a place like this. Nothing more than a plot and engraved piece of stone. It adds necessary context to troubled thoughts.'

I don't think I've ever heard him sound so defeated.

'I'm not giving up that easily,' I say more defiantly than I feel. 'This ring – these men who roam freely in the shadows – had something to do with my sister's disappearance, and I will not rest until I uncover every last one of them. I got Turgood with careful digging and pressure, and no amount of covering up and threats will stop me this time either.'

He is unmoved by my impassioned declaration. 'I wish you the best of luck, but you're going to have to continue alone. If and when Jack pulls out of his coma, he's been reassigned, and it wouldn't surprise me if he finds himself moved into a totally different area of the force and away from the cold case files he previously worked.'

I don't need to ask why he feels this way as I sense the decision has already been taken.

'That's fine,' I resolve. 'I started this thing alone, and I'm happy to conclude it that way too.' I turn to leave, but then I recall the second reason I sought out Rawani tonight. 'I could do with one final favour though. I'm looking for any information you can share about a missing child called Ruth Swaile.'

His eyes narrow. 'I can't be seen to be helping you on your quest.'

'She's nothing to do with Tomlinson, or at least I think she isn't. Can you just pull her file and let me see it? I think I might have found her, but I need background information on her, and there's nothing online.'

He studies my face as if trying to determine whether I'm telling the truth.

'I'll see what I can find. Is there anything else you can tell me about her?'

'Only that she went missing before 1988, and may or may not have dark orange hair. I'm sorry, that's all I have to go on.'

He looks like he's considering the request, but that may just be for show. I begin to move back the way we entered, but he isn't following, once again staring at the gravestones with the haunted look of a man who knows the dance is about to end.

Chapter Thirty-Six

NOW

Ealing, London

My nerves are still on edge as I make it back to Rachel's abandoned flat in Ealing. Don't ask me why I thought it was a good idea to come here, but with Rachel's phone switched off, and no hotel room booked for the night, I can't think where else she would go. My spare key gets me in through the communal entrance to the block of flats, but it's only when my second key won't turn in the lock of Rachel's door that I realise the lock has been changed and Sunday night's horror flashes back before my eyes. The burning smell that had been so pronounced inside the flat still hangs in the air in the corridor too.

I knock on the door, pressing my ear to the UPVC panel to listen for any movement within, but all I can hear is the gentle patter of a passing shower on the small pane of glass above the main entrance. They hadn't warned of rain, but given the warmth of the day, it doesn't surprise me that Mother Nature is easing the pressure and humidity.

'Rach, are you in there?' I call through the letterbox. 'It's Emma.'

I prise open the flap with my outstretched fingers but with the blinds drawn on the bay window, it's so dim inside that I can't make out anything. For all I know she's fast asleep in her room, but my instinct tells me she hasn't returned.

Of course, there's one person who will probably know whether Rachel has been past today, but asking her risks further discussions about her favourite writers, and whether or not I'm friends with them. Summoning my inner strength, I climb the stairs to Mrs Duvitski's flat and give three short, sharp knocks. The rattle of her fastening the security chain sounds her arrival, and the door slowly edges open.

'Oh, is you,' she says when our eyes meet.

She closes the door again and the chain rattles once more, before the door opens fully this time.

'Good evening, Mrs Duvitski,' I begin, adopting my warmest and least-threatening tone. 'I'm sorry to trouble you so late in the evening.'

'Is okay. I wasn't in bed yet.'

It's only just turned nine o'clock, but I wouldn't have judged if she had been tucked in for the night. I'd give anything to be in my pyjamas back in Weymouth right now.

'Good,' I acknowledge. 'I was just wondering whether you've seen or heard from Rachel Leeming today.'

She eyes me suspiciously, as if I've just asked her to betray her family. 'No. Haven't seen her.' It sounds as if she's clearing her throat every time she annunciates the 'h' sound.

'I noticed the lock has been changed on her—'

'Landlord order workman,' she cuts me off. 'He repair door and change lock.'

'That's good,' I smile, attempting to ward off her suspicion. 'But Rachel wasn't there when the door was repaired?'

'No. He leave new keys with me. I am to pass to Miss Leeming when she back.' The keys appear in her hand as if by magic, but she jangles them in case I missed their presence. 'You are going to see her soon?'

'Hopefully,' I reply, surprised by the lack of certainty in my own voice.

Mrs Duvitski thrusts her hand towards me, and I duck out of the way instinctively, before realising she's trying to give me the keychain. 'Is fine. You are her friend. I know this. Your responsibility now.'

I accept the keys, but she closes the door on me before I can offer any reassurance that I will ensure Rachel receives them. Heading back down the stairs, I'm not sure Rachel's landlord would be happy knowing Mrs Duvitski had so willingly handed over the keys to one of his flats, but at least I know I'm not a danger. The key is stiff in the lock and it takes some wiggling to get it to sit right, but the door does eventually open and the acrid burning pong hits me straight away. Holding my breath, I move through to the living room and do a quick recce to make sure nobody is inside the flat, and that no further damage has been caused. I'm relieved the sound of my racing heart is all that greets me.

The flat doesn't look any different to how we left it yesterday morning, and there's certainly no sign that Rachel has been back here today. I try her number again, but don't leave a message when prompted to do so. For all my inner assertions that Rachel is probably absolutely fine, I can't ignore the possibility that whoever is pulling strings to derail mine and Jack's investigation into Tomlinson's connections to the ring might wish harm on her.

I start at loud knocking at the door. There's no security chain I can rely on, nor a peephole for me to see who is there. Planting my foot just behind the door, I slowly open it, gasping with relief when I see the beady eyes and glasses of Mrs Duvitski.

'Key work okay then?' she says, without so much as a hello.

'Yes, thank you,' I reply, removing my foot, and opening the door wider.

She stands where she is, peering over my shoulder, as if expecting some kind of spectacle within.

'Was there anything else I can help with?' I ask, uncertain why she really came down here.

'You're writer, yes?'

Oh no, here we go.

'That's correct, Mrs Duvitski. As I explained the other night, I write non-fiction books.' I force a smile, hoping that will be the end of it. I'm not so fortunate.

'You want story to tell, you should write *my* life story.' She raises her eyebrows as she says this, hinting that – in her eyes at least – she has some story to tell.

'Oh yes?' I say, unable to think of a way out.

'My parents move to UK at end of second war. But my father was spy, and he return to Poland in 50s working for Soviet Union. When I was born, he defect to UK, and we live here ever since.'

She speaks so matter-of-factly that I don't doubt she's speaking the truth.

'Sounds fascinating,' I placate, 'but my books follow my

investigations, and so far have focused on missing children. That said, I'm sure there could be some interest in hearing some of your father's stories. I don't know any ghost writers personally, but—'

'I will not talk about my father's career,' she says, wrinkling her nose in derision. 'He was spy, but Moscow never forget.'

I'm not entirely sure what she expects me to do with this information, and it's one of those moments when I desperately wish Rachel or Jack was here to come to my rescue.

'As I said, Mrs Duvitski, I'm not a ghost writer or a biographer, so I'm not sure I can be of any use.'

I'm expecting her to make a hasty retreat, but she remains where she is. 'Do you know James Patterson? I am huge fan of his books.'

'I can't say I've ever met him, but I know he's a very popular crime fiction writer.'

'I think my life story could be told like that. Real page turner, I think.'

'Well, you could always try writing the story yourself. The first piece of advice always given to new authors is to write what you know, and who better to tell *your* story than you.'

Her brow furrows as she considers the suggestion. 'I wouldn't know where to start.'

'The beginning is as good a place as any.'

She stares at me glassy-eyed. 'Yes, I could do that. I write some pages about my life, and you read them and tell me if you want to write the story.'

I open my mouth to correct her, but she's already turned on her heel and is hurrying up the stairs. I'll just have to think of a way to let her down gently when she comes calling with pages. I'm about to close the door when the communal entrance bursts open and a drenched Rachel with panda-eyes sways into the hallway.

'Oh thank God,' I gasp, but have to hurry to catch her as she stumbles towards the new door.

The whisky on her breath stings my nose before she's even that close. Draping her arm over my shoulders, I manage her into the flat, and with the sofa-bed missing its stuffing, the only place I can think to put her is her bed. She collapses into a fit of giggles as she bounces slightly.

'I've been trying to call you all afternoon,' I admonish like a disappointed parent. 'Where have you been? What happened about the meeting with your editor?'

'Oh yeah, that,' she says, blinking rapidly as if the room is spinning and she's trying to find a focal point. 'So,' she slurs, 'they're making job cuts as part of a restructure, and moving lots of journalists into new areas. There's a big push on expanding digital distribution and advertising, but I'm not part of their plan.'

It was the news I'd been fearing, and judging by her drunken state, I'm guessing she's spent most of the afternoon squandering part of any redundancy package offered on drowning her sorrows.

'I'm sorry to hear that, Rach,' I say, dropping onto the mattress next to her. 'I wish you'd called me; I'd have come and kept you company.'

She looks over to me and presses a clammy hand against my cheek. 'That's because you're my best friend, and you love me. I mean, I love you. No, wait, I mean... What do I mean?'

I haven't seen drunk Rachel in years, and I don't know whether it's the stress of recent paranoia, or learning Zara's shocking secret, but I can't help but chuckle. I have nothing but sympathy for my best friend, but I also know there's nothing I can say or do tonight to ease her feelings of loss and disappointment.

'Have you spoken to Daniella yet?'

She shakes her head and pouts. 'I don't want to tell her until I find a new job.'

'Fair enough,' I sigh. 'I'm sure you'll have other journals begging you to join them.'

Her pout hardens into a frown. 'I told my editor where he could stick his job.' The wrinkles in her brow soften. 'Do you know, he had the nerve to say I might have kept my job if I hadn't spent so much time chasing around after you? Can you believe he said that? What an arse! I told him that you're one of the greatest investigators in the world, and that he'd be lucky to have you on his team.'

I'm not surprised to hear that even in her darkest hour, Rachel was still championing me. I need to replicate her effort.

'I reckon they'll regret letting you go, Rach. Once you start at a new paper or magazine, they'll see what a huge mistake they made and beg you to return.'

She gives up on the spinning room and closes her eyes.

'You know, if things get desperate,' I tease, 'you could always write Mrs Duvitski's life story. It's an international tale of espionage and Tupperware.'

I look over to see if she's laughing, but her slowly rising chest and gentle snore tell me she's fast asleep. Draping the blanket over her, I head back into the living room and open my laptop, loading up the page dedicated to Anna and searching for any new messages.

Chapter Thirty-Seven

THEN

Ruislip, London

She woke with a start, uncertain of her surroundings, her forehead soaked with sweat and her heart feeling as if it would erupt from the confines of her chest.

'You were screaming,' Tom commented, sitting up and rubbing his eyes with the ball of a fist. 'Bad dream again?'

She opened her mouth to speak, but it was as if the words were too terrified to peek out. There was terror, of that she had no doubt, but as the daylight shone through the thin curtains, and the items of furniture in the room became more discernible, she couldn't recall what the dream had been about.

'Should I get you a glass of water?' Tom tried again, his eyes now more alert, and adopting his usual knight-in-shining-armour routine.

'I'll be fine,' she manged to whisper in response. 'Go back to sleep.'

He didn't budge, watching her poke her legs from beneath

297

the duvet, hesitating before planting her feet on the carpet. She was too old to believe in monsters lurking under the bed, but she had believed it once, hadn't she? There'd been a reason she'd believed in it, but her fragile memory refused to connect the dots so soon after waking.

Reaching for her kimono from the hook on the back of the door, she pulled it around herself, closing the bedroom door as she left. She shouldn't have been surprised to find Angie sitting at the small island in the kitchen, a steaming mug of black coffee before her.

'Sorry, did the kettle wake you?' Angie asked absently.

'No, I'm just naturally an early riser these days.'

'You never used to be,' Angie scoffed, before thinking better of it. Her conversation with Emma had really put things in perspective for her, and she'd meant every word of the apology she'd offered last night. It was time to stop living in the past, and concentrate on the future.

'Tom not up yet?' she asked, in a less than subtle attempt to change the subject.

'He's usually up before me when he's working, so when he has a few days off, he likes to sleep in,' Zara replied, selecting a mug from the cupboard and locating the box of tea bags.

'Kettle's not long boiled,' Angie commented.

Zara pressed her hand against the side of the kettle, before filling her mug. 'Can I ask you something?' she asked, biting her lip subconsciously, her pulse once again quickening.

'So long as you're not just checking where I've hidden my will,' Angie chuckled awkwardly. 'Of course you can. Ask away.'

Zara pushed the tea bag around inside the mug, uncertain what voice was propelling her along, but without the strength to overcome it. 'What *was* I like before...? Before it all happened? I've never been able to properly distinguish memories from things I've read and photographs I've seen. To be honest, I struggle to remember much about life before *it*.'

Angie studied her daughter's face, trying to determine whether the question was genuine, or whether it was some kind of trap to catch whether last night's apology had been a lie.

'Sometimes it's better to let the past sleep. Especially when the future looks so bright and rosy for you. Don't think that sparkler on your hand hasn't caught my attention. When did Tom propose?'

Zara had almost forgotten she was wearing the ring; strange how it had become a part of her so quickly.

'Two nights ago,' Zara smiled, rotating the ring around her finger, her heart filling with love every time the diamond caught the increasing light from the kitchen window. 'He said he'd been carrying it around with him for weeks, waiting for the right moment, and then he just asked.'

Angie stood and quickly closed the space between them, embracing Zara. 'I'm so pleased for you, my darling. Tom is wonderful, and I can see from the way he looks at you that he's head over heels in love with you. I couldn't be happier.'

The hug had never felt so awkward and clumsy for Zara, but despite her best efforts, her shoulders refused to relax. 'Thank you,' she said, as the two women broke apart and Angie returned to the bar stool by her coffee mug.

'I take it you haven't set a date yet?' Angie asked.

'Oh no, not yet. I haven't really had time to think about any of that yet.'

'You know, I don't think I've ever heard you say what sort

of a wedding you'd like. I always assumed you just weren't interested in the institution, for which I blame myself and your father. We were hardly the best example, particularly after...' The word remained hanging between them. 'So are you thinking registry office, or church? In truth, I think you can get married almost anywhere these days. I read a story online last year about a couple who decided to tie the knot while skydiving out of a plane. The best man and maid of honour had to jump too, while the vicar tandem jumped, and shouted out the vows for them to repeat during the descent. Apparently the whole thing was filmed as evidence of the responses provided by the happy couple. And once they'd touched down, they signed the register and went for a good old knees-up.'

She smiled at the memory of the video clips she'd seen. 'Not that I want to give you any ideas,' Angie quickly corrected. 'I certainly have no intention of jumping out of an aeroplane at my age.'

Zara shook her head. 'Skydiving isn't on my bucket list either, but please don't mention it to Tom, as that's just the sort of thing he'd probably love. I'm sure he did a bungee jump the summer before he went to university. He's less active these days, but that doesn't mean the craving for adventure has left him.'

Angie took a sip from her drink. 'What would be *your* ideal scenario then?'

Zara discarded the tea bag and splashed in milk. 'I genuinely don't know. If you'd asked me about marriage a week ago, I'd have told you I have no interest in it. Yet, as soon as Tom said the words, I couldn't think of anything I wanted more than to be his wife and take his name.'

'You don't have to take your husband's name; not these days. You could remain an Edwards forever if you chose to.'

Zara looked away, the suggestion too painful to confront head on. 'Did we ever talk about weddings *before*, you know? It's what little girls are supposed to do, isn't it? Plan their weddings – what they'll wear, who they'll invite, and how enormous the cake will be – with their mothers. Did I ever...?'

Angie considered the question and Zara's motivation for asking it again, but deciding the query was genuine, she opted to answer. 'You had a scrap book for a time. I remember it was after we'd been invited to my cousin's wedding. It was held in a hotel not far from Poole. Do you remember it? We had to get up so early. They'd asked you to be a flower girl, but you must have been... ooh, I don't know, five or six maybe? It was such a hot day, and your dad and I decided it would be better for us all to travel down there in shorts and T-shirts, and change when we arrived at the hotel. But traffic was awful with everyone heading to the coast, and we ended up having to pull into the hard shoulder on some A-road, and change in the car. We made it to the ceremony with five minutes to spare, and it was a lovely day. There was a swimming pool at the hotel which you and other younger guests splashed about in after the food. On the drive back home that night you were telling us all about the sort of wedding you'd have when you were older. I think your dad went white trying to calculate how much it would all cost him.' She chuckled. 'The next day, which was a Sunday, you started going through my old glossy magazines, and trying to find pictures of dresses that you would wear, but also what your guests would wear. God knows whatever happened to that scrap book. I suppose it could still be in the loft somewhere. I don't know.'

Zara was grateful Angie hadn't asked how much of the story she remembered, because she wouldn't have been able to lie without bursting into tears.

'Is there anything you'd like to do today?' Zara asked instead, no longer wishing to verify any more of her missed history.

'I'd really like it if you and I could maybe go into Central London? A girls' day out. We could hit Oxford Street first, maybe stop for a spot of lunch or afternoon tea, and then move on to Harrods? What do you think? Would Tom mind us ditching him?'

Zara wasn't sure she wanted to ditch Tom, but the look of desperation in Angie's eyes was enough to have her agreeing straight away. 'I'm sure Tom will be relieved to get on with some work. He was only commenting last night that his inbox is fit to burst. I'll take him up a cup of tea, and see what he thinks.'

'We could maybe have a look at some wedding dresses too,' Angie said, raising her eyebrows excitedly. 'I'd let you use my old one, but I'm pretty sure it's been eaten by moths. Every bride should have the dress of their dreams anyway, and if it's okay with you, I'd like to buy you your wedding dress. My mother bought mine for me, so it kind of feels like a tradition we should continue, mother to daughter.'

Zara hurried from the room, with the tea in hand, before the sting behind her eyes materialised into inevitable tears. Tom hadn't returned to sleep yet, and was staring at his phone as she entered the room.

'Are you all right?' he asked.

'Fine,' she lied, stretching her lips into a smile. 'I made you tea.'

'Thanks,' he said, stifling a yawn. 'Have you decided when you're going to tell Angie about... you know, what we discussed with Emma?'

Zara gently shook her head. 'Not yet.'

He caught her wrist as she lowered the mug of tea to his nightstand. 'You don't have to say anything to her if you don't want to. After what she said last night, maybe it would just be better not to tell her. You and I know the truth, and there's no reason we can't keep digging without Angie realising. Emma seemed really keen to help, and maybe hypnotic regression could help stir other memories that will help connect the dots. All a DNA test will tell you is what you already know deep down. In my head, I'm not sure it's worth it, but it's your decision, and I'll support you either way.'

Zara leaned in and kissed him on the lips. 'She wants us to have a girls' day out in the West End today. Do you mind?'

She noticed the look of relief on his face, despite his efforts to cover it. 'Only if you're sure you don't want me there.'

'I won't say anything to her without you there, I promise. To be honest, I don't think I would be able to say anything without you at my side anyway. She mentioned wedding dress shopping.'

Tom's smile grew wider. 'Yeah, I suppose we will have to talk about setting a date and all that at some point. You two go and have a good day out, and maybe try to put all this behind you. I can't remember the last time I saw you not looking nervous or stressed. A day out with Angie could be just the distraction you need.'

'What will you do?'

'Log into work remotely and catch up on everything I've missed so far this week. I'll be fine.'

She excused herself with the intention of going for a shower, but paused as she reached the open door of the guest room. It smelled of Angie's perfume, a scent that had somehow always managed to relax Zara. Angie had left the duvet in a scrunched-up heap on the end of the bed, so Zara entered and straightened it, thinking it was the least she could do for her guest. But as she straightened the pillows, something caught her attention, and without thinking twice, she reached out and picked it up, holding it to the light. A single hair with the follicle intact. Zara dropped it into the pocket of her kimono and headed to the bathroom, wondering whether it would be enough for Emma's lab friends to perform the test.

Chapter Thirty-Eight

NOW

Park Lane, London

I've stayed in hotels in Central London before, but never as fancy as the one I find myself standing outside of now. The uniformed men at the door are old enough to be my father, but wear the warmest smiles as they greet guests and doff their caps at me as I pass as if I'm royalty. Once through the gilded swivel doors, I find myself in the most luxurious of lobbies. The carpet is bouncy, suggesting it's either new, or is treated with regular tender, loving care. There are more uniformed staff inside, each making sure to smile and greet me as I wander through, uncertain where I'm going or where I will find the mystery caller who had me out of bed so early in the morning.

'Can I help you, madam?' the model-like woman behind the check-in desk asks, as I approach.

'I'm looking for the hotel restaurant,' I admit, slightly

embarrassed that I haven't seen so much as a sign to its location.

'Do you mean The Armoury or Sports Bar?' she asks without missing a beat.

I honestly don't know, I don't admit. The only information I was given was the hotel's name and a prompt arrival time. She must sense I'm flummoxed, as her cheekbones rise into an even broader smile.

'Are you here to meet somebody?' she asks.

'Yes,' I nod eagerly.

'If you tell me your name, as well as the name of the guest you're meeting, I'll check and see if he *or she* has listed you as visiting.'

'Sure. My name is Emma Hunter,' I begin, relieved for once to meet someone with no clue as to my identity, 'and I'm here to meet with Miss Aurélie Lebrun.' I puff out my cheeks in satisfaction.

The woman before me scans her eyes against the screen in front of her. 'Ah yes, Miss Lebrun is taking breakfast in The Armoury,' she replies. 'She is at table fourteen. If you follow the carpet to the bank of lifts at the back of the hotel,' she indicates with her hand, 'and go up to floor one, the maître d' will be able to take you straight to her.'

I follow the line of her arm to the signposted lifts. 'Thank you.'

'You're very welcome, Miss Hunter. Don't hesitate to ask if we can be of any more service.'

I move away and hear an almost identical greeting delivered to the man who was waiting behind me in the queue. I've no idea how much a night at this venue must cost, but I don't doubt it's a small fortune. I assume Aurélie's parents are footing the bill.

This morning's phone call caught me off-guard, and when I heard Aurélie's timid tones asking me to meet with her, I was half-tempted to refuse. After how much she and her legal team messed me about on Saturday night, I'd be happy never to hear from either again. But she sounded frightened, and told me it would be a private meeting between the two of us, and was in my best interests. How could I refuse?

The lift carriage up to the first floor also resembles something I'd expect to find in a palace or theme park, and if I didn't know better, I'd say the panels were embossed with real gold. Exiting the lift, I see that the entire floor has been reserved for the two dining areas, with the Sports Bar to my right – resembling the type of 80s-themed establishment so popular with American tourists – and the more reserved and traditional Armoury to my left. Sure enough, the maître d' appears ready for me as I approach, and as soon as I offer my name, his eyes brighten and he leads me through the maze of tables to where Aurélie is sat waiting near the back. I accept his offer of coffee, as he returns to his station at the front of the restaurant. A waiter appears a moment later with a fresh pot of coffee, a jug of cream, and a small bowl of various sugar sachets.

'Thank you for coming,' Aurélie begins, tucking a segment of marmalade-covered toast into her mouth. 'I wasn't sure you'd actually turn up.'

'You asked me to come, and I wouldn't be so rude,' I admit.

When we first met, Aurélie had just emerged from a life trapped beneath the ground in Poole, claiming to have no understanding of the English language. Not long after she was released from the hospital into the care of her parents, her grasp of the language quickly improved, as did the truth about her relationship with the man who'd kept her trapped for so many years. If I'm ever allowed to publish the manuscript *Trafficked* you'll be able to read all about it.

'How have you been?' she asks when she's finished the toast and I've poured a generous volume of coffee into my cup.

'I'm keeping well, thank you,' I lie. 'And how are you?'

To be honest, she looks in better health than when we first met last year. Her hair has grown and has been styled into something more modern, with highlights added. The skin beneath her eyes now radiates good health, and the carefully applied lip gloss shimmers beneath the restaurant lighting. If you met her for the first time today you wouldn't be able to tell her apart from the other overnight stays in London for business meetings.

'I am very well, thank you,' she says, offering the remaining triangle of toast in my direction.

I gently shake my head, having scoffed a croissant on the tube journey over. Rachel was still snoring when I left, so I poured her a glass of water and hastily scribbled a note saying I would return before lunch. I also placed a bucket at her side of the bed just in case.

'What did you want to speak to me about?' I ask, cutting to the chase.

She looks over to the tables closest to us, but it's clear that the couple on one side and the man with his head buried in the *Financial Times* on the other have no interest in what we're discussing.

'I want to apologise for the other night. My father... he

wants to protect me, and it was his idea to hire the lawyers to protect my interests.'

This I can easily believe. It was Remy Lebrun who originally invited me to Poole to meet with his daughter, and it was his insistence that I write *her* story in my words. Which is what I did, although I'm not sure any of us were prepared for the truth she gave. I actually kept a lot of what she told me out of the final manuscript that was delivered to my publishers – a watered-down version that I thought would be agreeable to all parties. At least, that's what I thought prior to Saturday night's ambush.

'I didn't write anything that wasn't true,' I reply, more defensively than I intended.

'I know,' she says, dabbing the crumbs from her lips with a napkin. 'I have told my parents everything that I told you, but they don't like to hear the truth.'

Again, I don't doubt this. Remy insisted I hand over all the MP3 recordings of mine and Aurélie's interviews. I kept copies, of course, but he wanted to hear everything that was discussed. It wouldn't surprise me if the lawyers he hired have heard them too.

'I don't share my father's view,' she tells me now. 'I wanted to say something to you at the office on Saturday, but I wasn't sure you would believe me. That is why I have returned to London now to see you. I want you to believe that I am sorry for lying to you about your sister, Anna. As far as I know I never met her, but there were girls there who – like me – wanted to help their benefactors. It may sound strange to you, Emma, but when you are under their control… their spell, you would be willing to do almost anything they commanded. If Jasper told me to jump, I would.'

Jasper Derwent – Aurélie's captor – died shortly after the two of them tried to abscond with their daughter. His passing had seemed to unlock his hold over Aurélie – or at least partially so. I'm not convinced she's told me everything about her time under his manipulation, but I've heard enough to know she was compliant in helping people like Derwent to attract and snatch other children.

'Are you going to allow me to publish my book?' I ask now.

She tries to smile, but I can see she is struggling, and it reminds me that she is as much a victim in all of this as she is complicit. The tension disappears in an instant.

'I want to help you, Aurélie,' I say. 'Help me to stop the men who snatched you from that beach in Worthing; the men who sold you at an auction to Jasper Derwent; the men who physically and psychologically scarred you.'

'I want to help,' she admits, pressing the napkin to her moistening cheeks. 'I have told my father that I don't want his lawyers involved. He is not happy but if I have to fight him for you, I will. I am here today to say the same thing to your publisher's legal team.'

It is music to my ears, but I don't feel an urge to celebrate, given the gravity of the subject matter. 'Thank you, Aurélie. I think the story shows that it wasn't your fault, what happened to you. I think people need to understand that you had no control over what happened to you during that time.'

'There is more I have not told you,' she says, checking the diners closest to us again. 'Since we spoke before, I have been having dreams – memories – of my time before. I lived in that hole, but there were times we left too. I have remembered a place – a building – where I was taken in the early days. I don't know the address, but I remember it was a tall building, maybe four or five storeys high. There was a large statue of a bronze lion outside. I remember this because I wanted to climb on and to ride it away.' She grimaces at the admission. 'Inside the building there were important people, I think. I remember Jasper acted differently around them. He was... what's the word? *Submissive*. They were in charge, I think. They wanted to use me to help them, but Jasper, he didn't want me involved. I suppose he didn't win because I then remember being taken to a different place – a party of some sort – and being asked to dance for some older men... Here the memory... it starts to fade. I think we could find that building with the lion though. If we looked together?'

There is a pleading in her eyes that I can't say no to. 'Do you remember anything else that might help us determine where it was?'

'I want to say it was in London somewhere, but I am not certain.' She closes her eyes and a tear escapes. 'I see green leaves when I remember the lion, so I don't know if there was a garden or maybe a park nearby. And there is a strong smell of... you know, um, a fish smell, like maybe we were near the sea, but not.' She opens her eyes again. 'I'm sorry, I wish there was more.'

It isn't a lot to go on, but I unlock my phone and connect to the hotel's Wi-Fi network and begin searching for local buildings with large bronze statues. I show Aurélie some examples of the images I find, but she shakes her head at each one.

'Was there anybody else in the building you can describe? You said there were other men that Jasper seemed in awe of; can you tell me who they were, or what they looked like?'

She shakes her head. 'I'm sorry, but they were in a room,

and they closed the door on me. There was a boy there – older than me, quite tall. I remember now, he took me by the hand and told me we couldn't listen to the grown-ups' meeting. He was the one who led me outside, and told me the lion was called... Bartholomew.' She smiles momentarily as the scene plays out behind her eyes. 'I told him it was a silly name for a lion.' Her eyes widen now. 'I remember there were railings – a metal fence – the leaves were behind that, across a small road. There were other tall buildings all around us. In fact, I think they were in a square surrounding us. They all looked the same, apart from the lion beside us. Does that help?'

To a tourist like me, the description doesn't automatically narrow down the possibility of an address, but I have seen residential areas of central London that do match that description. Maybe someone with a broader understanding of the local geography would enable us to focus on exactly where she might be referring to.

'Would you come and meet someone with me?' I ask, with a slug of my coffee for renewed energy.

'Of course, who do you want me to meet?'

'He's a senior police officer, and the only person I trust to help. Grab your coat.'

Chapter Thirty-Nine

NOW

Rayners Lane, London

A call to Uxbridge Police Station, and a quick chat with PC Denier, reveals that DCS Rawani isn't due in the office today. She won't give me his home address, but reluctantly agrees to call him and ask him to message me urgently.

He does eventually, sending me the address of an American-style diner that's walking distance from his home. He is sitting in a booth when we arrive – the only customer so far – and I've never seen a man look so out of place. His turban is as tight and pressed as ever, and even though it's his day off, he's wearing a navy blazer and tie. The young servers behind the counter in bright red and yellow polo shirts look as though they're trying to guess exactly who he is and why he's chosen their place of business to mourn.

It's certainly an odd choice of location, given his resistance to meat, and the fact that there doesn't appear to be anything vegetarian on the menu. Maybe that's why he chose here: if you were trying to predict where he would arrange a clandestine rendezvous, this would probably be your last choice.

'How's the milkshake?' I ask, as I slide in across the table from him.

He lifts the paper cup and twirls the contents with the paper straw before lowering it again. 'I've had better.'

He looks uncertain as Aurélie slips into the booth beside me. There's the briefest moment of recognition, but it's gone in an instant.

'This is Aurélie Lebrun,' I feel compelled to quickly explain. 'She was abducted from Worthing as a child and held by associates of the ring for eighteen years.'

He considers her, before nodding for me to continue.

'Aurélie has started to have flashbacks to her time before captivity, and I think we can use her memories to uncover more about the ringleaders.' I turn to her, not wishing to exclude her from proceedings, and hoping her version of recent recollections will have him as excited as I am.

'It is true,' she says. 'I remember being at a building with many powerful men, somewhere in Central London, I think. I remember this enormous statue of a lion.'

'And the enclosed garden,' I encourage, 'don't forget about the enclosed garden.'

She nods along. 'I remember that Jasper – my captor – he was scared of these men, and when they demanded I help he made sure I did.'

I don't want to get bogged down with the unnatural relationship between Jasper Derwent and Aurélie, and steer the conversation back to how it can help us now. 'I reckon this building with the lion could be some kind of headquarters for operations, and if we can find it, it might bring us a step closer to whomever is behind it.'

'Where is this building?' he asks.

'We don't know, but the way Aurélie described it reminded me of those enclosed gardens and residential streets that litter Central London. Tall townhouses with black wrought-iron gates. The large lion statue must be fairly unique, so I was thinking you could use the city's network of CCTV cameras to find and rule out similar properties to narrow down the search.'

He scoffs at this suggestion. 'On what grounds? I can't make that kind of request on a whim, and to explain the truth will only throw more light on what you were trying to investigate.'

'Make up a story,' I suggest. 'You could say you're looking for... I don't know, some kind of drugs operation or something. It doesn't matter. If we can find the property, we can find out who owns the building, what its intended purpose was, and whether it's still in use.'

Rawani looks nonplussed by what he's heard. 'I told you last night: the investigation is over.'

'Only if we let them win,' I counter. 'Who's to say we don't just go back to how things were before Jack was seconded to the NCA? Me and him – with your help – reviewing missing child cold case files and finding other victims we can tie to them. Something so big can't have covered its tracks that well.'

He takes a long slurp of his milkshake until I finish speaking. 'No.'

I frown. 'What do you mean, no?'

'The investigation is over. Jack has been reassigned, and I...
I will be retiring. It's over, Miss Hunter.'

Even I start as my hand slams down on the table. 'You can't
let them win, Jagtar. *This* is precisely what they want. They
know we're onto them and they're doing everything they can
to shut us down: intimidation, threats, violence in Jack's case.
You know, they've even managed to get my best friend Rachel
released by her newspaper, and threatened the AH Foundation
with an audit from the Charity Commission. They're scared,
but that shouldn't frighten us off; we need to move in for the
kill and finally expose them.'

My impassioned plea is falling on deaf ears. 'I'm sorry, but
it's too late for that. We have no *real* evidence that such a ring
exists, only hearsay and supposition. It isn't enough. When
starting a criminal investigation the burden is on the police to
prove that a crime has been committed. We're not even close to
that stage.'

I can't believe he's given up the fight. When I first met him
– a stern man who still saw the world as black and white,
rather than as multiple shades of grey – I never would have
thought he'd cave so easily.

'These men *do* exist,' Aurélie speaks up. 'I witnessed
meetings and parties hosted by such people. I will make a
formal statement.'

Rawani's stare turns to her, but his face remains
emotionless. 'And what will you say, Mademoiselle Lebrun?
Can you name names? Can you specifically testify that a
named individual brought harm to another named individual?
If so, who and who?'

I'd love it if she could answer the question and put him on
the back foot, but she remains quiet.

'Saying an unidentified group is responsible for abducting, trafficking, and abusing a group of unnamed children is nothing more than anecdotal—'

'We have the names of victims,' I interrupt. 'Jemima Hooper, Cormack Fitzpatrick, Faye McKenna, Aurélie Lebrun, Zara Edwards, and…' I take a deep breath, 'Anna Hunter.'

He narrows his eyes but doesn't speak.

'All these children have been identified on the videos retrieved from Arthur Turgood's hard drive, save for Zara and Aurélie, but we know from their witness accounts that their abductions and captivity were undertaken by more than one person. It is my belief that we've barely scratched the surface, but we've managed to find all these children in under two years. This isn't the end, Jagtar. This is just the beginning.'

'Zara Edwards,' he says. 'I don't recognise that name.'

'She was the Brighton Rock Girl, who was abducted in the mid-80s and supposedly recovered nearly two years later.'

His frown deepens. 'And what makes you think she was taken by the same people?'

I lean closer and lower my voice. 'Because I have it on good authority that the girl who came back was *not* Zara Edwards.'

He waits for me to expand further, but I'm not prepared to go into the specifics with him if he's turned his back on us.

'You have time left to help us,' I say instead. 'Even if they're forcing you out, you'll still be in role for a few months, right?'

'Weeks, rather than months,' he responds sourly as if doling out a death sentence.

'Even so, there's a lot we could do in a few weeks. When I came to you after Jack and I found Cassie Hilliard, you believed me when I said that her grandfather had been

317

involved, and you told me you wished you had a way to prove it. Do you remember?'

He doesn't argue.

'*Help* me to find these monsters, Jagtar. Please?'

He slides the paper cup to the edge of the table, discarded. 'I'm sorry, Miss Hunter, but there is nothing further I can do for you. It is with regret that our professional relationship has to end in such a disappointing manner, but there's nothing more I can do. For your own safety, I'd think long and hard about whether or not pursuing your inquiry is worth it.'

He shuffles out of the booth, straightening his suit jacket and tie. 'My wife is adamant she wants to organise a small retirement party for me, and I would be honoured if you would attend as well. It won't be anything too wild, just a few former colleagues at a local Bangladeshi restaurant. If it's okay with you, I'll pass on your email address?'

As disappointed as I am with his decision, I appreciate the thought, and nod. 'I will see you then.'

He moves away from the table, and it's only then that I notice he has left a brown paper envelope on the table. I reach for it and call after him.

'Jagtar, aren't you forgetting something?'

He pauses and considers us both, before shaking his head. 'Best of luck with your endeavours, Miss Hunter.'

He turns and leaves the restaurant, and I feel duty-bound to offer Aurélie some kind of apology and reassurance. 'We don't need him,' I say. 'We can use Google Maps Streetview to look at different roads, or failing that, get hold of a map and stalk the streets ourselves. It won't be as quick, but with a bit of luck, we'll find it.'

My eyes fall back on the brown envelope that Rawani left

behind, and curiosity gets the better of me. The envelope isn't sealed, and as I lift the flap, I find several printed pages inside. Sliding them out, I spread the pages across the table, quickly realising what I'm looking at.

I could kiss the man!

'What is all this?' Aurélie asks, confused.

'It's background on a girl named Ruth Swaile,' I tell her. 'It's another step towards the truth.'

Chapter Forty

THEN

Ruislip, London

Emerging from the shower, Zara hurried to her bedroom. She closed the door, grateful to hear the hum of Tom and Angie's voices in the kitchen. Moving quickly to her dressing table, she opened each of the three drawers and shuffled items around, searching for anything she could use to protect the hair she had recovered from the spare room.

Carefully extracting the hair from the pocket of her kimono, she rested it on the top of the dresser and studied it in greater detail. Would it be enough for scientists to perform the necessary test? These days she was pretty sure they would have preferred a mouth swab; at least that seemed to be how they did it in the forensic shows on the television. To ask Angie for a mouth swab would give away her intentions before she was ready. At least this way, she would have certainty when crossing that bridge.

But in truth she wasn't sure if she wanted to know for

certain. It was one thing to prove she wasn't the Zara Edwards that Angie had brought into the world, but it still didn't narrow down who she really was. The name Ruth was little to go on, and even as she played the name around in her head, she wasn't sure it was actually ringing the bells she'd believed she'd heard yesterday. It was definitely a familiar name, but as she said the word out loud, it didn't feel as though it was calling to her in the same way that Zara did. Maybe it was simply a case of her mind not wanting to remember the past.

Tom's voice grew louder as he approached, and she quickly hunted for something to keep the hair safe, but finding nothing suitable, she pulled a tissue from the box on the corner of the dresser and rested it over the hair so that Tom wouldn't see it. He entered the room a moment later, his hair skewed to one side as it appeared to be most mornings. Without his top on, she could see where a few pounds had now taken a firm hold around his waist – not that she minded. It was a sign of contentment on his part, and gave reassurance that he wasn't going out of his way to try and impress anyone else. Not that he wasn't still in pretty good shape for a man of his age. The grey and white hairs that had broken out on his chest had yet to fully take control of the hairs on top of his head, but his hairline had receded more in the last couple of years. She wouldn't swap him for another though.

'You all right?' he asked, catching her watching him in the reflection of the large mirror on the dresser.

She spun around on the stool and moved towards him with a playful smile, not in keeping with the weight of thoughts on her mind. 'I was just admiring my handsome fiancé,' she said, running a pointy finger across his shoulders and down his back, giggling as he writhed with the satisfaction.

'Stop it, your mum's just down the hall,' he patiently warned, though she sensed he wouldn't have been able to stop himself if she were to slip off her kimono.

'Spoilsport,' she teased, continuing around to her side of the bed before opening the wardrobe and picking her outfit for the day.

'I'm going to hit the shower,' he advised, coming across and kissing her passionately. 'But we'll continue this conversation later. Hey, see if you can't get your mum a bit tipsy this afternoon, and then she might have an early night.' He waggled his eyebrows suggestively, and she nodded in agreement, watching him leave, before rushing back to her dresser and locating an envelope from amongst Tom's things. Not perfect, but it would have to do.

An hour later, and with Tom now in his small office, talking on the phone, Zara opened the front door for Angie, and the two of them hustled out. Both stopped short when they saw Emma half-walking, half-running towards them, clutching a large brown-coloured envelope. She seemed equally surprised to find the two of them together.

'Emma, we weren't supposed to be catching up today were we?' Zara asked, suddenly worried that she'd forgotten an engagement.

Emma stopped as she reached the two of them, momentarily out of breath. 'No, and I'm sorry if you're on your way out, but I have something to share with you.' She tilted the envelope indicatively.

'Mum came down to visit last night,' Zara said to explain Angie's presence.

'It's nice to see you again, Angie,' Emma commented, 'and it's good to see you two together.'

An awkward silence descended on the three of them as they all considered what each knew about the other.

'We were just on our way out to Central London,' Zara said, changing the subject. 'Can whatever you need to share wait?'

'Not exactly,' Emma replied, looking down at the envelope. 'Perhaps it would be better if we talked inside. It's helpful that you're here to hear what I have to say, Angie.'

Zara's eyes widened as she realised that Emma might believe they'd already had the conversation about Zara's true identity, and panic set in.

'Actually, no,' she stammered. 'It *will* have to wait, I'm afraid. I promised Mum a day out, and that's what we're going to have.' She emphasised the word *Mum* in an effort to subtly tell Emma that Angie was none the wiser, but it didn't seem to have worked.

'This really is important news,' Emma continued. 'It has to do with what happened to you thirty-five years ago.'

'Oh well, if it's important, we can always postpone our plans,' Angie offered, turning and smiling apologetically at Zara.

'No, Mum, you were looking forward to going out today. I'm sure whatever Emma has to say can wait *until after you've returned to Brighton*.' The gritted teeth were a veiled message to Emma, who only now seemed to realise the precarious situation she found herself in.

'Oh, I see. Well, Zara, do you think I might talk to you very quickly? It will only take five or ten minutes, and then the two of you can be on your way.'

Tom must have heard all the chatter as he appeared at the front door, a confused look hanging from his face.

'Emma's come to talk to me about that thing,' she said. 'Do you think you could take Mum into town for a cup of coffee and a slice of cake, and I'll catch up with you after?'

He began to open his mouth to protest, but resisted as Zara fired him a hard glare.

'Sure. I'll take her to Giuseppe's and see you there in, what, ten, twenty minutes?'

Zara nodded and caught the door from him as he grabbed a hoodie and escorted Angie up the driveway as the two younger women dived into the house.

'She doesn't know,' Zara whispered quickly. 'She was here when we got back last night, and I wanted to tell her, but then I couldn't, and I just—'

'It's okay, Zara, I won't say anything to Angie until you're ready, but I think it's really important you see what I've found.'

Zara showed her through to the conservatory at the back of the house, as if putting even more distance between herself and Angie would make the conversation easier.

Emma removed her jacket and sat in one of the wicker chairs, as Zara followed suit, her eyes never leaving the envelope.

'This is a file I managed to get hold of from a police officer friend of mine. It is detail on a child called Ruth Swaile who went missing from Limerick in 1983, aged six, which would make her forty-four now, as you will be in June. I've had a look through the file, and whilst there are no guarantees, I'd argue there's a strong possibility that the person described here could in fact... *could* be you. I must emphasise that I'm basing this purely on the image that came with the file that the Garda used when searching for her.' Emma paused and extracted a number of pages from the envelope, flipping through them until she found what she was looking for. Handing the photograph over, the breath caught in Zara's throat.

'The red hair, the soft-set nose, and the small smattering of freckles are all attributes Ruth shared with Zara Edwards.'

Zara's hands were suddenly clammy as she held onto the image, studying the pretty face of the child with a gap in her upper teeth as she smiled awkwardly for the photograph in a green-coloured cardigan emblazoned with a school crest of some sort.

Emma unlocked her phone, located the image of the Brighton Rock Girl and lined it up with the image Zara was grasping. 'The two girls could be sisters,' she commented. 'Or at least first cousins. Given the two-year age gap, it would be easy to mistakenly assume one grew into the other.'

Zara looked from one image to the other, but neither felt familiar. 'What can you tell me about Ruth's life?'

Emma shuffled back into her chair and skimmed through the pages on her lap. 'I only know what I've read in this file, and I couldn't find anything useful online. I can only assume that if Ruth's disappearance was reported to the press in Limerick in 1983, those pages are in some kind of offline archive. Ruth's parents – Connor and Margaret – were known to the Garda, both having spent a lot of time in and out of prison from a young age. The details in the file are scarce but there are references to drug use, violence, and aggravated burglary. There's also a report from social services about Ruth and her younger brother Joseph.'

Zara's tear-streaked eyes snapped up to Emma's face. 'I have a brother?'

'Ruth had a brother called Joseph, well *has* a brother called Joseph from what I've managed to find. He lives in Bristol and runs his own software company. Connor and Margaret are both deceased, I'm afraid to tell you.'

A tear escaped, but Zara made no effort to wipe it away. 'When?'

'As I say, things are a bit sketchy, and I only just started to look in the taxi ride over, having received the file this morning. Connor Swaile was arrested and charged with the murder of Margaret two years after Ruth's disappearance. Based on what I read in the file, the lead detectives suspected both parents of killing Ruth and then covering it up. Her blood was found in the council house where the family were living at the time, as well as an unexplained blood stain on one of the car mats in the back of their car. It wasn't enough to charge either parent, but the case has remained unsolved. Connor died in prison, as a result of a fight during a riot in the late 80s. Given that the police assumed Ruth had died in 1983, it isn't a huge leap to understand why nobody thought to question the similarities to Zara when you were discovered in 1988.'

Zara stared back at both images again, and couldn't doubt the facial similarities between the girls. Was it possible that she'd had a childhood in and out of social care in southern Ireland prior to being discovered in Callum Gerrard's house? She couldn't recollect any such life, but equally she couldn't rule it out.

'What happens next?' Zara asked, handing the picture and phone back. 'Where do we go from here?'

Emma returned the pages to the file. 'Well, that's kind of up to you. These days there are ways and means of determining such things scientifically, and as I said to you yesterday, a sample of Angie's DNA and your own could be compared. If there's no match, then the next step would be to reach out to Joseph Swaile and see whether he'd be willing to offer one for comparison.'

Ruth stretched the collar of her top, attempting to fan her suddenly hot neck, even though it felt as though the blood had drained from her body. She remembered the last time she'd felt such a contradiction, and quickly excused herself, hurrying to the bathroom.

Emma remained where she was, going over the file again, looking for any clue to confirm or dispute the theory.

'Here,' Zara said, thrusting a small paper envelope towards her, five minutes later. 'It's a hair from Angie. I'll give you one of mine too. How quickly can you get them checked?'

Emma stood, and accepted the envelope. 'I'll see what I can do. Meanwhile, if it's okay with you, I think we should go and see Joseph Swaile. Maybe he can shed some more light on Ruth.'

Chapter Forty-One

NOW

Ruislip, London

Zara looked shell-shocked as I left her home in Ruislip and made my way into the town centre to find somewhere I could get my head down and with a decent Wi-Fi signal. Two caramel lattes later, and with little more light I can shed on the background of Ruth Swaile, I'm just about done with London. My head is clouded, and I am certain that it's the lack of Weymouth's fresh and salty air in my system that has me so adrift. I don't think I've spent so few days at home since moving to university, but even then I'd visit Mum at least once every other weekend to check on her.

Pam Ratchett called last night and said the doctors are happy for Mum to be released back into the home's care, and I can't tell you what a relief it is; at least that's one less trouble for me to keep up in the air with all the other balls I'm currently juggling. The sooner I can get back home to her the better.

I emailed Joseph Swaile, introduced myself, and advised him that I'm doing background research on a potential new project and want to meet him to discuss his missing sister. He phoned me back within an hour, and has reluctantly agreed to meet me at his home in Clifton tomorrow. I've booked train tickets for Zara and me, though I have my doubts that she'll agree to come. I'd thought she would have been thrilled by the prospect of a long-lost brother, but she showed little excitement. Maybe she just needs to sleep on it; I only hope my news hasn't spoiled the day Angie had planned with her. Despite the potential repercussions of the DNA test results, I fear Zara is going to need Angie a lot more than she realises.

I have spoken to the lab, and have an appointment to drop the two samples in this afternoon. They have promised to turn them around as quickly as they can – for once I was only too happy to play on the infamy that comes with my name. One way or another, tomorrow is going to be a huge day in the life of Zara Edwards. I've promised myself that I will stay in London only as long as it takes for Zara to come to terms with the results, and then I'll be heading home. Butterflies are already fluttering in my gut at the thought of fish and chips from the little place on the corner.

I'm just shutting down my laptop when my phone catches my attention. Expecting it to be Rachel, I'm surprised when the number on the screen is withheld. I don't tend to answer anonymous callers, preferring to listen to a voice message, but I make an exception and put the phone to my ear.

'Emma Hunter,' I say cheerfully, running my finger around the rim of the coffee glass and savouring the last of the sweet froth.

'Miss Hunter? My name is Deidre and I'm one of the senior

nurses at the ICU at Hillingdon Hospital. I'm phoning with regards to a Jack Serrovitz?'

'It's Serro-vich,' I correct subconsciously, before my chest tightens, and a cold shadow creeps over my arms.

'Yes, well, Mr Serrovitz has you listed as his next of kin—'

'What?' I can't keep the shock out of my voice. I had no clue that Jack had listed my name and number on his records, nor when he would have done it. We're friends, sure, but wouldn't he have listed Mila's mum, or a relative?

The feeling of dread spreads from my arms to my shoulders, thinking of only one reason a hospital would contact the next of kin of a critically ill patient.

Oh God, no. Say it isn't so!

'What's happened? Is he...?' But I don't have the strength to finish the thought.

'Oh, no, no, don't panic, he's fine. He's awake. That's why I'm calling. He asked me to phone you and ask you to come in and see him.'

I don't wait for her to finish. I shove my laptop into my satchel and race from the café without looking back.

———————

The taxi takes the longest twenty minutes I've ever experienced to reach the hospital, and I can't get out quickly enough, hurrying up the small incline and in through the main entrance, past the robed and probed sucking on their cancer sticks to the side. I already know my way up to the ICU, and I decide against waiting for the lift, instead tearing up the stairs, taking them two at a time and arriving at Jack's room breathless.

The officer at the door recognises me, and allows me a moment to regain my composure before checking my identification and logging the time in his notebook. I enter the room, so relieved to see Jack sitting up in bed, even though his face still resembles a bruised banana. He's busy talking to someone, but stops the moment he sees me and simply smiles – that broad, goofy, slightly unhinged grin of his that I've missed more than I'm prepared to admit to myself.

I hurry into the room, and it's only when I'm practically on top of him that I remember we're not friends who peck cheeks, and at the last minute I thrust out my hand, which he limply shakes with a confused frown.

'Thanks for coming,' he says croakily. 'It's good to see you.'

'It's great to see you too,' I reply, the butterflies flapping incessantly again.

'How have you been?'

'Better than you, clearly,' I tease. 'How's your head?'

'Feel like I went ten rounds against the Ultimate Fight Champion… and *lost*. I can't believe it's Wednesday already.'

I have so many questions. I can't get them straight in my head and I don't want to overwhelm him, but we have so much to catch up on.

'You're just in time,' he croaks. 'I was just explaining to the DCS what happened.'

I hadn't noticed Rawani sitting in the corner of the room, but he nods at me now, still wearing the suit jacket and tie I saw him in earlier at the diner. It doesn't surprise me that Jack has requested us both to come in, though part of me is curious to know which of us he called for first. I don't ask.

Rawani stands and moves across to the bed, carrying the chair with him. He offers it to me, but sits in it himself when I decline. There is too much nervous energy coursing through my veins to sit still.

'The last time I spoke to you, on Saturday night, you said you were following up on some lead into the case, but I've subsequently learned from Jagtar that you'd already been told the investigation was over the day before. Why didn't you tell me, Jack?'

'I didn't want to upset you,' he says ruefully, firing a frustrated look at Rawani for exposing his secret. 'Besides, as far as I'm concerned it isn't over. I promised you we would find out what happened to your sister, and it feels like we're making progress. I'm not going to stop even if I'm reassigned.' He has to stop to cough.

'It doesn't matter; you still should have told me. It isn't your fault that the NCA is pulling its resources. I would have understood.'

'I'm sorry,' he says, taking a lungful of oxygen from the mask hanging around his neck.

The nurse on the phone had said Jack was awake, but she hadn't given any clues as to his condition, and the fact that he still has access to oxygen leads me to conclude he probably shouldn't be so animated so soon after regaining consciousness.

'I shouldn't have misled you, but my stance hasn't changed. I'm not giving up on this.'

Rawani folds his arms across his chest. 'Pursuing personal vendettas is exactly the kind of behaviour that will bring trouble.'

'With all due respect, sir, this isn't personal; this is about bringing an end to a devious circle of men who have been above the law for too long.'

'You've already been reassigned, PC Serrovitz. As soon as you are passed fit to return to work, you will be stationed out of Brixton.'

'That won't stop me, sir.'

'It should, Jack,' Rawani says forcefully. 'You gave it your best shot, but we swung and missed. It's over.'

I'm grateful Jack isn't so easily swayed, but I'm also worried about the way he's speaking. Rather than discouraging him, his accident has renewed his motivation, and I agree with Rawani that trouble lies that way.

'You agree with me, Emma, don't you?' I hear Jack say, his eyes burning into mine for moral support. 'We can't give up now. We've got them running scared, and if this was the jungle, now would be the time to move in for the kill.'

'What happened on Saturday night, Jack?' I say, steering the conversation away from my own personal feelings on the matter.

Jack takes another slug of oxygen from the mask. 'I received an anonymous phone call from some woman telling me she had information that would help with my investigation. It sounded suspicious because she seemed to know exactly what I was working on without me confirming any details. She said she had proof that senior figures in the Metropolitan Police had been covering up child abuse for years, and would supply me with the names of those figures if I met her. She didn't name Tomlinson on the phone, but I couldn't see who else she'd be referring to. Don't get me wrong, it smelled fishy, and I assumed it probably wouldn't pan out, but I had to pursue it just in case.

'That's when I phoned you, Emma. I was going to tell you all about it, but I stopped myself at the last minute. As soon as

I heard your voice, I kept thinking about how they could have found out about our suspicions about Tomlinson. I knew I hadn't mentioned his name to anyone but you two, and that neither of you would disclose it. And then I had this alarming thought that maybe they'd managed to hack our phones. So I didn't mention the woman directly, not wanting to put her – or you, Emma – in danger.'

He pauses for another intake of oxygen, and I let his supposition filter through my thoughts: the audit of the AH Foundation, the burglary at Rachel's, the attack on Saskia, Rachel's redundancy – all indirect threats that could have been spurred by splintered conversations. But if that's the case, then the people we're chasing are far more powerful – and dangerous – than we've given them credit for.

'So I drive to Richmond to this pub called The Lucky Horseshoe. It was a bit of a dive, but I go in, looking for this woman. That's when I come across Dean O'Farrell, sitting there, lording it up. It feels too much of a coincidence that he happens to be there after what had happened between his daughter and Mila at school, and I guess frustration got the better of me, and I had a go at him. Stupid, I know. We had a scuffle outside, but it was no more than that, and then I got back into my car. I knew at that point that the anonymous phone call was aimed at getting me to the pub to see O'Farrell, and so I decided to head home. I didn't see the large van until it was already slamming into the side of my car. I did what I could to correct my steering, but then... I woke up here. I know the van was navy blue in colour, but the registration plates had been removed. The only person I saw inside the van was wearing some kind of balaclava, so I can't even identify who was responsible. They wanted me there, to drive me off the road.'

'And yet you still think it's a good idea to keep going?' Rawani mutters.

'All the more reason to keep going,' Jack wheezes back. 'But we can't keep... tiptoeing around. We... we need to hit them... where it hurts. Their activities need to be exposed to the world.'

I take the mask out of Jack's hand and press it over his nose and mouth. He looks about to argue, but then thinks better of it. The silence brings a respite to think. I've never been one to rush decisions, nor to take actions without careful consideration. Even when I felt certain I had enough evidence to expose Turgood for his crimes at the St Francis Home, I checked and rechecked my facts before I went back to the police.

Jack pats my hand and I let go of the mask, allowing him to lower it again. 'We need to cast the spotlight on them instead. Take what we have and put it out there; let the public decide about the likes of Tomlinson, Turgood, and Saltzing.' He looks me dead in the eye. 'Could you use your platform to share the truth? Write a blog, or do an interview with someone where you can talk about what we're looking into? They can bully and intimidate because we're bustling in the shadows. If we step into the light, they won't be able to attack us without exposing themselves to further enquiry—'

'That's a terrible idea,' Rawani interrupts. 'There are laws against naming and shaming individuals without sufficient evidence. You'd both be throwing away your careers, and could potentially face custodial sentences.'

'It's a risk worth taking,' Jack says firmly. 'I became a police officer to fight injustice and bring restitution to those who deserve it. How many victims have this group left in their wake? Enough is enough!'

I love Jack's passion, but I agree one hundred per cent with Rawani. 'We don't have enough, Jack. The only thing tying Tomlinson to any of this is that photograph with Turgood and Saltzing, but it could be perfectly innocent.'

'But equally it could help us unlock so much more. Haven't you noticed how the pressure has increased since we were sent it? Somebody out there trusted us to use that photograph for the better, and by sitting on it, we're as bad as the police officers who didn't intervene when complaints were first made against Turgood by his victims. I've had enough of keeping their secrets for them.'

Rawani stands. 'I can't listen to any more of this. I implore you both to consider the repercussions of what you're suggesting. Not only will it impact those you're chasing, but how many others will suffer as a result? You don't even have enough evidence to obtain a warrant, let alone bring a successful prosecution.'

We both watch him leave, and in that moment, I'm half-tempted to hurry after him.

Jack picks up my hand. 'I know it's frightening, and it puts your reputation at risk, but just think for a moment how good it *could* be. What if it encourages other victims to come forward? What if it exposes more culprits? What if it finally sheds some light on how your sister wound up in their clutches?'

I extract my hand from Jack's and put the mask back over his face. 'I'll think about it.'

He's about to argue when there is a commotion at the door

behind, and Mila comes haring into the room, immediately leaping to her father's side and resting her head on his chest. And in that moment I see their shared bond and remember that this isn't just about finding Anna and exposing Tomlinson; Jack's motivation for pursuing this is deep-rooted in his role as father and protector.

Chapter Forty-Two

NOW

Clifton, Bristol

There wasn't a lot of information I could find out about Joseph Swaile online, and as we arrive at the large wooden gates at the front of the property, I can't help but feel like I've underestimated how today will go. The property beyond the gates is tall and modern, and spread across at least two plots. Whatever Joseph has made of himself, the property reeks of wealth.

The man who meets us at the gate isn't what I was expecting either. Despite being several years younger than Ruth would have been, the years have not been kind. His head is shaved, but shows where patches of baldness would have been obvious if any hair had remained. He carries an excess of weight around his middle, and appears squeezed into the designer leather jacket he's wearing despite the mild climate. The expression he wears shows a lack of trust and plenty of wariness about our presence at his home.

I show him my business card as confirmation of my identity, and when he scrutinises Zara beside me, I quickly explain that she is my research assistant. I do check whether there is any recognition between the two, but there's nothing obvious.

He keeps hold of my card and leads us up to the main door, beyond which two large dogs are sitting and growling. I'm uncertain of the breed, but they yield the moment he clicks his tongue and issues the command to do so. I sense they would willingly strip the skin from our lifeless bodies if he gave the order, and so I'm already on edge as I perch on the armchair in the living room, which is larger than my entire flat's floor space. He doesn't offer us drinks.

'I was going to have my solicitor present, but he's been held up in town,' Joseph says, with no trace of an Irish accent.

'I'm sorry?' I reply. 'You called for a solicitor?'

I casually glance around the room in an effort to get a better sense of who this man is, but the cream walls are bare of photograph frames. In fact, there are few personal touches in this place, and I can't help feeling like we're in a show home, rather than somewhere lived in and chaotic.

'Well your email said you wanted to ask questions about my sister, so I thought I might be safer with legal counsel here.'

I glance at Zara, missing his point.

'We're not from the police, Mr Swaile. As I explained in my email, I'm just trying to understand what happened at the time when your sister went missing.'

He stares at my business card pinched between his fingers. 'But you do work as some kind of consultant with the police, no?'

Something is definitely off here. He's glaring at us like

we're something that needs wiping off his shoe, and he's made no effort to make us feel welcome.

'I looked you up,' he continues, flicking the card against his chin, before using it to scratch his clean-shaven neck. 'You're working with the Met Police on unsolved missing children cases, aren't you?'

Clearly, Joseph Swaile has preconceptions about the purpose of our visit and I need to put his mind at ease if I'm to break the ice.

'I have historically helped the police with some cold cases, but I'm not here in that capacity, Mr Swaile. I came across your sister's case, and I'm hoping to determine exactly what happened to her, and whether there's any possibility that she might still be alive—'

'Did my wife put you up to this?'

The question not only cuts off my words, but throws my thoughts into disarray.

'I'm sorry, your wife?'

He raises his eyebrows as if he's caught me in a lie. 'I imagine she told you that I'd be happy to talk to you about my sister, but what you don't realise is just how twisted that bitch is.'

He looks from me to Zara and then back again.

'Did she also suggest that you bring a red-headed assistant with you to stick the knife in and appeal to my better side? This is so typical of her tricks and games. Well you can tell her from me that I'm not buying it, and that if she thinks this will win her a bigger settlement in our divorce, then she's got another think coming.'

Suddenly, the lack of personal touch in the room makes sense. Whether she's taken those items with her, or he's only recently moved in, this is a man who isn't going to welcome intrusion in his life.

'I assure you, Mr Swaile, that I don't know your wife, nor am I here acting on anybody's instruction. I just want to know more about Ruth.'

He suddenly sits forward and thrusts my business card towards me. 'You're wasting your time, Miss Hunter. My sister died thirty-odd years ago. My parents were suspected of killing her and covering it up. To be honest, I don't remember a lot about that time, nor about her. I spent most of my childhood in social care, and having been kicked from one home to another, the memories get a bit jumbled.'

I look at Zara, trying to determine what she's thinking, but her eyes are fixed on the notebook on her lap before her. Bringing her here was a mistake. I should have met with Joseph separately and assessed his willingness to consider a DNA test before raising Zara's hopes of a family reunion. There was a part of me that hoped they'd recognise each other after all these years and we'd return to London with more answers.

'What can you remember about your sister?' I try. An open question is always a good place to start.

He doesn't immediately respond and I instantly check for the dogs, before he puffs out his cheeks, deciding he will indulge me further.

'I remember that life was difficult back then. I remember little about life before being taken into care. I know a lot of people that survived the system paint pictures of poor treatment and neglect, but to be honest, I think that's when my life properly started. I can't explain why, nor give you specific examples, but once I was on my own, things just got better. I can only assume that mine and Ruth's upbringing wasn't always great, but I can't say for certain why I think that.'

I glance at Zara again, but I still can't read what she's thinking.

'She was three years older than you, right?' I say to Joseph.

'From what I understand, but I really don't remember having an older sister. I'd say my earliest memory is Christmas in one of the homes I was in – my third apparently – and I was bought a Gameboy for Christmas by the family I was living with. I think it was the happiest I'd ever been, and I lived with them for a few years before I moved on again. Pat and Mitch – I'm still in touch with them to this day.'

'You have no pictures of her,' Zara suddenly says, her tear-strained eyes glaring at him.

'No,' he shrugs.

I try to catch Zara's eye, to warn her that confrontation is not going to aid our cause, and that maybe she'd be better stepping outside for a breath of air, but her gaze is fixed on him.

'Don't you care that she might still be alive out there in need of your help?'

Joseph now narrows his eyes and focuses his full attention on Zara. 'No, I don't, and even if she is, she never came looking for me, so why should I care what she's done with her life?'

Zara shoots up and moves closer to him. 'Maybe she didn't know she had a brother. Maybe she couldn't remember her life before she was taken. Maybe—'

'Look, what is all this?' he fires back, standing as well, and pushing her away from him. 'As far as I'm concerned, my sister was part of a life I was lucky to escape from. She represents a chapter in my life that's closed as far as I'm concerned.'

He crosses the room and arrives at a dog-shaped jar that he lifts the lid off, and pulls out a large brown cigar, which he promptly lights and puffs on, eyeing the pair of us: the redhead who is shaking and looks as if she will tumble like a house of cards, and the terrified writer hunched over.

I stand and quickly cross to Zara, placing a protective arm around her shoulders. I try to coax her back to her seat, but she brushes off my attempt.

'You must have wondered at the possibility that she's still alive out there over the years, surely?' she shouts at him.

He puffs on the cigar, the cloud of smoke obscuring his face. 'I really haven't. If my sister was out there somewhere with her own life, I'd wish her all the best, but it's been too long for me and her to have any kind of connection. I've moved on, and I don't want my past dragging up.'

Zara's shoulders tauten beneath my arm, and before I can say anything to quell the tense atmosphere, she stomps out of my grasp towards the smoke.

'Here it is,' she growls at him, 'your past dragged up and laid before you. Nice to meet you, brother.'

Nobody reacts. If any of us could move, we'd be able to hear a pin drop, but it's like someone's paused us on the screen. Even the smoke emanating from Joseph's cigar looks as though it's in freeze-frame.

They're staring at each other and I can't tell if he's about to hug her or thump her. He does neither, instead peering around the side of Zara and glaring at me.

'Is this really the best you could do?' His eyes inspect Zara from head to toe as her shoulders bounce in time with her rapid breathing. 'I mean, the hair colour, sure, but facially she looks nothing like my sister.'

He still thinks we're here as part of some vindictive scheming with his soon-to-be ex-wife. He doesn't appreciate the significance of Zara's admission.

'Zara, I think we should...' I begin to say, but she isn't listening.

'Look at me, brother. Look at me! I am Ruth. I was abducted and sold into a sex-trafficking ring, and I repressed the memories, but I'm here. Now. I'm back. Just look at me!'

He shoves the cigar back between his lips but peels away from her and heads towards the door. 'I want you both out of here *now*. I don't know if this is usually how you get your stories, but I must say I am disgusted that you would dare to take such a painful incident from my past and try to use it against me. How dare you?'

The dogs growl somewhere outside of the room, sensing their owner's anger, but I need to get control of the situation.

Zara storms over to him, leaning into the smoke, as he steps back and clatters into the door. 'You think you've had it hard? You have no idea what I went through! Locked up. Abused. Wishing for death. And despite almost getting my wish, I battled back from the edge of despair and rebuilt my life. How dare *we*? How dare *you*, Joseph? I came to you out of some kind of loyalty, but I see the apple didn't fall far from the tree.'

His temporarily intimidated state quickly passes. 'Get the hell out of my house!'

Zara doesn't hesitate, rushing towards the front door, pulling it open and haring off into the street. I immediately begin to give chase, but Joseph grabs my elbow as I'm passing him.

'I don't know what you were hoping to gain from me today, Miss Hunter, but I want no part of my family's history being dragged up for a writing project. Nothing you can say or do will change my mind on that matter either.'

Right now, I don't care what he thinks of me. My instinct is telling me to get to Zara before she does something from which there'll be no return.

Chapter Forty-Three

THEN

Clifton, Bristol

The road beyond Joseph's house was sodden as the grey clouds overhead heaved with the torrential downpour that had been brewing all day. Zara raced down the drive and through the still-open gates, immediately turning right but with no idea where she was heading, just knowing she had to keep running. She'd been fighting all her life, and just when she'd thought her race was over, rejection had slapped her hard across the cheek, and jeered.

She could hear Emma calling after her as the rain and wind spurred her on. She hadn't expected Joseph to be so unforgiving, and now she hated that she'd dared to dream of a happy ending.

I should have died in that fire, she told herself, pounding the pavement and not caring when water from the puddles splashed up against her jeans. Her escape that day should have meant a fresh start, a chance to put it all behind her and start living, but in truth, despite her efforts to forget and repress, it had always been there, lurking and waiting to catch up to her. She'd been naïve to think it would ever let her go.

And poor Tom… she'd willingly dragged him into her nightmare too. She'd allowed him to believe she was this ordinary, normal character, betraying his trust with every word spoken and every breath taken. She'd robbed him of the chance to know true love, built on a foundation of honesty, rather than a closet of skeletons and half-truths.

But it wasn't just Tom she'd kept in the dark for so long. How many times had Angie shown her compassion and support, even though deep down she must have known that Zara wasn't the little girl she'd lost. Zara's selfishness and refusal to see the truth had brought nothing but pain and suffering to those around her, and as she spotted the sign and saw the deep valley pouring out on the horizon, she reached the only decision that made any sense.

It was time to stop running. It was time to accept that she couldn't change the past and couldn't fix the future. In some way she'd been hurtling towards this destination since she emerged from the fiery window, but had been too blind or unwilling to see it.

As her feet splashed against the pavement leading to the suspension bridge, she felt the wind almost lifting her into the air, helping her see the only logical conclusion she could draw over her life of lies and fear.

Vehicles moved alongside the barrier, oblivious to the proximity of death. Stopping, she looked back along the hill she'd climbed, and could see Emma pursuing, desperately trying to swallow the distance. She wouldn't be able to scale the inward-sloping anti-climb barrier, but she could make it up onto the wall before the barrier started, and from there she could scale out far enough to make the most of the seventy-five-metre drop to the muddy banks of the River Avon. There was no way she would survive the fall, and like the swan sensing its own demise she could take one final flight.

With a deep breath she planted her hands on the top of the shoulder-high wall, as far as she could stretch them, feeling the rough edges of the brickwork beneath her fingertips, before planting a foot on the edge of the barrier. With a second breath, she heaved herself upwards, pushing into the barrier as her chest pressed against the top of the wall, but the breath left her instantly as she found herself staring down to the mud and fast-flowing water below.

Emma's voice calling her name was louder now; she was obviously able to see what she was doing, but Zara refused to look back. With a second heave, she was able to straighten her arms and shuffle her body around so that her bottom was atop the brick column, her hands still gripping the edge of it, fearful of falling. The wind whipped at her boots as her legs dangled over the ravine. Somewhere behind her a car's brakes screeched, but she wouldn't be put off, gently lowering herself to the narrow ledge beyond the wall, still clinging onto the wall for dear life.

But now that she was facing back towards the bridge, she could see that several cars had stopped, and their drivers were rapidly emerging, some with phones pressed to their faces, others nervous about getting too close and startling her into falling.

'St-stay back,' she warned them, as she stepped sideways onto the anti-climb barrier, holding onto the rim as she slowly edged along it.

'Zara, stop, please,' Emma called out, now only metres away from her.

'Stay back,' Zara warned again, fixing her with a determined yet sympathetic stare.

Emma edged slowly along the footpath, separated by the barrier but close enough that she didn't need to shout. 'Think about Tom.'

Zara's heart broke at mention of his name. 'I am thinking about him,' she whispered back as the wind clawed at the edges of her eyes. 'He's better off without me.'

'He wouldn't agree. He loves you, Zara. He wants to marry you.'

Zara shook her head. 'He doesn't know the real me. He loves the projection I offered, but that isn't who I am. He wouldn't like who I am on the inside.'

Emma remained rooted to the spot, and Zara couldn't tell if the moisture on her face was the rain or tears.

'I'm sorry I involved you in any of this,' Zara offered, edging further along the narrow ledge. 'I should have ended things sooner.'

'I understand that you're angry about what happened to you, Zara, and I am too, but you can't give up like this.'

'I'm not giving up. I'm giving in. I'm tired of living a lie, Emma. You tried to help me, and I know you tried your hardest, but not everyone can be saved. You have to let me go.'

Emma suddenly swallowed the distance between them, and threw her arms out through the barrier and wrapped them around Zara's waist, pinning her.

Zara tried to bat her away, but she couldn't hold the barrier and swat at Emma's arms at the same time. 'Get off me. This isn't your concern.'

'I can't let you go. I watched a young, troubled woman plummet to her death last year, and I can't watch history repeat itself. The police are on their way, and I just have to hold onto you until they arrive.'

Zara looked back over Emma's shoulder as mobile phones were held out, videoing the encounter.

'You won't be able to hold onto me if I let go and step off this ledge, Emma. Are you sure you want to be remembered as the woman who let me slip and fall? Let me go and allow me to take this final step alone.'

'I'm not going to let you go until you've heard what I have to say. The lab phoned me while I was chasing after you. They have your DNA results.'

'It doesn't matter anymore. We both know I'm Ruth, even if Joseph isn't prepared to accept it.'

Emma leaned in closer, barely able to keep her hands together as the storm swarmed around them. 'The results were a match, Zara. You *are* Angie's daughter.'

Zara stopped struggling, blinking against the rain as she tried to make sense of what she'd heard.

'You *are* Zara Edwards,' Emma said again. 'The results are conclusive. Regardless of what you believe or recall from that time, Angie is your mum and you are the Zara Edwards who was abducted from that pier.'

'You're just saying that to get me off this bridge.'

'I'm not. They emailed me too. I forwarded it to your phone. Check for yourself.'

Zara curled her left arm around the barrier and reached into her trouser pocket with her right. She unlocked the phone and stared at the email, not wanting to believe the words, but unable to escape them in black and white.

'But I don't...' she stammered. 'I never... I can't be...'

Emma pressed her face against the wire. 'You suffered greatly because of those people, and if you give in now, you'll let them win. You deserve a future not plagued by doubt and sorrow. I can help you get the support you need if you'll let me. Please, Zara, come back to us, and I will do whatever I can to bring down those who've caused all of this.'

Zara glanced back over her shoulder at the grey sky and the picturesque landscape beyond. It represented freedom from the torment, and all she would need to do was jump back and plummet. But as her gaze returned to Emma she pictured Tom at her graveside, and instead of letting go, she grabbed hold of Emma.

'Help me back to the edge. I don't want to fall today.'

Chapter Forty-Four

NOW

Weymouth, Dorset

Five days have passed since I helped Zara back from the edge of the Clifton suspension bridge, but the nightmares have yet to subside. In my dreams we are back on that bridge, only I don't manage to talk her down, or I do but then she slips and falls from my grasp. I wake screaming, and I have to check online news articles to make sure I didn't imagine her scrambling back over the wall just as the paramedics arrived.

She was kept in hospital overnight and warned by the police, but I did my best to explain the delicate nature of the situation, and then Tom escorted her back to Ruislip. Since that first time I saw her ghost-like figure at Maddie's window, I don't think I've fully appreciated just how much damage was inflicted on her at that time, and in the subsequent years when she's tortured herself with those doubts. I thought she'd survived her experience, but in truth she's still living it. Maybe she will never be free of those demons, but at least she has something to live for now. She assures me she wants to get better and the promise of a future with Tom beside her will support that journey.

I can't begin to imagine how difficult it will be for her and Angie to come to terms with the DNA results, but they're taking it one day at a time. Tom suggested the two of them go away for the weekend somewhere they can just talk and be open with one another, and I've provided the contact details of a couple of private psychologists with good reputations. Time will tell whether the two of them manage to heal the chasm of the wound that grew between them. I'm hopeful.

Subconsciously, I've drawn so many comparisons between Zara's situation and Anna's, and whilst I can't prove it yet, I am certain now that there may be a connection between what happened to them both. The more Jack and I learn about the ring of traffickers on the south coast, the less I can believe that such abductions aren't connected.

I've promised Zara I won't write a tell-all book about her journey until it's closer to resolution. In return, she's agreed to keep me posted about memories uncovered during her counselling sessions. Maybe the key to finding out what happened to Anna lurks somewhere buried in Zara's memories. There's a part of me tempted to show her the image of Turgood, Saltzing, and Tomlinson, but she's buried those memories so deep that it probably wouldn't do any good.

It feels so great being back home where the seagulls squawk their life's story and the waves applaud everyone who stops by to say hello. I slept soundly for the first time in a long time that first night back here. Slept so well, in fact, that I didn't hear my alarm sounding. It's amazing how familiar surroundings can clear the mind. I began sketching notes, pulling together everything that happened in the aftermath of completing *Trafficked*, and it was like I could suddenly see where all this has been heading.

'Is it ready yet?' Jack asks, pacing as much as his limp will allow.

'Nearly,' I tell him, buying myself a few extra seconds of thinking time.

He's been staying here with me as part of his recuperation ahead of his transfer to Brixton. Given the state of his injuries and his need to properly rest, I have been kipping on the sofa in the lounge – not that he was happy for me to give up my bed. But now he knows just how stubborn and assertive I can be on my own territory.

He's limp-pacing again, which is possibly one of the oddest movements I've ever seen. Because of significant bruising to his shoulders in the car accident, and his broken wrist in a sling, he's half-hunched over. Add to that the bruised-banana skin shading of his face, and his swollen knee, his walk resembles that of a doll whose limbs have been put back in the wrong sockets. He assures me he's not in any pain, but I catch him wincing every time he has to turn and come back the other way. He'd be far more comfortable lying on the sofa or in bed, but he can't settle. It wouldn't surprise me if he feels a bit like a fish out of water being away from the grind of London.

As soon as we got back here, Jack whipped out a device from his bag and had me scan my flat for any kind of surveillance devices. Neither of us can understand how else certain people found out about our investigation, but we didn't find any bugs planted. He then ran detection software on my phone and laptop, finding apps that have been secretly monitoring my keystrokes and GPS for God knows how long. I certainly didn't download them to my devices, and as far as I'm aware neither have been out of my sight, but they were there regardless. Jack tells me there's no way of tracing who put them there, or when, but they've been removed now. He said he found something similar on his phone too, which provided scant consolation. It is an invasion of our privacy, pure and simple, and the only silver lining I can draw is that we've got them worried enough to take that kind of risk.

And that's why I've been collating all my notes and extracts this last week, ordering and understanding. I've plotted two books to reveal the journey that's brought us to this point, and I'm just putting the finishing touches to the outline I plan to send to Maddie and my publishers. I've resisted Jack's urging to go public via a blog post. My platform is my books, and if we are to turn the tables on those pressuring us to stop, it has to be done on my terms. Rachel offered to leak the story to one of her former colleagues, but I'm not ready to push anyone else into harm's way just yet. That's why I'm trying to delay pressing the send button. I want to speak to Maddie, to warn her about how serious this investigation is getting. That's the least she deserves.

'The sooner you press send, the sooner you can take me out and show me the many delights the old town has to offer,' Jack says.

So far we've survived on a diet of takeaways and bits I can fetch from the corner shop sixty seconds away. I've been promising Jack that there's more to Weymouth than the beach and the fish and chips, and I'm determined to prove him wrong.

'Send it, send it, send it,' Jack is bouncing at the edge of my desk like a puppy chasing its tail. I'm grateful when his ringing phone distracts him.

'Hello?' he says into the receiver. 'Hold on, hold on… Emma's here too. Do you want—? No, okay, sure, I'll put it on.'

I frown at him as he lowers the phone to my desk. He hobbles across the room to the sofa, dropping the remote as he attempts to pick it up. I can see Rawani's name at the top of the phone screen, showing that the call is still active.

The television flickers to life and I recognise newsreader Kirstie Greenacre's face from when she was reporting on Aurélie's emergence in Poole at the start of the year. Her hair has been softened to a strawberry-blonde bob, more conservative, and better suited for a mainstream audience, since she was promoted to an anchor role. At first I want to question why Jack is scrutinising the image so quietly, until I see the words 'Fatal Shooting' at the bottom of the screen.

I instantly tense, certain now that whoever has been killed this morning is known to Jack and Rawani, and I fear the worst. Kirstie Greenacre's neon-green suit jacket is so bright that my eyes ache, so I allow the image to fade to a soft focus and concentrate on her voice instead.

'The suspect in the shooting is in police custody, not far from the victim's home in Market Harborough, a town that has been left stunned by this morning's developments. Neighbours heard shots ring out shortly before six o'clock this morning, and immediately called the local police. A patrol car happened to be nearby and arrived at the site, a small cul-de-sac at the north end of the town, within two minutes, trapping the suspect inside.'

I am racking my brain for anyone I could know who lives in Leicestershire, but I'm stumped, yet Jack's face has drained of blood, so I'm loath to ask him who they're talking about for fear of upsetting him further.

'A tense standoff with armed response officers ended shortly after 10am,' Kirstie's voice continues, 'when the suspect allowed officers entry to the property, and was led away in cuffs and under a blanket cover. We are still waiting for the lead investigator to make a formal statement about this morning's tragedy, but expect something before lunchtime.'

I'm about to ask Jack who they're talking about when Kirstie drops a bombshell. 'Tributes have been pouring in for the former Metropolitan Police Commissioner, who returned to the Leicestershire town shortly after his retirement more than a decade ago.'

My mouth drops when a still of Anthony Tomlinson's face appears on the screen. It can't be a coincidence that this has happened the moment we're about to expose his crimes.

Jack mutes the television and switches his mobile to speaker phone. 'We've seen it,' he says loudly. 'It changes nothing.'

'It could just be a coincidence,' I hear Rawani suggest, but his voice lacks any kind of conviction.

'I can't believe they killed him,' I say, shocked and saddened by what I've just seen.

'They're tying up loose ends,' Jack says defiantly. 'They know we're coming for them, and that Tomlinson was the target of our investigation, so they've silenced him before he can reveal anything more about them.'

My brow furrows. 'Can you hear yourself? This isn't some tin-pot Hollywood thriller where nobody really cares when culprits get their comeuppance. Whether Tomlinson was involved with the ring or not, he has been shot and killed today. Show some respect, Jack. For all he *might* have done wrong, no person is wholly evil.'

I breathe heavily as the blood boils in my cheeks. Jack mouths the word *sorry*.

'I think we need to tread even more carefully,' Rawani says next, concern dripping from every syllable. 'If Tomlinson's murder has anything to do with the work you've been undertaking, they could be coming for you next. Apart from Emma's friend Rachel Leeming, have you told anyone else about the investigation?'

I look at the draft email to Maddie and my publisher. 'We were about to. Maybe we should hold back, Jack.'

But he's shaking his head. 'There's greater safety in numbers. The more people we tell, the safer we'll be, I'm sure of it. They might have been trying to tie up a loose end this morning, but they've made things worse because the person who shot him is in police custody. If anything, they've exposed themselves even more. I think we stick with the plan and keep the heat on them.'

'Only you two can decide how you want to proceed,' Rawani says. 'All I'll ask is that you're careful. I don't want to see any harm come to either of you.'

Jack ends the call and looks at me. 'Think about it for a second: if Tomlinson has nothing to do with the people who abducted and abused your sister and the others, why did he end up shot today?'

Jack has tunnel vision. I close my laptop screen and move away from him, trying to get the words straight in my mind before facing him again. 'We don't know for certain what happened this morning. He could have disturbed a burglar and things got out of hand. Or maybe the perpetrator is someone he helped send down years ago who's come back for revenge. Or there could be any other number of possible hideous reasons a man has lost his life. You need to take a step back and put things into perspective.'

'Don't chicken out on me now, Emma; we've come too far. It was you who started all of this when you helped Freddie bring justice to Turgood and the others at St Francis. It was you who asked me to review your sister's casefile. I'm not saying any of this is your fault, but you can't just relinquish responsibility because you don't like how it tastes.'

'I'm not relinquishing anything,' I say through gritted teeth. 'I happen to agree with your theory that we're safer in numbers. I just don't want you leaping too far ahead with your imagination. I haven't formally named Tomlinson in the outlines I've prepared, and the first book is practically written already, based on the notes I've been making; it just needs stitching together in the edit. But I also think Rawani is right to warn us to rein things in a bit. Let's see what else we can find out about Tomlinson's shooter before we draw any conclusions. Agreed?'

He looks confused, but nods. 'So you'll send it?'

I nod as I cross the room and open the laptop lid. The cursor hovers over the send button on the screen. 'Are you sure?'

He fixes his eyes on mine. 'Send it.'

I start as my phone bursts to life on the desk.

'The number's withheld,' I tell him.

'You want me to answer it?'

I shake my head and accept the call, switching on the speaker so Jack can hear whatever is said too.

'I'm phoning for Emma Hunter? Is she available please?' a friendly enough woman's voice asks.

'This is Emma Hunter,' I say quickly. 'What is this with regards to, please?'

'Oh hi Emma, I'm DS Sarah Yates, and I'm calling from Leicestershire Constabulary. I need to speak to you as a matter of urgency. Have I called at a bad time?'

A murder in Market Harborough, and now a call to me from Leicestershire Police. Alarm bells are ringing.

I frown at Jack. 'No, now is fine. What can I help you with?'

She sighs. 'Well, it's all a little unusual. My DI has asked me to phone you to ask whether you know a woman by the name of Miss Kylie Shakespeare.'

There's something there, scratching at the back of my mind like a kitten chasing a loose thread, yet no matter how hard I try and tug on it, it won't come. I want to say there was a reference to a Kylie in what we've been investigating, but my mind is too in shock to comprehend.

'No, I'm sorry, I don't think I do. Can I ask what this is about?'

'It's a bit sensitive, and it would be easier face to face. Would it be possible for you to come up this afternoon?'

'To Leicester?'

'Yes, well, Market Harborough actually.'

Jack's worried face reflects how I'm feeling.

'I'm sorry, not without more of an explanation.'

There is a pause on the line, and when DS Yates returns, she sounds louder even though she is talking more quietly. I assume she's pressed her lips closer to the microphone. 'Are you aware that there was a fatal shooting at a home in Market Harborough this morning?'

'I just heard about it on the news.'

'Yes, well, the suspect arrested on the scene has refused to provide any details about why she was at the victim's home this morning. All she will say – and keeps repeating – is that she wants to speak to you first.'

'Me?'

'Yes, Emma, you. She was pretty insistent that we contact Emma Hunter the writer, and not to make a mistake. She says she's happy to make a full confession to her crime but only after speaking to you.'

Jack is shaking his head and mouthing *no*.

'Why does she want to speak to me? I don't know her.'

'She won't explain why, but my DI asked me to ask whether you could come and help us get through to her. It's not something we would usually entertain, but my DI is under serious pressure to get a result on this, owing to who the victim was, so you'd be doing us a huge favour if you could come up. I can send a patrol car to collect you if transport is an issue, but if you can make your own way it would be quicker.'

'Will Emma be safe?' Jack asks now. 'I take it the suspect has been strip searched for weapons?'

'Who is this, sorry?' Yates asks.

'PC Jack Serrovitz. I'm with Emma now.'

'The suspect's clothing has been taken for forensic examination. She is wearing tracksuit bottoms and a T-shirt that we provided.'

'What about weapons secreted in her hair?'

'There was a lot of blood, and she showered before dressing again. Her hair is shaved, so, there are no hidden weapons.'

'I could drive you up there if you want?' Jack whispers now.

'You can barely walk, let alone drive.'

'Please? I'd rather not leave you at anyone's mercy. I'm not due back at work until after the weekend. What do you say?'

I tap his hand away from the phone. 'Very well, I'll come up now. Do I need to bring anything else with me?'

'A form of photo identification like a passport will be sufficient. Any idea how long it will take you to get here?'

'Three to four hours, dependent on traffic.'

'Thank you, Emma. I'll let my DI know to expect you. Many thanks.'

The line dies and I plough into my bedroom, filling my satchel with a change of clothes and underwear, taking a look around my room and feeling as though I've barely been back long enough to be heading off again. Jack is fiddling with his phone as I emerge.

'I've plotted our route,' he tells me. 'We can grab some food on the way up, but we could be there by 5pm, all things being equal.'

I don't argue, closing down my laptop and packing it without sending the email to Maddie and my publishers. My mind is a blur with thoughts. Who is Kylie Shakespeare, and why do I feel like that name should mean something to me? How does Tomlinson's killer know who I am? Is this part of some ploy to derail our investigation? Have they arranged for their suspect to somehow try to tar my name?

Opening the desk drawer, I locate my passport. I'm trying to determine if I need anything else as I open the door, bumping into the tall figure of Rick Underwood, who is holding a floral bouquet. It's been weeks since we last spoke, and now that he spots the passport in my hand, his face crumples in puzzlement.

'Are you going somewhere already? You've barely been home a week.'

I open my mouth to speak, but Jack bumps into the back of me carrying his holdall. 'Who's this?' Jack asks.

Rick thrusts out his hand before I have chance to introduce them. 'I'm Rick, Emma's boyfriend. We met before. At the vicarage on Hayling Island?'

Jack makes no effort to shake Rick's hand, and although I feel obliged to correct Rick on his statement – we haven't yet had the boyfriend–girlfriend conversation – I can't process what is unfolding.

'I'll wait in the car,' Jack says in a huff, pushing past the two of us and hobbling down the steps and towards his car.

'What's his beef?' Rick says, pained.

I don't have time to be worrying about romantic implications. I need to know who Kylie Shakespeare is and what she wants from me.

The thread in my head comes slightly looser: wasn't Kylie the name spotted on the lanyard by the beady-eyed post office worker? Could the woman who sent me the photographs be the same woman now in custody?

I grasp the doorframe as I swoon with light-headedness.

'It's not what you think,' I tell Rick, glancing over to Jack tapping his watch at the car. 'I'm sorry, but I don't have time to get into this now.'

'You don't need to explain. The two of you are going off on holiday somewhere and have a plane to catch; I don't want to get in your way.' He steps aside, dropping the flowers to the ground.

'No, Rick, listen you've got the wrong end of the—'

He holds his hand up and cuts me off. 'You know, I thought

it was odd that you'd come back here and hadn't phoned to let me know, or ask if I wanted to hook up, but I kept telling myself you have a lot on your plate and to give you some space. I should have realised there was something going to happen between the two of you. It was inevitable from your first two books.'

He deserves more of an explanation, and if he would actually allow me to get my words straight, I'm sure he would understand that there's nothing going on between me and Jack but work, but I resent that this is the conclusion Rick has automatically jumped to, and so I keep my mouth shut.

'I'll see you around,' he says, skulking away, but I let him go.

He's a nice guy who deserves better than a woman who can't decide what she wants. Slamming my door, I lock it and hurry to Jack's car.

'Don't ask,' is all I say to him as he starts the engine. I could be wrong, but I'm sure I spot a slight smile on his face as he watches Rick disappearing into the distance from the rear-view mirror.

Everything we've investigated over the last couple of years is racing to the front of my mind and vying for attention: Freddie's plea for justice that first night we met and the hurt that is keeping him from returning my calls; the presumption that Cassie Hilliard was dead, only for her to be discovered a year later; the role Sally Curtis's abuser played in her disappearance; Aurélie's emergence from the pit of hell and her telling us about the ring; the murders of Cormack Fitzpatrick and Faye McKenna under assumed identities; and now Zara's repressed memories blurring her true identity.

What if... what if Kylie Shakespeare is someone whose path we've crossed before?

What if she's the key to finally exposing the paedophiles and corrupt senior figures that have wilfully turned a blind eye for all these years?

As signs for Market Harborough start to whizz past our speeding car, I can't escape the sense that our journey is nearing its end.

THE END

Emma Hunter will return for the last time in *Exposed*...

Acknowledgments

Writing acknowledgements gets harder with every book, because the more I write and publish, the wider the pool of supporters I find are helping me realise my dream.

It seems a no-brainer to start with thanking my family for their love and support, and for putting up with my mind wandering mid-conversation when creativity strikes. How my wife in particular puts up with long car journeys in stark silence is beyond me! But she does because she knows it's part of the writing process. There have been nights when she's been woken by the brightness of my phone screen when a clever twist has struck at three in the morning. For all the times you don't roll your eyes and tell me off, thank you.

My children are an inspiration to me every day, and as they continue to grow so quickly, I am eternally grateful that I get to play such an important role in their development. I know neither has found it easy during lockdown and home-schooling (who of us has?), but they continue to show one another affection, patience and kindness, and make being their dad that bit easier. The role of parents, whether present or absent, is a constant theme in this series, and that's because my parental role is so key in my life.

I'd like to thank my own parents and my parents-in-law for continuing to offer words of encouragement when I'm struggling to engage with my muse.

Thank you as ever to my best friend Dr Parashar Ramanuj who never shies away from the awkward medical questions I ask him. Thank you to Alex Shaw and Paul Grzegorzek – authors and dear friends – who are happy to listen to me moan and whinge about the pitfalls of the publishing industry, offering words of encouragement along the way.

I want to thank every member of the One More Chapter team who've played some part in the production of this series. I'm always nervous to hear what my editor Bethan Morgan thinks about the latest book because she was there at the start and helped flesh out Emma's character and friends, but she's always so positive and constructive that she's been a joy to work with.

Thanks to Lucy Bennett for her work in producing the series' covers; to Tony Russell, whose copyediting is always relatively painless; and to Simon Fox who kindly completed the proofread to pull out those all embarrassing spelling mistakes. Finally, no book release is complete without the fervent effort of the marketing team, so big thanks to Melanie Price for all you've done to raise awareness of the series and encourage new readers to pick up the books.

And thanks must also go to YOU for buying and reading *Repressed*. Did you love it as much as Emma's previous encounters? Are you desperate to see how the story will play out after *that* ending? Please do post a review to wherever you purchased the book from so that other readers can be enticed to follow Emma's quest. It takes less than two minutes to share your opinion, and I ask you do me this small kindness.

I am active on Facebook, Twitter, and Instagram, so please do stop by with any messages, observations, or questions. Hearing from readers of my books truly brightens my days and encourages me to keep writing, so don't be a stranger. I promise I *will* respond to every message and comment.

YOUR NUMBER ONE STOP

ONE MORE CHAPTER

FOR PAGETURNING BOOKS

One More Chapter is an
award-winning global
division of HarperCollins.

Sign up to our newsletter to get our
latest eBook deals and stay up to date
with our weekly Book Club!
<u>Subscribe here.</u>

Meet the team at
<u>www.onemorechapter.com</u>

Follow us!

 @OneMoreChapter_
 @OneMoreChapter
 @onemorechapterhc

Do you write unputdownable fiction?
We love to hear from new voices.
Find out how to submit your novel at
<u>www.onemorechapter.com/submissions</u>